Inoculated

Inoculated

Scott Michael Decker

Thanks to the following beta-readers:
Anne Potter
Elise Abram

Titles by the Author

If you like this novel, please post a review on the website where you purchased it, and consider other novels from among these titles by Scott Michael Decker:

Science Fiction:
Cube Rube
Doorport
Drink the Water
Edifice Abandoned
Glad You're Born
Half-Breed
Inoculated
Legends of Lemuria
The Gael Gates
War Child

Fantasy:
Bandit and Heir (Series)
Gemstone Wyverns
Sword Scroll Stone

Look for these titles at your favorite e-book retailer.

Chapter 1

Lydia brought the amoeba-class ship out of sub-ether above a cloud-shrouded planet in the Mnemosyne Constellation and threw a glance at her companion. "I swear, Xsirh, I don't know what those Homo sapiens are thinking. Look at her! Ugly as pondscum! Why does she get to become Empress?"

On the holo, a dainty tiara glittered in the human female's dishwater hair. Her skin was white and rough as plaster. Her lips were the color of rutabagas and poised in a perpetual pout. The nose was squished into the face, a wart the size of a snail perched on a cheekbone, the close-set eyes peering from beneath a unibrow. The holonet was alive with the upcoming coronation of the Homo sapiens Empress, and it didn't matter where Lydia surfed or what program she watched, the hype inundated all the media.

The blob of protoplasm in the copilot's chair, Xsirhglksvi Xlmhgzmgrmrwvh, nodded in agreement. "With your radiant beauty, you're far more deserving to be Empress," Xsirh said. A series of slurps, burps, and chirps comprised the language of her companion, inviting inevitable comparisons to human flatulence. Xsirh's green exoderm mottled with laughter, cilia writhing around his face.

Detecting sarcasm, Lydia glanced at the upper portion of his physiognomy, where his optical organelles were located. "And you became an expert on human beauty when?" Reared by the Kziznvxrfn, she knew their language better than any other human, and sometimes better than they themselves did.

"When I met you, Lydia." His coloration took on a blue shade, a sign he was blushing. "I knew you were special from the moment I saw you."

Mollified, she smiled. "Thank you, Xsirh." He was the father she'd never had, the mother she'd always wanted, and the brother she was always competing with, all in one. He gets maudlin at the oddest of times, she thought. Of all the Kziznvxrfn, he knew her the best. He'd reared her

2

since she was four. The Paramecium way of life had been difficult for her to adapt to. Without his protection, she would have perished. He'd risked censure and ostracism to help her, relations between human and Kziznvxrfn tenuous at best.

She replaced the holo with a view of the planet below. Their destination outlined, the capital Helios occupied an archipelago on the water-bound planet. Lydia and Xsirh had come to negotiate a contract for its didinium exports, which the Kziznvxrfn considered a delicacy.

One of the few humans who understood the Kziznvxrfn's near-addictive craving for the unicellular protists, Lydia had started buying didinium harvested on human worlds for the Kziznvxrfn market and now was the number-one supplier, with a seventy-five percent market share and a fleet of cargo transports. Always on the lookout for new sources, she'd come to Mnemosyne with her adoptive father to scout out the quality of its product.

"Atmospheric entry in one minute," the ship computer blurted. "Zgnlhksvirx vmgib rm gdl nrmfgvh," it repeated in Kziznvxrz.

She checked her five-point and glanced at Xsirh.

A transparent shell dropped from the ceiling to cover him, his periplast far more permeable than her epidermis and his body lacking bones. In a multi-g descent, he'd ooze right through five-point restraints, even with anti-grav absorbing the brunt of the torsion forces.

The ship began to shudder and shake. Lydia concentrated on breathing deeply, atmospheric entry the worst part. Twenty-four years ago, during just such a descent, she'd been orphaned on Kziznvxrfn, her parents dying in the crash. She gripped the armrests with both hands, sweat breaking out on her brow, her stomach doing pirouettes up to her craw, her heart hammering in her ears.

Then the shudder ceased.

"Imperial Infection Control to inbound Paramecia vessel, please assume a holding pattern at fifty-thousand feet while your ship is being imaged."

"Acknowledged," Lydia said, barely finding her voice in time.

"Imaged?" Xsirh said, the shell retracting into the ceiling. "Why do they need to image our ship?"

"Contraband, probably." She shrugged, frowning. She'd commed with a complete flight plan and had been cleared by the authorities. She couldn't imagine what the holdup was.

"Oh, I'll bet it's the coronation."

Intuitively, she knew he was right, the hoopla reaching even Theogony on the galactic rim, a hoopla they couldn't avoid no matter how hard they tried.

"Infection Control requesting visual contact," the ship computer said. "Rmuvxgrlm Xlmgilo ivjfvhgrmt erhfzo xlmgzxg."

"On screen," Lydia ordered.

"Commander Sarantos here, Imperial Infection Control. Lydia Procopio, I presume?" A smile lit up his face. "My, aren't you pretty!"

Prettier than that pondscum Empress of yours, she thought. "What's the hold-up, Commander? All the clearances are in the flight plan filed a week ago with Space Traffic Control."

"We've had some changes in protocol due to the recent outbreaks, Ms. Procopio, clearances or not. We're detecting alien life aboard the ship. We'll need to sterilize the vessel."

"Of course there's alien life aboard—my Kzizn-vxrfn companion, Xsirh."

"Kzizn? You have a Kzizn aboard? We'll need to do a visual and the alien will have to be dealt with."

"He's been inoculated per protocol, Commander. We've both been inoculated. It's all on file." Humans everywhere were paranoid about infectious agents and invasive species. Recent infectious outbreaks had ratcheted up their paranoia to a persecutory fervor.

"Prepare to be boarded," Commander Sarantos said. The screen winked out.

"I don't like the sound of this, Lydia," Xsirh said.

Her stomach ground and heaved, and not from the rough atmospheric entry. "It's never been a problem before. We've been to how many worlds belonging to these supposed Sapiens?" She frowned at him, dreading the inspection. And what had the Commander meant by "the alien will have to be dealt with"? Lydia and Xsirh had learned how difficult relations could be, their first few attempts to establish trade contacts having failed spectacularly.

"Not very sapient, are they?" Xsirh said. "I'd better get into my envirosuit before they board." His exoderm extended as his periplast retracted, protecting the attached cilia. He looked as if he were folding himself inside out. Xsirh slithered to the floor and squirmed toward his cabin on his exoderm, the mucousy periplast better suited to semi-aquatic environments.

The ship lurched violently to one side. "Tractor beam," the amoeba said, its voice eerily calm. "Gizxgli yvzn."

Thrown against her restraints, she wondered if Xsirh was all right. "Xsirh?" She tried to look over her shoulder. "Xsirh?" Unable to see him, she unbuckled herself. Bracing herself to keep from sliding down the slanted floor, she made her way into the corridor.

"Just a bruise," he said, holding twenty tentacles to a mottled patch of his periplast.

"Nothing broken?" she asked.

He shook his head and laughed, his optical organelles meeting her gaze. He had no bones to break. "Right in the micronuclei, though," he added, his organelles squinting in pain. His micronuclei were the equivalent of human gonads, one of four ways that Kziznvxrz reproduced.

I wish we'd been using the sub-ether drives, Lydia thought. They'd have put us beyond reach of any tractor beam.

"Unauthorized entry being attempted," the ship said. "Fmzfgsliravw vmgib yvrmt zggvnkgvw."

Infection Control, she thought. "Entry authorized. Let them in." She turned to Xsirh. "Better that than they blow our hatches."

"This won't be pretty."

She knew that as well as he did. The amoeba-class vessel righted, and she stepped toward the hatch, which opened.

The face of Field Commander Sarantos was a mix of a leer and a wretch. "What's that stench?! Smells like a sewer!" His face settled on a wretch, his skin turning green.

"Kzizn atmosphere, Commander," Lydia said. "In such a hurry to board, you can't wait for us to change the air? Hitting us with that tractor beam without warning injured my shipmate. If he requires medical care, you'll be getting the bill."

His face turned from green to red. "Inspect the ship!" he barked over his shoulder. "And you stay right here."

"Watch for Xsirh on the corridor floor," she told the marines as they surged past. She turned to Sarantos. "The next time you visit Kzizn, I'd like to offer you a complimentary kick to the testicles. Like the one you gave him."

A vein pulsed at his temple, his hand on his sidearm.

"Got the Kzizn, Commander!"

A blood-curdling squelch came from the back, Xsirh blatting in pain.

She whirled. "What are you doing to him?!"

Commander Sarantos slammed her to the bulkhead, his arm to her neck. "I said, 'Stay'! Take the Kzizn aboard," he said over his shoulder.

"You can't do that! He's done nothing wrong!" she choked out, trying to push his arm off her.

"R'ev wlmv mlgsrmt dilmt!" Xsirh said.

The Commander made another face. "What the hell was that noise? It sounded like really bad gas. Is that speech? What'd he say?"

"He said he's done nothing wrong!"

They'd wrapped Xsirh in a net and were hauling him onto the other ship.

Commander Sarantos let her go. "I'd advise you lay low for the next few days, Ms. Procopio. Whatever business you have can wait."

"My first order of business will be to file a complaint with the embassy, and my second, to do whatever I can to get you bounced out on your incompetent backside!"

"It's just a Kzizn, Ms. Procopio."

"That's my father, Commander!"

* * *

Lydia frowned at the line ahead of her. A queue of a couple hundred people snaked away from the Imperial Infection Control kiosk at the Helios spaceport, all of them awaiting clearance.

"What's the holdup?" she asked the person in front of her.

A rough-faced old man, his back bent from years of labor, gave her a look up and down. "Where you been livin', some backwater bayou? Outbreaks on Pyrgos Five and Cygnus Twenty, both planets under quarantine." He shook his head at her. "Ought to surf the holonet more often."

She blinked blankly at him and snorted. "Brain rot," she said. Anxious already to get Xsirh out of custody, she was tempted to raise a stink just to get past the line. She was certainly going to file multiple complaints about the rough, unwarranted treatment they'd received. "Where are you coming from?"

"Neither of those places, thank the stars."

She estimated how long she'd be standing in line, saw immediately she'd have to postpone her appointment with the CEO of Titanide Aquafoods. And who knew how long it'd take to get Xsirh released. Or if. She didn't have a lot of faith in human bureaucracy.

"Lydia." She extended her hand to the halfbent old fart in front of her.

"Nick," he said, shaking. "Short for Nikephoros. Pleased."

"Mutual," she replied. "What do you do here?"

"What else on a soupy planet like this? I fish—run a trawler for Titanide. Not much else to do either."

Lydia saw a bureaucrat making his way through the line, asking quick questions of each person he passed. "Titanide? I'm here to see Orrin."

"Runs a tight ship, he does. What's he gonna do with a pretty one like you?"

Lydia blushed and snorted. "Strictly business."

The bureaucrat pulled a man aside and led him over to an arch, where a glowing biodetector sat, its bulk twice the man's height. The man walked under the arch, alarms sounded, the arch flashed red, and a squad of armed soldiers appeared from nowhere.

"But I've been inoculated!" the man said, his voice quailing with fear as they hauled him away.

"What'll they do with him?" Lydia asked.

"Sterilize him," Nick told her with a shrug.

"Will he be able to reproduce after that?"

"Depends on whether or not it kills him."

Lydia stared after the squad, the man in their midst struggling. "How long has it been like this?"

"Happens whenever there's an outbreak. And those quarantines may not be enough." Nick shook his head.

Lydia had read up a little on immunology and disease prevention. Her father Dorian had been a Professor of Xenobiology before he died in the shipwreck, and among his effects had been some preliminary research. The fact that Imperial Infection Control was screening people after they made planetfall seemed to her to border on incompetence.

The bureaucrat was back at it, asking people questions, passing most of them by.

"What do you suppose he's asking?"

"Whether they've been to Pyrgos Five or Cygnus Twenty in the past year."

Lydia frowned, having been to both planets multiple times on business. Pyrgos Five manufactured shipping containers, and Cygnus Twenty supplied packaging. "What's it like to fish on Theogony?"

"Terrible! Didinium are all over the place. They get in your boots, they get in the nets, they clog up the exhaust pipes, they swim up inside the sewers, and worst of all, they get mixed in with the catch. You ever see a didinium? Those slugs can grow to the size of your head."

Lydia grinned and nodded. "On Kziznvxrz, they're ferocious little beasts." In their early evolution on Xsirh's home planet, the Kziznvxrfn and Didinium had fought for preeminence across a million years, each devouring the other relentlessly, and only in the last five hundred thousand had the Kziznvxrfn waded onto dry land from the planet's primordial soup as the dominant species. And the Kziznvxrfn had never lost their liking for didinium, despite its being nearly extinct. "They're considered a delicacy. If you can catch them."

"A delicacy? They taste awful! Who in their right minds would think they're a delicacy?"

Lydia shrugged at him. "I have relatives with some pretty strange tastes."

The bureaucrat approached the old man. "Any travel to Pyrgos Five or Cygnus Twenty in the past year?"

Nick shook his head. "No, Sir, never been either place."

The head moved slightly in Lydia's direction, the bureaucrat's eyes remaining fixed to his palmcom. "Any travel to Pyrgos Five or Cygnus Twenty in the past year?"

"Several times to both," she said.

Nick instantly stepped back, as did several people around them.

"I've been inoculated," she told them all, "if that's any help." Lydia already knew nothing she could say would sway a bureaucrat, always gumming things up like didinium in the fishing nets.

"Inoculation didn't help five hundred million people on Cygnus Twenty," the bureaucrat said. "Is that a rash?" he asked her.

"Huh?"

"Those spots on your arm, is that a rash?"

"Oh, that? I don't know," Lydia said. "It's been itching off and on since I left Kziznvxrz."

"I'll have to ask you to come with me, miss. What's your name?" The bureaucrat gestured toward the glowing biodetector.

"Lydia Procopio." She followed him to the arch. Blue lights twinkled around its insides, the hum of its motors faintly audible. It soared over her, dwarfing her slight form.

"On my signal, just walk slowly through, Ms. Procopio. Don't make any sudden moves." The lights began to blink. The hum went up two octaves. "Go ahead, please."

She stepped slowly through the machine. When she reached the far side without setting off the alarms, Lydia turned to the bureaucrat. "I told you I've been inoculated."

Chapter 2

"Unlike Imperial Infection Control to revoke its clearances without warning," Orrin Stamos told the fetching young woman across from him. "And I'm so sorry they treated your ... father so badly. After her coronation, the Empress will be touring the outlying colonies. Based on the level of activity here, I'm guessing Theogony will be her first stop. I'm afraid an Imperial visit is going to complicate things."

The CEO of Titanide Aquafoods hoped she hadn't heard his hesitation. His company was the largest exporter of fish on Theogony. Orrin frowned, distressed at the way she'd been treated, but having difficulty believing the alien was so important to her.

Now their deal was about to fall apart.

Her company was the biggest importer of didinium on Kzizn. Trawlers on Theogony dredged up didinium by the trillions, the creatures ubiquitous. A carnivorous unicellular ciliate protist, its gelatinous texture nauseated the human palate. The didinium preyed upon Titanide's main catch, so throwing them back wasn't an option, and disposing their carcasses into the sea had earned the company the castigation of local environmentalists. Selling the didinium to the Kzizn seemed like the perfect solution.

Orrin didn't want to lose the contract because of a diplomatic snafu.

When he'd met her at the spaceport, Orrin had seen how distressed she was, and she'd insisted on being taken immediately to the consulate. En route, she'd been furious and disconsolate by turns.

"How's Xsirh's detainment being received at home?" he asked hesitantly.

"I don't know yet," Lydia replied, her gaze on the floor. "They probably won't release him any time soon, will they?"

"Difficult to say. Why do you ask?"

"My father's throwing a birthday party for me on Kziznvxrz three days from now."

"Well, I hope you don't have to spend your birthday here."

He could feel the contract slipping through his hands, as though coated in slime. He knew the creature who'd accompanied her to Theogony couldn't possibly be her biological father, but clearly, she regarded him highly. Her biographical information indicated she'd been reared by the Kzizn after being shipwrecked on the planet as a child. All right, Orrin asked himself, if I were visiting Kzizn with my father, and they detained him, how would I want to be treated?

"Look, why don't we go see him, make sure he's being treated all right?" Orrin knew he wouldn't be endearing himself to Immigration, but he was in exports, not tourism.

"Oh, could we?" she said, brightening immediately. "That'd be wonderful! They probably don't even know what to feed him. And he'll dehydrate within hours if he's not immersed. Oh, thank you, Orrin!"

She looks about to leap across the desk! he thought. Himself, he wouldn't mind, the young woman quite attractive, but his girlfriend certainly would. I'd better com her, he thought, I'll probably be late for our date.

Orrin had Lydia wait in the foyer while he made arrangements, having to reschedule two afternoon meetings with suppliers.

He wondered what he was getting himself into.

* * *

Carissa Minas, Warden at the Helios Immigration Detention Center, frowned at the uproar.

We're Immigration! she thought in disgust. We should be trained for this!

Instead of a calm and orderly detention, chaos had erupted from the moment the detainee had arrived, the Kzizn's odor causing revulsion and nausea. Carissa had nearly fainted when she'd entered the holding area.

Now, watching on holo, she struggled to keep her face impassive, her bowels grinding and heaving, just like everyone else's in the facility. The creature's stupefying smell pervaded the place, and the sights and sounds hovering above her desk made it worse.

The elliptical glob of shimmering muck squirmed and writhed on the cell floor, bright mucous green along most its length. The purple splotching on its midriff almost looked like bruises. And it emitted a constant stream of blurts, blats, phorts, and phlats, the sounds a human might make when undergoing extreme gastrointestinal ejection.

"Sounds like C-Diff in there," said the man across from her, Lieutenant Simon Hatzis, her second in command. "Smells like it, too."

"What? What's that?" Carissa asked, looking at him through the holo.

"Clostridium difficile," he said immediately. "A bacteria in the human intestine which releases toxins that attack the intestinal lining. Causes projectile diarrhea, highly infectious."

"It's infectious?!" she asked, pointing at the writhing creature. The recent infectious outbreaks on two nearby planets were causing considerable consternation.

"Well, not according to the ship's manifest," Simon replied, looking at a hand-held holo, text swirling above it. "'All passengers inoculated and assured to be free of infectious pathogens per interstellar protocols.' It's even signed off by Imperial Infection Control." He extended the holo toward her.

"I don't need to see it, thank you." She hated his manner, redolent of a teacher lecturing young boys on imitating bathroom sounds.

The holographic figure blatted sonorously.

"Oh, my! What I wouldn't give to have been able to emit such sounds in grade school!"

Her stomach cramped as if in sympathy, and she realized she had to pass gas.

No! she thought, not in front of Lieutenant Hatzis! She couldn't stop the flatulence, but thankfully, it was silent, and the cloud of miasma that seeped up around her head wasn't terribly different from the stench already pervading the facility.

It wasn't enough that Imperial Infection Control had issued a detain-all-aliens order for Theogony. Then that insufferable Field Commander, Sarantos, had foisted upon her a detainee that the facility was unprepared to care for, one who appeared to be in distress, perhaps injured. And then this idiot Lieutenant waltzes into my office and spews his discursive diffiwhatever dissertation! Carissa fumed, wondering what she'd done to deserve such a fate.

"Visitor to see the Kzizn, Warden," her intercom blatted.

Maybe someone from the embassy to tell us how to care for the creature, she thought. Carissa had commed them immediately after the alien's arrival, needing a translator. She'd quickly realized she needed more than translation. "Thank you, Stan, and can you ask environmental services to do something about the smell?"

"Yes, Warden." Stan's voice over the intercom was almost as unpleasant as the sounds from the cell, the equipment ancient.

"Shall we, Lieutenant?" She gestured him to go first. I'd do anything to get his officious ass out of my office! Carissa thought, carefully keeping her sentiments off her face.

He preceded her into the corridor and turned toward the foyer.

There, in the septic-smelling, antiseptic waiting room, they found not another Kzizn from the embassy but two humans, both of them looking distraught.

"I'm Orrin Stamos, CEO of Titanide Aquafoods," the man said.

"Lydia Procopio," the woman said. "I'm told my father is being detained here."

Carissa shook both their hands, introducing herself. Even in her distress, the woman was stunning. "I'm afraid you must be mistaken, Ms. Procopio. Our only current detainee is an alien."

"A Kziznvxrfn," the woman said. "I know he's here."

For a moment, Carissa was baffled. She'd never heard the full, non-diminutive name for the aliens spoken by someone fluent in the Kziznvxrfn language. Nonplussed by the bizarre sounds issuing from the beautiful woman's mouth, Carissa was befuddled by what she was trying to tell her. "Forgive me, a what?"

"A Kzizn."

"Your father's a..." She coughed, taken aback. "Forgive me, but ..."

"He adopted me when I was four. He's the only father I've ever known."

Spoken with such simplicity, the words moved her. Further, the woman looked as if she'd been crying.

"I know he's here, Warden."

A bit difficult to disguise that fact, Carissa thought sardonically. "Yes, the Kzizn is here. Uh, er, what's his name?"

"Xsirh."

" 'Sure'?" Carissa repeated.

"Well, almost. It's short for Xsirhglksvi, spelled X-S-I-R-H."

"Xsirh?" Carissa marveled that anyone could master such difficult sounds. She could see Lieutenant Hatzis suppressing his laughter. I'll pummel him later, she thought.

"Please, I have to see him. He was injured when Infection Control put a tractor beam on our ship. And he has to be immersed every few hours or he'll die from dehydration."

"Of course, Ms. Procopio." Even better than a translator from the embassy, Carissa thought. They didn't have a machine that could translate a language as difficult as Kziznvxrz. Even among human settlements across the galaxy, the proliferation of languages challenged even the most sophisticated translation equipment, despite the near ubiquity of Galactim, the lingua franca. "A few questions, first, if I may?" Carissa asked. "What was the purpose of your visit?"

"They were meeting with me to negotiate a didinium export contract," the man said.

Orrin is his name, she reminded herself. "Thank you, Mr. Stamos." She looked at the woman. "You mentioned injury, Ms. Procopio. How was he injured, and how severely?"

"He got up from his chair to get into an envirosuit after Infection Control said they were boarding our vessel. The tractor beam caused our ship to lurch, throwing him against the wall and bruising his micronuclei, the human equivalent of testicles."

Carissa saw the two men squirm. "Sorry to hear he was injured, Ms. Procopio. You mentioned immersion?"

"Yes, Warden, preferably in salt water to maintain his electrolytes. Fresh water will work for a day or two, but will eventually cause delirium, seizures, coma, and respiratory arrest."

"Lieutenant Hatzis, secure what he needs."

"Huh?"

She whirled on him. "Get on it, man! He's in our care. His health is our responsibility."

Hatzis hesitated again.

She stepped up to him, shoved her face into his, and ground her heel into his foot. "Now, please," she said sweetly. Carissa turned to the woman as the Lieutenant limped away. "Ms. Procopio, we'll do everything we can to insure he's well. Typically, visitors aren't allowed, but given the circumstances, we'll make an exception. If you'll give us a few minutes, I'll escort you back myself."

* * *

Wait for it! Erastus thought, wait for it!

He was Erastus Doukas, Agent Provocateur from the Imperial Bureau of Suspicion, and he watched the Immigration Detention Center like a hawk for anyone exiting.

He'd seen his target entering with an unknown man ten minutes ago.

Wait for it! he told himself yet again.

For the next two minutes, no one else entered or exited the building.

The detention center was isolated, sitting on the point, perched atop an escarpment overlooking the sea. Purposively so. No one got in or out without being observed. And there was only one bridge.

He surveilled the facility from across an estuary where rough seas surged. Erastus was somewhat dismayed at how close the facility was to the water. Not that anyone would dare try to escape into the roiling seas, waves battering rocks just a few feet below the facility's foundation. What do they do in a storm? he wondered.

But no matter. She'd gone in the facility, and hadn't come out.

And if everything went well, she never would. Not of her own volition.

He grinned, his mission nearly finished. "T-minus three minutes," he said into his com.

Rarely did he complete such missions so fast, but this one had been unusual from the start. A month ago, he'd been contacted by agent control in a brightly-lit alley on Lucina IX.

A woman wearing a fedora and a long trench coat was slumped against the alley wall between two malodorous bins of refuse, glaring radon lamps high overhead throwing every object into sharp relief. "Agent Doukas," she said, her eyes barely visible under the wide brim, her nose as perfect as an axe blade.

"If you're gonna do the cloak-and-dagger routine, you might consider a darker alley," he told her.

"What concern of yours is that?" she snapped. "Besides, dark alleys are spooky."

He could see the fine, classic lines of her face, the perfect nose, the luscious lips. "They don't find dead dames in bright alleys."

"Precisely my point, Doukas," she snarled, mispronouncing his name like a homophobic slur. "I've a special assignment for you. One which has the bouquet of a fine Metaxa."

He immediately went on high alert. As exalted as it was rare, Metaxa was a distilled blend of brandy, spices, and wine from Pelopone VI. Nearly no one except the Imperial Family could afford it. Nearly no one but the Imperials drank it. He knew what she meant but he didn't say it: Orders from the Palace.

"You are to travel immediately to Erato IV in the Mnemosyne Constellation. The planet is locally known as Theogony. You're familiar?"

"Adjacent to the system of that alien species with the unpronounceable name, right? The Kzizn?"

"That's the one. In fact, that's your task. Secure the planet under the Bureau's auspices, capture all aliens and their human companions, and ship them back to Gaea for interrogation."

"All of them?"

"Did I specify any exemptions?" Her tone was as sharp as her nose.

"What about indigenous species?"

"There's no intelligent life on Theogony!"

Taken aback, he realized the orders applied only to … "Ah, sentient aliens," he said. Sentience was a characteristic ascribed to just a few elite forms of life in the galaxy, a category rumored to exclude Homo sapiens.

"Of course I mean 'sentient,' idiot!"

Proving once again that an assumption on his part would have made an anatomical posterior of them both. She doesn't need my help in that regard, he thought. He suspected he didn't need hers, either. "How long do I have?"

"A month."

At first, he thought to object, Theogony just a parsec from Kziznvxrz. But how do I know any Kzizn are even there? he wondered.

"Relations between the two species aren't spectacular," the woman said, "so you might not have any difficulty at all."

"Which means very few human companions, too," he said, nodding. "What about the embassy?"

"Don't worry about it. Cleared by Immigration, and technically, not even Imperial Territory."

And he and a crew of ten subordinates had come to Theogony and had scoured the planet for any sentient aliens, not just Kzizn. Within a week, they'd secured their removal to Gaea for interrogation.

Done, he commed agent control to say he'd finished early. "What do you mean, I gotta stay?" he objected to the shadowy, fedora-obscured woman.

The blade-nosed face in the holocom nearly leaped from the machine into his hotel room. "I told you a month, do you hear?!"

And the very next day, Emperor Zenon died, throwing the Empire into an uproar. Fortunately, Princess Hecuba stepped into the breach and declared herself Empress, a startling move for a young woman at the tender age of twenty-four.

Watching events on Gaea from the border planet Theogony, Erastus couldn't help but notice that in the background of every vid or still of the Empress-designate lurked the Dowager Empress, Narcissa Thanos, the Emperor's surviving second wife. The first wife had died in childbirth some thirty years ago.

Doukas wasn't a genius, but he wasn't ingenuous either. Rot in the rarified air of a palace smelled the same as that in brightly-lit alleys. And something smelled rotten in Denmark, wherever that was.

And then, that morning, a Kzizn ship had commed Helios Control for permission to land on Theogony. Aboard were a Kzizn and a human. Intuitively, he knew his bird had alighted.

Watching the building to assure for himself that not a soul emerged from the Immigration Detention Center, he lifted his com to his mouth. "All right, katáskopos, time to capture our bird. Go, go, go!"

Hovers and ground cars descended upon the facility like a swarm of bees. Instantly, the place was surrounded, and the ordnance aimed at it was enough to blast it off the precipice and into the sea.

Doukas and two subordinates brandishing sidearms blew into the waiting room, badges out. "IBS," he intoned in his deepest voice, displaying his badge in one hand. With the other, he held his weapon at his shoulder, its point glowing and ready.

The stench was hideous, and he nearly gagged.

Behind partitioned glass, the receptionist quailed and slowly sank to the floor, his hands in the air.

Three agents surged in behind him, one going left, one going right, and one staying at the door. Three more entered behind them, all of them looking bilious.

Two agents on his heels, Doukas headed straight in, toward the holding tanks, already familiar with the layout. He opened his trake to the paging system, trying to contain his gag reflex.

"This is Agent Erastus Doukas of the Imperial Bureau of Suspicion." His voice boomed back at him from overhead. "This facility is being commandeered by Imperial authority. All planetary Immigration officers are hereby deputized as IBS agents under my command. You will lower yourself to the floor immediately. You will be shot after the count of five if you are not on the floor. Five, four, three, two, one."

Six agents reported all clear.

Doukas marched past wormwire-reinforced glasma panes toward a set of double doors.

A uniformed female burst through the doors. "What's the meaning of this!?"

"Hold your fire!" he told his agents, two guns trained on her. "Warden Minas, I hope. If you're not, you're dead."

"Indeed. What the stars is going on?"

"Your detention center is now under my command by order of her Imperial Majesty. All your staff are now my staff, and all your prisoners are now my prisoners."

"Fine by me. How are you going to care for the Kzizn?"

Doukas was taken aback, not quite the response he expected. "I'm not. It's to be transported to Gaea immediately for interrogation. And its companion, the woman it arrived with. Who's the man?" He strode through the next set of doors, the Warden on his heels.

"A business associate, a Theogony native."

In the corridor beyond, the stench intensified. "The Kzizn's through this door?" Doukas stopped abruptly before going through.

"In the holding tank, yes," Warden Minas said.

He signaled to the two agents with him, both of them female.

All three burst through the door.

Partitioned cells lined the walls, their shiny, carbo-nick alloy bars stretching from plascrete floor to plascrete ceiling. Bare loomglobes hung near the ceiling, bathing the scene in stark, surreal light.

A woman lay on the floor in front of the rearmost cage, her wide-eyed stare on the agents.

Nearby lay a man, the Theogony native. Just beyond the bars lay a lump of green protoplasm, a large purple splotch in its middle.

The stench was overpowering, and Doukas nearly retched.

His two agents turned the same putrid green as the creature beyond the bars from the stench. They pounced upon the couple. His other two Kzizn detainees had worn envirosuits, the Theogony atmosphere eventually fatal to the Kzizn. None of them had had human companions.

"What's the meaning of this?" the woman asked, a plaster barrel to the base of her skull.

He saw she was exceptionally pretty, even face down on the floor. Doukas knelt where they could both see him. He flipped out his badge and repocketed it, so practiced at the maneuver that no one had time to peruse it. "Agent Erastus Doukas, Imperial Bureau of Suspicion. You're under arrest."

"On what charges?!" the man demanded. "I want to speak with my lawyer!"

"He wants his lawyer," Doukas mocked, his voice a high-pitch whine. "Sequester them," he ordered. "No further contact between the prisoners until after interrogation. Put the female in isolation and take the male immediately to interrogation room two. I'll question him first."

Other agents converged to assist, and as they hauled the female to isolation, Doukas was taken aback by her breath-taking beauty.

"My father needs help," she protested as she was dragged away. "He'll die if he' not immersed within an hour!"

Father? Doukas wondered, bewildered for a moment. Then he realized she was talking about the Kzizn.

"R'oo yv zoo irtsg uli z grnv," the alien inside the cage blatted.

Doukas cringed at the sound, as if to dodge projectile diarrhea. He stepped to the bars to look at the amorphous figure, its cilia writhing helplessly in the air. "Get a Kzizn envirosuit," he told the agent beside him, Lieutenant Special Agent Jace Eliades.

"Why do you suppose she called it 'Father'?" Eliades asked.

Doukas shrugged. "And then get me her dossier, Lieutenant."

"Yes, Sir."

Warden Minas stepped up beside him. "How soon can you get them going to Gaea?"

"An hour maybe. Lieutenant Eliades, secure transport. We'll be ready by the time they get here."

"Yes, Sir." Eliades had his hand to his ear, his lips moving soundlessly as he issued a series of orders.

"I can't believe the smell," Doukas said. "And she calls this thing her father?" he asked the Warden.

Minas shrugged. "Reared by the Kzizn since she was four, apparently."

He glanced over his shoulder toward the isolation cell where his agents had taken her, wondering what the palace wanted from her.

Erastus Doukas, Agent Provocateur from the Imperial Bureau of Suspicion, was convinced she was the reason he'd been sent to this backwater planet.

But why her? he wondered.

Chapter 3

"Colonel," the com squawked on her desk, "I've just received a request for a dossier on the subject."

Colonel Melanctha Remes looked up from her desk at the back of the theater at IBS Command on Lucina IX. Atop the fine classical lines of her face was a nose as sharp as an axe blade, perfect for cutting through the red tape of Imperial bureaucracy. She peered through the glasma pane separating her from operations.

Beyond the glasma was a darkened room lit solely by the myriad of holo displays hovering above the staff. Five rings of desks encircled a central pit, where her immediate subordinate stood, directing the surveillance technicians around him like an orchestra conductor.

"I'll be there in a moment, Lieutenant-Colonel." All squawk-box coms recorded, she wanted this information off-record, the mission to Theogony having that fine Metaxa bouquet.

Why the hell is the palace so interested in the Kzizn? she wondered, standing and making her way to the command theater center.

The entire Delta Quadrant under her surveillance, Colonel Remes was mystified by the sudden attention to an isolated planet on the outer Scutum-Centaurus Arm, where virtually nothing happened. Further, the focus on the Kzizn was downright enigmatic.

The Empire had somewhat recovered from the uproar over Emperor Athanasios Zenon's untimely demise three weeks ago, the initial shock throwing everything into chaos. Yesterday, Colonel Remes had floated an inquiry to IBS Command whether to abort the mission to Theogony.

The impersonal, imperious reply had been, "All current missions will be pursued in extreme vigor with all due diligence and dispatch." An emphatic no, and cloaked within the message, the threat of dismissal should the mission fail, worded vaguely enough to slather the communiqué with a viscous layer of plausible deniability.

And then this morning, Doukas had commed about a new arrival.

The original mission had emphasized the detainment of all sentient alien life and any human companions. The proximity of Kziznvxrz to Theogony had suggested the emphasis on the Kzizn, but they were such a reclusive race, devoid of hegemonic ambitions, languishing on their septic, swampy world like limp, amorphous blobs of protoplasm, that Colonel Remes wondered what threat they could possibly pose. They were a race of peaceful if repulsive aliens, no threat to anyone.

Had they had any such ambition, they'd be formidable, their aspects repulsive. Further, their advanced technological development gave them a tactical advantage over their Homo sapiens neighbors, their interstellar ships diaphanous and difficult to track, their weaponry virtually unknown.

Diplomatic relations with the Kzizn had always been tenuous, their appearance, language, and aroma all so repulsive to humans that missions to Kziznvxrz had been brief and unproductive. Theogony was the only planet where the Kzizn maintained an embassy, their diplomats exchanged yearly, their human hosts as attractive to the Kzizn as they were to the humans. Further, the Theogony atmosphere was deleterious to Kzizn health.

Colonel Remes threaded her way up the aisle, nodding to subordinates, most the technicians at their desks so focused on their work they didn't even notice her. On one holo was a feed from Gaea, the capital, the pomp and pageantry of the upcoming Imperial Coronation glutting the media.

Lieutenant-Colonel Urian Nikitas saluted her as she stepped into the conductor's pit, a holographic image of the Delta Sector swirling above them, multiple points of attention highlighted to indicate threat level, the Theogony region outlined in red.

"All coms off?" she asked.

Lieutenant-Colonel Nikitas nodded.

"Who's requesting the dossier?"

"Agent Doukas, on Theogony," Nikitas replied. "Damn it, Colonel, why him? Forgive me for asking, but he's as slimy as those Kzizn."

"I know it. I had to scrub my backside raw just to rid myself of his stench. Deny his request for the dossier. Don't tell him why, not even that it's ultra-confidential. Tell him there is none, all right? That'd be best. There is none." She questioned the wisdom of telling her trusted second-in-command what its status was, much less that it existed at all.

"Yes, Colonel," he said, giving her a brief salute.

She stepped back to the pit edge, watching as he commed Agent Doukas in the field.

"One moment, Agent Doukas," Nikitas said, turning to her. "Colonel, Agent Doukas says no transport's available for the two prisoners. He's asking for further instruction."

"No transport, in this day and age? There must be hundreds of ships he can charter, and thousands he can commandeer!"

"I told him the same. He swears up and down there's not a single interstellar vessel in the Mnemosyne Constellation except the vessel the two prisoners arrived on. Something about security measures being taken in the sector, he says."

"Security measures? But we're security," she protested. "If there're security measures to be taken, we're the ones to taking them. Unless…" Colonel Remes blanched, only one possibility coming to mind.

The Secret Service.

That small, ultra-clandestine law enforcement agency whose sole task was to protect the Imperial family. And the Empress-to-be.

If the IBS mission to Theogony had befuddled her before this, now it flummoxed her completely.

Colonel Melanctha Remes wondered what was going on.

* * *

Vasilios Xenakis, Imperial Secret Service Special Agent Ad-hoc, issued the order to halt.

A squadron of vessels stopped as a unit in the Oort cloud of the Erato subsystem. Highlighted on his holo were six planets orbiting a dull yellow primary. Their squadron was the main expeditionary force sent to secure the region prior to the Empress-to-be's arrival some three days hence.

Already, his pre-containment unit had interdicted any inbound ships, except for that slimy Kzizn vessel whose diaphanous hull had baffled all sensors, and whose sub-ether drive had obscured its emissions.

And just why, Vasilios wondered, would her Royal Assness choose this stinking backwater?

Xenakis wasn't bitter.

No, why would he be bitter?

In fact, he had every reason to be grateful. He was an upstanding officer in the most clandestine law-enforcement organization known to the Milky Way, and four weeks ago, he'd been awarded Employee of the Month.

Either I did something stupid or I'm about to be fired, he'd thought as he received the plaque at the awards ceremony back on Gaea. Or I'm about to get an assignment so reprehensible that I'll wish I could crawl back into my Petrie dish.

Mother, forgive me my thoughts, Vasilios said silently to the cockpit ceiling.

And the day before Emperor Athanasios Zenon died, the dreaded orders had appeared on his desk, commanding him to embark on his current mission.

Vasilios thought back through his last thirty years of service to the Imperial family, wondering where he might have slipped up. Where there might have occurred that single perceived slight to precisely the wrong person, whose ire he'd provoked and who'd harbored this most-minute of grudges for decades, the insult festering like a puss-filled boil on the buttocks of hindsight, seething with noxious poisons, its insidious discontent slowly oozing infectious dissatisfaction, until the diseased tumor had burst three weeks ago, and had unleashed its vitriol onto his otherwise-pristine career.

Twenty-nine years ago, he'd met the now-Dowager Empress, Narcissa Thanos, Emperor Zenon's second wife, then only a servant applying to his Majesty's service, whom Vasilios was considering as a new hire to attend upon the Empress Consort, Ambrosia Lillis.

The scion of a shipping magnate, Ambrosia Lillis was beautiful, as intoxicating to look at as

46

her name. She'd have risen to fame without her father's wealth just on her looks alone. Cultured and suave, demure as a fog-shrouded sunrise, Ambrosia was introduced to Gaean high society at an Imperial ball thrown to announce the official appointment of the Imperial Heir, Athanasios Zenon, as the Regent Emperor.

At thirty-five years old, Athanasios was ready to assume the Emperor's duties and become the nominal Emperor, his father hale and hearty but seeking to assure a smooth transition and avoid a nasty interregnum. Single, and the most desirable bachelor in the Empire, Athanasios had taken few lovers and seemed annoyed with the usual crop of high-society debutantes being thrown under his feet by their scheming aristocratic parents.

Despite the ball having been thrown in Athanasios's honor, Ambrosia stole the evening. And the Prince's heart. The romance had set fire to wagging tongues and had torched the Imperial ambitions of many an aristocratic parent.

And it had immediately invoked Imperial Secret Service protection for Ambrosia, whose personal safety had become the charge of Special

Agent Ad-hoc Vasilios Xenakis. Further, it had merited a retinue of personal servants, personally selected by said Special Agent.

One servant girl during the interviews had struck Vasilios Xenakis as incredibly competent and perceptive. Narcissa Thanos, her dossier had told him, was a peasant girl from a minor city on the far side of Gaea whose mother had died in childbirth and whose father's tsipouro vats produced only enough of the alcoholic beverage for him. Despite these desultory origins, Narcissa had worked her way quickly through several aristocratic Gaean families. Just after the Imperial ball, she'd applied to enter the Empress Consort's personal service as a Lady's Maid.

Ambrosia's personal safety his charge, Vasilios had screened Narcissa thoroughly. Her meteoric and blemish-less career in servitude had struck him as overly ambitious, but in multiple interviews, she'd assuaged his concerns, as had his interviews of all her previous employers.

At the bedside of the near-term Empress Consort, that competence had become starkly evident.

"I fear her Ladyship will have a difficult time," Narcissa had told him the day before Ambrosia went into labor. It'd been an odd pronouncement, quite in opposition to the opinion of a cadre of physicians in attendance upon the Empress Consort.

At the birth, medical personnel swarming around the Consort, and her favorite servant Narcissa right beside her, Vasilios had kept a personal eye on the Empress Consort for as long as he could, as if he might guard her from the clutches of Thanatos himself.

But no one had been able to protect her, and Ambrosia had died in childbirth.

Twenty-eight years later, looking down at the Erato subsystem, Vasilios Xenakis sighed.

Six planets orbited a dull yellow primary, the fourth one a pure blue marble, over ninety percent ocean.

How the hell did I end up here? he wondered, his task to secure a beautiful if backwater planet in a backwater system in a backwater constellation at the lightly-populated end of a galactic arm for the arrival of the Empress, the second daughter of Emperor Athanasios Zenon by his second wife, Narcissa Thanos.

Far from the center of power.

Far from the grave of the Empress Consort Ambrosia Lillis, the only person he'd ever loved.

* * *

Outside the door of the mausoleum where the ashes of the Empress Consort Ambrosia Lillis lay interred, a woman laid a single rose on the lowest step, said a brief prayer, and then moved on.

Drucilla Kanelos hadn't wanted to get any closer nor stay any longer.

Someone immediately took her place from a long line of waiting supplicants snaking through the graveyard into the distance, each with flowers, cards, and other mementos of sorrow in hand.

In two days, the usurper gets crowned, Drucilla thought, shedding a silent tear for Ambrosia and her unnamed daughter, wherever she was at, if she were alive at all.

A Laundry Maid who'd washed the personal undergarments of the Empress-to-be from the time she'd been an infant, and before that, who'd laundered the bed sheets of the Empress Consort Ambrosia Lillis, Drucilla hadn't let her lifetime of laundering dirty linens for the Imperial family either corrupt her or depress her. She was proud to have laundered the matrimonial sheets of the Empress Consort.

But ashamed of those she'd laundered later.

For within that laundering duty had come the august responsibility of verifying the breach of hymenal tissues by the Imperial pestle.

It was a singular honor to have done it the first time for the Empress Consort, her Ladyship Ambrosia Lillis. And a person might think that a second such instance of this sacred duty might have lifted Drucilla to the heights of Laundry-Maid heaven.

Pulling her hood far forward, Drucilla Kanelos hurried away from the mausoleum for fear of being seen, casting furtive glances all directions.

She'd wanted to honor the deceased Consort on the anniversary of her death two days hence, but the usurper's mother had conveniently scheduled the coronation for that very same day.

Deliberately, at least in Drucilla's mind.

Hired from the same pool of Lady's Maids, Housekeepers, Head Nurses, Chamber Maids, Parlor Maids, House Maids, Between Maids, Nurses, Under Cooks, Kitchen Maids, Scullery Maids, and Laundry Maids, Drucilla knew Narcissa from previous posts among the Gaean aristocratic households.

If she finds out I came here, she thought, I'll wake up dead tomorrow.

Drucilla had had the singular disgrace of verifying the Imperial-pestle breach of the hymenal tissues belonging to the upstart maid-become-Empress, Narcissa Thanos, an act which might have earned Drucilla the Dowager Empress's undying enmity.

But somehow had not.

Hurrying back toward the palace, Drucilla made her way along a busy avenue, an occasional hover whining past, pneumatubes crisscrossing the air above her like spaghetti noodles, a rainbow of people inside the tubes being whisked to their myriad destinations like so many corpuscles. Only Drucilla used the sidewalk, other travelers safe in their vehicles or tucked in their tubes, secure in anonymity.

Footsteps behind her!

Bewildered, she glanced back.

An ungainly figure with an egg-shaped body and stick-like legs hurried along, going the same direction she was.

She increased her pace, the tap of feet behind her sounding not like shoes but more like metal spikes striking pavement.

The tapping increased in tempo. "Dzrg, kovzhv."

What the stars kind of language is that? she wondered. What Drucilla had just heard had sounded more like a bad case of flatulence. Galactim was used for the routine business of government, but the people of Gaea could be frequently heard speaking their native Greek, from which Galactim was derived.

"Wait, please." Similar sounds, but this time with a simultaneous overlay of Galactim. A translator! And somehow in the mechanized translation, hints of desperation were audible. The tinny steps were right behind her.

Drucilla saw an alley ahead. Much as any woman disliked being in a confined space alone with a stranger, she feared Imperial surveillance worse. She turned abruptly into the alley. Impersonal plascrete soared overhead on both sides. The whine of hover and whoosh of pneumatube were muted here.

She looked at the figure.

Below each dress-slack pant leg poked a metal spike. The slacks were hung from the rim of what appeared to be a gigantic egg cup, like the ones they used at the palace during breakfast, when they inevitably argued over which end to break first, the big-endians and little-endians often coming to blows over the issue. Attached to the egg-holder edges was a frame whose only purpose, it appeared, was to give the blazer some shoulders to hang from and someplace for the bizarre head to perch. It could only be called a head because of the position it occupied on the anatomy, the clownish features looking as if they'd been copied from some children's morning holo show.

But what really drew her attention was the green amoebic creature inside the egg holder, its cilia flailing at the controls of the contraption. Indentations atop the amoeba looked vaguely like eyes, and a pocket just below them opened and closed in time with the gurgles, burbles, and squelches.

"Thank you," it said.

She suppressed the urge to duck, the sounds reminding her of projectile emesis. "What the hell are you?" She saw a thin veil of some material between them.

"I'm a Kziznvxrfn," the creature said.

"A who-what?" She realized it wasn't a material at all, but some sort of field, one of those science-fictiony force fields.

The creature emitted a series of blats and burps, its translation machine beeping back in protest. "Ah, bewilderment expressed. I'm a Kzizn," it said, finally. "From beyond the Erato subsystem, in the Mnemosyne Constellation."

"One of them. Always wondered what you looked like."

"Diplomatic relations between our people are somewhat fraught with difficulty."

"I'll bet. You sound violently ill."

"Yes, a side effect of our aspiration and expiration."

"You're gonna die on me?"

Again a series of blats, burps, and gurgles, the machine blatting back in shrill tones. "Oh, uh, 'breathing' is the proper word, I'm being told."

"Oh, heavens, I was wondering. What's that shimmering around you, anyway?"

"A vovxgilnztmvgrx field to separate the air I breathe from the air you breathe."

"A what field?"

"Vovxgilnztmvgrx," it said. Its translator burbled back at it. "Oh, uh, I'm being told there isn't a translation for that particular concept. Hasn't been developed by humans, apparently. Anyway, it keeps your air from harming me and my air from offending you."

"Now, why would I be offended?"

"You don't want to know. Oh, this is all so difficult. Listen, I know your government doesn't want you talking to me—"

"Now, why would they be offended?" Drucilla knew the creature was right, but how did it know? She'd lived in the palace for the last thirty years. She'd seen the consequences of the slightest offense, many of them imagined. Among the offenses that wasn't a product of the imagination was simply knowing too much. Many a domestic servant hadn't survived until morning because, under the cover of night, or under the night covers, he or she had found out something damaging about his or her charge.

"Never mind," she told the creature. "What's your name, by the way?"

"I'm Svkszvhgfh Ezhrozprh. Just call me Ezra. You're Drucilla Kanelos, Laundry Maid on staff with the Dowager Empress. You're going to Theogony with the Empress-to-be the day after her coronation."

"I am?" It was the first she'd heard about it. And usually the servants knew before members of the Imperial family. "How do you know?"

"I have a message for the Kzizn Embassy there, a message I can't get to them any other way."

She noticed Ezra hadn't answered her question. "And you want me to help? And get my ass thrown into prison?"

The translation machine beeped, clicked, clattered, and slurped, stuck on some word.

"Forgive me, but what is 'ass'?"

She smacked her backside. "This thing."

"This is a colloquialism?"

"A who-what?"

"Bewilderment again. Immaterial. I understand 'prison.' I assure you, you'll be protected, and there isn't any way you'll be caught."

"How do you know?"

The breathing orifice became a crescent moon, ends upturned; a mock smile. "The message is verbal, and they'll find you when you arrive. They're expecting you."

"What's the message?"

" 'Gsv likszm rh uzi nliv gszm hsv hvvnh.' "

"Huh?"

"Bewilderment expressed. Pardon, but I'm wondering why you're puzzled. It's very simple. 'Gsv likszm rh uzi nliv gszm hsv hvvnh.' "

"How am I supposed to remember that? What am I, a human voice recorder?"

"Oh, that's right, my apologies. I forget that humans have imperfect recall. A curious trait, that. Very well, I suppose I'll have to have you remember its Galactim translation. Ready?"

"All right," Drucilla said, "go ahead."

" 'The orphan is far more than she seems.' "

Chapter 4

She should have died in the crash! Deion thought, sweating.

In the palace security center, buried five hundred feet below the palace proper, Chief of Palace Security for the Imperial Secret Service Deion Goulas reviewed the measures thus far implemented for the Imperial Entourage. Touring the Empire was de rigueur for all incoming sovereigns. Making sure the tour was safe was his responsibility.

And to his knowledge, Deion was the only person who knew the ultimate fate of everyone aboard the diplomatic mission to the Kziznvxrz home world a quarter-century ago.

Upon arrival, as the ship was entering the atmosphere, hull integrity had failed, and the burning hulk had plunged into the ocean. Those aboard had been killed instantly, the Ambassador, her husband, and their four-year-old daughter.

Or so everyone thought. Only Deion suspected otherwise.

Three years ago, rumors had begun circulating of a Human-Kzizn pair of entrepreneurs in the Mnemosyne Constellation at the end of the Scutum-Centaurus galactic arm. Since the region was beyond the reach of the major space lanes and nearly devoid of interstellar traffic, the pair had made a killing in shipping and commerce, quickly assembling a fleet of Kzizn-manufacture freighters whose diaphanous hulls and sub-ether drives confounded conventional sensory equipment.

Slowly, Deion had come to the personal conclusion that the human could only be the four-year-old Ambassador's daughter, now grown.

It hadn't been a conclusion he'd arrived at suddenly, but one he'd reached after years of random sightings, several dozen stills, a few security cam vids, and interviews of two people who'd done business with her.

Information which had previously been superfluous to his primary duty—Palace Security.

Until now.

Now, the Dowager Empress wanted to go there, the first stop on the Imperial tour.

Why there? he wondered, the information niggling at him in ways he couldn't quite fathom.

Further, he'd been unable to say just what it was about the crash twenty-four years ago that so intrigued him. The crash of an Ambassador's ship on a distant, swampy world of no particular diplomatic, cultural, economic, or military significance was a blip on the radar. Diplomatic missions went awry all the time, more often than the public realized, these events typically kept out of the galactic headlines.

The crash itself had not struck anyone at the time as particularly momentous. A minor Ambassador, Viscountess Basilissa Procopio had taken her Professor husband and four-year-old daughter on what was considered among the aristocracy a futile and repulsive mission. Not only was Kziznvxrz far from the centers of haute culture, couture, and cuisine, the planet was also revolting, triggering the basal ganglia of human beings in ways that nothing else could. The lizard brain of Homo sapiens had developed an aversion to vomit and excrement as one of its earliest neurological responses. Finding someone brave enough to resist these deeply embedded autonomic responses and live on a swamp at the threshold of oblivion had been a challenge. Not a single member of the aristocracy would touch it.

The Emperor, young Athanasios Zenon, had offered the Ambassadorship to any among the aristocracy who would take it, and for several years, that offer lay open, the position unfilled, without takers. Further, ruling with a benign autocracy, he'd been unwilling to foist it upon anyone, even those who'd incurred his displeasure.

Having just started as a junior officer in the Secret Service, Deion Goulas remembered the minor stir in the Imperial household, just four short years after the death in childbirth of the Empress Consort, Ambrosia Lillis, the event plunging the Empire into deep despair. But the stir, a tempest in a teapot, really, and such a minor breach of protocol that nearly no one outside the administration had noticed, had alarmed everyone in the Imperial household.

About a year after Ambrosia's death, Emperor Zenon took up with the servant girl, Narcissa

Thanos, his deceased Consort's Lady's Maid. The affair would have scandalized the Empire, but everyone assumed it would fizzle out after a time. Except that it hadn't.

In three years, she'd taken over his bedchamber and had spread her influence like an insidious cancer throughout the Imperial household. The fait accompli of her coup d'état was to order Viscountess Basilissa Procopio to Kziznvxrz to take up the unwanted, perennially-vacant ambassadorship. The Lady's Maid wasn't so brazen as to order it outright, using instead a combination of poison and honey to engineer the appointment, but that was the effect.

A minor incident, to be sure, but of profound importance, for it had signaled a shift in power from the Emperor to his new unofficial consort. The move cemented her influence over Imperial affairs.

Deion remembered the incident vaguely, and the Ambassador's tragic end was even more obscure. All of these events, however, were being brought into sharp relief by a decision whose origin had left upon it the taint he'd come to know as the power behind the throne.

Why does the Dowager Empress Narcissa Thanos want her daughter Hecuba, the Empress-to-be, to start her Imperial tour in the Mnemosyne Constellation the day after her coronation?

* * *

Licensed Behavioral Technician Baptiste Tomaras knew he had it easy, his job as cushy as it got.

He was a member of the hand-selected team caring for the daughter of the just-deceased Gaean Emperor, Athanasios Zenon. When he told people what he did, sometimes they misunderstood him, and one response he often got was, "Oh, I didn't know she was so impaired!"

And then he had to explain that no, it wasn't the Empress-to-be, Hecuba Zenon, whom he cared for, but the Emperor's other daughter, the first one, Cybill Zenon, whose mother, Ambrosia Lillis, had so tragically died in childbirth.

"Cybill, this way, please," Baptiste said, trying to draw her away from the window.

She was pressing her face against the glasma again, an afternoon ritual for her. There wasn't any danger, the glasma impervious from either side to all but a boson-beam bomb.

He was simply implementing her behavior plan. He didn't know why the doctor didn't want her to mash her face against the glasma and slather so much drool that the window sill had started to soften. "Cybill wants to color, doesn't she? Coloring is her favorite."

"Cybill not like Bap," she said.

"Cybill doesn't like Baptiste, maybe, but she loves to color." He dangled a marker near the window where she could see it, even with her face plastered to the glasma.

Slowly, he lured her away, and soon she was at the easel, laughing and swiping randomly at the holocanvas. As much as they tried to stimulate her language skills, she was as about as expressive as she would ever get, the functional equivalent of a two-year-old.

And yes, as true of any two-year-old, she threw fits. A minor drawback of the job.

Most of the time, she was so zonked on limbic-system suppressants, she couldn't summon the adrenalin to throw them. It was rare she had to be restrained.

She threw a glance over his shoulder and said, "Bad room."

"Good coloring," Baptiste said instantly, attempting to redirect, already knowing he was too late. She was referring to the "quiet room" behind him, a door they typically kept closed. Inside the room was a bed with six-point mechanical restraints, there in case she ever got so out of control as to make chemical and manual restraints ineffective to insure her safety.

For some reason known only within the primal impulses regularly issuing forth from the underdeveloped brain of the twenty-eight year old woman, she'd begun to focus on the quiet room. Last restrained there six months ago, she would look longingly toward the room and then soil herself. Six months in her impaired retention might as well have been the Paleocene Epoch.

Another minor drawback of the job, Baptiste thought.

A few times, he'd redirected her without problem, distracting her successfully before these stimulatory signals traveled from her brain to her bladder. But once she got the words out, urination soon followed.

On cue, she wet herself, a bright yellow stain spreading down the legs of her pants.

Per the behavioral plan, Baptiste paid it no attention. "Time for Bap to go."

Two female co-workers, both behavioral techs like him, emerged from the office. One, Talitha, gave Baptiste a raised eyebrow as she passed. They escorted Cybill to the shower, Talitha talking happily, and per the behavioral plan, neither mentioning the incontinence.

Baptiste retreated to the office, where Doctor Jack Eliopolis waited, frowning at the surveillance holos, only the sounds from the shower piped into the office. "Drooling at the window, saying she doesn't like you, redirected, happily coloring, glimpses the QR, says, 'bad room,' and then wets herself." Doctor Jack looked at Baptiste. "Which one do you suppose was the antecedent?"

"We should have the QR door closed, frankly. I think it's seeing the restraints." Baptiste sat at a holoterm to do his notes, seeing his shift was over a half-hour hence.

"Good point," Doctor Jack said, nodding. "Let's do it, see whether the behavior changes."

Cybill their only patient, the team was able to refine their behavioral intervention plans with nuances not available to most facilities. The Emperor's daughter received the most advanced behavioral modification interventions and pharmacologic regimens.

"Good work today, Bap," Doctor Jack said as Baptiste was going out the door.

Navigating his way through palace security, Baptiste walked to the pneumatube station right outside palace grounds. Ten glasma tubes stood in a vertical row, the sun glinting off their shiny surfaces, lines of people at each tube, the pop-and-whoosh of capsules audible under inane music.

Rush hour, he thought glumly. Within a minute, it was his turn, and a capsule popped to a stop in front of him. He climbed in, and the pneumatube scanned his face and asked him, "Home?"

"Home, James," he replied.

The capsule took off with a whoosh, the pressure changes causing his ears to pop.

Bewildered, he watched the scenery around him change, the tube taking him toward the Acropolis at the center of New Athens. The pneumatube wasn't taking him home. Baptiste hit the emergency communicator inside the capsule.

A red light lit up, and the serotonic voice of automation asked him, "What is your emergency, please?"

"I'm being taken somewhere other than home!" he complained.

"Your vital signs are within normal parameters. Are you injured?"

"No," he said.

"Are you bleeding?"

"No," he conceded.

"Are you unconscious?"

"I damn well hope not!"

"Then it's not an emergency. Please restrict your use of the emergency communicator to emergencies. Thank you." The communicator went silent and the light went off.

Baptiste wondered what would have happened if he'd answered affirmatively to any of the annoying questions. The capsule took a side tube and dropped toward the ground. It eased into place at a station, and Baptiste stumbled to the platform.

The Acropolis was right in front of him. A symbol of civilization for four thousand years, the Acropolis on Gaea had been duplicated from the original on Earth, its soaring columns dominating the New Athens skyline.

"Inspiring, isn't it?"

The Galactim was mixed in with gurgling sounds which Baptiste could only associate with extreme digestive upset. Cybill had once eaten half a pillow before they could stop her and then had gagged for an hour, making similar sounds. He looked at the figure who'd emitted the sounds.

Inside a metal cup was a green mass of writhing goop, a thousand tendrils sliding over a control panel. Sockets near the top looked somewhat like eyes, and below that was an orifice which flapped in mistimed sequence with the sounds, "Rmhkrirmt, rhm'g rg?" The cup was held aloft at waist-height by a pair of metal extensors protruding from a motor housing mounted on the underside of the cup. A frame sprouted from the cup edges and met over the creature's head. A veil of distortion hung around the alien, like a sheet of plastic.

Baptiste quickly forgot his own distress. "What the hell are you?"

"A Kziznvxrfn. My name is Svkszvhgfh Ezhrozprh, but you can just call me Ezra."

"Uh, all right, Ezra." Baptiste glanced over his shoulder at the malfunctioning tube that had dumped him here. "I've never met a real Kzizn."

"We're really an affable bunch, once you get past the smell."

"And the sound."

"Yes, well, that too," Ezra said. The tendrils waved in unison in what looked to be a shrug.

Baptiste decided to venture a hunch. "So why'd you bring me here? How'd you bring me here?"

"You're a sharp one. Hmm, yes, the why and the how. You're one of the caretakers for Princess Cybill Zenon. She calls you Bap."

"It's the only part of my name she can remember."

"A terribly impaired young woman. Tragic, what happened at her birth."

"Tragic," Baptiste repeated.

Her mother dying in childbirth, and a life severely restricted by a stunted development. If the Empress Consort's death during childbirth hadn't been painful enough, the daughter's failure to thrive must have doubled the Emperor's grief. Not one, but two tragedies. It wasn't a wonder why Emperor Athanasios had succumbed in subsequent years to the wiles of the upstart Lady's Maid, Narcissa Thanos.

He looked at the creature. "Ok, so you know a lot about me." He opened his palms beside his shoulders.

"Er, uh, forgive me, I'm not completely conversant with Homo sapiens body language. What does that mean?"

"It means, so what? You know who I am, you got me here somehow. Now what?"

"This isn't going quite the way I expected. You humans are terribly impetuous. I didn't say that out loud, did I? Oh, my, I'll never figure out this translator." The cilia danced wildly in obvious distress, the longer tendrils slithering in circles.

"How did you get me here, anyway?" Baptiste was intrigued that the creature had managed to infiltrate the pneumatube control system.

"Electrons behave the same whether they're traveling along a wire or propagated as waves. It was easy to beam in an alternate set of instructions in response to your face."

"But the whole system's encrypted."

"You call that encryption? Hmligrmt! A newly germinated Kziznvxrfn could develop a cipher more complex than that."

The sounds the creature made were remarkably similar to those Cybill generated in her imbecile oblivion. "Ok, and now the why, please."

"Why? I don't know why your systems are so quaint. Perhaps it's the rudimentary human evolution."

Baptiste was getting annoyed. "Why did you bring me here, Ezra?"

"Oh, that, well, yes. Xovzirmtgsvgsilzg." The creature paused, all the tendrils going suddenly still. "The Kzizn think a great deception has been perpetrated upon the Gaean Empire."

* * *

Retired Governess Eugenia Ioannou considered herself a member of a specialized class of Gaean Citizen.

"Gigia, look at me!" squealed a child on the jungle gym.

"Look at you!" Eugenia replied, enjoying an afternoon in the park with her niece's daughter.

Governesses occupied a curious kind of social ambiguity. They cared for the female children of the aristocracy from the moment of birth until the age of majority, male children under the charge of governors. Governesses were typically unmarried, were considered unmarriageable, and often came from aristocratic families who'd fallen on hard times, either through misfortune, misadventure, or debauchery. Without the resources to live comfortably on their meager inheritances, they had to go into service to support themselves. Highly educated and cultured, they thought it unseemly for them to stoop to one of the myriad positions within the ranks of maids. As governesses, they were expected to bring their education and culture to bear in helping rear the scions of their more fortunate peers, and perhaps retain a modicum of dignity.

"Look what I can do!" the child screeched, hanging upside down, her dress falling over her face.

"Look what pretty panties you have!" Eugenia called back.

The girl screamed in mock dismay and righted herself.

Holding themselves aloof from the service staff, governesses were nevertheless looked down upon by their employers, in large measure because they represented what might happen to the family should similar misfortune befall them. Further, governesses represented contradiction, on the one hand retaining their gentility and on the other, having to work for a living. They typically were treated badly by their host families and the service staff. They had few rights, might be dismissed at whim, were expected to work all hours of the night, often found themselves victimized by male family members, and were inevitably blamed for the victimization that had been perpetrated upon them. Worse yet, they were expected to be disciplinarians and were prohibited from imposing consequences for misbehavior. They had to be models of comportment in the face of sometimes savage treatment.

"Come jump rope with me, Gigia!"

"I'm too old to jump rope, Darling," she called from the park bench.

Governesses however were glorified in vids that showed them granted privileges beyond those accorded house servants, such as walking through the front door. Partly because of that fictional depiction, retired Governess Eugenia Ioannou considered herself special, her status made loftier because of the family she had previously served.

The Imperial Family.

She was revered among governesses for a singular accomplishment within that service: She'd survived it.

She'd survived *Her.*

Yes, *Her.*

There was only one *Her.* And if an interlocutor didn't know whom Eugenia referred to when she mentioned *Her*, Eugenia dismissed that person as unworthy of her time and attention.

Her was of course the Dowager Empress, Narcissa Thanos.

Eugenia heaped contempt on anyone she had to explain that to.

Further, Eugenia had not only survived her service as governess to the Imperial Family and *Her*, she'd guaranteed that she and her family would be spared the Imperial Wrath in perpetuity. Although childless, she did have nephews and nieces whom she doted upon, and their future was secure.

Because she, Eugenia, had outsmarted *Her*.

The curious episode had begun with the tragic deathbed of the Empress Consort, Ambrosia Lillis, giving birth to the Princess Cybill Zenon. In preparation, they'd hired Governess Eugenia Ioannou, who was expected and prepared to care for the child from the instant she and her mother left the birthing chamber.

But instead of both leaving it, only one of them had.

The death of the Empress Consort Ambrosia Lillis had thrown her entire coterie of servants into unemployment, all of whom sought service positions elsewhere. All except the Lady's Maid, Narcissa Thanos.

Eugenia remembered that first terrible week, the palace in chaos, the Empire prostrate with grief over the tragic end to the fairytale romance. Having been enthralled with the courtship between the Emperor and his Consort, Eugenia was stricken too, having plunged herself nightly into immersivids of the royal couple, hurling herself into Ambrosia's part like every other female throughout the Empire, even sneaking home a few of the hormone-infused, black-market seduction scenarios, orgasm guaranteed or your money back. Against this backdrop of a fairytale romance and a fairytale pregnancy, the Consort's death in childbirth had left the Empire devastated.

Heartbroken, Eugenia hadn't been able to refuse the entreaties of the Lady's Maid, Narcissa Thanos, to see the baby, Princess Cybill Zenon.

Unlike everyone else, who seemed entranced by the vulnerable, day-old child, Narcissa recoiled, her hand to her mouth. "Don't you think she looks ... slow?"

"Not as if she'll have mastered several languages by now," Eugenia retorted.

"Well, no, of course not, but … I must be mistaken."

And each time, twice per day, that Narcissa laid eyes on the child, she'd initially have that ill-concealed look of concern, as though something were abnormal about the child's development. The two of them took to having afternoon tea, Narcissa seeming disconsolate over the late Consort, berating herself for inattention in letting her charge slip away. During that first week, while the Lady's Maid secured the late Empress Consort's effects and quietly resolved the estate, these visits were not considered inappropriate, as long as they remained brief and untoward.

"I've applied to become your nurse assistant," Narcissa told Eugenia abruptly on day seven.

Taken aback, Eugenia did her best to conceal her response. It was presumptuous of a lowly Lady's Maid to think she might give succor to one so delicate as the Infant Princess, a task ill-suited to anyone not belonging to the aristocracy. Only a member of the lesser nobility might be entrusted with her care.

She was livid when she found the next day that Narcissa had been added to her staff. No coattail-riding upstart member of the service staff was going to wriggle her way into the Imperial Family's good graces under her watch. Not if Eugenia could help it!

But as Lady's Maid to the Empress Consort, Narcissa apparently had been consulted on a frequent basis as to the Consort's druthers, inquiries made on behalf of the Emperor himself, and to Eugenia's utter horror, by the Emperor himself, who it appeared had taken a liking to the Lady's Maid.

So Narcissa stayed.

Perhaps she reminds him of his lost betrothed, Eugenia told herself at the time. But as a precaution, being a suspicious one, Eugenia began archiving the nursery vid feeds. Just in case, she told herself.

"If it's all right with you, Lady Governess," Narcissa told Eugenia just a day or two into her new position, "I'd like to spend part of my day with the Procopio family. Their daughter's but a few hours older than Princess Cybill, and mayhap I might learn a thing or two from Governess Filmena."

She certainly needs to learn manners, Eugenia thought, welcoming any excuse to get the upstart commoner out of her hair for a few hours each day. Not that the social graces a princess was required to acquire could be imparted by someone so debased as a servant.

The Procopio family was of the lesser nobility like Eugenia herself, but unlike her, they'd enjoyed continued prosperity and Imperial favor, living just outside the palace grounds on an estate of enviable size. Eugenia did not begrudge them their good fortune.

She knew Governess Filmena personally, the two women consulting each other sometimes on matters of care. Eugenia pitied Filmena for the task ahead of her, for it was rumored that the Procopio child's genetic profile indicated a difficult development. While such genetic syndromes as fragile-x, Turner's, and de-novo dysmorphia had been eradicated from the gene-pool, new infirmities in gene structure cropped up as fast as old ones were eliminated. Many genetic disorders could not be traced to a single gene but were instead spread among several genes. In Lydia Procopio's gene structure, no specific abnormality had been identified, but an aggregate of lesser oddities prognosticated trouble for her development.

Princess Cybill Zenon's genetic structure was clear of any oddities.

"We should make a day of it, you know, an outing of sorts, on the palace grounds, of course," Narcissa said one day, the babies nearing two weeks old.

Eugenia thought hard, disliking the idea but knowing the grounds secure in every way, hard-pressed to demur without causing the overly-persuasive Narcissa to run to the Emperor in complaint.

Sugar pines encircled a glade whose succulent grasses glowed with emerald brilliance, dew scintillating in the morning sun, each baby in a carriage, gurgling happily.

"Eugenia, might I talk with you a moment?" Governess Filmena asked.

Eugenia looked at her, her counterpart from the Procopio household. The two of them knew a common tragedy. A swindler out of Bellona XI had suckered both their forebears into investing nearly all their assets into a pyramid scheme of massive proportion and had absconded with the lot of it, leaving a substantial number of the lesser nobility impoverished.

Narcissa was doting over the girls in their respective carriages, paying the two governesses no attention whatsoever.

Filmena looked to one side and inclined her head that direction, indicating her desire to speak privately. The two Governesses turned their backs on Narcissa with the two infants.

"What the hell is he thinking, hiring that strumpet?" Filmena immediately asked her the moment they were out of earshot, her voice low, her speech fast, her face furious. "Not that I'm questioning the Emperor's wisdom, but it's just not right!"

Eugenia was relieved that someone else shared her opinion. She'd not been able to garner an iota of support in her opposition to the strumpet's appointment.

"Anyway, seems she feels a bit miffed at your haughty treatment and tried to inveigle me into getting you let up a little on her. If anything, you're not hard enough with her, Eugenia. Seems to have assumed airs in her uppity little mind that she knows better than you how to rear a princess. The utter gall!"

The two of them twittered.

"I'm given to understand Lydia's genetic profile doesn't look good," Eugenia said.

Filmena frowned and nodded, giving her counterpart that look.

The look Eugenia had seen on Narcissa's face.

Alarmed, Eugenia turned.

Fifty feet behind them, Narcissa was still bent over the two carriages, her lilting voice carrying across the meadow.

That look.

Her intuition screaming that Narcissa had just done something to Princess Cybill Zenon, Governess Eugenia scurried back to the carriages. "Got me a fright, I did," she said to Narcissa as she poked her head into the Imperial carriage.

The bonnet was a bit askew, but the baby stared at her, a bewildered look in her face.

Odd, Eugenia thought, she's usually happy to see me. Concerned, she lifted the infant out of the carrier. Immediately, the child began to cry.

"Oh, dear me, I've gone and upset you, haven't I?" And she hurried to take the squalling infant back to the nursery, carrying her the whole way, the afternoon outing a disaster.

Not terribly long after that, at the daily Imperial showing, a ritual in which Emperor Athanasios deigned to gaze upon his child, Eugenia saw something between the Emperor and the upstart Maid-turned-nurse. Just a glance, but enough to raise Eugenia's suspicion.

And she discovered shortly afterward that Narcissa was retiring most evenings not to the servant's quarters toward the rear of the palace grounds, but to the Emperor's chambers.

The information was nearly as devastating as the death of the Empress Consort, Ambrosia Lillis.

In her daily routine of bringing the infant to a viewing room to await the Emperor's arrival, Eugenia was sometimes alone with the Imperial infant, Narcissa with her at other times. Eugenia took advantage of the times she was alone to place miniature holocams in a few of the viewing rooms.

Within a month, she had on holocam the information she needed to secure Narcissa's immediate dismissal, the encounter reminding

Eugenia of the seduction-scenario immersivids she'd furtively watched during the Emperor's courtship of his Consort.

First, before confronting the strumpet with the incriminating vid, Eugenia placed a physical copy in two secure locations and then rigged a dead-man switch. A term borrowed from days of yore when electrical devices ran on slim filaments of metal known as wires, a dead-man switch was a device that automatically signaled at regular intervals unless stopped by the person who held the switch. If the person ever died, the switch then flipped when no one stopped it. Eugenia's dead-man switch was her sending a message to ghost holomail account. If Eugenia didn't send the message once per week, the ghost account would then auto-send the incriminating vid to multiple news outlets and a frivolous litigation firm she'd employed named Dewey, Treatem, Likashose, and Howe.

"Gigia, look at that man!" the child on the jungle gym squealed.

Eugenia leapt to her feet, startled out of her reverie.

A bizarre-looking figure in a trench coat tottered toward her through the park.

She almost grabbed her great-niece and fled.

The features looked to be those of a clown, a bulbous red nose protruding from a garish, white-cream face, where two green-rimmed eyes were mounted, looking different directions, an oversize smile in ruby-red lips permanently plastered between the cheeks. The face might have come directly out of some children's morning holo show. A long, limp trench coat hung from narrow, angular shoulders, giving glimpses of a livid-green torso. Dress slacks hung from a bowlish, protrusive stomach, and from each pant leg protruded a metal spike, which rang with a metallic twang each time they struck the plascrete.

"Please, don't be frightened."

The words reached her over the nearly-simultaneous sounds of extreme digestive distress, "Kovzhv, wlm'g yv uirtsgvmvw."

The creature was now close enough that Eugenia could see that the livid-green torso was a mass of jiggling jelly covered with writhing cilia, a few longer tentacles slithering over a device mounted just inside the trench coat.

"Ewww!" her great-niece said, holding her nose.

"Did I leak a little? I apologize for my terrible-smelling breath."

"That's your breath?" the girl said. "And what are those sounds? Can you teach me how to make 'em?"

The creature issued a series of snarts and forkles, which sent the girl into a tizzy, and soon, Eugenia too was laughing uncontrollably, delighted to hear the girl's hilarity.

The retired Governess later wiped the tears from her eyes, unable to remember the last time she'd laughed so hard.

And by then the mass of alien green protoplasm was burbling contentedly, turning from one to the other, as if looking at each in turn with its optical organelles.

"Well, thank you, whoever you are," Eugenia said. "I haven't laughed that much in a long time."

"I am Svkszvhgfh Ezhrozprh, but you may call me 'Ezra,' if that is easier for you to pronounce.

I'd like to talk with you about what happened in the days following the death of the Empress Consort, Ambrosia Lillis."

Chapter 5

"You're who?!" Lydia stared through the bars at the badge.

"Imperial Bureau of Suspicion," it said in bright red letters, the man's name, "Doukas," prominent below that. And then the man holding it whisked it away.

"What'd you say your name was?" she asked again with a sneer.

Furious that they'd imprisoned her father for no good reason, she was now doubly furious that she'd been detained. The foul atmosphere of Theogony didn't help, its air without the methanogens that thickened and sweetened Kziznvxrz. The atmosphere of her home world contained nearly five percent ammonia, hydrogen, carbon dioxide, and methane, giving it the sweet smells of anaerobic decomposition.

"Listen, Dickass, I'm a citizen of Kziznvxrz. You can't hold me against my will. You've got no jurisdiction."

The ugly face beyond the bars grew uglier. "You're in Imperial territory, where I can do what I damn well please."

"My father and I have been trading in Gaean territory with Gaean approval for over five years. We've never had a glop of trouble from any Imperial representative, and we've never had a ship impounded for contraband. Look it up, Detective Doukas. None of our ships have so much as a moving violation. Further, our company is under contract with the Gaean Empire to deliver critical lithofuels to Cygnus Twenty. If we give the word, Cygnus Twenty goes without."

"That's Agent, by the way," Doukas said.

"All right, Agent. What are we being held for?"

"Where'd you come from in that fancy vehicle?"

Not answering my questions, Lydia thought. Two can play that game, but is it a game I really want to play? All she really wanted was to wrap up the contract with Titanide Aquafoods and get off this foul-smelling Terran planet back to Kziznvxrz. Longing for the open, mud-brown expanses of semi-liquefied tidal flats, whose constant, quiet percolation burbled with such delectable aromas, Lydia sighed. "Look, we just want to go home, all right?"

"The faster you answer my questions, the faster you get home."

"I heard you talking to Warden Minas. You're planning to send us both to Gaea, halfway across the galaxy. You don't have any intention of letting us go home." She stared at him. "Deny it, Agent Dickass."

He stared at her silently, denying her even the comfort of being right.

"Look, whatever my father and I are being arrested for, Orrin hasn't done anything. How about we make a deal? You let Orrin go, and I'll stop calling you Dickass."

"I've been called worse."

Not budging. She should have expected as much and wondered whether he was amenable to bribery. Not that she'd consider it, but she'd been given to understand that the closer to Gaea one got, the more grease these Grecians expected.

"I've already turned him loose, by the way."

She saw the cold calculation in his dull, compassion-less eyes. I'll bet he thinks he can gain my trust by telling me that. Not that he's actually let Orrin go, either, she thought, knowing these humans capable of deceit.

When her father had first introduced the concept to her, he'd been telling her about the tragic accident that had orphaned her on Kziznvxrz.

"It may not have been an accident. Someone may have sabotaged the ship in such a way as to hide the fact they tampered with it," Xsirh told her.

"Why would someone hide anything, Papa?" the girl said, now eight years old, her memories of Gaea distant. The sight, sound, odor, and texture of the Kziznvxrfn were as familiar to her as her human parents had once been. Xsirhglksvi was particularly familiar to her, he who had reared her over the objections of his peers and despite the vehement opposition from a dissident Kziznvxrfn splinter group, the Wrwrmrfn.

Of course, technically, Xsirhglksvi Xlmhgzmgrmrwvh wasn't even male, the Kzizn able to perform in either role, changing their reproductive organelles as needed for the circumstance. Kzizn reproduced in four ways, most often preferring to reproduce asexually through fission, in which they would split in two by pinching through their long axis. They could also reproduce through an interaction with other Kzizn-vxrz known as heterogeneous conjugation, the human equivalent of copulation, either partner taking either role, or through endogenous autogamy, otherwise known as self-fertilization. Thus, they really couldn't be insulted by telling them to go procreate with themselves.

Something Lydia was tempted to tell this pinch-faced troglodyte in front of her. "Liar."

"Where'd you come from?"

It was clear to Lydia that the Agent was at least as stubborn as she was. And so she let loose on him, telling him to procreate with himself in his own back passage, something her variation on his name had already suggested.

The pinched face went purple, and he stormed out in a tizzy, leaving Lydia alone in the isolation cell.

Well, that was really effective in securing my release, she thought, looking around.

A set of carbo-nick alloy bars stretched from plascrete floor to plascrete ceiling. Around the cage door were solid plascrete walls, easily a foot thick. A single bare loomglobe hung near the ceiling, at a height at least double Lydia's. The walls on either side were more plascrete, and the back wall of her cell was the native bedrock. There were no windows, and she saw that the only vents were in the ceiling twelve feet above her, obscured by the loomglobe.

She stepped to the back of the cell and put her hands against the wall.

Somewhere close, she felt the pounding of surf, the wild seas of Theogony beating persistently against the few archipelagos that dared raise themselves like upstarts above the turbulent waters. The sounds of ocean transmitted to her hands through rock reminded Lydia of Kziznvxrz, and her longing for home returned.

She turned, put her back to the wall, and bunched her fists.

I will not cry! she ordered herself.

She slid down the wall, hugged her legs to her chest, put her forehead to her knees.

And wept.

* * *

"What do you mean, you can't get me a ship?! I have to endure this stench another day?!"

Colonel Melanctha Remes, commander of the IBS Command Outpost on Lucina IX, recoiled at the vituperation in the voice of Agent Erastus Doukas on Theogony. His holoimage hung above her desk like a miniature incubus. At any moment, she expected the diaphanous figurine to whip out a trident and sprout a forked tail. Immediately upon hearing that Agent Doukas hadn't been able to procure transport to Gaea, Colonel Remes had requisitioned a patrol from nearby Momus XVIII, but it had been forced to halt at exactly midnight GMT or Gaean Mean Time.

"Nothing is moving today, Doukas," she said, "not a single vessel anywhere in the Empire."

Today was the coronation of Princess Hecuba Zenon, daughter of the just-deceased Emperor Athanasios Zenon and the upstart Lady's Maid, and now Dowager Empress, Narcissa Thanos.

"Can't we get an exemption?" the IBS Agent asked, his holoimage distorted by multiple layers of encryption. "Didn't the palace itself order their detainment?"

"Don't say that!" Remes remonstrated, cringing. Now, she'd have to purge the transmission from any and all systematic recording and archiving devices here on Lucina IX, there on Theogony, and at every intervening retransmission station between the two planets. She put in an immediate trace to record those holonet hops. But it wasn't the hours of work ahead she regretted. "Fool! You'll be lucky if you aren't detained for interrogation on Gaea yourself! Out!"

She cut the connection, and the incubus dematerialized from above her desk. Colonel Remes knew she was reamed, her career over.

Doukas really stuck his dick up his ass this time, she thought, and mine too. There was no concealing such a major blunder from the Imperial Secret Service, whose clandestine tentacles reached into every skeleton-filled closet throughout the Empire, no matter what level of encryption nor how many layers of security obscured it from scrutiny.

With bulldog persistence, Melanctha method-ically retrieved the incriminating utterance from the Command Outpost archives and destroyed it, and then did the same for every holonet re-lay between Lucina IX and Theogony, her bowels grinding, her palms sweating, her hands trem-bling. Each relay would record her actions, of course. There was no obscuring the fact that she was destroying the transmission, but she hoped against hope that when she was tried for con-spiracy in Imperial courts that her having done so would mitigate her role and perhaps result in a lighter sentence than she might have otherwise received.

She held no hope she wouldn't be arrested and tried. Those were inevitable from the moment Doukass had said "palace."

It didn't matter that it was true. All that mat-tered was he'd said it.

Once she was finished, Colonel Melanctha Remes summoned a live holofeed of the festivi-ties on Gaea, finding comfort in Hecuba Zenon's coronation and its attendant Pangaea.

In ancient times, the festival of Pangaea con-sisted of numerous sacrifices to the Earth Goddess Gaea and her mate, the Star God Heaven, whose joining gave birth to all the lesser Titanide gods and goddesses, Oceanus, Coeus, Crius, Hyperion, Iapetus, Theia, Rhea, Themis, Mnemosyne, Phoebe, Tethys, and lastly the immutable Cronus. In modern times, Pangaea simply referred to the bacchanalia and saturnalia common to licentious celebrations.

Pangaean debauchery was already evident on Gaea, the spigots of the Imperial vaults opened wide, fueling a grand celebration.

The festivities helped to assuage Colonel Remes' feelings of impending doom.

* * *

Vasilios Xenakis, Special Agent Ad-hoc of the Imperial Secret Service, picked up on the transmission immediately, and before Colonel Remes had deleted it, he'd obtained a copy and was already forwarding it to his superiors.

Maybe it'll redeem my career and earn me a post somewhere closer to Gaea, Vasilios thought, closer to the grave of the only person I've ever loved.

He hadn't meant to fall in love with the Empress Consort, Ambrosia Lillis.

She'd be fifty years old today, he realized.

He'd been assigned to head security at another coronation at the innocent age of twenty-five. For a Kalamata native, an extraordinary first assignment, but not unexpected for a graduate of the Corfu Institute of Military Studies, the finest academy on Gaea. The coronation of Athanasios Zenon as Acting Emperor was as lavish as that being held today for his second daughter Hecuba. But that first one might as well have been Ambrosia's debutante ball.

Vasilios watched the festivities on one holo, and on another, he watched the planet Theogony in the Erato subsystem of the Mnemosyne Constellation. It did not strike him as ironic that the coronation of Hecuba Zenon was being held on the anniversary of Ambrosia's death.

It was deliberate, arranged by the Dowager Empress, Narcissa Thanos.

Agent Xenakis sent a com to the other nineteen ships under his command, their placement in the Oort cloud forming a perfect dodecahedron, ensuring complete visual and sensory coverage of the entire Erato subsystem. Each ship in the squadron acknowledged.

Like his counterpart in the domestic security branch, the Imperial Bureau of Suspicion, Xenakis knew precisely where his orders had originated, but he was not so foolish as to disclose it. Erastus Doukas had earned himself an early retirement to a dungeon on Gaea, or at least to a cell on Tyrintha, the prison planet.

From his position in the dodecahedron, Vasilios saw only one star beyond Erato, between him and the vast void of empty space, Andromeda the next nearest galaxy at 2.5 million light years away. That one star was a dull, blue-white primary with barely enough lumens to cut through the dense atmosphere of its only planet.

The Kziznvxrz subsystem was the outermost in the constellation, so far beyond the nearest space lane that the region had no strategic worth whatsoever. The Kzizn home world, a murky, muddy ball, hovered relatively close to the cold blue sun. The half-a-dozen diplomatic missions to the worthless planet had all ended abruptly, the two races mutually repulsive to each other. The last attempt to establish an embassy on Kzizn some twenty-four years ago had ended in tragedy, the ship coming apart on atmospheric entry.

Doukas's bungled efforts to clear Theogony of any sentient aliens would certainly aggravate diplomatic relations, especially his transporting the five Kzizn citizens to Gaea for interrogation, three of whom were already en route.

Vasilios had seen the notation that one of the two Kzizn citizens awaiting transport to Gaea was a human female. It had struck him as odd, the Kziznvxrz ecology offensive to human sensibilities and deleterious to human health. He couldn't imagine anyone living there, much less obtaining citizenship.

The image on the holo in front of Vasilios shimmered.

What was that? he wondered, examining the Kzizn primary closely.

"Agent Xenakis," his com squawked, "I've got some odd signals from Kzizn, unusual disruptions in the sub-ether. Spectral analyses appear normal. Please advise."

The shimmering, Vasilios thought. "Get me an analysis of the Kzizn propulsion technology."

"Yes, Sir."

Everyone knew their technology was superior. A reclusive race, the Kzizn had declined several entreaties for technological exchange. Further, all attempts to purloin one of their vessels had failed. The only reason the Gaean Empire hadn't invaded was the Kzizn's utter lack of ambition. And the fact that any such invasion was likely to be repulsed. As long as they didn't attack Gaea outposts or try to annex Gaean territory, the Empire seemed willing to let them alone.

No one had seen a Kzizn weapon either, although they were rumored to exist.

"Agent Xenakis, there, uh, apparently isn't an analysis to be had. The Kzizn propulsion technology hasn't been studied to any appreciable depth."

"There must be some information on it somewhere." Maybe their sub-ether drives are beyond our understanding, he thought.

"Just a few observations of their ships flying at low speeds. And even then they're difficult to look at. They're often described as 'diaphanous' and 'illusory.' We've never been able to replicate the technology."

"In other words, we don't know how they travel, do we?"

"No, Agent, we don't."

"They could be invading Theogony right now, and we wouldn't know it."

"I guess that's theoretically possible, Sir."

Vasilios amplified Theogony on his holo.

As he watched, the planet began to shimmer.

Agent Xenakis hit the red alert.

Chapter 6

It's a party for them, but not for us, Drucilla thought, pausing to look at a holo.

Imperial Laundry Maid Drucilla Kanelos frowned at the bustle around her, all ten thousand of the Empress's personal staff in an uproar. In the middle of the night, the order to pack had descended upon the service staff like a cloud of locusts.

A tour of the Empire was an obligatory part of any Emperor's investiture. The service staff could have guessed they'd have to pack for an extended excursion. The Imperial space liner, the Prince George, named after the first Monarch of Greece back on Earth, was kept in orbit, stocked, provisioned, and ready to depart at a moment's notice for exactly such occasions. The exigencies of ruling such vast domains as the Gaean Empire were likely to whisk its ruling family anywhere throughout the galaxy, and the space liner's always being ready kept the chaos barely within manageable limits.

Drucilla and the other nine-thousand, nine-hundred-ninety-nine service staff members usually got wind of such excursions long before the departure date, but the untimely demise of Emperor Athanasios and the swift investiture of his second daughter Hecuba as Empress had launched the Empire into a state of high confusion.

Further, Drucilla was expected to make a compulsory appearance at the coronation and Imperial ball in a show of fealty. Disregarding this requisite duty would certainly invite the castigation of the Dowager Empress and an immediate dismissal, if not criminal charges of disloyalty.

And the Dowager Empress never forgot a slight. Not even the ones she'd imagined.

Drucilla was nearing retirement, at least ten years senior to Narcissa. She had trained Narcissa in the skills required of a Laundry Maid when Narcissa was but fifteen, newly entering maid service in the Procopio household, and as fresh from the provinces as a rutabaga from the ground. Like any attractive girl from a rural background nearing the age of legal consent, Narcissa had found herself in a swarm of male service staff. Only Drucilla's swift intervention had kept her from getting pregnant and therefore fired. But the incident had awakened Narcissa from her provincial slumber.

In Drucilla's mind, at least, it was probably the only reason she had kept her job and her life. She had to attribute her longanimous service to the Imperial family to something.

The Dowager Empress, it appeared, never forgot a favor, either.

She wasn't the only one with a long memory. Throughout her decades of service, Laundry Maid Drucilla Kanelos hadn't forgotten a single incident.

Especially not *the* incident.

Checking the Imperial bed sheets for hymenal blood on the morning after the Imperial consummation was the highest duty accorded to a Laundry Maid. A duty so sacred that Laundry Maids were sworn to secrecy before being initiated into the art. And not all Laundry Maids were initiated, only the select few who'd be handling the matrimonial linen. When a succession was in doubt, or when a blushing bride's extra virgin olive oil was thought to have been spoiled, the Laundry Maid handling the matrimonial linens was sure to be called upon to verify having seen the hymenal stains. The lives of many a Laundry Maid had been placed in danger to prevent verification.

This practice had spread throughout the nobility, and even upper-class commoners were said to have taken on the airs of this rare bird of passage, its spread accompanied by old maid's tales of how to mimic the telltale break, dyed-red robin's egg among them.

If you're that distrustful, Drucilla was inclined to tell them, just don't marry the meretrix!

And why commoners would adopt the practice baffled her completely, as if their ranks weren't already tainted with commoner blood.

The second time Drucilla was called to check the matrimonial linens had challenged her principles of propriety. The first time, she'd been deeply honored, the bride-to-be having been the Imperial Consort, Ambrosia Lillis, daughter of Countess Giorgi Lillis, hers a hymen worth breaking.

But the second had been that of Narcissa Thanos, she who'd entered the service profession as a Laundry Maid in the House of Procopio at age fifteen, a rutabaga who'd just fallen off the proverbial vegetable truck, whom Drucilla had trained in the arts of matrimonial linen handling.

And the ways a hymenal stain might be mimicked.

Try as she might, Drucilla hadn't been able to prove the hymenal stains fraudulent. Narcissa, she knew, was too cunning not to devise a foolproof guise. The Imperial succession depended upon it.

Drucilla remembered being called to audience with Emperor Regent Athanasios, his first Consort dead five years, his only child from that joining a functional idiot who required specialized, twenty-four hour care, his new wife ruling the Imperial household with an iron fist.

The dull gaze tracked her approach but seemed to be empty of the spirit that most forty-year-olds would have. His father ailing and having withdrawn years ago from any active role in governing, the Emperor Regent exerted full control over his empire, but he seemed to Drucilla to lack any control over his own life.

Pitiable, she'd have said, had she been asked to describe him.

"You're Drucilla, yes?" he said simply. The courtiers on either side of him had verified her identity five times in the last hour. And the Imperial Secret Service had done the same.

"Yes, your Imperial Highness, Laundry Maid to Her Imperial Highness, Empress Narcissa," she said, dropping instantly to both knees, the carpet so thick she thought she'd dropped onto a cloud. Drucilla kept her gaze on the floor in front of her. It was considered defiance to look upon his August Person. The guards lining the walls were ready to leap upon her at the first sign of the least hostility.

"Yes, and she tells me, the person who trained her in the very arts you've now employed on her behalf."

"Yes, your Highness." Respond only to the question asked, and do not elaborate, she'd been told by the courtiers who briefed everyone prior to entering the Imperial presence.

"Ironic, isn't it?"

"Some might say, your Highness."

"I ask you, Drucilla, Maid of the matrimonial laundry, to look at me."

She shuddered, the request unexpected.

"Please, it's important."

The request was elegant for its simplicity, and Drucilla raised her gaze. She was no spring chicken, of a similar age as Emperor Athanasios, and she knew he'd suffered. She found she was looking not at the ruler of the human-occupied universe, but at a person who found himself trapped by events seeking one bit of solace, the slightest consolation, that might make all his suffering worth something.

And the realization slammed into her mind: He wants me to deny she was a virgin.

Reeling, she struggled to keep her gaze on him, the walls warping, the room skewing. It was one thing to be asked such a question, but it was quite surreal to know that the person asking— one's own Sovereign Emperor—wanted a particular answer, a particularly damning answer.

"Tell me what you found this morning on the conjugal sheets, Drucilla."

Her throat closed on her, and sweat sprang up on her brow. Her heart thundered in her breast, and her palms were chill and clammy. Her bowels cramped and heaved, and her gorge rose in her gullet. "Your ... Highness," she said, her voice catching, "I found ... a stain that appeared to have come ... from a broken hymen."

"Appeared?" His gaze didn't change, as though he asked by rote.

"It passed all the required tests, your Highness."

He sighed.

An Imperial sigh was far too ambiguous for Drucilla's concrete mind to interpret. In retrospect, she'd wished she'd asked, but it would have been presumptuous of her to do so, in violation of all convention. And it would have certainly come to Empress Narcissa's attention.

She'd been ready to retreat, thinking the audience over, thinking she'd been dismissed from the Imperial Presence.

"You applied all the required tests to the best of your ability?"

This time, before answering, she glanced furtively to each side of the throne.

"Leave us," the Emperor said.

The courtiers glanced amongst themselves, hesitating.

"Now, please. Guards too."

"But—"

"Now, please." His voice hadn't changed, but something had.

And now Drucilla was frightened.

Being granted a solitary audience with such an August Person was analogous to receiving the Employee of the Month award. Either she'd done something stupid or she was about to be fired.

The moment they were alone, the Emperor sighed again. "And turn off the recording equipment," he said aloud to no one. "I order it!" He cast a baleful glare around the room as if to sear shut with just his gaze any lens that might still be open.

"You may speak freely, Drucilla. You know Narcissa as well as anyone."

Taken aback, Drucilla felt an inkling of hope, seeing now for the first time a spark of spirit. "She talks like a snake that bites its own ass," she blurted.

He looked at her, and then chuckled inanely. "But snakes don't have asses."

"You see how she twists things? Just what I'm talking about, your Highness."

"Not quite the question I was asking." He gave a giddy giggle. "Hymenal tissues be damned! Archaic practice that someone should have banned long ago. Tell me truthfully, Drucilla. Is Narcissa faithful?"

It was so direct a question that Drucilla couldn't have answered with anything other than a direct answer. "Panta pisti," she said in Greek. "Always faithful, your Highness." And then she looked at him directly. "To herself."

"And no one else, eh?" Emperor Athanasios threw his head back and laughed, then stopped abruptly. "Yes, that's my observation of the conniving bitch, too." He leaned forward and peered at her. "You tried very hard to prove that the stains weren't from her hymen, didn't you?"

And now Drucilla was no longer afraid. "Yes, your Highness. I tried to prove they weren't with every test at my disposal. And I'm disappointed to report that I was unsuccessful."

The Emperor grunted, frowning. "Thank you for trying, Drucilla. It appears we're now completely ensnared in her web, doesn't it?"

Twenty-odd years later, as she finished packing her bag for the requisite sovereign tour of the Empire, Drucilla glanced over at the holo.

An image of the Empress-to-be, Hecuba Zenon, waved at unseen crowds, a glittering, diamond-encrusted dress draping her to her feet, being paraded to the Parthenon in central New Athens to be crowned Empress.

Are you really the daughter of Emperor Athanasios Zenon and the Laundry Maid Narcissa Thanos?

* * *

Erastus Doukas, Agent Provocateur with the Imperial Bureau of Suspicion, stared dumbly at the woman in front of him.

She whipped out her badge and thrust it back where it came from with pickpocket agility. "Agent Nellie Roussos, Secret Service, Internal Investigations Unit. We're here to take your detainees back to Gaea."

He'd barely had time to read her badge. He looked over her shoulder.

A group of muscular suits in dark glasses and gum-soled shoes stood in two silent ranks behind her. And beyond them was a Gaean patrol cruiser, Imperial emblems emblazoned on its sides, the dull rumble of its idling engines audible. They'd managed to land the ship astride the estuary between the detention center and the main island, the seas roiling beneath the ship as though angry that it hovered just out of reach.

"I'm glad you're here," Erastus said. "I thought I'd have to languish in paradise another day. How'd you get permission to travel on coronation day?" He entered the building and headed toward the cages at the rear.

"Special dispensation," the woman said, following briskly, her nose wrinkling. "What's that smell?" Her speech was as devoid of expression as her face. The twin ranks of muscular suits followed her with uncanny precision.

"The alien. And most of the smell is now contained by his envirosuit. You should have smelled it before." Erastus pushed through the first set of double doors.

"The Kziznvxrfn, right? What's his name, Agent Doukas?"

He glanced askance at her. "You said that almost as well as the female prisoner. She calls him 'Xsirh,' but his full name is much longer. You should hear her say it. Tongue-twister doesn't do it justice."

" 'Xsirh?' "

"Yeah, just like that, better than I can pronounce it. You a linguinologist, or something?" The word didn't sound quite right to him. Erastus hoped he wasn't displaying his ignorance again. They went through another set of double doors. "I thought I was gonna have to suffer that stench for days. Oh, by the way, she calls him her father." He glanced at her.

"That is a curiosity, Agent Doukas," the woman said, looking at him dully.

"Yeah, funny thing, that. Raised her since she was four, she says." Doukas was put off by Agent Roussos, her nonchalant manner, her clipped speech, her abrupt manner, her impassive face.

"Four. On Kziznvxrz. How odd."

Perfect pronunciation again, Doukas noted. They approached the final set of doors, a guard of his on either side of it. "I put her in isolation so she couldn't talk to the alien. But if you need a translator, she's your man."

"She's a man?"

Erastus stopped and looked at Agent Roussos. "No, I said, 'She's your man.' Never heard the expression before? Where you been livin'? Some backwater swamp somewhere?"

"Oh, pardon. A misunderstanding, Agent Doukas. Through these doors?"

"Her cell is beyond the door to the right, his is straight ahead to the rear. I'd suggest keeping them apart on that little boat of yours. They're pretty slippery, these two. Might start a mutiny if you let 'em near each other."

"I will note your suggestion, Agent Doukas."

They went through the doors, four of the muscular suits moving toward the alien in the last cell, four heading down a short corridor toward the woman's isolation cell.

Agent Doukas and Agent Roussos watched them carry the limp alien in its envirosuit, the reinforced material easily holding the creature's weight. Kzizn were terribly slow on dry land, far better adapted to mudflats and bogs.

Moments later, the other quartet of guards emerged with the woman, her wrists cuffed in bright glasma circlets.

Erastus was struck again by her breathtaking beauty.

"Lydia Procopio?" Agent Roussos asked, her voice as dull as ever.

"That's me," the woman said. "Who're you?"

"Agent Nellie Roussos, Secret Service, Internal Investigations Unit. You're not under arrest. We'd just like to ask you and the alien a few questions."

"We haven't done anything. We've both been inoculated. Where are you taking us?"

"Immaterial. Your ship will be safe in the meantime, won't it, Agent Doukas?"

Roussos hadn't looked at Erastus. "Uh, yeah, it'll be safe." He wasn't sure why, but he got the feeling there was more to Agent Roussos than met the eye. She was just too damned tidy.

"Well, all right," Lydia said, throwing a glance his way.

"Pleased to meet you, Ms. Procopio."

"Mutual, Agent Dickass," she said pleasantly.

He recoiled, blinking at her as they hauled her out the door and down the corridor. "While you're at it, Agent, beat some humility into her."

"Not authorized, Agent Doukas." The woman turned to look at him. "What did she call you? Was that a colloquial pejorative?"

"Uh, yeah, that's what it was." He smiled to cover his bewilderment and walked with her to the entrance of the building.

"Oh, uh, Agent Doukas?" Agent Roussos stopped just beyond the threshold and turned to look at him. "We weren't here."

"Yes, of course. You may rely on my complete dereliction." He hoped he'd said that right.

She hesitated momentarily. "Thank you." She shook his hand with a limb as limp as a fish and stepped toward her ship, its boarding ramp just a few feet from the base of the steps.

He watched the boarding ramp retract. The engines began to rev, the dull rumble escalating to a high-pitched whine.

Erastus Doukas, Agent Provocateur with the Imperial Bureau of Suspicion, couldn't quite pinpoint why the whole episode had been so disconcerting, from the clandestine meeting in a brightly-lit alley to this bewildering transfer of detainees on coronation day. It was all too bizarre for the small-minded Doukas.

Then the patrol vessel with Imperial emblems lifted slightly from its perch and dematerialized in front of him.

* * *

"What was that?!" Vasilios called to his navigator on the com. The image of Theogony on the holoscreen had shimmered again.

"More sub-ether disruptions, Sir," his com squawked over the roar of engines.

The second set of such disruptions from the surface of Theogony.

His vessel plummeted toward the planet, all engines blazing, the nineteen other ships in the flotilla also scorching their way toward Theogony.

Special Agent Ad-hoc Xenakis of the Imperial Secret Service began to sweat. Even if they managed to spot a Kzizn ship, the tractor beams aboard his ship would be unlikely to latch onto the slippery alien vessel. Not a physicist, Vasilios had a limited understanding of sub-ether principles. But he knew that a ship in sub-ether couldn't be latched onto or fired upon. Sub-ether was like a window into another universe, he'd been told. His Musca-class vessel was perfect for surveillance but a poor vehicle for interception.

The autopilot turned on the retros, the deceleration slamming Vasilios against the restraints.

You'd think I'd get used to this by now, he thought idly, his eyes glued to the holo, his face stretching. "Tractor beams ready?"

"Yes, Sir, but uh ..."

"I know they won't work on a ship in sub-ether, but we have to try."

"Yes, Sir."

He didn't blame the young navigator. Theirs was a thankless task. They were as likely to be executed if something went wrong as not. Simply because the Dowager Empress had turned her face from him. She never forgot a slight, Vasilios knew.

Not that she needs one to order my removal.

"Contact Gaean Command and alert them to a possible alien infiltration of Theogony."

"Yes, Sir," the com squawked back at him.

You'd think they'd make better equipment in this day and age, he thought, his ship starting to shake as it entered the atmosphere.

White clouds streaked the surface of the blue marble below him, the capital Helios outlined on the holo. The detention center stood at one end of an archipelago, alone, only a bridge connecting the building with the rest of the city.

"Enlarge," he said. The holo detected what he was looking at and amplified.

The edifice ballooned to life on the holo. Two figures stood at the top of the steps in front of its doors, gesturing wildly at each other. Suddenly, they both looked up.

Toward him.

Twenty ships converged on the compound, his touching down on the bridge.

Vasilios leaped from the hatch, blasma gun poised at his shoulder, its tip white hot. "Special Agent Ad-hoc Vasilios Xenakis of the Imperial Secret Service," he said to the pair, one of them a low-browed gumshoe, the other a woman in an Immigration uniform.

"Where's your badge?" Low Brow said.

"I don't need a stinking badge."

"Yeah? Never heard that before. Your badge now, or I blow your head off." A kalashmakov pistol appeared in Low Brow's hand.

He'd be stupid enough to use it, too, Vasilios thought, sighing. He pulled out his badge. "The aliens got your detainees."

"How'd you know?" the woman asked.

"They were disguised as you guys," Low Brow said. "She said her name was Nellie Roussos, Imperial Secret Service, Internal Investigations Unit."

"I'm Carissa Minas, Warden, Helios Immigration Detention Center," the woman said.

They shook. "Pleased," Vasilios said, glad someone here had some competence. "Saw the sub-ether disruptions once on Kzizn, and then twice on Theogony," he told her. "On arrival, and then again on departure." He looked at Low Brow. "I'll have my assistant check on the identity."

"Erastus Doukas, Agent Provocateur, Imperial Bureau of Suspicion," the man said.

They shook. "Pleased," Vasilios said. All he's likely to provoke is gales of laughter, Agent Xenakis thought, keeping it off his face.

"How come you get to travel on coronation day?" Low Brow asked him.

"Lead containment contingent for the visit of her Imperial Highness." He jerked his thumb over his shoulder at the nineteen Musca-class ships hovering over the island. "Warden Minas, I'll need holos of the entire incident. Every minute from every cam since the alien detainee's arrival, please, not just today's events."

"That's a whole lot of holo," she said. "Let me get started on it. Back in a moment." She retreated into the building.

Vasilios commed the name he'd been given to his navigator. "Start from the beginning, Agent Doukas," he said. "Just the facts, Agent, just the facts."

Chapter 7

Lydia Procopio turned to her escort the moment they boarded the ship. "Thank you so much," she said in Kziznvxrz. She'd smelled them the instant they'd taken custody of her. If she hadn't lived among them for twenty-four years, she wouldn't have known they were Kzizn.

The four beefy humanoid-shaped Kzizn stared blankly at her. "Please proceed peacefully," one said, also in Kziznvxrz, pointing along the corridor.

"Aren't you going to take off these handcuffs?" Lydia held up her bound hands, the bright glasma circlets glinting in the dim interior light.

"Go, please."

"Where's my father?" she demanded, fear beginning to knot up her bowels. "He was hurt, and he may need medical attention."

126

"Xsirhglksvi will be taken care of. Your cell is that way. Cooperate, or we will escort you manually. Now, please."

Lydia obeyed immediately. Now, she was really afraid. "What are you, Wrwrmrfn?" she asked, not expecting an answer.

A Kziznvxrfn splinter group, the Wrwrmrfn had lurked for millennia in the remote bayous of Kziznvxrfn politics, their xenophobic philosophy and take-no-prisoners rhetoric at odds with moderate mainstream Kziznvxrfn views. She wondered how they'd managed to morph themselves into near-perfect humanoid shapes, the female even mastering Galactim, a near impossible feat for a Kzizn.

But if she and Xsirh were now their hostages, it meant that the Wrwrmrfn had moved from rhetoric to terrorism.

They directed her through the ship to a cargo hold, where a cube stood, fifteen feet to a side, gleaming and polished as though newly manufactured. Its hatch stood open.

They took off the circlets. "In," the one Kzizn ordered.

"Pondscum," she snarled.

They shoved her into the cube and slammed the hatch closed, the sounds from outside indicating they were locking her in.

The cell was devoid of comforts. An excretory, a bed, a sink, a chair.

But at least they were all designed for a human. She sat immediately and secured the five-point, guessing they were taking off quickly.

The lurch of acceleration added its upset to the anxiety gnawing at her innards.

They've been planning this for a long time, Lydia thought. She wished she knew what "this" was. It didn't surprise her that they'd taken her hostage, the group having long advocated her extermination, the most vocal among those objecting to Xsirh's rearing her.

Xsirhglksvi had described the bureaucratic battles he'd had to wage just to keep her on Kziznvxrz. Everything from what school she attended, what immunizations she got, what food she ate, what to do with her excrement (which proved a powerful catalyst to Kzizn waste products), what clothes she wore, and even what air she breathed.

At four years old, all she had understood was that she wasn't looked upon favorably, and that Xsirh struggled every day just to meet her basic needs. Those first few years had been horrible for her, the atmosphere noxious, the swampy tidal flats difficult for her to navigate, and the wet, clammy weather giving her perpetual goose bumps.

But for Xsirh, the struggle had been worse, even though she hadn't known it at the time. The simple mechanics of providing for her basic needs had nearly overwhelmed him. The political opposition to his adopting her had nearly resulted in criminal charges. And of course he'd been ostracized from his pod for having taken on the care of this foul-smelling, funny-sounding, bizarre-looking offspring of that widely-derided alien race known as Homo sapiens.

Or as the Kzizn pronounced it, "Slnl hzkrvmh." The Galactim approximation sounded like "Silinil" but lacked the glottal stops, affricates, and lateral clicks that thickened the Paramecium tongue.

Lydia examined the cabin thoroughly from her chair. Of standard Kzizn manufacture and materials, it'd been designed with human dimensions and physiognomy in mind. They must have copied some of my father's designs, she thought, the chair fitting her perfectly. Further, the air in the cabin had little of the sharp ammonium scents common to the Kzizn tidal flats. They'd invested considerable resources into manufacturing this cabin alone.

The more they'd invested, the greater her disquietude became.

Come on, she told herself, think!

She brought to mind what she knew about the Wrwrmrfn. A radical fringe group, they appeared to be an evolutionary throwback, preferring not the tidal flats where their moderate cousins lived but the gentle surf just beyond, a liminal existence inhabited by rotting seaweed, water-logged driftwood, and bloated graptolite, trilobite, and brachiopod carcasses. They eschewed the comforts of warm tidal pools, the lovely aromas of mud, the pleasant buzz of swarming cyclorrhapha. One of the pillars of their reversionary philosophy was their aversion to technology.

It doesn't stop them from using it to their advantage, Lydia noted, looking around.

Another of their philosophical pillars was the extinction of Homo sapiens and the takeover of the galaxy. They alone among the peaceful Kzizn had any ambition to extend the Paramecium dominion. Fortunately, theirs was quite a minority view, and war with the nearby Gaean Empire had never been considered a viable political option.

The Gaeans had never attacked Kziznvxrz either, despite each race finding the other repulsive. Their mutual indifference far exceeded their mutual revulsion, the Wrwrmrfn philosophy notwithstanding.

So what are they trying to accomplish by kidnapping me from Theogony? Lydia wondered, dreading the answer.

* * *

First among equals, Bishop of the Orthodoxy Dea Papadopoulos swept across the stage, the picture of regality, her smile affixed to her face with carbo-nacreous adhesive.

I don't know why I dressed up, the Bishop thought. The Dowager Empress has never graced our pews with a single thread from her satin-clad backside.

Bishop Papadopoulos, or "Bish Pap" to her intimates, was layered with the vestments of her office. A glittering kolpak or miter perched atop her head, its dome undercloth woven from the finest damask, its outer platinum cage encrusted with diamonds, and atop the miter, a cross of pure gold, the Savior depicted in fine relief. Beneath all her finery, she wore the humble alb, a pure-white garment reaching her ankles, a cincture girdling her waist. Over the alb, she wore the dalmatic, a long tunic with wide sleeves, today's color a shimmering gold lame. Over the top of that was the phelonion, or chasuble, usually the outermost vestment. On this august occasion, she wore on the top of everything the revered sakkos, its name derived from the ancient Greek word for sackcloth. This outer garment symbolized the tunic of disgrace worn by the Savior at his humiliation.

How apropos, the Bishop thought, I get to wear a sakkos at my humiliation. Even a fully-enclosed hazmat suit won't keep me from feeling sullied.

She was in her element, but out of her element. As the Deity's representative on Gaea, she was responsible for administering to the Lord's worldly affairs and for dispensing the ecstasy of eternity to the faithful. This was her calling. But today, the Bishop would minister to the High Thief herself and would consecrate the ascension of Princess Hecuba Zenon to the Empirate.

Bishop Papadopoulos halted at the Acropolis altar and knelt. Lit thuribles awaited, the burning incense inside sending its perfumed tendrils cascading down the steps. "Dear Lord," she murmured, sure no one was near enough to hear, "forgive me my blasphemy and save my ass today."

Then she rose, spread her arms elaborately, and turned to face the crowd, her robes flying around her in a whirlwind of cloth.

The seething mass of humanity below her roared. The cacophony was nearly a physical blow against her chest, leaving her gasping for breath. From her perch atop the steps of the Parthenon, she could see nearly all of New

Athens, the city occupying a bowl ringed by mountains. Orbit-scraping structures spiked the valley floor. Pneumatubes noodled in between, a veritable bowl of vermicelli. Faces sprouted from every bit of open space between buildings and every window of every building, all peering in her direction.

This many people hadn't gathered for the coronation of Hecuba's father, Athanasios.

Bish Pap wondered why. Do they sense the presumption of commoner blood to the royal throne? The decline of Empire before their very eyes? The mad theater of mockery?

But it wasn't Hecuba's coronation they feared.

The Dowager Empress Narcissa Thanos watched like a hawk from the Imperial seats, a bunting-plastered box to one side of the Parthenon steps.

Atop the steps to one side of Bish Pap was a bejeweled pedestal, on it the Imperial Scepter, symbol of might. To the other side of her was the Imperial Shield, symbol of protection. To the immediate right of the altar was the Imperial Cloak, symbol of unity. And to the immediate left of the altar was the Imperial Crown, symbol of infalli-bility.

Princess Hecuba knelt at the base of the Parthenon steps, her head bare of her dainty tiara for the first time in her life.

Bish Pap couldn't remember seeing Hecuba without the tiara atop her revolting little head, the symbol of her position.

Eidolon of beauty, Hecuba wasn't. The pinched lips were poised in a perpetual pout. The nose was squished into the face between cheeks too close together. A wart the size of a snail perched on one cheekbone. The close-set eyes peered from beneath a beetled unibrow, the single line of black hair across her forehead looking like a giant umlaut. The hair was dull blond, the color of water used to wash a thousand dishes. The coif had been sculpted with the implements of modern hairdressing for naught, the thin hair defying all efforts to tame it. She wore cloaks of silk and damask, so diaphanous and fine of manufacture they did little to hide the dumpy body beneath. Her appearance was a cracked foundation, through and through, and no amount of inspired cosmetology could straighten the building atop it. It would have taken a faceplant to improve her looks. She was ugly.

Bish Pap raised her gaze above the Princess and wielded her perfect smile across the crowd like a sword, slashing first one direction and then the other, palms in and hands up. Then she lowered them slowly.

And the roar died.

"Gaeans here and throughout the Empire, welcome today to this sacred event," she said, her voice booming across the assembled masses, her image appearing on a hundred trillion holos across the watching Empire. "We gather to honor the passing of our beloved Athanasios and to welcome the arrival of our adored Hecuba."

Bish Pap had almost said "adorable," but she wouldn't have been able to stomach such a blatant lie. "His Highness is dead, long live her Highness!" She thrust her arms into the air.

The crowd roared, their arms raised as well.

She brought hers down, and the crowd went silent. They're learning, she thought. "We gather for the coronation of her Highness, the Empress Hecuba, may she rule wisely and well. Long live her Highness!" Again, she thrust her arms into the air.

Again, the crowd roared, their arms raised.

She brought hers down, and the crowd went silent. Soon, I'll have them drooling at bells, she thought. "We gather in the might of our Creator and ask that He bless this Scepter, symbol of her power. Long live her Highness!"

The crowd roared and raised their arms in time with hers.

"We gather in the light of our Creator and ask that He bless this Shield, symbol of her protection. Long live her Highness!"

Again, the crowd roared and raised their arms with hers.

"We gather in the sight with our Creator and ask that He bless this Cloak, symbol of her unity. Long live her Highness!"

In synch with her, the crowd roared and raised their arms.

"We gather in the right of our Creator and ask that He bless this Crown, symbol of her infallibility. Long live her Highness!"

A last time they roared and raised their arms.

"Now," Bish Pap announced, "to place in the Imperial Hand the symbol of Her power, Chief Admiral of the Gaean Naval Forces, the handsome and honorable Hector Kritikos!"

A figure stood from the bunting-plastered Imperial box, his immaculate uniform bedecked in medals.

Bish Pap greeted him effusively. Then with great ceremony, she retrieved the Scepter from its mount, returned it to the altar, and knelt to say a prayer. She picked up a thurible and swung the smoking metal ball around her head once, its path leaving a trail of vapor. Standing, she handed the now-blessed Scepter to the Chief Admiral.

While she waited beside the altar, Admiral Kritikos carried the Scepter reverently down the steps toward the waiting Hecuba. The young woman had not moved, her head bowed. While Admiral Kritikos hectored her in haughty tones, extracting from the Princess a solemn oath to exert her military power judiciously, Bish Pap wished he'd get on with it, already bored with the pomp and finery.

In the crowd beyond a solid line of kneeling guards, a figure perhaps twenty deep looked to be maneuvering through the crowd.

The Chief Admiral finally quit blathering and handed the Scepter to Princess Hecuba.

One down, three to go, Bish Pap thought. "Now," she intoned, "to place upon the Imperial Arm the symbol of Her protection, House Speaker of the Gaean Assembly, the high and mighty Elke Drivas!"

A figure stood from the bunting-plastered Imperial box. Her smart, slick suit shimmered in burnished blues. She looked like an immaculate angel devoid of taint.

Bish Pap greeted Speaker Drivas expansively. Then with great ceremony, she retrieved the Shield from its mount, and returned to the altar for the ritual purification by thurible. A trail of vapor ringing her, she handed the now-blessed Shield to the House Speaker.

She carried the Shield reverently down the steps toward the waiting Princess. While Representative Drivas driveled to Hecuba in a booming voice from her soapbox on the purity of politicking, extracting from the Princess a solemn oath to negotiate with bipartisan compromise, Bish Pap groaned at the utter folly, not a soul believing any compromise possible, the House already plotting its recalcitrant postures.

In the crowd, the figure looked to be wriggling his or her way nearer to the front.

Two down, Bish Pap thought, two to go. "Now," she pronounced, "to place upon the Imperial Shoulders the symbol of Her unity, Premier of the Gaean Administration, the hale and hearty Flavian Galanis!"

From behind the bunting-plastered Imperial box emerged a man. His sultry, smooth suit shone in black, like a dark devil of death. If Thanos weren't already in the Imperial box, the Bishop might have believed him death.

Bish Pap greeted Premier Galanis effusively. Then with great ceremony, she retrieved the Cloak and purified it, the thurible leaving its ring of smoke. She handed the now-blessed Cloak to the Premier.

Galanis carried the Cloak reverently down the steps. While he propounded in an amplified voice to Hecuba upon the efficiency of bureaucracy, Bish Pap sniggered at the blatant contradiction, even the Savior recoiling in spirit at the oxymoron, the administration ready to bury the next Imperial edict under mountains of red tape.

In the crowd, the figure now stood at the front line of the audience, just beyond a kneeling soldier's shoulder.

Three down and one remains, she thought, thank the Deity! "Now," Bish Pap announced, "to place upon the Imperial Head the symbol of Her righteousness, Chief Justice of the Gaean Empire, the right and holy Daphne Carras!"

The long black robes of the Chief Justice moved her stoically across the steps, like a wraith devoid of legs.

Bish Pap greeted Justice Carras reverently. She retrieved the Crown for purification, swinging the smoking thurible around her head not once, not twice, but thrice. Standing, she stepped through the triple rings and handed the now-blessed Crown to the Chief Justice.

While she waited beside the altar, Justice Carras carried the Crown down the steps toward the waiting Hecuba. While Justice Carras spoke in sonorous tones, extracting from the Princess a solemn oath to exert her righteous wisdom judiciously, Bish Pap wished she'd get it over with and crown the ugly bitch, trying not to wet her britches. She'd have fallen asleep if she hadn't had to pee so badly.

The Chief Justice finally blithered herself into silence. She raised the Crown and began to lower it into place upon Princess Hecuba's head.

"Stop!" the figure at the front of the crowd declared, the voice boomeranging over the crowd.

Chapter 8

It wasn't far from Theogony to Kziznvxrz, and Lydia didn't have much time.

She shrugged out of the restraints and immediately inspected the door to the container. The Kzizn were remarkably adept at harnessing fluids to their purposes, but equally inept with solids.

They'd put the hinges on the insides of the doors.

She smirked, shaking her head, and got to work.

Without prisons—or the need for them—the Kzizn were virtually without experience in containing each other. The first time Lydia had come across a jail cell on a human-colonized planet, she'd stared at it for hours, trying to warp her mind around what it meant. Depriving another creature of its liberty was as untenable to Kzizn-vxrz as a tidal mudflat to humans.

Patiently, she unscrewed the hinges using a hairpin, the process tedious.

She wished she were back on the tidal mud-flats. The constant vertigo of standing upright on land for three days had been disconcerting. Her human trading partners seemed oblivious to the strain, walking around all day on their lower limbs as if born to it. On rare occasion, she'd heard them complain of sore feet. The one time she'd tried to describe mudflats to these land-based bipeds, the reaction had nearly sundered the contract negotiations. Lydia hadn't raised the subject again.

The last screw coming out, she wondered where they were keeping Xsirh, if at all.

Stepping back, she eyed the door.

On one human world, she'd taken a round of self-defense classes at the advice of another fe-male of her species. "A pretty woman like you might have to fend off a lusty male," the woman had told her. In the classes, Lydia had learned just how remarkably effective her limbs were as weapons.

Okay, here goes, she thought. She raised her foot and kicked.

The door careened from its frame.

She poked her head out into the cargo hold. It looked unoccupied except for the container.

The Wrwrmrfn, the rogue Kzizn who'd captured her and her father, were probably having a round of distilled dihydroxyl with him, the beverage intoxicating to them. The purified beverage was ultimately poisonous, diluting Kzizn electrolytes quickly. In small amounts, it lowered their inhibitions and tended to put them in a convivial mood. Lydia had found ethyl alcohol to have similar effects on her.

She sidled up to the cargo bay door. She couldn't hear anything through it. Good, she thought, guessing they hadn't heard her kick her way from the container. They hadn't thought to lock the cargo bay door. Probably hadn't imagined she might escape. She slipped into the corridor beyond, the tubular shape easier to navigate than those rectangular human corridors.

She heard sounds of revelry from the galley. Similar in layout to her own Kzizn-manufacture ship, she guessed where the cockpit was, wondering how to commandeer the vessel. Do I disable the environmental systems first, create a diversion, or what? Lydia wondered.

Homo sapiens were frightening for their violence. The Kzizn had never been to war with themselves and had only developed weapons as a defense against the barbaric humans. Kzizncide was unheard of, and the most extreme conflict on Kziznvxrz was the horrific schism between the Wrwrmrfn and mainstream Kziznvxrfn, which had forced the latter to banish the former to the ocean surf. Ostracism was equivalent to death, for without the pod, how could a Kzizn survive?

Thinking through her options, Lydia decided direct action was probably the best.

She slithered up the corridor past the galley and into the cockpit.

Only the copilot was in her chair, the pilot probably in the galley having a little distilled dihydroxyl with the other Wrwrmrfn.

"What are you doing?" the woman said.

"Taking us home. I'm Lydia Procopio." In the Kzizn language, her name was pronounced, "Obwrz Kilxlkrl."

"I'm Mvoorv Ilfhhlh. Pleased to meet you." Mvoorv extended a tentacle in greeting.

Lydia grasped and shook it, recognizing her as the one who'd led the incursion into the detention center. The woman looked a lot different in her Kzizn guise, the human disguise having given her an unhealthy pallor. "How did you do that, Mvoorv?" She hiked her thumb over her shoulder to indicate Theogony behind them, a gesture she'd picked up on Eos XI.

"You mean imitate those Slnl hzkrvmh?"

Lydia giggled at the pejorative, the Kzizn name for Homo sapiens making a mockery of their supposed intelligence. What really amused her was how the Kzizn used the name openly to their faces, insulting humans without their knowing it.

"Our Slnl clandestine pods developed a short-acting catalyst to solidify our exoderms," Mvoorv said. "What I'd really like to get my tentacles on is that long-acting catalyst they're supposed to be developing."

"Long-acting? And look like me for the rest of your days?"

Mvoorv laughed aloud, her green mass jiggling like jelly, the sound not dissimilar to a series of human farts. "Xsirh said you'd be delightful."

Lydia grinned and squeezed herself into the pilot's chair. A perfect bowl, it wasn't very comfortable for her. Having bones, she didn't have the same fluidity as the Kzizn, who could fit into just about any space they chose to occupy. Similarly, her hands weren't as adaptable as Kzizn tentacles, and she really had to stretch her fingers to get them on the controls.

"What are you doing, Obwrz?" Mvoorv asked again. A Kzizn asking the same question twice was equivalent to astonishment.

Lydia had already answered and didn't repeat herself. No self-respecting Kzizn did. Say something once, why say it again? She took the controls and adjusted their course to take them to the Kzizn capital, Dzhsrmtglm, near Xsvhzkvzpv Bay. The entire mudded-out west side of this gargantuan bay was the perfect environment for the miasma-loving Kzizn. The thought of home was comforting.

"How might I persuade you not to take us to Dzhsrmtglm?"

"You can't," Lydia replied. "I appreciate your rescuing us from that detention center, Mvoorv, but Xsirh and I don't agree with your philosophy. We're not going to cooperate. Whatever you hoped to achieve, you'll have to accomplish it without us."

Mvoorv issued a high-pitched blat, the Kzizn equivalent of a sigh. "We will accomplish our goal, you know. In fact, we almost have." Her tentacles slithered over the controls in front of her, and a sub-ether image appeared.

The image was a projection of events in the human capital of New Athens, on Gaea, adapted from a human holonet broadcast. The constant broadcast of images on the sub-ether created disturbances for Kzizn transport, all of which was powered by sub-ether drives. Modulating these ripples had required the Kzizn to retool their propulsion technology with built-in dampening units. The human invasion of the sub-ethernet had been cause for great concern among the Kzizn, since their sub-ether technology was all that kept Homo sapiens off Kziznvxrz. Humans were the worst invasive species known to the galaxy.

The image showed the front steps of the edifice known as the Parthenon. At the top of the steps was a thickly-clad human wearing a flamboyant hat, the high priestess of their bizarre religion. Spiritual practices among Homo sapiens were risible at best, in the opinion of Kzizn scholars.

Bishop Dea Papadopoulos, the subtitle said. She was swinging above her head a metal ball on the end of a chain, the ball leaving a stream of smoke, a cleansing ritual, Lydia knew. She was mystified how introducing toxins into the air was supposed to cleanse anything.

"Why are you showing me this, Mvoorv?" she asked.

"The new Empress will herald a change in our favor, Obwrz."

She looked over at the female Kzizn.

Gender roles among the Kzizn were temporary states, assumed for reproductive purposes. The multiple means of replication available to the Kzizn bewildered their human neighbors. Whenever Lydia tried to tell a Kzizn she would always be female, it usually provoked gales of laughter, the concept of remaining one gender nonsensical to the multimorphic Kzizn.

Lydia didn't like the look of evasion in Mvoorv's visual organelles, evasion a trait that the Kzizn had learned from their Homo sapiens neighbors. She wasn't telling Lydia everything.

"You don't need to cooperate with us any further," Mvoorv said. "You've already done your part."

Lydia raised her eyebrow at the woman. On the holo, the Bishop handed the Crown to the Chief Justice, who descended the steps toward the ugly Princess.

For some reason, as she listened to the Chief Justice spout a lot of nonsense, Lydia was convinced that that should have been her.

The Chief Justice lowered the Crown toward the head.

"Stop!" a figure at the front of the crowd declared, the voice boomeranging over the crowd.

Lydia recognized the Kzizn immediately. "Ezra, no!"

* * *

As the words reverberated across the crowd, Bishop Dea Papadopoulos wondered how the creature had infiltrated the public address system.

"I beg you, do not do this! It's a mistake!" the alien blatted, the sickening sounds of its own language underneath the monotone translation.

The first blasma blast blew a score of human spectators and a few guards into their next lives, the beam of destabilizing ions causing their flesh to disintegrate into sticky red plasma.

Bish Pap looked over just in time to see the Dowager Empress fire a second time, a shot that didn't miss its mark.

Alien slime splashed the crowd, and screams erupted as its acids etched their way into human flesh.

"Crown her, or you're next," Narcissa Thanos said, taking aim at Chief Justice Daphne Carras.

The woman in long black robes lowered the crown onto Hecuba's lopsided head.

* * *

Special Agent Ad-hoc Vasilios Xenakis watched the coronation ceremony over the holonet just as his vessel achieved escape velocity from Theogony for his return to the Oort cloud. Satisfied at least that the system had been adequately secured, Vasilios gaped at the holo, watching incredulously as Narcissa Thanos blasted the alien apart, then aimed the blasma gun at Chief Justice Carras. "Crown her, or you're next."

Justice Carras lowered the crown.

A curious burbling sound in the cockpit behind Vasilios caused him to turn.

A bright-green slug easily six inches around hurled itself at his face and wrapped its tentacles around his head. His hands came up too late, the creature already slipping tentacles into his mouth and nostrils.

The two tentacles in his mouth slithered down his throat, punched a hole in his esophagus and wrapped his heart in a vice-like grip. The other two in his nostrils punctured the ceiling of his nasal cavity and sent their spike-like tips into his basal ganglia.

Vasilios Xenakis died, at last joining his beloved Consort Empress in the afterlife.

* * *

Imperial Laundry Maid Drucilla Kanelos stood on the crowded ante-promenade deck of the Imperial cruise liner George the First with barely enough room to breathe. She watched a giant holo of the Dowager Empress aim the blasma gun at Chief Justice Carras. "Crown her, or you're next."

The top judge of the Gaean Empire lowered the Crown.

And the crowd aboard the cruise liner went wild.

The cold started just under the hem of Drucilla's evening gown and slithered up the insides of her thighs to her anus. She'd have liked the sensation in other circumstances, but in these, her titillation turned to terror as pain ripped through her innards, the mass inside her wriggling relentlessly toward her heart, shredding any flesh in its way. Drucilla's dying scream was drowned out by cheers in the crush of humanity around her.

And there the body of Drucilla Kanelos remained for several more minutes, suspended upright in the tightly-packed crowd.

* * *

Chief of Palace Security Deion Goulas watched a holo of the coronation from Security Command twenty stories beneath the palace, the ventilation system working overtime to cool the crowded underground compound. Deion leaped to his feet the instant the alien said, "Stop!" the voice booming over the loudspeakers, the figure at the front of the crowd a bright, lime green.

"Who let that alien get so close?!" Deion demanded.

Security Command erupted in chaos just outside his office.

"I beg you, do not do this! It's a mistake!" the alien said, the nauseous sounds of its language underneath the monotone translation.

A blasma beam blew a huge hole in the line of spectators, missing the alien. A fountain of liquefied flesh splashed the crowd. A second blast splashed green alien goop at least twenty spectators back, many of them writhing from the acids.

Narcissa Thanos took aim at Chief Justice Daphne Carras. "Crown her, or you're next."

Justice Carras lowered the crown.

Deion looked up at the vent. A ball of bright green goop slithered through the grill, a six-inch round globule of oozing protoplasm.

The same bright lime green as the creature at the coronation.

The slug launched itself at Deion's face, and his hands came up too late. The creature's tentacles in his mouth slithered down his throat and bit through his carotid artery. The other two in his nostrils wrapped themselves around his basal ganglia and squeezed.

Chief of Palace Security Deion Goulas was dead before he hit the floor.

* * *

Former Governess to Lydia Procopio, Filmena Sotiropoulos, who had resigned rather than accompany Ambassador Procopio to the planet Kziznvxrz, watched in dismay as the Crown descended toward the head of Princess Hecuba Zenon. It struck her as ironic, really, that Hecuba Zenon, the second child of Athanasios, born to him by his second wife, the Lady's Maid, Narcissa Thanos, would be the one to receive the Crown upon her repulsive little head.

An object splatted against the glasma of her sixteenth-floor apartment window, and Filmena stared at it dully. It looked like a large slug, its footprint against the glasma nearly six inches across. The creature convulsed and surged through the outer glasma pane, spreading itself across the inner layer. Filmena didn't know whether to be disgusted or alarmed. Then the slug convulsed again and oozed through the glasma into her apartment.

She stood, her terror rising, and stepped toward the door.

It flung itself toward her face as she turned and splatted against the back of her head. Screaming, she ran toward the door, but before she reached it, the creature wrapped her neck with tentacles and strangled her scream. Two more tentacles positioned themselves at her upper back and shoved their points between her third and fourth cervical vertebrae to sever her spine.

The body of Filmena Sotiropoulos fell against the inside of her apartment door, where it was found days later, partially decomposed.

* * *

Eugenia Ioannou, Retired Governess of Princess Cybill Zenon, attempted to watch a holo of the coronation from her barstool at the nearly-empty pub. She could barely keep her head up.

The first blasma blast stirred her slightly from her drunken stupor, the fountain of liquefied human remains splashing across the crowd. She just caught sight of the second blast, and she wondered why the fountain of flesh had turned a putrid green.

"Crown her, or you're next."

The voice of Narcissa Thanos penetrated through the alcohol-saturated cerebral cortex to Eugenia's amygdala, and fear sent a sobering shock of adrenalin shooting from Eugenia's hypothalamus.

We're in for it now, she thought, picking up her beer from the bar.

She didn't notice that the beer wasn't amber anymore but had somehow turned bright green. Thinking she was hallucinating, she upended the glass anyway. The thick sludge slithered into her trachea, pierced the lung and severed the aorta.

Retired Governess Eugenia Ioannou fell backward off the barstool, the glass shattering as it hit the floor at the same time she did, and she died.

Chapter 9

"Revered Leader, I bring you my fellow Paramecia, a group of Wrwrmrfn who have acted to the detriment of the pod, for whom I beg your forbearance." Lydia Procopio lowered herself to her knee. The six-inch layer of muck on the floor gave a satisfying squelch.

She had just arrived in the presence of the oldest Kziznvxrfn, Mrxlwvnfh Gzelfozirh.

Beside Lydia was Xsirh, looking wan but recovering from the injury to his reproductive organelles. The noxious human air and dry environment had done more to exacerbate the injury and damage his system than the actual impact with the corridor wall.

Behind Lydia and Xsirh was the group of Wrwrmrfn, looking abashed. Their leader, Mvoorv Ilfhhlh, stood at their front, her exoderm a sickly pale green, her tentacles drooping at her sides, her cilia flat and limp. She looked the picture of capitulation.

All thirteen of them were crowded into a room large enough to hold twenty people standing. The walls were a slimy brown color, shiny as though wet. Along each side wall a few inches off the floor were cups for sitting. On the floor was six inches of the finest putrescent mud to be found, none but the best for the Revered Leader.

Mrxlwvnfh Gzelfozirh, the Ivevivw Ovzwvi of the Kziznvxrz, occupied a similar cup, its position at one end of the room the only indication it held any importance. The closest approximate translation of his title, Ivevivw Ovzwvi, meant "Revered Leader," but it also carried with it hints of his age and lineage. Mrxlwvnfh Gzelfozirh was several thousand years old, had reproduced at least a hundred times in each of the four ways available to the Kziznvxrz, and had even outlived some of those he'd spawned.

Mrxlwvnfh looked past her to the group of Wrwrmrfn, and then returned his optical organelles to her. "The Homo sapiens have crowned a new Empress," Mrxlwvnfh said.

"What do you know of these events, child Lydia?"

"Little, Revered Leader," she said.

He turned his optical organelles onto Xsirh. "What do you know, Grandchild?" Mrxlwvnfh was Xsirh's grandparent, having spawned Xsirh's spawner.

The term Mrxlwvnfh had used for Xsirh translated clumsily but literally as "offspring conceived through conjugation." The word was pronounced "luuhkirmt-xlmxvrevw-gsilfts-xlmqftzgrlm," and Lydia found it a tongue-twister, in spite of being reared by Xsirh since age four. There were subtle distinctions to parentage among the Kziznvxrz. How one was spawned made a huge difference in one's social status. The individuals accorded the most status were produced through the conjugation of two Kzizn. Since each Kzizn could choose to be the male, inseminating the female bearing the young, these were considered distinct and separate means of reproduction. Evolutionarily, these Kzizn tended to be more vigorous and hardy, and were subject to fewer infirmities. Kzizn spawned through fission, the pinching of a Kzizn through the center to form two new Kzizn, carried all the genetic irregularities that they'd been born with and any that might have developed during the lifetime of the Kzizn who had spawned them. Self-fertilization, the third method of reproduction, was also the most reviled. Offspring produced this way were derided as "jerk-offs."

Xsirh looked at his grand-sire, his organelles swiveling to focus. "Revered Leader, alas, I also know little. Svkszvhgfh Ezhrozprh left for Gaea some months ago. Lydia tells me Ezra tried to stop the Homo sapiens ceremony. I am aggrieved that the plasma of my pod-mate and my co-parent of five offspring has rejoined the food chain."

Lydia held out her hand to comfort him. Xsirh's tentacles wrapped themselves around it.

"I am sorry to hear of Ezra's loss," Mrxlwvnfh said. "He was a free-thinker."

Lydia blanched, someone's thinking for themselves and not in cohesive accord with the pod often taken as derogatory.

"He went to Gaea at my bidding," Mrxlwvnfh continued, "and if anyone is responsible for his rejoining the food chain, Xsirh, it is I. Forgive me."

"But surely, Revered Leader," Xsirh objected, "you didn't ask Ezra to stop the ceremony."

"No, you speak factually, I did not, but I did ask that he go to Gaea, which placed him there, where any Kzizn would object to such a wrongness." The Revered Leader's optical organelles swiveled toward Lydia. "Human child, I desire to confer with you in private. Let me dispense with these Wrwrmrfn, and then we will talk."

Lydia and Xsirh stepped aside, her father taking one of the side cups. Lydia knelt in the mud beside him, the cups too uncomfortable for her to sit in for long.

The dissident Wrwrmrfn moved toward the Revered Leader as a group, Mvoorv Ilfhhlh at their head. All of them melted to the floor in obeisance.

"You invaded a Homo sapiens planet by disguising yourselves as them," Mrxlwvnfh said. "Worse, you did it not to rescue your fellow Kzizn and his human daughter, but to incite our Homo sapiens neighbors. An act of provocation." He uttered the word with the full expulsive emission of his digestive tract—disgust.

Further, provocation was an act repulsive to the capacity of a Kzizn, a peace-loving species whose only predatory enemy on Kziznvxrz, the didinium, was nearly extinct. Lydia tried to understand what might have motivated the splinter group to take such an opprobrious action.

Mrxlwvnfh's upper cell sprouted livid purple spots, a sign he was furious. "Further, with this act of provocation, you have incited the ire of these Homo sapiens, and even now, they amass in the Oort cloud of our system in preparation for an attack.

"One that you provoked," he added. "What do you have to say for yourselves?"

Mvoorv Ilfhhlh raised her tentacles in supplication. "May I address the Revered Leader?"

"You may."

"Revered Leader," Mvoorv said, her organelles popping up from the top of her head, "there are subtleties within subtleties at work here. We are too timid a race to live beside these voracious Homo sapiens. We lack the spine—to borrow one of their phrases—to compete with them. Therefore, we must destroy them, as we once did the didinium. Our technology is superior to theirs, and all we lack is the will to extirpate all trace of them from the galaxy." She turned toward the imagers. "Rise up, pod-siblings, and—"

"Silence!" blatted Mrxlwvnfh.

Mvoorv went silent.

"You have revoked your right to remain members of the pod. You have demonstrated beyond all doubt that you are neither worthy of living in Paramecium society, nor of receiving the mutual support of its members. You are banished, all of you, to the middle of the sea."

Lydia gasped, and all the Kzizn in the room emitted exhalations of horror, similar only in feeling to her expression, theirs the rapid opening and closing of orifices around small pockets of air.

Already ostracized and living on the fringes of mainstream Kziznvxrfn society, these Wrwrmrfn were denied access to the mudflats, the rich primordial soup found on those vast stretches of semi-liquefied tidal basin whose yield of anaerobic organisms fed billions of Kziznvxrz. Forced to live in the surf already, they eked out a modicum of food from the cold, rough waves. Now these ten Wrwrmrfn were banished even from the surf. They would not survive long in the open sea, where microorganisms were too sparse to support a Kzizn and where the few remaining didinium prowled, voracious.

"Go now, unfaithful Wrwrmrfn," Mrxlwvnfh said, his voice deep and sad, "and suffer the consequences that you have brought upon yourselves."

Lydia watched as the goop of Wrwrmrfn slithered from the room, their cilia wilted, their tentacles hanging limp.

Xsirh murmured to her, "I need to attend to Ezra's affairs. Besides, I think Mrxlwvnfh wishes to speak with you alone."

She'd gotten that impression, too. "Give my love to his family," she said. Ezra had been one of her father's many reproductive partners, but they hadn't been on intimate terms since Lydia's first few years with the pod. She remembered him fondly. He'd been among the few pod members to have fully supported Xsirh by helping to nurture Lydia.

Why had Ezra tried to stop the ceremony? she wondered, waiting patiently in the mud while the Revered Leader's attendants replaced the six-inch layer of muck with fresh tidal-basin ooze.

The audience room restored to its original freshness, Lydia took a deep satisfying breath of the wonderful miasma, the air redolent of child-hood mud-bath frolics with her father.

"Xsirh took great risks when he decided to rear you," Mrxlwvnfh said.

"I know, Revered Leader. He nurtured me beyond all expectation."

"Please, call me Marx," Mrxlwvnfh said, gesturing with his tentacles for her to approach.

She rose and eased herself into the fresh puddle of mud beside him. Instinctively, she leaned into his embrace. His tentacles wrapped around her, and his cilia began to massage her skin. Among Homo sapiens, such physical proximity and intimacy with one's leader was unthinkable. Lydia's excursions to multiple human-occupied worlds had taught her a few difficult lessons about their bizarre views of intimacy. The men just wanted to put their reproductive organelles into hers, and their female life-partners, whom they called wives, objected to that—vehemently, as Lydia had found out on one occasion. She'd been fortunate, Xsirh had later told her, not to have engaged in the act of conjugation with the paired Homo sapiens male.

"Your aroma has changed since you first joined us, child Lydia."

Twenty-eight years old, and they still call me child, she thought, bemused. At nearly six thousand years old, Mrxlwvnfh probably couldn't think of her as anything else. "You remember me when I was young?" she asked. Lydia did smell better now, her diet consisting of the thick zoylmwrtzh soup made from thickened algae. The main Kzizn diet of microorganisms was unsuited to her gullet, and no matter how many times she tried it, she usually ended up ill. As long as she stuck to a vegetarian diet, properly prepared, she experienced no adverse side effects.

"Of course I remember. We tried many times to return you to your people, but our entreaties fell on non-functioning auditory organelles. It was a trying time for us all. We were certain if we didn't return you that the Homo sapiens would surely invade Kziznvxrz to rescue you."

She turned her head to look at him. "Marx, why didn't they?"

The upper, sloped sides of his oblong shape slid upward—a shrug. "For a long time, we didn't know, but Ezra discovered a few things in his last days on Gaea."

"Why did he go there, Marx? Why did you send him there? Did he have to be punished because he won the Kzizn-of-the-month award?"

Mrxlwvnfh turned his upper nodule from side to side. "No, child Lydia, he went at my bidding to find out about you."

* * *

Lydia waded through the swamp toward home, pensive. What Mrxlwvnfh had told her was deeply disturbing. The coronation yesterday of Hecuba Zenon as the new Empress of the Gaean Empire was the culmination of a series of events that had begun before she was born.

Ezra's death had interrupted his quest for the truth, however, and the information he'd retrieved was incomplete. Amidst the information was a salient fact: Twenty-four years ago, a lowly Lady's Maid who was bedding the Emperor, Narcissa Thanos, had somehow engineered the appointment of Viscountess Basilissa Procopio, Lydia's mother, to the ambassadorship of Kziznvxrz. How and why Narcissa Thanos had done it remained a mystery.

Home for Lydia and Xsirh was inland somewhat, near the edge of the habitable tidal flat, where the thick slurry of mud began to dry, heights where seawater rose only during storms (Kziznvxrz lacked a moon), where amphibious creatures ventured to tread. There, at the edge of Kziznvxrz society, she and her father lived, their house one of the few structures with a dry floor, its above-water elevation making it difficult to access for the Kzizn, except with great effort. Fortunately, Xsirh was a young Kzizn, only a thousand years old, still vigorous with youth.

The wrong side of town, as the Homo sapiens said. Xsirh's choice of abode had been a cross product of social pressures and practicability. Members of his pod had disapproved of his decision to take on the care of the Homo sapiens waif. She smelled bad, made noxious noises reminiscent of their elimination process, and behaved like a child. Given that she was four years old at the time, there was a logical explanation for the latter. Further complicating the situation was her urine, which contained a catalyst whose interaction with Kzizn waste products precipitated the release of poisonous gasses. And on the practical side of things, the four-year-old simply couldn't have survived in the mud. She'd have drowned within a few days. So Xsirh had found an abode just above the tide line, among the least desirable locations. Lydia had been teased mercilessly by her Kzizn peers for living on the wrong side of town.

She waded from the muck and stepped through the doorway, glad to be back home, the familiar surroundings a comfort to her. She and her father weren't here much anymore, she realized, their business in trade frequently taking them off planet. Behind the house was an elevated platform, empty now of their amoeba-class vessel, which was still on Theogony.

How are we ever going to get it back? Lydia wondered.

She rinsed herself off in the cleansall just inside the doorway, a feature most Kziznvxrfn homes didn't have. Xsirh had outfitted the home in deference to Lydia's comfort, eschewing the six-inch layer of muck that covered the floor of every other home on the planet.

She stepped from the cleansall and opened the cupboard beside it to reach for a clean set of formalls.

A didinium leaped from the cupboard, glanced off her hand, and wrapped itself around her face.

Lydia dropped and rolled and managed to slip her hand between the creature and her cheek.

It tried to wrap its tentacles around her neck to strangle her.

Her arm in its way, she banged her forehead on the floor and stunned it somewhat. She brought her other hand up and pried the slug partway away from her mouth, and then spat into the didinium's intake orifice.

Her spittle hit its mark, and her pre-digestive enzymes catalyzed the lining of its intake exoderm. She ripped it off her head and flung it against the wall as the flesh began to sizzle. The slug slid to the floor, leaving an excrement-brown streak down the wall. The mass of proto-plasm slowly fizzled into a puddle of protoplasm, smoke billowing up toward the ceiling.

Gasping, she stumbled to the door, the smell revolting.

She'd gotten lucky. She'd been reaching into the cupboard when it leaped out. Her hand had deflected it away from her lower face and neck. Had it landed where it intended, it would have choked her in less than three minutes.

She sat beside the door, breathing roughly, wondering how the didinium had gotten into the house. A deep-sea predator, didinium were rarely found near the coastal areas and almost never this far inland. The didinium and Paramecium had been mutual predators for nearly a million years, and only in the last five hundred thousand years had the Paramecium emerged as the dom-inant species, nearly wiping out the didinium in the coastal areas. Now, didinium was a del-icacy among the Kziznvxrz, but one that Lydia couldn't stomach.

Relieved to have survived the attack, she set about cleaning up the mess.

Finished, she stepped into the cleansall a second time.

Not quite the homecoming greeting she'd expected.

Xsirh hadn't returned from visiting Ezra's pod, where he'd gone after their audience with the Revered Leader. Guessing he'd be home soon, Lydia set about preparing a meal, knowing he'd be hungry when he did return, fixing his favorite anaerobic soup, and preparing a lichen salad for herself.

From the direction of the tidal flat came the sounds of someone sloshing through the muck. Xsirh, she thought, recognizing his slither.

He came in on his exoderm, his cilia folded into his middle, a bundle of tentacles sprouting like a fern from the center of his abdomen. He set an object near the door and wiggled across the floor toward the kitchen. "I smell anaerobic soup! My favorite! You spoil me terribly, Lydia."

"A little spoiling makes us all smell better," she replied, the saying an adage as old as the Kzizn language.

"I have something to show you after we eat." He climbed into his seat at the low table, a cup that looked like a gigantic egg-holder.

Lydia sat in her own chair, one built for her physiology. As she ate, she reached across the table, and he wrapped his tentacles around it. Together they dined, home again, father and daughter, the picture of perfection. She told him about the didinium ambushing her from the cupboard.

"A didinium, this far inland?" Xsirh said. "I thought I smelled something when I got home. That's quite odd. How do you suppose it got in?"

Lydia shook her head, not knowing.

"Here, let me show you what I brought," he said. Xsirh slithered back to the door and returned with the object he'd set there.

Clearly of alien manufacture, the object was angular; bolts on the intact end held together a casing, the other end exploded outward, sharp shards of a dull gray metal protruding wickedly.

"What is it?"

"The casing of an A-warp core."

She laughed and shook her head. "Must be Homo sapiens in manufacture. They're the only ones using such a primitive technology."

"It is of human manufacture," Xsirh said. "You're familiar with how A-warp works?"

"It's third-grade physics, father, of course. The torsion to the foliated hyperleaves compresses space in front of the ship and expands space behind it, moving the ship across space faster than the speed of light. Simple stuff." She couldn't help but giggle. "Primitive, too."

His intake orifice curved upward at the edges. "What do you suppose caused it to explode?"

She looked at the exploded end, thinking through what she knew. Although not an engineer or physicist, she had mastered the rudimentary principles that governed A-warp technology alongside all the other Kzizn children. "Well, I couldn't say for sure, but there aren't any fissile materials in an A-warp core. Something foreign must have been introduced."

Again, Xsirh smiled. "Chemical traces of a thermonuclear microfusion event were found embedded in the casing."

"A microfusion generator? In an A-warp core? No wonder it exploded. Would have had to have happened at or near peak load, though."

"Exactly." Xsirh sat up, obvious pride in his optical organelles. "And peak load for any spaceship engine occurs when?"

"Leaving or entering a significant gravity well, most likely a planet." Lydia looked at him. "Who would put a microfusion generator inside an A-warp core? That's either outright stupidity or sabotage. Why are you showing this to me, father?"

Xsirh held up the A-warp core. "Ezra had this among his possessions. His notes indicate it's from the Homo sapiens ship that attempted to land on Kziznvxrz twenty-four years ago, the ship carrying Viscountess Ambassador Basilissa Procopio and her family."

Carrying me, Lydia thought, staring at Xsirh.

Chapter 10

She strode up the hill behind the house, perhaps the highest point of land for miles around,
a place Xsirh had difficulty getting to, his exoderm not well adapted for dry, rocky terrain. She
scratched an itch on her arm.

All Kziznvxrz lived on the planet's tidal flats.
None of the other species on Kziznvxrz had risen
from the muck and adapted to the environments
on either side, the deep blue sea and hills like the
one Lydia now climbed, nor had they developed
the intelligence, language, and technology that
the Kzizn had.

She was grateful that Ezra had recovered
something from the crash site. The damage
to the A-warp core casing indicated sabotage.
Among other items her father had recovered
from the crash site were tissue samples from
both her father and mother, kept in zero-kelvin

cryo. When Lydia had learned of the Homo sapiens death customs, she'd laughed herself silly. The Kziznvxrfn had nothing similar, probably since death was so rare among them, their lifespans often exceeding five thousand years. So her parents had never had a proper burial, or any sort of obsequy. Lydia wondered whether the Procopio family on Gaea had held any ceremonies for the deceased Viscountess Ambassador, her husband, and their daughter.

She reached the hilltop and stared at the stars. Nightfall on Kziznvxrz tended to be sudden and sharp. Without a moon, its nights were dark. Given the system's position near the edge of the Milky Way, only a slim strip of stars was visible in the night sky. She'd seen the night skies on worlds relatively close to the galactic bar, where brilliant bands of stars bathed planets with near-daylight intensity. Lydia didn't sleep well in the presence of light—any light—and she couldn't imagine living on a planet with a moon.

The Kzizn didn't have the Homo sapiens equivalent of a religion. Having an average lifespan of five thousand years, they'd never developed the concept of an afterlife. The thought of one was ludicrous. Why would anyone have any desire for an afterlife after having lived five thousand years? They were ecstatic when it was time for them to contribute their protoplasm to the food chain. After that amount of time, Kzizn were practically begging to be released from the doldrums of existence.

Lydia wondered which star was Gaea's. She knew for a fact she couldn't see it, but she might have found a smidgen of comfort in looking its direction. It was where she'd been born. While the Kzizn had nurtured her and given her succor, they weren't her people. They'd allowed her to live with them, had educated her, and had made allowances for her human foibles, such as her lack of an eidetic memory, which all Kzizn had, but they wouldn't ever be able to bring her fully into their society. She simply would never live long enough, her life expectancy a fraction of theirs.

The thin strip of Milky Way stars directly above her stretched across a twenty-degree arc of sky. So far away, Lydia thought, wondering why someone had felt it necessary to sabotage the Ambassador's ship twenty-four years ago. As if the post itself weren't remote enough.

What possible threat could my mother have been to the ambitious and cunning Lady's Maid, Narcissa Thanos? Lydia silently asked the stars. She didn't know, and Xsirh didn't either.

"Known only to the stars," the Homo sapiens adage went.

Lydia looked at them overhead, wishing they would tell her.

The thin strip of stars shimmered.

What's that? she wondered. And as she watched, the patch of shimmering stars grew slowly wider. They shouldn't be doing that!

The oddity was like an artifact you could see only in your peripheral vision, the objects beyond it distorted. The artifact grew larger as she watched, its size difficult to gauge against the nearly black sky.

It settled just below the hilltop, on the other side of her house, a faint hum audible.

Then it appeared. From behind a diaphanous curtain manifested her amoeba-class vessel, the one she'd left on Theogony.

But who's flying it? Lydia wondered.

* * *

Erastus Doukas, Agent Provocateur with the Imperial Bureau of Suspicion, leveled the blasma pistol at the young woman. "Hands up, Lydia Procopio. You're under arrest."

She put her hands in the air instantly.

He hustled down the boarding ramp. Pistol aimed with one hand, he clamped a circlet onto her arm and twisted it down behind her back.

"Oww!" she complained.

"Now the other," he said, reaching up for it and wrenching it behind her back. There, he clamped them together. "All right, aboard." He grasped her upper arm with his free hand and dragged her toward the boarding ramp.

She didn't resist. "Where are you taking me?"

"A little out of the way place I know called the Andromeda Galaxy. Where do you *think* I'm taking you?" He couldn't believe how stupid she was, asking him something so simple. Doukas herded her onto the ship, and the ramp retracted behind them.

"You're taking me to Gaea, then. Guess I de-served the sarcasm. You'll let them know you've captured me?"

"No, I'm going to waltz right into an audience with the Empress and her fatuous mother the Dowager Empress saying I've a pleasant surprise for them personally." He guided her over to the cup-shaped Kzizn chair and strapped her into it, and then took the pilot's chair. Erastus felt her eyes upon him, watching his every move. He struggled to keep his attention on what he was doing.

She was so beautiful, all he wanted to do was look at her. He'd felt the same when he'd first taken custody of her on Theogony. If she hadn't called him that taunting pejorative he'd heard all his life, he might have remained spellbound, transfixed by the elfin face and bottomless-blue eyes.

Focus! he told himself, looking over the bewil-dering, unfamiliar controls. The Kzizn ship was difficult to fly, his hands ill-adapted to the con-trols, better suited to tentacles than hands. It'd been a challenge to fly it here from Theogony.

"The blue button, over there," she told him.

Oh, yeah, he thought. A low hum became audible, a far more pleasant sound than the dull roar of Gaean-designed ships. He'd actually found it quite pleasant to fly, other than the difficult controls. "Ridiculous for these ships not to have any type of security systems," he said, activating the engines.

"Well, when you don't have theft, you don't worry about thieves," she replied.

Sensing sarcasm, he grabbed the nav, spreading his hands across a two-foot square of fine-motor controls. The ship began to rise, wobbling awkwardly.

"It's got voice command," she said.

"But I don't speak that awful-sounding language."

"I adapted it to Galactim, too."

"Why didn't it say so?" He looked at her suspiciously. "You're not going to take over the ship, are you?"

"No, of course not."

"Ship, take us into orbit, and then set a course for Lucina Nine."

"Orbit, and then set a course for Lucina Nine, acknowledged," the ship said in Galactim, and then it repeated itself in Kzizn, "Liyrg, zmw gsvm hvg z xlfihv uli Ofxrmz Mrmv, zxpmldovwtvw."

"Eww!" Erastus cringed at the sounds. "Any way to turn that off?"

"Ship, Galactim only, please."

"Galactim only," the ship said. "Tzozxgrn lmob," it repeated.

"You sure it'll obey?" he asked the young woman. "That language is awful enough to make someone vomit!"

"It'll obey."

The ship engines engaged, pressing him into his seat. He glanced over at her.

She was pressed into the cup awkwardly, looking uncomfortable in the upended hemisphere, as if in pain.

She seems to be taking this all without much complaint, Erastus thought, wondering why.

The planet below retreated in the holoscreen, its left side lit by the setting sun. The mudded-out bay they'd just lifted off from was cloaked in darkness, no lights to indicate inhabited areas, as on most human-occupied worlds. Thinking the lack of lights odd, Doukas asked her about it.

"Their optical organelles perceive a wider range of frequencies than our eyes. And they're much more sensitive to ambient light, no matter how little of it there is."

"You mean they can see better." He didn't know what organelles were, but he didn't want to seem stupid by asking. He struggled enough with that as it was.

"Orbit achieved," the ship said in its dreary monotone. "Course plotted for Lucina Nine. Engage at what speed, please?"

Shoulders hunched up near his ears, he cringed, waiting for the ship to start blatting in that foul-sounding language.

The ship didn't say anything further.

Erastus threw her a glance. "How fast can this thing go?"

"Sub-ether transport requires no time at all. We can arrive at Lucina Nine in moments."

"Captured the Kzizn transport technology and the most wanted criminal alive, all in one trip." Erastus could feel the glory already. "Ship, open a sub-ether channel to Colonel Melanctha Remes, IBS Command Outpost, Lucina Nine."

"Warning, sub-ether transmission will disrupt our drives," the ship said without emotion. "Engines will have to be shut down while transmitting. Open sub-ether channel?"

"So we sit here vulnerable while I transmit, eh?"

The young woman shrugged at him. "No one's chasing us, in case you hadn't noticed."

He had noticed, and he thought it odd. "Why aren't your people chasing us? What's the matter with them? And why are you just letting me kidnap you?"

"It's not complacency, I can tell you that. I am uncomfortable, and I'd appreciate it if you'd take off these bracelets."

Startled, he nearly got whiplash looking at her. "You'll go with me willingly?"

"Of course."

He stared at her, aghast. "But why? You should be doing everything you can to get away from me!"

"If taking me to Lucina Nine stops the Empire from attacking Kziznvxrz, then take me."

Not exactly a genius, Erastus had to think through what he was doing. Not that he cared one whit whether Kziznvxrz was annihilated with a planetary core detonator, turning the ball of mud into a ball of fire. All he wanted was to clear his name of the fiasco on Theogony, where somehow the Kzizn had impersonated Imperial Secret Service agents and had whisked the human captive and her father from under his very nose. He didn't care what happened beyond that.

An Agent Provocateur, he cared nothing about interstellar relations and even less about the bizarre interest that the Palace seemed to have in the young woman now in his custody. All he cared about was avoiding looking bad, his physical appearance notwithstanding. Like the newly-crowned Empress, his ugliness was irremediable.

He turned to the control consol, happy he wasn't being pursued. "Ship, open a sub-ether channel to Lucina Nine."

"Shutting down engines, opening sub-ether channel to Lucina Nine."

"One of these days," the woman said, "you humans will devise a better means of communication."

He snorted at her, and realized the sound was uncomfortably like a word from the Kzizn language, which he didn't speak. "You've got room to talk."

"I'd have more room if I didn't have these bracelets on."

Trusting that she wouldn't try anything, he got up to remove them. He took one off, watching her carefully.

"Thank you," she said, giving him a brief smile.

Her charm sent warmth coursing down into his toes. He smiled back and then took the other one off.

"Channel open."

"Agent Erastus, is that you?" A holo of Colonel Melanctha Remes materialized above the controls.

"I have a present for her Highness, the Empress Hecuba." He gestured at the young woman.

Remes' jaw dropped, and her face blanched. "Fool!" Remes snarled, and the holo collapsed.

Erastus stared at the empty space above the control panel, wondering what had happened. Not the reaction I expected, he thought, wondering why she hadn't been overjoyed.

"I don't think she wanted to hear that," Lydia said.

He whirled on her. "Shut up! What do you know?!" Flummoxed, he didn't need his captive telling him what he already knew. "Engage course!" he snarled.

"Passengers in unsafe locations," the ship said. "Please secure all passengers."

"I said 'engage'!" he screamed at the holoscreen, tendons popping out at his neck, a vein wriggling at his temple.

"Engaged."

The acceleration slammed him into a bulkhead, knocking him unconscious.

* * *

"Colonel Remes, incoming!" Lieutenant-Colonel Urian Nikitas squawked on her com. "Vessel of unknown make and model just appeared in orbit above Lucina Nine!"

Colonel Melanctha Remes of IBS Command nearly soiled herself. "Sub-space disruptions?"

"Yes, Colonel."

"Kzizn! Squadrons three, five and eight, scramble! Intruder alert! Squadrons three, five and eight, scramble! Intruder alert!" What the Hades is Dickass thinking? she wondered.

"Squadrons three, five and eight scrambling, Colonel!"

Klaxons began to sound, lights dimmed, and red strobes took over.

Now I can't see a blasted thing! she thought, tearing out of her office into the command theater. The five rings of monitoring stations had come alive with activity, Lieutenant-Colonel Nikitas at the center, spouting orders.

She reminded herself that she wasn't certain it was Doukas, but his transmission hadn't contained the sub-space signatures built into all Gaean ships, military or otherwise, indicating he'd pirated a vessel of Kzizn manufacture. Melanctha had ordered a scan of the Kziznvxrz system immediately after closing the com channel, and sensors had detected sub-space disruptions just moments after the holocom. It was a fair assumption that the Kzizn-manufacture ship was piloted by Doukas, but it was still an assumption.

The fiasco just yesterday on Theogony had set them all on edge. The Kzizns' disguised as Imperial Secret Service personnel purloining the captives from the Detention Center was an interstellar incident of major proportions. Melanctha had placed IBS Command for the Delta Sector on high alert, prepared for the order to assist the Gaean Armada in its assault on Kziznvxrz. Ships were now amassed in the Oort cloud of the lonely system at the edge of the Mnemosyne Constellation, more collecting every moment. But thus far, no attack had been ordered.

Colonel Remes joined Lieutenant-Colonel Nikitas in the center ring. "Status?"

"They're surrounding the unknown vessel now, Colonel," Urian said.

On high alert already, they'd been able to scramble quickly. "That's the second time in two days that Gaean territory has suffered Kzizn encroachment."

Nikitas shot her a glance. "You don't think this is Doukas?"

"I do, but he's caused me more work in the past week than a bureaucrat from Gaea." She rolled her eyes. "I'd rather blast his ass into the next galaxy and apologize later. Get me a secured channel to all three squadrons, and then a separate unsecure channel to the Kzizn vessel, muted."

"Channels open," Nikitas told her moments later.

"All fighters, arm neutredoes at full power. This is the second Kzizn incursion in two days. Prepare to blast."

She waited until they acknowledged. "Unmute," she ordered, awaited his nod and then said, "Attention Kzizn vessel, you have violated Gaean territory. Shut down your engines immediately or be blasted out of the sky."

The static of a regular radio signal screeched from the speaker. No holo appeared. "Agent Doukas is hurt and needs immediate medical attention," an assertive female voice said. "I'm taking him to the hospital. Out."

"Non-sub-space transmission, Colonel," Nikitas told her.

"Belay there, Kzizn vessel," she said.

"It's gone!" squawked their com. "The Kzizn ship has vanished!"

Several monitoring stations confirmed. "Slipped away without a trace, Colonel," one tech said.

"Colonel, sub-space disruptions detected at Tyrnavos Hospital."

"On screen!"

The sprawling hospital complex appeared, and atop the tallest structure perched a gleaming blue-metal vessel, its sleek design nothing like any ship of Gaean manufacture that Melanctha had seen. The boarding ramp was already out, and a figure awkwardly carrying a bundle stumbled down the ramp. A hospital crew hustled out to meet them.

A close-up showed medical personnel taking a limp and bloody Agent Doukas from the arms of a young woman, blood covering the front of her formalls. Her hair brown, her face triangular and soft, and her eyes a vivid blue, the young woman was striking for both her bloody clothes and her elfin beauty.

Melanctha Remes drew a sharp breath, the face unforgettable.

Chapter 11

Lydia walked along an endless corridor inside a tight cordon of captors, keeping her composure in spite of her fear.

For Kziznvxrz, she kept telling herself, anything to avert an attack on Kziznvxrz.

The squad of uniformed soldiers had converged on the hospital helopad within minutes of her landing. A hundred blasma rifles aimed at her, they'd ordered her away from the ship and then had swarmed around her, bundled her into a waiting hover, and whisked her away to a military compound surrounded by barbed wire, gun emplacements, and watchtowers.

On arrival at the compound, they'd whisked her over to a gigantic biodetector, the arch twice as tall as her, its sides glowing blue.

"But I've been inoculated!" she'd insisted. They'd shoved her through it anyway, and the machine had turned green, indicating she was clear of pathogens.

The phalanx of soldiers marched her down the corridor. At a checkpoint, where carbo-nick alloy bars reinforced clear glasma panes, female soldiers replaced all the males in the phalanx, and they took her down another corridor, this one equally sterile. They passed through three more checkpoints, ID-ing the prisoner and every member of her escort each time.

A woman at the last checkpoint stepped up and stuck her face into Lydia's. "I'm Sergeant Glavan. Your Kzizn pals try any of their tricks here, and they'll have *me* to deal with." She poked a thumb at her own chest.

"Yes, Ma'am."

"Now, if you agree to cooperate, we'll get you out of those bloody rags and into a shower. One wrong move, and we blast your ass."

"Yes, Ma'am." Lydia would have saluted if she could have done so without irony. Doukas had bled all over her, and all she wanted was to get out of the sticky, clingy garment.

They led her into the containment area. Two of the female soldiers indicated a cleansall stall, and a third retrieved a fresh pair of formalls. "Slowly now," one of them told her. "No sudden moves."

Methodically, she stripped, trying not to feel naked.

"Just leave it. Into the stall."

"Stunning, isn't she?" one said to another.

"Plug it!" the detail commander said.

She got into the stall, its door clear glasma. She closed her eyes, and the cleansall cycled through a wash, a rinse, and a dry. A hairhelm descended from the ceiling and gave her a quick, utilitarian coif.

She stepped out and dressed in the pair of proffered formalls.

They led her along another sterile corridor to a cell. "In," a soldier said, "Chow in five. You hungry?"

She entered the cell, wondering what they'd be feeding her. "Famished," she said, "and I'm a vegetarian."

"This ain't the Hilton, sister."

She bit her tongue on a sarcastic reply. She'd never been able to stomach the protein-rich protozoa steaks on Kzizn, and standard human fare hadn't proved any more digestible.

They closed the door and locked it, the carbonick reinforced glasma giving her no privacy.

Another cell, the third in three days, Lydia thought. The cell wasn't terribly different from the one on Theogony, the materials more durable here. Detainment cells didn't differ much, she surmised. On Kziznvxrz, there weren't any, so she didn't have much to compare them with.

What the hell did I do? she wondered. Easing herself to the bunk, she squelched her despair. For Kziznvxrz, she told herself again.

She looked up to find a woman staring at her.

Her ramrod posture declared her status as loudly as the epaulets on her shoulders. She had a sharp, blade-like nose. "Colonel Melanctha Remes, IBS Commander here at the Lucina Nine. Lydia Procopio?"

Lydia nodded.

"You could've escaped—easily. Instead, you took Doukas to the hospital. And then you stayed there on the helopad until we got there, again giving up an opportunity to escape. Why did you want to be captured?"

"Maybe stop an attack on the Kziznvxrfn," she said, shrugging. She felt the woman's scrutiny, as though Colonel Remes recognized her.

"At the Immigration Detention Center on Theogony, you called the Kzizn your father."

"He reared me since I was four. My mother, Viscountess Ambassador Basilissa Procopio, and my father, Professor Dorian Procopio, were killed when our ship broke up entering the Kziznvxrz atmosphere."

"And you've lived there ever since?"

Lydia shrugged. "Nearly twenty-five years now. My father and I have a small shipping company. We have every Imperial clearance we need, Colonel. I've been to three dozen Gaean planets. We've never had a problem before. And it was a dissident group called the Wrwrmrfn that kidnapped us from Theogony. They're trying to stir up conflict between Gaea and Kziznvxrz."

"Kziznvxrfn Dissidents?"

"You pronounce that pretty well, for a human."

"Thank you."

"Why all this trouble, Colonel?" Lydia asked. "We didn't do anything wrong. We've both been inoculated."

The other woman's face was impassive.

Either she won't tell me or doesn't know, Lydia thought, and she doesn't want to betray which it is. "Look, you don't have to tell me anything, but you could do something for me."

"What would that be?"

"Make sure they don't attack my home."

* * *

"I can't make any guarantees, Lydia," Colonel Melanctha Remes said, looking over the waif.

Her small frame and elfin face gave the impression of adolescence. The refulgent beauty of her face was compelling, as though an angel had stepped from heaven into the cell. Lydia Procopio had the heroic face of ancient tales, like the ones Melanctha had heard as a child. A face so perfect and fine that it caused the breath to catch and the heart to skip. Further, the face reminded Melanctha of someone. The face of someone she'd never forget.

"I've ordered double vegetables and half the meat. No guarantees it'll be anything like your usual diet on Kziznvxrfn." Then Melanctha met

Lydia's gaze. "I'll do what I can about the naval buildup."

She turned and was headed out the door when a faint "Thank you" followed her from the cell far behind her.

Your first duty is the Empire's security, Melanctha remonstrated herself, the face of her captive threatening to break through the hard shell that she'd built over the memories of her youth, layer by layer.

"Get me a secure channel to Kastela. Admiral Vlahos on holo," she said to the air, striding down the corridor, knowing Lieutenant-Colonel Nikitas was monitoring her.

"Yes, Colonel," he said. "Obtaining channel."

Melanctha gritted her teeth, her jaw muscles rippling, her stride nearly the march of an automaton. No, she ordered herself, you will not think about him! She took the stairs rather than the lift, blindly charging through the checkpoints, her face carefully composed, her mind in turmoil.

"Colonel, I have an encrypted channel to Rear Admiral Vlahos, Kastela Headquarters," Nikitas said. "Go ahead."

She passed the last checkpoint. "I need privacy for this one, Urian." Melanctha hoped using his first name would soften the request. She turned a corner toward her personal suite.

"Certainly, Colonel. Monitoring off."

She entered the underground apartment she'd occupied for six years, a palatial suite of five rooms.

Rear Admiral Cleon Vlahos was waiting for her, leaning against the mantel in the living room. His holo image, rather.

"Clever bastard," she told him. "How are you, my friend?"

"None the worse for the wear and tear of acquiring a new Emperor, Mela," the holojection said, coming away from the faux hearth. "Good to see you, my friend. I've missed you, but I'm glad you were spared the hullabaloo here on Gaea."

"I don't know what shocked me more," she told her boss, "seeing the narcissistic bitch aim her blasma pistol at doddering Daphne or watching the High Justice soil herself again in public."

The Rear Admiral's image threw his head back and laughed. "Classic Narcissa, wasn't it?"

"In fine form, the both of them," she replied, laughing too.

He sobered suddenly. "But you didn't com me for that, did you?"

"I've got the girl, Cleon."

The sharp intake of breath told Melanctha all she needed to know.

"Not another word," she told him. "For your safety and mine, eh?"

"That's wise, Mela. Thank you for the caution. It's too easy to think the encryption impenetrable."

She smiled. He hadn't said, and wouldn't ever say, that the IBS had incorporated backdoor decoding methods into every type of encryption used throughout the Empire. "Two things I need, Cleon. And what I don't want is a word of assent or even acknowledgment."

"Not and maintain plausible deniability, of course," the Rear Admiral replied. "Not a very clear transmission to start with, Colonel. Your image is fuzzy, difficult to hear you through the static." His image was perfect, his voice crystal clear.

She smiled. "First, see if you can delay the attack on Kziznvxrz. A splinter group called the Wrwrmrfn carried out the extraction raid on Theogony. Second, get me the file on Count Terzi's only child, the one who died at age ten."

"What? What was that, Colonel Remes? The signal is really bad. I didn't hear a thing you were saying. I can't even see your face anymore, Colonel. Colonel Remes? Colonel? Oh, blast it. Signal's gone. Holo out!" The expression on his face as the holovid collapsed was a broad grin.

Melanctha felt the smile slide off her face like a mud mask at a beauty parlor, and she lowered herself to the divan, the memories too vivid to contain anymore. Memories of the freak hover accident and horrific explosion that had taken the life of her childhood friend right in front of her. The life of Count Terzi's son, Icarus, the next in line for the crown after the new infant child, Hecuba Zenon.

Colonel Melanctha Remes wept.

Chapter 12

Lydia looked up from the half-eaten meal.

A lab-coated man stood in front of the glasma door, a biometer in hand. "Nurse Galen Liakos," he said. "Please step out of the cell so I can examine you. Colonel's orders."

She frowned, bewildered. The female guards on either side of the nurse looked as puzzled as she felt. "I'm a prisoner. Why would Colonel Remes give a grape leaf?"

The nurse shrugged. "Patient refusing to cooperate," he said to the air, as if reciting to a machine.

"I didn't say I wouldn't cooperate." She rose and stepped to the door, which slid aside.

The two guards held their blasma pistols at ready, their tips glowing.

"Step this way and stop here," the nurse said. "Now turn around. Pull the formall off your shoulders and lower it to your waist."

Lydia did as she was bidden, the chill air on her exposed back and front making her skin prickle.

"These leads will be cold."

Icy points of sticky tape pegged her, one to each shoulder just below the clavicle, one to each side on the lowest rib. Her skin sucked in the adhesive, accustomed to environments much more moist than this one.

"Breath deep and release," Nurse Liakos said.

She did so dutifully, feeling a bit warmer on the exhale.

The sterile setting helped her feel somewhat comfortable being half-exposed in front of the man. On Kziznvxrz, she rarely wore clothes. The humid environment and constant presence of mud made it difficult to keep anything clean. A quick rinse just before entering the house was far easier without clothes to contend with. Studying a human-occupied world before she'd arrived, she'd been bewildered by the outer coverings they always wore. And she'd learned what a disturbance the sight of an unclothed woman caused without having to experience it firsthand.

He ran the biometer up and down her back while she breathed, the hand-held machine humming. "Is that a rash?"

"Huh?"

"Those spots on your right arm, is that a rash?"

"Oh, that? I don't know," Lydia said. "It's been itching off and on since I left Kziznvxrz. I've been inoculated."

"All right, taking off the leads now. These are usually pretty sticky." They came off easily, with only a slight tug. "That was odd. Formalls back on, please."

Lydia pulled the cloth back over her shoulders, wriggling into the form-fitting suit. While she secured it in front, Nurse Liakos started asking her questions.

Endless questions. As many questions as Imperial Immigration had asked when she'd first applied for a trade visa. Personal questions about her procreation history (none), psycho-chemo alteration history (none), abuse history (what's abuse? none), family history (unknown, orphaned at four), violence history (none), ad nauseam.

At the end, Nurse Liakos thanked her politely and apologized for the invasive questions.

"Galen," she asked, "did your parents want you to be a doctor?"

He grinned at her. "Couldn't tell from my name, could you?" With a nod, he punched a few buttons on the biometer, and the hum died. "Pleasure to make your acquaintance."

"Likewise," she replied as the guards herded her back into the cell.

He nodded and nearly ran into Colonel Remes as he exited.

Lydia watched them retreat into the corridor, unable to hear their conversation from inside her cell. She saw Colonel Remes slip something into her pocket as she entered the detainment area.

"Come with me, Ms. Procopio."

"Where are you taking me?"

"Gaea, Ms. Procopio. You're going to Gaea."

* * *

Lydia boarded the mini-cargo vessel waiting on the tarmac, her phalanx of guards walking her up the ramp.

The cell aboard the ship was a container in the cargo hold beside her amoeba-class Kzizn vessel, looking as sleek as a wasp.

They'll dismantle it and try to re-engineer its drive, Lydia thought, knowing the sub-ether transport technology superior to the Homo sapiens' A-warp drive.

The phalanx of guards marched her into the cell, a sterile box with seat, toilet, shower, and bunk. It looked remarkably like the cell aboard the Wrwrmrfn vessel that had taken her back to Kziznvxrz. They secured the door behind her, the carbo-nick reinforced glasma giving her a view of the cargo hold entrance. The guards left the ship, and mechanical whining indicated the boarding ramp was retracting.

She strapped herself into the seat, guessing lift off was imminent.

Another twenty minutes passed however before warning lights began to flash.

Gaea finally, Lydia thought.

It'd always been a curiosity, that distant planet she was supposedly from. Not that she had much interest in going there, just that it was an unknown feature of her life, a place she'd heard about and imagined things about, where her relatives were thought to live. She'd always had a faint yearning to visit Gaea, and once she'd even inquired into the process. The bureaucratic hurdles had seemed daunting at the time, far greater than her vague desire to overcome them.

And whatever family she might have on Gaea, they'd either lacked the will or the political influence to persuade the government to have the accident investigated. Kziznvxrfn requests to have the Homo sapiens take back the Ambassador's surviving daughter had been met with silence.

Lydia didn't understand why they hadn't, nor did she begrudge it. She'd been so overwhelmed with the sudden loss of her parents, the horror of the crash itself, and the difficulties of her new environment, that she'd given little thought to Gaea. And she'd been four years old, barely old enough to know what death was, bewildered that Mommy and Daddy weren't ever coming back.

As to the things that Mrxlwvnfh Gzelfozirh, the oldest Paramecium, had told her, information gathered by Ezra on Gaea before the coronation, Lydia didn't quite know how to put it in context. It seemed such a pastiche of random facts, splotches of paint spread out on a canvas, no two splotches touching, no way to connect the information together.

The ship rumbling under her, the acceleration pressing her into the seat, Lydia hoped she was making the right decision.

Going to Gaea seemed the only way to stop an attack on Kziznvxrz.

Why, she couldn't have said. What possible interest could I be to these Homo sapiens now?

The acceleration eased, and the warning lights blinked off.

She unbuckled herself and looked at the bunk. She was tempted, the utter boredom inside these cells difficult to endure. Ironic, she thought, that I've become such an expert on prison cells.

Somewhere, a hatch opened.

Lydia looked toward the cage door.

Colonel Melanctha Remes appeared beyond the glasma. Without a word, she opened the cell.

"Join me in the mess? There's a proper synth we can program to your liking."

She stared at the other woman, really looking at her. Not much experienced at estimating age, Lydia guessed the woman was in her late forties, early fifties. She held herself stiffly erect, but beyond the sharp-bladed nose, her gaze was gentle, her face having a hint of regality, plain but not unpleasant. Soft confidence exuded from her, the confidence of command.

"I didn't expect to see *you* aboard, Colonel Remes."

"I've taken the initiative to bring you to Gaea personally. Given circumstances, it seemed the prudent thing to do."

"What circumstances are those?" Lydia still hadn't moved, bewildered.

"The back and forth, and the interest in you displayed by our capital. Come along, then. Provided you won't try to escape, there's no need for you to remain in that cell."

Lydia shrugged. "I won't, which you already knew."

"I did."

She stepped toward the door, and the Colonel led the way. The rectangular corridors were disconcerting to Lydia, Kzizn ships having tubular passageways. As they moved through the ship, Lydia got the distinct impression they were alone, no one else aboard. In the galley, the table and chairs were uncomfortably high, Kzizn cup-seats just inches above the floor and their tables usually not more than a foot.

Colonel Remes gestured her to sit and stepped to a machine.

Lydia watched as the device beeped and blipped back at the Colonel.

"Stubborn thing doesn't have a setting for vegetarians. Call me Mela, by the way."

"Pleased," Lydia said. "Thank you, Mela."

"What do the Kzizn call you?"

"Obwrz," she said. "They have as difficult a time pronouncing Galactim as we do Kziznvxrz."

Melanctha sat across from her and pushed a steaming bowl toward her.

The green bubbling liquid looked appetizing and smelled delicious. "What is it?"

"Protoplasm soup. I had your stool sampled, by the way, and this concoction is as close to your usual diet as I could get. Hopefully, it's adequate."

Lydia tasted it. The warm protoplasm soup was good. Somewhat odd in taste, but not objectionable. She found the Homo sapiens animal protein diet nauseating, and this soup was a welcome change. "Thank you, very kind of you." She looked at Melanctha. "Why the personal interest, Mela? What am I to you?"

Lydia saw the woman change. It wasn't overt or dramatic, but enough to indicate something profound had once happened to her.

"I had a friend in childhood, and I saw him die. You look uncannily like him, Lydia. His name was Icarus Terzi, and before Empress Hecuba Zenon was born, Icarus was the heir apparent, the next nearest relative to Emperor Athanasios Zenon."

* * *

Rear Admiral Cleon Vlahos, Chief of the Imperial Bureau of Suspicion, brought his gaze up from the dossier of Icarus Terzi and looked out the window of his office at Kastela Headquarters on the outskirts of New Athens.

Initially, he'd delegated obtaining the file to his administrative assistant.

"Sir, my apologies, access to Icarus Terzi's dossier is restricted."

"But you've got top-secret clearance."

"Access requires top-top-secret clearance, Sir."

"So I have to retrieve the damn thing myself, eh?"

"Yes, Sir, I'm afraid so."

"Why do you suppose that is?"

Outside the triple-paned glasma window, in the distance, the palace gleamed like a jewel.

Icarus Terzi had been the son of Count Ilias Terzi, cousin to Emperor Athanasios Zenon, and the heir-presumptive if the Emperor failed to spawn a viable candidate for the throne. At the time of the boy's death, the Emperor's first daughter, Cybill, was beginning to show signs of developmental difficulties. Her failure to meet several expected milestones was generally perceived as a sign she would be passed over for the succession. More than one member of the aristocracy had cast an envious eye in the direction of Icarus, the next obvious heir apparent.

Tragic, Cleon thought, how the boy died. A hover had veered out of traffic, had upended, and had plummeted to the ground, erupting in a fireball, right on top of Icarus Terzi. A freak accident, few hovers malfunctioning in such a spectacular way.

The boy had been playing on the private grounds of the Terzi estate with his friend, Melanctha Remes, the two ten-year-olds being watched from a distance by his governor, an old gentleman named Giles Sotiropoulos. Blameless in the boy's death, Giles had been fired nonetheless, and the file indicated that he'd committed suicide not long afterward, destitute and without the means to support himself.

Vlahos got up from his desk, disturbed by the similarity in feature between the boy, Icarus Terzi, and the captive, Lydia Procopio.

The aristocracy, being a somewhat insular group of scions, most of them so fabulously wealthy that fortunes might be made in their footsteps, were not immune to trysts, liaisons, and infidelities. In fact, it might be said that they had far more opportunity to indulge themselves in such foibles.

Rear Admiral Vlahos remembered the Kzizn ambassador, Viscountess Basilissa Procopio, a suave woman of immaculate breeding whose husband, Dorian, was a Professor of Xenobiology and a scion from among the lesser nobility. Vlahos had admired Viscountess Procopio's staunch resolve in accepting the ambassadorship to such a distant backwater.

He'd been a newly-appointed sub-secretary of Military Intelligence to the Imperial Bureau of Suspicion and had been at the palace to brief the Emperor on an uprising along the outer Perseus Arm. So it was just by chance he'd been present when Emperor Zenon had formally asked Viscountess Procopio to take the appointment.

Palace personnel had become aware of a subtle shift in the bureaucracy. No official documentation of this shift could ever be found, but the upper echelons felt its impact on daily-decision making. The guerilla bureaucracy adjusted to such changes with alacrity. Power was like water, having an undeniable need to flow, finding its way around or over obstructions, eating away at vulnerabilities until it had etched a channel where it might flow unrestricted, often seeping silently through thicker obstructions, eroding insidiously at the bedrock of people's moral character, saturating their inhibitions and slaking their thirst for power. Everyone had become aware that Emperor Athanasios had lost his grip on power. Four years of grieving for his beloved Consort, Ambrosia, had wrung him dry as a sponge.

Power had begun to flow through a new, unofficial consort, one whose station prevented her from ever being recognized in any official capacity, the Lady's Maid, Narcissa Thanos.

Newly-appointed to a position didn't mean Vlahos was new to bureaucracies. Thirty-three years old, Lieutenant Vlahos had previously served as Chief of Counter-Intelligence in the Gaean Navy. His graduation at twenty-three from the Hellenic post-graduate naval academy with triple degrees in encryption, linguistics, and interstellar relations had nearly guaranteed him a fast-track to Admiral. Alas it was not to be, the IBS having somehow pulled some strings to get Vlahos transferred to a civilian intelligence role.

Strings, he'd discovered, that had been closer in size to hawsers. They'd hauled his career ship by its hawsers over to civilian intelligence.

Now, as he compared the two stills, one of the boy, Icarus Terzi, and one of the captive, Lydia Procopio, the Chief of the Imperial Bureau of Suspicion knew his ship had come in.

He considered his options: withhold the dossier from Colonel Melanctha Remes, his erstwhile lover with whom he'd shared many a romantic evening; take his information directly to Empress Hecuba and the Dowager Empress Narcissa; consult with his colleague the Chief of the Imperial Secret Service; or simply take the initiative and annihilate Remes and her captive en route from Lucina IX.

Vlahos knew the latter the most prudent course.

It was what the Empress would order him to do, anyway. And if he didn't do it now, he was likely to incur the Dowager's wrath in having hesitated.

If he'd had some way of killing the captive without hurting Melanctha, he wouldn't have blinked.

And since they're both going to die, Vlahos thought, why don't I send the information anyway? In his estimation, it wouldn't hurt. In fact, if he didn't send it, Melanctha might become suspicious.

In the dossier on Icarus Terzi, he saw a genetic profile. He was certain Melanctha had obtained a tissue sample from her captive. A comparison of their genomes would prove irrefutably what Melanctha certainly suspected: That the captive, Lydia Procopio, daughter of the Ambassador to Kziznvxrz, Basilissa Procopio, was a close relative of the just-deceased Emperor Athanasios Zenon.

How and why was immaterial.

Emperors don't think the same way as normal people, Vlahos told himself. They hold in mind the long view and aren't averse to a little intrigue.

Not averse to a little intrigue.

He smiled at his minimizing Imperial misdeeds.

Perhaps Athanasios had impregnated Basilissa as a hedge against his legitimate children through Ambrosia not surviving childhood. Likely targets of assassination from multiple directions, the aristocracy included, such children rarely lived lives with a modicum of normalcy, under constant guard, their food and water always taste-tested, every interlocutor screened heavily and vetted thoroughly.

Vlahos was convinced Lydia was of Imperial blood. His only question was the degree of consanguinity. No matter what the degree, however, the Dowager Empress wanted her dead.

Looking out his office window, Vlahos queued up a holomail message for Melanctha and attached the dossier on Icarus Terzi. In the distance, the palace sparkled.

"Encryption, please," he said, as though to the air.

"What level encryption, Sir?"

Cryptology one of three degrees he'd earned at post-graduate, Vlahos smiled. "Quadruple, please." With such deep encryption, even someone with his considerable skills would have difficulty decrypting it.

"Ultra-top-secret priority, Sir?"

"No. In fact, no priority at all," he told his desk computer. Better not to bring attention to it, he thought. "Send immediately."

"Sir, there is no subject or message, only an attachment. Send anyway?"

"Send immediately," he repeated.

"Message sent, Sir."

Rear Admiral Cleon Vlahos admired the wonderful view from atop Kastela Headquarters on the outskirts of New Athens, the city spread before him in the bowl-like valley, the ring of mountains on one side soaring into the clouds, the seas on the other like blue blankets of water.

The splat against the glasma didn't alarm him, the window triple-paned and impervious. The smear on the other side looked odd, like some gigantic gastropod without a shell. It burrowed a hole through the first pane, and then began to work on the second.

Disbelief and revulsion held Vlahos entranced. His mind tried to apprehend what chemical synthesis might be required to tunnel through the impervious glasma.

The slug burrowed through the second pane and spread itself onto the third.

Should I be alarmed? Vlahos wondered.

The innermost pane of glasma melted quickly. A tentacle leapt to his throat and yanked his head into the glasma, splattering his brains across the lovely view.

Chapter 13

"Huh? You took a tissue sample?!" Lydia didn't know whether to be honored or alarmed. "Forgive me, but what possible importance does my genetic profile have? What's going on here, Mela?"

The other woman looked at her from across the table. In her gaze was a terrifying concern. She had just told Lydia she'd received the dossier on Icarus Terzi.

Lydia continued when the only response she got was silence. "First, you tell me I look like the Emperor's nephew, once removed, and now, you want to compare my genes with his? What in Hades is going on?"

"Don't get upset, Lydia. I realize how difficult this must be for you. Detained by Imperial Infection Control, kidnapped by a faction among your own people, arrested by the Imperial Bureau of Suspicion. And now all this."

Lydia snorted. "Upset? Why should I be upset? Not a single Homo sapiens has exhibited a whit of interest in me for the last twenty-four years. The moment Empress Hecuba gets crowned, they're all coming after me with fishing nets. The next thing you know, the Imperial Secret Service will try to kill me. Why should I be upset?" She heard her own voice echoing back at her from the galley walls, and she realized how loud she'd gotten. "I'm sorry, Mela." She took a deep breath and sighed, looking down at the empty bowl in front of her.

"All true," Melanctha replied.

"When I got back to Paramecia, my father showed me the A-warp casing from the shipwreck twenty-four years ago. Traces of a thermonuclear microfusion event were found in its lining." Lydia watched the Colonel's face as the information worked its way to its logical conclusion.

The color drained from Colonel Remes' face. "Your mother's ship was sabotaged." She stared at the wall behind Lydia.

"And did you see those obituaries the day after Empress Hecuba's coronation?"

"Obituaries?"

"Of Drucilla Kanelos, Eugenia Ioannou, and Filmena Sotiropoulos?" Lydia had happened to see a name from among the list of people on Gaea whom Svkszvhgfh Ezhrozprh had interviewed. The time of death had coincided with Hecuba's coronation. Alarmed, Lydia had searched the holonet for the other names. "All of them died when Hecuba was crowned. Ezra spoke with them in the days leading up to the coronation."

"Must be a coincidence, Lydia."

"Do you even know who they were?" Lydia recited their positions. "The Laundry Maid to the Dowager Empress, the Governess to the first-born child of Emperor Zenon, and my Governess when I was an infant. You tell me, Mela, how do all three die on the same day at the same time that the second-born child is crowned Empress?"

Colonel Melanctha Remes was shaking her head.

"I don't know, either, Colonel," Lydia said quietly. "But it certainly isn't a coincidence."

"Let me contact my superior, Cleon. He's the Bureau Director. He'll have some ideas."

Lydia watched Colonel Remes' jaw work, the mouth moving as the woman subvocalized on her trake. She'd considered getting similar hardware when she'd found out at twenty years old that ninety-eight percent of Homo sapiens had such electronics installed between the ages of eight and ten. Somehow, she'd never gotten around to it. Only the aristocracy eschewed such implants.

"What do you mean, he isn't available? He just sent me an h-mail!"

Lydia didn't like the sound of that. She put her hands on either side of her chair as if to steady herself. Fixed in place to the floor, it offered insubstantial comfort.

Remes stood as if to head to the cockpit. "Well, damn it, then, check on him!"

She probably doesn't realize she's verbalizing, Lydia thought.

The ship lurched and howled, Remes careening into a wall, the empty bowl with her. Lydia clung to her chair, the momentum threatening to hurl her too.

Tractor beam! Lydia thought. Klaxons blaring, the ship slewed the other way, steel complaining, her bowl bouncing back the other way, the unconscious Remes slamming into that wall. Then the motion ceased.

All the loudspeakers blared, "Micro-cargo vessel, this is the Department of Infection Control, prepare to be boarded."

This isn't a coincidence either, she thought, her heart pounding heavily, panic threatening to overwhelm her. Lydia didn't hesitate. Remes was insensate and bleeding from a head wound. Lydia grabbed Melanctha by the waist and hauled her into the corridor, the gravity at a half-G helping. She carried the unconscious woman into the cargo hold to the entrance of her amoeba-class vessel.

A heavy thunk struck the micro-cargo vessel amidships.

Boarding party, Lydia thought. The amoeba's boarding ramp seemed to take hours to extend itself.

"Power up," she called to the ship as she hauled Melanctha aboard. The boarding ramp retracted behind her, the amoeba coming alive under her. Lydia secured Melanctha in a sleeping net.

"Direct sub-ether jump!" Lydia dived for her chair, the holo display coming to life. She buckled her restraints.

Fists pounded on the amoeba hull. The display showed three figures in full envirosuits outside.

"Destination, please?"

"Anywhere!"

One of the three drew a weapon and aimed it.

"Jumping," the ship replied. And the vessel shifted, leaving Lydia with that slight twinge of nausea she always got.

The display changed, stars wheeling around the ship in scintillating profusion.

"Where are we?" Lydia didn't recognize the configuration of stars, their brilliance causing her to squint. Why are there so many?

"Two parsecs from the Galactic core," the amoeba said, "three parsecs from Gaea."

Too close to the capital. "Jump to Istra Six," she said immediately, the first place she could think of.

"Jumping," the amoeba said. Again, that nausea, and the stars around the ship changed.

A planet three-fourths covered in jungle appeared below the amoeba. Istra VI sat half-way
out the Scutum-Centaurus arm on a side spur,
a politically unimportant system whose primary
attractions were its lush jungles and fabulous
beaches. She and Xsirhglksvi had gone there
once, and she'd had a wonderful time, Xsirh not
so much, the climate wet enough but far too hot
for him.

"Orbit, please." She struggled out of her restraints.

Colonel Remes was barely conscious as Lydia
checked her wounds. The bleeding had stopped
on its own. Globules floated around the cabin
and coagulated on multiple surfaces.

"Where are we?" she said groggily.

Lydia told her. "They hit us with a tractor
beam and boarded."

"I know you're not an engineer, but any idea
how they did that while we were in A-warp?"

She shook her head. "We need to get you examined. You hit the wall pretty hard both times."

"Both times? I barely remember the first."
The other woman smiled at her weakly. "You're

pretty resourceful. You saved our lives, you know."

Lydia shrugged. "I did what I could."

"Thank you." Melanctha tried to struggle free from the sleeping net. "Here, help me out of this thing. Look, uh, we can't go planet side. We'll be ID'd instantly."

She's right, Lydia told herself, helping Melanctha into the cockpit. Lydia sat the other woman in her chair and wiggled her behind awkwardly into Xsirh's cup-chair. "We need to get you medical attention. What do you suggest?"

"I know a few shady characters on Amphitrite Three who might be able to help. At the Bureau of Suspicion, we get to know a lot of the local pondscum."

"Jump to Amphitrite Three," Lydia ordered. Pondscum was one of her favorite dishes, repulsive to the eye but delectable to the palate.

"Jumping," the amoeba replied, and she felt that twinge of nausea.

A blue-white ball materialized on the holo-screen. A cold, forbidding planet, nearly all the infrastructure underground, Amphitrite III seemed to Lydia the perfect place to go underground for a few days. "How do we avoid being ID'd here?"

"I'll take care of that," Melanctha said.

"Sub-ether holomail received," the amoeba said.

Lydia and Melanctha exchanged a glance. "Who do you suppose—?"

"Identify source," Lydia said. Who would be contacting us? she wondered.

"Holonet trace indicates the origin as Lucina Nine, and sender identified as Lieutenant-Colonel Urian Nikitas."

Again, Lydia exchanged a glance with Melanctha. She wondered how he'd acquired her holomail address.

"Let's see what Urian has to say."

The Lieutenant-Colonel's face protruded from the holo. "Colonel Remes, are you all right? A-warp disruptions were detected along your flight path. It appears that the Department of Infection Control has seized your ship. To search for infectious pathogens, I suppose. I've lodged a complaint against them. Ridiculous for them to be suspicious of the Bureau of Suspicion. I'm h-mailing you just to make sure you're all right.

Why are you personally taking the prisoner to Gaea in the first place? Let me know what your disposition is, Colonel." The face collapsed.

"They weren't searching for infectious pathogens, were they?" Lydia asked.

"I'm afraid they weren't," Melanctha said. "Can you get a visual on the micro-cargo vessel?"

"Not from this distance," she told the Colonel. "We'd have to be within a parsec. Are you going to reply?"

"You don't have any special equipment aboard to prevent its being traced, do you?"

Lydia shook her head. "They tell me that Kzizn vessels are difficult to trace because of their hulls and sub-ether drives, but the holomail that this ship uses is Gaean technology, not Kzizn."

"Then perhaps I'd better not reply. It's odd. I've worked beside Urian for six years now, but I can't really say I know him."

"I'd say we've got bigger problems than that. Why do you suppose Director Vlahos wasn't available?"

"I don't know. Suspicious, how he sent that dossier, and minutes later couldn't be raised."

"Do you have access to other dossiers?"

Melanctha looked at her.

"The two governesses and the Laundry Maid."

"Not easy to obtain without someone at headquarters to get them for me," Melanctha replied.

"Gl szwvh drgs rg zoo!" Lydia cursed in Kziznvxrz, and then switched back to Galactim. "We need more information, Mela."

Melanctha turned to look at her. "Such as what's really going on on Gaea."

* * *

Licensed Behavioral Technician Baptiste Tomaras knew he was hip-deep in human waste.

Ever since that Kzizn had commandeered his pneumatube capsule, Baptiste had felt he'd been thrust into some really bad spy movie, spooks following his every move, the feel of eyes on his back like an ice pick between the vertebrae, blasma rifle sights queuing up his head for the next shot.

And what does the Kzizn do after I get him a tissue sample from Princess Cybill Zenon? Baptiste asked himself rhetorically. Goes and gets splattered by the Dowager Empress herself!

If Baptiste hadn't felt paranoid before that, the sight of liquefied alien flesh spewing in a green cloud of spray on holovid was certainly enough to cause him to void all over himself.

Hip-deep in his own waste.

Baptiste hustled from the pneumatube station toward the palace. Going to work each day was a task now so onerous he could barely face it.

He joined the long line of palace employees getting their daily biodetector scan. The pathogen check had detected the empty vial, but he'd justified his having it on some pretext. Now, three days after the Empress's coronation and that idiot Kzizn's sacrificing himself, Baptiste shuffled forward, sweating profusely, his heart pounding in his ears like a bass drum.

"Hey, you all right, Bap?"

Oh, no, his coworker, Talitha. He'd been trying to avoid her. She was far too perceptive. It didn't help that he'd fallen instantly in love with her their first day on the job two years ago.

"You're not all right, are you?"

Consumed with guilt, afraid he'd be shot dead any moment, terrified his name and face would be plastered across the galactic tabloids, certain he'd be cited in the Encyclopedia Galactica as a traitor. "I'm fine," he said. His quavering voice betrayed that he wasn't. "Of course, I'm fine." A little better, a little more convincing.

"Then why are you sweating? A touch of fever, Bap?"

He nodded mutely. He wished Talitha wouldn't call him that. It's what Princess Cybill called him. It's all she could remember.

The line ahead was getting shorter, the biodetector an arc that glowed green as people passed through it. The guards on either side looked terribly bored. They seemed to focus as he and Talitha approached.

They asked the usual questions, got the usual responses.

"He ok? Looks ill," one guard said to Talitha.

"Touch of fever, I think."

The biodetector arch glowed green, and he was through, Talitha right behind him.

She walked the long path to the palace beside him in silence, the immaculately manicured grounds on either side like some fairyland paradise, preserved in perfect symmetry.

Baptiste saw none of it, the cold nipping at his cheeks.

The employee entrance looked as if it might have once served lesser dignitaries. A huge portico crowned a colonnaded entrance, the flaking gold leaf paint on the handrails the only indication it wasn't public anymore.

"Come with me," she said the moment they entered the building. Instead of heading toward Princess Cybill's wing, she hauled him toward the break room.

She wrestled him into a chair and got him a cup of coffee. "You've been acting like a ghost for a week, Bap. Something to do with the coronation?"

He realized he'd been on edge since Ezra had asked him to obtain the tissue sample. At the time, it'd seemed like the right thing to do, given the circumstances. What the alien had told him was deeply disturbing. And getting a sample of Cybill's tissue for analysis had seemed not only prudent, but deeply patriotic.

The morning of the coronation, he'd delivered the sample to Ezra.

The alien, whose name was impossible to pronounce and even more difficult to spell, had
thanked Baptiste. "You will know a deep satis-
faction when the lie is exposed."

"What are you going to do with it now?" he'd
asked the green, pulsating blob of alien flesh.

"Genetic analysis," Ezra had said, his real voice
burbling under the translator's soft contralto.
"Try to prove that she's unrelated to Emperor
Zenon."

And within hours, live on galactic holo, Ezra
had been reduced to a bubbling pool of protoplasm. Baptiste had no idea whether Ezra had
had the opportunity to do the analysis.

"Bap, you've got to tell me what's going on."

He looked up at Talitha, so beautiful, so vulnerable, so naïve. "You're being very kind, and
I'm grateful, but it's better if you don't get involved. The fewer who know, the better."

She just stared at him, a soft smile on her face,
the silent question in her eyes.

Baptiste knew he couldn't resist her entreaties. When she looked at him that way, he
couldn't have denied her if she'd asked him to

scrub a toilet with his own toothbrush. "Why don't I tell you after work, over dinner?"

"My place," she said instantly. "I'll fix."

He met her gaze and nearly wept in relief. The burden of knowing what he knew, of doing what he'd done, had somehow become lighter. "I'd like that."

On their way to Princess Cybill's wing, he looked over at her. "Thank you."

"You're welcome." She met his gaze and giggled.

And for the first day since he'd obtained the tissue sample from Princess Cybill, Baptiste felt as though he were really present with his charge, doing his job with all the mindfulness that a Licensed Behavioral Technician should have.

Chapter 14

"Incoming holomail," the amoeba said.

Her head pounding, Colonel Melanctha Remes threw a grin at Lydia. "That'll be my contact." She'd sent a holomail to the top bottom-feeder she knew on Amphitrite III and had secured the amoeba a landing berth at an off-grid spaceport near the South Pole. Geologic analysis indicated Amphitrite III was deep in a quaternary glaciation, its fossil record revealing rich and varied fauna and flora extant during previous interglacial periods.

Nearly all underground, the planetary infrastructure seemed ripe for the kind of illicit traffic the Bureau was empowered to interdict: Exotic substances with psychogenic properties, illegal weapons of poor manufacture, enslaved hordes of humans, and businesses catering to licentious libidinality, catering to every whim, no matter how depraved. Every conceivable form of power, pain, and pleasure might be had on Amphitrite III, all of it obscured under thick ice sheets, if not bed sheets.

Melanctha glanced at Lydia for permission to activate the message. The amoeba was a strange ship, all smooth surfaces inside, not an angle to be found. She supposed if she were a soft-skinned invertebrate, she'd have designed her vessels similarly.

"On-screen," she said. Despite her pounding head and possible concussion, Melanctha was relatively confident they'd be able to get the care she needed. Even criminals need medical care, she told herself, especially cosmetic surgery.

A face materialized, obscured by a fedora. Melanctha realized how ridiculous she must have looked to Agent Doukas back on Lucina IX.

"The boss doesn't like you Imperialists hanging around, so you can't stay long, all right?" The fedora and the face underneath it collapsed.

Imperialist was the name given Bureau agents by the underworld—anyone remotely connected to Imperial authority.

Embedded in the message were the coordinates of the spaceport entrance, which likely consisted of a gigantic hole in the side of a glacier. Such entrances could be quickly constructed and quickly destroyed, making them ideal for smugglers.

"Plot course for coordinates," Lydia said to the ship. "You sure about these people, Mela?"

"Of course not," Melanctha admitted. "They're a slimy bunch of slugs. But at least we'll have the chance to recoup and recover."

She thought about Icarus and what he'd meant to her. They'd fallen in love, the two pre-teens, to the degree two pre-teens could fall in love, a latency-age infatuation. Many of their games on the grounds of the Terzi Estate had consisted of how to outwit the boy's Governor.

"Listen, Lydia," she said, "about Count Icarus Terzi."

The young woman looked over when she didn't continue.

On the holo, licks of bright red at the edges accompanied a slight rumbling. The deceleration pressed Melanctha into her seat. Her headache grew sharply worse.

"Entry," Lydia said, her face looking drawn.

The atmosphere of Amphitrite III was low in carbon dioxide, the surface below them so bright it was difficult to look at.

"The reason he and I were playmates as kids, that I spent long hours at his family's estate on the outskirts of New Athens," she said, turning to look at Lydia, "was that my father and his mother were having an affair. I was ten years old and infatuated with him, and in my child-like mind, my father took me there under the guise of cementing my marriage to the future Count. Years later, I realized otherwise. Anyway, Countess Terzi ended up pregnant, and her son, the current Count Ioan Terzi, is my half-brother."

"Ioan," Lydia repeated, as if fixing it in her memory.

The amoeba's shuddering ceased as their speed dropped, and the young woman took the controls, a flashing cross-hairs on the holo indicating their destination.

"You're telling me this because you think Count Terzi will help me?"

Melanctha nodded. "Ioan never knew his older brother, and the scandal around his mother's affair with my father was widespread enough that everyone knew he wasn't Count Ilias' son, and therefore—"

"Not a threat to the succession."

She looked over at Lydia. "You're sharp. Yes, an illicit child. But Count Ilias refused to disown him, perhaps out of grief for his own son, who died so tragically."

"He'll be younger than me, won't he?"

"He's twenty-three now," Melanctha replied, watching the craggy, ice-locked landscape below. "A year younger than Empress Hecuba."

Amphitrite III was the kind of world few people dreamed of colonizing, especially at the poles. The equatorial regions weren't much warmer, the small oceans unfreezing for just a single month during the equator's two summers, only a narrow band of earth directly below the sun experiencing a thaw. Nearly all the planet's surface water was locked up in ice, the oceans briny and inhospitable except to the hardiest of aquatic species. Nearly all agriculture on the planet was hydroponic. The little arable land was difficult to till and couldn't be farmed with Terran crops due to the foreshortened growing season. A few indigenous specimens with rapid gestation cycles were farmed, but produced too little food to sustain the populace.

The spaceport entrance, she saw, was a hole at the base of a glacier. As the ship dropped in elevation and the landscape revealed its features, Melanctha watched in awe.

Miles-tall mountains of ice sawed at the sky with jagged teeth. Many of them glowed a deep blue with trapped air, a sign of rapid freezing. Sheer escarpments jutted from mountainsides, their edges wicked, as though slashing at the passing ship.

"Not a place I'd come for vacation," Lydia said.

Melanctha felt cold just looking at the landscape.

In a cleft between two mountains, where a snow-filled crevasse hid activity from all but the most prying of eyes, was the spaceport entrance. At first it looked to be an overhang, the massive slab of ice above it looking ready to smash to smithereens anything under it, but the area underneath kept reaching farther and farther back under the mountain.

The amoeba was soon enveloped in darkness, the overhang having long since become a cave.

Lydia was poised above the controls and looked ready to punch in an evasion course.

"Can you get us out of here if this cave collapses?"

"I can try," she replied.

Melanctha prayed she could. She'd been to the planet once before, and its ever changing glacial landscape at the equator—floods, storms, avalanches—had frightened her.

The cave became a tunnel, rock replacing ice all around them, its scale large enough to contain whole cities. Structures began to appear in the cave sides, and the floor below them began to sprout buildings, vehicles darting between them like ants.

"You could fly an armada out of this place."

Melanctha nodded, seeing a clearing ahead, the crosshairs on the holoscreen indicating the area as their destination. On the tarmac was a variety of vessels. All of them looked like private vehicles, and she didn't see one among them that looked to be from a law-enforcement agency.

Did I expect them to meet us here? she wondered.

As she thought about it, the possibility seemed very real indeed.

* * *

Lydia stepped through the biodetector at the hospital entrance. The arch above her glowed green, indicating she was clean of pathogens.

"I'm Chelsais Bouras, but you can call me Steve," the man said.

Lydia shook his hand, his grip firm and confident. "I'm Lydia, Steve. Pleased." She wasn't pleased at all. He struck her as a thew-bound thug with beefy shoulders.

The man turned to Melanctha, who'd also just stepped through the biodetector. "Boss wants to see you once you're done here." He glanced at her wound.

"Of course, Steve," the Colonel said.

"How'd that happen?"

"Ship got hit with a tractor beam while I was in the galley."

His eyes searched hers.

Lydia could see the conclusions he reached with just that little amount of information. She'd heard his name before when she and Xsirh had visited the region two years ago. They'd been warned to steer clear of him and his organization.

They stood at the emergency room nursing station just a few miles from the spaceport, where she and Melanctha had been immediately escorted. Steve had walked in moments later and then had sidled up to the counter to the front of the line.

Steve turned to the nurse behind the counter. "Nurse Wretched, get my friend here some medical attention, would you?"

"The name's Riga," the nurse said, "and she'll have to wait her turn, like everyone else."

His fist slammed the counter and he pointed to himself. "The name's Bouras. Get her some attention, or your name will be wretched."

Nurse Riga's eyes widened, and she hesitated.

"Please," Steve added, spreading his hands in apology.

They were soon in an examination room, a doctor asking rapid-fire questions, Steve listening placidly from the door, his gaze on the corridor.

Lydia imagined he was constantly vigilant.

"Let's get that imaged," the doctor said. "She was unconscious how long?"

Lydia shrugged. "A few minutes, maybe, not more than ten."

"And the wound occurred the first time she struck the wall, or the second?"

"First time, if I recall correctly."

"Is that a rash?" the doctor asked.

"Huh?"

"Those spots on your arm, is that a rash?"

"Oh, that? I don't know," Lydia said. "It's been itching off and on since I left home."

The doctor brought a machine down from the ceiling. "If I could ask you to step over there near the door, Ms—?"

"Procopio," Lydia said, complying and moving toward the door.

Steve glanced at her and returned his gaze to the corridor. "Where were you going?"

She didn't know how much to tell him, but given his activities, she suspected that the less he knew, the better. "A little excursion to the Maldives," she said. En route to Gaea, the Maldives had been in the direction they'd been headed.

"Sleek little rig you got. I ain't seen its like before. Who's the manufacturer?"

Difficult to hide where it's from if someone really wants to know, she thought. "Outer Scutum-Centaurus arm, near Theogony." She watched the doctor tend to Melanctha, not looking at Steve. For a human male, he hadn't given her much attention. She was accustomed to drawing numerous prolonged stares, particularly from the males.

The sexual dimorphism among Homo sapiens was a curiosity to her. Reared among the Kziznvxrz, Lydia had found the preening of her female peers and male paramours annoying. They seemed to be constantly posturing toward each other, as if continuously fertile. The monomorphic Kzizn transformed themselves as needed and found the posturing superfluous, even risible.

She felt Steve's glances, which were fewer and shorter than the stares she usually got.

"You're good," Steve said. "I don't blame you for being cautious. The bloodsuckers around here will drain you dry the moment you drop your guard."

"You included?"

"Me included."

She was startled by the honesty of his response.

"You come back and see me, next time you're in the area. I like you."

Not much chance of that, Lydia thought.

* * *

The hover ride took them up the side of the gargantuan tunnel. From inside the amoeba, it hadn't looked daunting, but walking in open air below the jagged crystalline roof of stone and ice gave Lydia the constant feeling of impending doom, as though it were about to collapse.

Riding up the slope in a hover helped somewhat, but not much.

"What holds up the ceiling?" she'd asked Steve immediately after they'd left the hospital.

"Antigrav units," he'd said, paying more attention to her now, while driving, than he had before.

252

"Hey, watch out!" Melanctha said from the back seat.

Steve swerved to avoid another hover, bleating the horn and shaking a meaty fist out the window. The air coming in was frightfully cold, but he didn't seem to feel it.

What have we gotten ourselves into? Lydia wondered.

"We just need a place to lay low for a few days," Melanctha was telling him.

"You're in the right place," Steve reassured her, grinning madly at Lydia, paying no attention to Melanctha, as if she hadn't spoken.

She didn't feel reassured and kept herself from glancing back at Melanctha. There was something in Steve's manner that left Lydia feeling … sticky. As if she'd just waded through a hip-deep pool of mud. Kziznvxrz didn't have criminals, and although Lydia had heard about them among human populations, she'd never knowingly interacted with one. Until now.

The experience wasn't exactly pleasant.

His intimidating the nurse at the hospital hadn't endeared him to her. And his brusque and truculent manner with nearly everyone else was at odds with how he treated them.

Lydia could make a pretty good guess which one was the true Steve.

The hover climbed steadily, the road narrowing and the drop-off getting increasingly steep.

"Where you goin' after this?"

The extent of his speech seemed to be two-syllable words and five-word questions. Lydia wondered if multiplying them gave his approximate IQ. Feeling naïve, she let Melanctha answer the ill-disguised probes for information. A brilliant conversationalist, Steve was not.

"Here we are." The hover pulled up under an escarpment that jutted out from the tunnel wall nearly a hundred feet. "The boss would like to see you before you get settled."

Another vehicle pulled in behind them as they got out. Lydia hadn't realized they'd been followed. She saw the overhang was encircled by guards spaced every thirty feet. Lydia suddenly felt trapped. Melanctha didn't look capable of an escape attempt, not with a new bandage on her head.

"The boss just wants to talk," Steve said, grinning and gesturing to a door.

Columns framed a corridor leading up to the door, and Lydia glimpsed one last slice of the far cavern wall as she and Melanctha were herded inside.

She was startled by the flooring. The soft, cushioned layer of deep burgundy fabric on the floor silenced their progress. She thought she was walking on a cloud. Steve led the way through corridors decorated with statuary and portraiture. Holo-flame sconces lit their way, their joyous flames even giving off wisps of holo-smoke.

They turned a corner and approached a set of double doors. On either side of them stood a large man in a bulky suit. At Steve's nod, they opened the doors outward.

In a sun-drenched courtyard, a man in a white three-piece suit enjoyed a mai-tai at pool-side, fanning himself.

The near-tropical warmth hit Lydia as she stepped into the room, the smells reminiscent of her vacation to the jungle-shrouded world of Istra VI, the scents of palm and coconut battling a thick, salt-brine breeze.

But how … and then she realized that it was all artificial, that the environment had been manufactured. Tropical climates simply didn't exist on Amphitrite III.

Steve led them toward the pool. "Father," he said, "this is Melanctha Remes and Lydia Pro-copio."

The man in the white suit turned his head slowly to look at them. First at Melanctha for thirty continuous seconds, and then at Lydia for a full minute.

She began to feel uncomfortable under his scrutiny, and offered a tentative smile.

"You may call me Dmitri," he said finally, his voice a half-whisper.

"Pleased to meet you, Dmitri," Melanctha said. "Thank you for your assistance today."

"Don't be a γουρούνι, Son, and get them chairs." He looked at Lydia. "Forgive him, he hasn't learned manners yet."

Steve got them chairs, and Lydia thanked him as she took hers. She hadn't caught the word his father had used but it'd sounded derogatory.

Steve didn't look the slightest bit nonplussed by the interaction.

"May I get you something to drink?" he asked.

"Thank you, yes. Some water, please."

"We have a variety of beverages from all points of the galaxy, Ms. Procopio," Dmitri said. "Are you sure you won't try something a bit more exotic?"

"No, thank you, Dmitri. Water is sufficient." She'd found their alcohol-infused concoctions quite overwhelming.

"A martian on the rocks, stirred, not shaken," Melanctha told Steve.

"Aristocratic names you both have," Dmitri said the moment Steve was gone. He looked around his pool and leaned his head back for a moment.

The walls were painted to look like a beach somewhere near New Athens, where the winds might be hot siroccos off the Meditian Sea. As a child, Lydia had found a still of one such beach on Gaea and had projected it on all four walls of her room.

"Not often that members of the nobility seek sanctuary among their less-fortunate cousins."

He turned his head slowly their direction, his gaze alighting on Lydia. "You're the Viscountess Ambassador's daughter."

She nodded. "Reared by the Kzizn when my mother's people wouldn't accept me back."

His gaze shifted to Melanctha. "Your father was acquainted with Count and Countess Terzi."

"He was," Melanctha replied.

Steve returned with their beverages and then retreated.

Dmitri sipped slowly off his drink, a dark brown liquid so turbid it looked as if it absorbed light. He set down the glass and adjusted his cuff. Then he returned his gaze to Melanctha, his eyes on the bandage. "The doctor seems to think you'll live."

"I think I will," she replied, a smile touching her face.

Dmitri's gaze grew unfocused. "It is fate that brought you here. Princess Hecuba tours her domains, our new sovereign deigning to show the people the trappings of her majestic person." His gaze bore into Lydia. "Trappings it is said that belong to another."

"We know the true power behind the throne," Melanctha ventured. "She who threatened the Chief Justice."

"True power, Colonel, or false power? The power of the pretender. Yes, mighty power, but illegitimate. It is sad that the first child of Emperor Athanasios is so … incapacitated, no? The power of a pretender cannot hold fast against the truth. But for fate, you yourself might have been an Empress, married to the Emperor Terzi. Is this not a fact, Colonel?"

Melanctha's gaze dropped to the tile. "Yes, Dmitri, I might have."

"And yet you're here with an orphan on a planet known for its ties to the guerilla economy, to put it delicately. How strange fate is."

Lydia looked between the two, sensing more than what was being said. Clearly, Dmitri knew far more about the inner workings of the Empire than his tenuous position on its periphery should allow.

"I have a friend on Gaea you should see," he said, looking at Lydia, "if you ever find yourself there. My enturm, Chiron Likashose, a counselor

259

who sees after my affairs on the capital, is to be trusted in any circumstance."

"Thank you, that's very kind," Lydia said, bewildered that this man, this criminal, would extend such generosity.

"You're welcome, Ms. Procopio. I would be delighted if the both of you could join me for dinner this evening. Between now and then, I imagine you'd like to freshen up." Dmitri looked over toward his son. "You may show them the guest wing, my son."

Chapter 15

"Mela, Why do I get the impression that all he wanted was to tell us about this counselor on Gaea?"

"He has a cunning to him, that's for certain," Melanctha replied, admiring herself in a mirror.

"He's pretty resourceful too," Lydia said, looking at herself beside the other woman.

Their suite of three rooms was palatial. One common room contained a kitchen-dining area and a lounging area, floor-to-ceiling glasma on one end overlooking the gargantuan tunnel. On either side of the common room were bed-bath units, the accommodations commodious enough for a princess.

After changing Melanctha's bandages, Lydia had retreated to her unit and availed herself to the cleansall. Her meager wardrobe consisted of a clean pair of formalls. Frowning, she looked in the closet and found an evening dress scandalous for its scantiness, and in her exact size. In the jewelry case on the vanity was a necklace, earrings, and bracelet, the diamonds shining with the blue-white brilliance of glaciers, all matching. Melanctha had found similar couture in her room.

They both looked stunning.

"We're going to leave them gasping," the Colonel said, turning from her reflection.

Lydia smiled, feeling beautiful and wondering how Dmitri had managed to make such arrangements in so little time.

There was a knock on the door, and Melanctha went to answer. "Time already?" she asked. "We'll be along in a moment."

The plush corridors obscured the sound of their passage even from them. The high heels were somewhat awkward for Lydia, and she was afraid the stiletto points would puncture the floor. "I hope I don't have to run from anything," she said.

Melanctha threw a grin over her shoulder. Her stern, sharp face seemed softened somehow by the diaphanous dress hanging tentatively from her shoulders. "Maybe from Steve. But your heels are lethal, if you know how to use them."

My lessons in self-defense might be helpful, she thought.

They entered the dining area, where a long table of the finest Zortaxian pine split the room, whorls of blond and tan spinning through the tortured wood.

Steve greeted Melanctha first, and then looked at Lydia. His eyes bulged from their sockets, and his complection flushed. "M-M-Ms. Procopio," he managed from around a tongue twisted from titillation. He seemed rooted to the floor, his eyes fixed to her bosom.

Melanctha sniggered.

"Mr. Bouras," Lydia replied, giving him a slight curtsy, wishing now she'd just worn formalls.

"Ah, you're here!" Dmitri said, entering with a flourish. "Lovely, the both of you. I do hope I wasn't presumptuous in my choice of dress for you. Ms. Remes, you look positively statuesque. And Ms. Procopio, oh my!" He put the back of his hand to his forehead and feigned a swoon.

Once they were seated at the far end of the table, Melanctha across from Dmitri and Lydia across from Steve, the glasma window looking out onto the glittering tunnel just feet away, Lydia began to relax. Anything that put distance between her and the clearly-enamored younger man across from her was a comfort.

He looked besotted, flush creeping up his neck to his jaw. His father was focused almost exclusively on Melanctha, his admiration plain, but at least he kept his eyes on her face. Steve couldn't seem to get his eyes off Lydia's bust. Melanctha, oddly, seemed to be drinking in Dmitri's attentions like a parched traveler alone and forsaken in the desert.

Ubiquitous but unobtrusive servants served them dinner.

Lydia could see how the other woman's evening was going to end, but she wasn't interested in her evening ending in a similar fashion with the brute across from her. She wondered as she dined how she was going to engineer a graceful exit.

A blob of protoplasm smacked the glasma. It looked like a giant slug, its footprint against the glasma nearly six inches across.

"What is that disgusting thing?" Dmitri asked. "Apologies, my darling Melanctha, while I dispense with this nuisance."

Lydia knew exactly what it was: A didinium, a deep-sea predator, scourge of the Kziznvxrfn, their roasted flesh considered a delicacy. Their digestive acids ate through nearly everything. This one looked to be of similar size and ferocity as the one she'd killed upon returning home. Was that just three days ago? Lydia wondered, amazed so little time had passed.

Dmitri returned to the room. "An attendant is taking care of the pest."

"They're pretty voracious," Lydia said. "How many panes of glasma are there?"

The didinium convulsed and surged through the outer pane, spreading itself across the next layer.

"Uh, three," Steve said, his eyes now bulging for a different reason. "You know what it is?"

The attendant stepped out onto the balcony from another door, a scraper in hand.

She didn't know they lived on planets as cold as this one. She'd always thought they thrived only on semi-tropical worlds. It occurred to her that the staff might not know how to handle a didinium. "Mr. Bouras, does your attendant know what to do?"

The slug slung a tendril at the approaching attendant, wrapped his neck, and hurled him off the balcony. A distant scream faded from earshot.

"Apparently not," Dmitri said, his eyes bulging too.

Again the slug convulsed, and squeezed itself onto the innermost pane.

"Oh my god, it's coming after us!"

Lydia rose and approached the glasma. She positioned her face right in front of the creature and readied herself.

"What are you doing?"

"Our spit is poisonous to them, but only if they ingest it. Their exoderm neutralizes it. So I have to spit into its intake orifice."

The slug convulsed itself through the glasma and slung a tendril at her. She caught it, pulled it aside and spat into the didinium's intake orifice. Her spittle hit its flesh, and the slug disintegrated with a sizzle, its protoplasm streaking down the glasma in brown, excrement-colored smears, smoke wafting upward both inside and outside the triple panes. The smell was noxious.

"What the Hades *was* that?"

"A didinium," she replied. "One of the most ferocious predators on Kziznvxrz. The Didinium and Paramecium fought for dominance for nearly a megaannus."

"A what?" Steve asked.

"Me-ga-an-nus," Lydia repeated, separating its syllables. "A million years."

"Oh, I thought you were calling me names."

She'd considered it. "But what's it doing here? This planet's climate can't possibly support a creature like that."

Dmitri threw a glance at the cavern beyond the glasma. "We've been infiltrated. Steve, double the guard and alert the perimeter to an intruder. The question is, who was it after?"

"One tried to get me on Kziznvxrz just three days ago," Lydia said.

"How dare they try to assassinate you in my home?!" Dmitri seemed more offended that it had occurred under his roof.

"That also means they know where you're at," Melanctha said. "Mr. Bouras, I'm afraid I can't put your household at further risk. My apologies for the inconvenience we've already caused and for the attendant's death. We'll leave immediately."

"But where will you go?" Steve asked, managing somehow to compose a five-word question.

"There's only one place we *can* go," Lydia said, hating the word as it came out of her mouth. "Gaea."

* * *

"This is syndicate spaceport control," the computerized contralto voice intoned. "There's a delay in your clearance for takeoff. Please wait."

Lydia and Melanctha exchanged a glance. They both wore their evening dresses. Necks had broken as Lydia strode swiftly through the spaceport, heads spinning in her direction, the haute couture better suited for a fashion runway than a spaceport runway. The high heels hadn't slowed them at all.

And now they wanted Lydia and Melanctha to delay their departure. The spaceport tower on the holoscreen brooded at them, the small, squat building staring back at them with darkened glasma panes, like some secret agent.

"Doesn't smell so good, does it?"

"Sure doesn't. And besides," Melanctha added, "what self-respecting thief pays attention to rules?"

Lydia's fingers danced across the controls, her fingers splayed over the Kziznvxrfn controls.

On screen, several vehicles spat from the terminal and headed their direction.

"Engage course!" she told the amoeba.

"Engaging course," it replied. "Vmtztrmt xl-fihv," it repeated in Kzizn.

The ship shuddered and rose above the tarmac, and then swung up toward the tunnel ceiling. The ship lurched sharply, the screen flashing. "Hit taken to starboard!" the amoeba said, repeating it in Kzizn.

"Maintain course with evasion," Lydia told it. She glanced at Melanctha, strapped in her usual chair, Lydia buckled into Xsirh's egg-cup. "Hold on."

"Those fools'll bring the ceiling down!" she said, throwing a glance at Lydia, a sudden swerve throwing her to one side.

"Close up of tarmac!" Lydia said. A second swerve threw them the other direction.

The holoscreen zoomed in. Ten people in plain business suits stood in two even rows, their weapons aimed up at the ship. To one side stood their commander, her sidearm in hand at her waist.

"They look like IBS," Melanctha said.

Lydia was afraid of that. It meant they'd been traced, somehow. "Amplify sound," she told the ship.

"Hold your fire!" the commander was saying. "We found 'em once. We'll find 'em again."

"That's Lieutenant Christakos from Infection Control. Get us out of here, Lydia."

She programmed in a jump for the Thalassa Constellation. "If we jump from here, Mela, our sudden displacement will cause a sonic shock."

"Enough to bring the ceiling down?"

Lydia shook her head. "I don't know, but I don't think we should risk it. Not here, with all those people below us."

The amoeba's acceleration had taken them much farther along the immense tunnel, icy rock glittering above them. The way so far was clear as the syndicate settlement receded farther behind them.

"How do you think they found us?"

"Not sure," Melanctha said. "Not only found us, but infiltrated the base within hours."

Lydia turned to stare at the Colonel. "The didinium that came after me ..."

The other woman returned her gaze. "What are you thinking?"

"The second in three days—first on Kzizn, and now here. There's a faction on Kziznvxrz whose tenets include the extermination of humankind and the takeover of the galaxy."

"The ones who kidnapped you from Theogony?"

Lydia nodded. "They live in the surf, at the edge of Kzizn society, much closer to the deep sea, where the didinium still survive. The didinium are endangered due to overfishing, but I wonder if it's possible ..." She looked at Melanctha. "Does your species ever domesticate other species?"

"Well, yes. Many, as a matter of fact. Cats, dogs, horses—quite a few."

"I wonder whether the Wrwrmrfn have domesticated the didinium."

"Or perhaps breed them in captivity?"

"More likely, given how feral they are."

Ahead, the tunnel bent sharply to the right.

Beyond was a phalanx of starships, an entire squadron of under-cover, patrol-class vessels armed to the teeth, blasma cannons mounted between their incisors.

"Amoeba, jump!"

A tractor beam hit them, and the ship slewed as it entered sub-ether. And the tunnel disappeared from around them.

Chapter 16

"Where are we?" Colonel Melanctha Remes looked over at her companion.

Lydia shook her head. "Coordinates, please."

"Navigation module damaged, galactic positioning unavailable." And then it repeated, "Mzertzgrlm nlwfov wznztvw, tzozxgrx klhrglmrmt fmzezrozyov."

Melanctha cringed, the awful-sounding language more nauseating than the maneuver they'd just executed. She had no idea how a tractor beam might affect sub-ether navigation, but she knew what one did to A-warp.

"Kzizn translation off," Lydia said.

"Paramecia translation off," the amoeba said. "Kziznvxrz gizmhozgrlm luu."

"Attempt to determine position visually," the young woman said, sighing. "We could be anywhere."

"Attempting," the ship said.

Melanctha glanced at her. "What now?"

Lydia met her gaze. "Now, we wait. If the ship can't figure out where we are, we try a jump to a known location. Risky, but it's one way to do it."

"Don't we have to know where we're at first before we can jump someplace?"

Lydia shook her head. "Not necessarily, since all locations in the galaxy are pre-determined. Sub-ether engines are calibrated to the galactic core, and all jumps are simply translations in space to a fixed distance and direction from that core, irrespective of origin."

"Instantaneous translations, too. A-warp is pretty primitive in comparison, isn't it?"

Lydia nodded. "Compressing space does seem somewhat elementary compared with translating across it."

Melanctha could see Lydia was trying not to smile. We must seem so backward to her, she thought. She tried to wrap her mind around the Paramecium lifestyle, living in near-complete harmony with their environment, experiencing none of the ills that plagued human society. No robbery, no wars, no prisons, no poverty, no slavery.

The worst abuse they ever inflicted on each other was ostracism, and from what Lydia had told her, it wasn't often imposed. Very rarely was someone banished to the open sea, as the Werewormer contingent had been.

"Location visually determined," the amoeba said. A map appeared on the holoscreen, their position highlighted, nearby systems aglow. "Our coordinates are thirty-three-point-two-three-two degrees by eighty-seven-point-two-three parsecs, two-point-two parsecs above the galactic plane."

"Isn't that the Thalassa Constellation?" she asked.

"Not too far away from our destination," Lydia replied. "We must have escaped the brunt of the tractor beam."

"I wonder what our jump did to the cavern." She exchanged a glance with Lydia. "Why here?" Melanctha asked.

"I've an old friend on Eris Eleven, Economics Professor Zenais Demo. She helped me organize my business plan when my father and I started the shipping company. The Kzizn know virtually nothing about business. She can help me get in touch with Father."

Melanctha heard the strain in the younger woman's voice. "You miss him, don't you?"

Lydia blinked rapidly, nodding. "And I'm worried about him."

"You think the Were-wormer faction might try to hurt him?" She'd pronounced it the best she could.

"Either them, or the faction on Gaea that seems to be after me."

* * *

Professor Zenais Demo stepped off the shuttle and into the crowded transit station in the town of Irakleio, a backwater of no significance on Eris XI. She saw Lydia instantly, standing beside a taller, older woman whose ramrod posture and sharp, sere face bespoke a military discipline, a fact not obscured at all by the plain civilian formalls.

"Lydia, how are you?" she said effusively, giving the young woman a peck on each cheek.

"You look wonderful. How's business?" She exchanged pleasantries with the other woman as Lydia introduced them.

Then Zenais leaned in close and spoke rapidly in Lydia's ear. "Now, I know you're not here for a social call. The proprietor of the Caged Bull Tavern six blocks away can insure we'll have privacy. Follow me but only at a distance." She stepped back and smiled broadly. "So nice to see you here. Call me soon, and we'll have lunch. So long!" She waved and walked off.

Zenais had instantly been alerted to Lydia's distress by the odd location she'd specified, a backwater town halfway around Eris XI from the university. Irakleio lacked any attraction whatsoever and didn't even have a spaceport, the nearest one in Kifissia, six hundred miles away.

A consultant on the side, Professor Demo had helped Lydia and her father, the only Kzizn she'd ever met, assemble a viable business plan for the trading firm they'd wanted to start. After the consultation, Zenais had looked into Lydia Procopio's past, placing a few delicate inquiries with colleagues at the University of New Athens.

The Procopio Family had been among the most prominent of the noble families until falling into disfavor for reasons no one could seem to fathom. Viscountess Basilissa Procopio was suddenly appointed Ambassador to Kziznvxrz, a post vacant for nearly ten years, its location utterly remote and its conditions onerous. Living on tidal mud flats under a cloudy gray sky on a lonely planet at the end of the Scutum-Centaurus galactic arm wasn't anyone's idea of paradise.

The Ambassador's ship had crashed on arrival, all passengers presumed deceased, the vessel lost under the vast seas of a nine-tenths water planet. Or thought to be deceased. How Lydia Procopio had turned up on Kziznvxrz twenty years later, alive, well, and thriving, was remarkable.

Professor Zenais Demo's delicate inquiries had stirred up a minor tempest on Gaea, and one of her colleagues had warned her that the information she was seeking was so sensitive that it was redolent of a fine Metaxa.

Zenais didn't need to have it spelled out any further.

At the pub, she greeted the proprietor and asked for the most private booth he had. "Meeting with friends from out-of-system," she said simply.

He showed her to a back room, where the heavy smoke of illicit substances clung to the walls like ghosts. Customers liked to mix their pleasures, legal and otherwise. The dimly-lit room heralded a long-past age on Earth, when men on massive beasts thrust lances at each other to win over maidens whose chastity exceeded their beauty.

Zenais didn't have to wait long, the other two women arriving within minutes. "Mythos all around," she told the proprietor.

"Oh, I'd love a Mythos," the taller, older woman said.

"Melanctha, right?" Zenais asked, wondering whether she'd remembered correctly.

"Indeed, but call me Mela."

"This Mythos, does it have any ethanol?" Lydia asked, sitting across from Zenais.

"You mean alcohol? Of course, it does."

The young woman demurred. "I'm afraid I can't, Professor. At the first sip, I melt to the floor in a puddle of protoplasm."

"I'll have hers," Melanctha said.

Zenais shrugged. "Something to do with where you grew up?"

"I think so. My tissues seem to absorb fluids more readily."

She talked pleasantries with them while they were being served. A large tankard of brew in front of her, Zenais turned her attention to Lydia. "After you and Xsirh consulted me on your start-up trading firm eight years ago, I looked into your past. Not something I usually do, but I was curious. My inquiries were met with silence, mostly, but a few of my colleagues at the University of New Athens knew your father, your human one. Xenobiology Professor Selene Toccim, in particular, was very helpful. I suggest you see her when you get to Gaea." Then Zenais took a deep draught from her tankard. "Is that a rash?"

"Huh?"

"Those spots on your arm, is that a rash?"

"Oh, that? I don't know," Lydia said. "It's been itching off and on since I left Kziznvxrz. I've been inoculated."

"Anything come up during the screening?" Zenais knew they'd been screening for xenopathogens since the outbreaks on Pyrgos Five and Cygnus Twenty.

Lydia shook her head, frowning.

Zenais frowned back. "You're in trouble."

The young woman nearly burst into tears and began a tale that left Zenais amazed and gasping. At first, she just let the young woman talk, sensing her need to vent. As her speech grew a little less pressured and her story a little more coherent, Zenais inserted a question or two to help clarify the tale. "And these didinium are deep-sea creatures, you say. They can't live on worlds as cold as Amphitrite Three."

"Exactly. But we don't know who's planting them or why. It's easy to think they're after me, since it's happened twice now. Finding one in my home might have just been chance. Someone's trying to assassinate a syndicate boss wouldn't be unexpected, either."

"The method is rather insidious," Zenais said. "Gives me the shudders. Anyway, it's clear there's an effort to capture or kill you. How can I help you?"

"I don't have a way of contacting my father without giving away my location."

"I was wondering why you contacted me using a public holocom."

"And they found us on Amphitrite Three, so I think they tagged my ship with a galactic-locator."

"They fired on us as we were taking off from Amphitrite," Melanctha added. "Damaged the nav unit."

"So you need him to bring you a new vessel."

Lydia nodded. "I know I'm asking you to take a risk. Just meeting with us is risky, but I just don't know where else to go."

"Except to Gaea," Zenais said.

The young woman met her gaze. "But on my terms, and not as a captive."

* * *

"There've been some new developments," Xsirh told her. The machine beside him babbled in Galactim so Melanctha could understand him.

Lydia turned around in the pilot's chair. "New developments?"

He'd dropped in an archeota from orbit around Eris XI into an abandoned warehouse on the outskirts of Irakleio, where Lydia and Melanctha had been waiting, and had immediately launched. The ship had been outfitted with two human-style seats. Like her amoeba-class vessel, this archaeota was equipped with a sub-ether drive, capable of instantaneous transport. Further, it was smaller, sleeker, and far more nimble. They'd already executed several jumps to deter any followers.

They hovered in orbit over Kziznvxrz, Lydia now at the controls, ready to drop her father off at home before venturing to Gaea to confront the fate that awaited her.

"What new developments?"

Xsirh's optical organelles swiveled toward her, and his intake orifice turned downward at the edges. "Remember those tissue samples I kept in zero-kelvin cryo?" Xsirh asked.

Lydia felt the blood drain from her face, knowing where this conversation was going. "You did a genetic analysis."

The upper portion of Xsirh's physiognomy bobbed up and down. "Yes, Lydia, I did."

"And you compared my parents' genes with mine."

Again, Xsirh nodded.

"I'm not their daughter, am I?"

"No, child, I'm afraid you aren't."

Lydia had experienced difficulties in the past. The death of her parents, the wreck of their ship, the struggle to adapt to the alien environment and learn the alien language. The limitations of her physiology had caused her terrible trials in more than the environment and the language. She'd never really fit in with the other Kziznvxrfn, as much as she might have liked to. They were a gentle and loving people who rarely quarreled even amongst themselves, and those around her had extended themselves in a thousand ways to help her feel more comfortable.

But she'd never been one of them and never would be. And one tiny dream had helped Lydia to keep going when she felt she couldn't go on any longer, when her school subjects seemed overwhelming or her peers treated her condescendingly because her neurology prevented her from remembering the way they did and from learning at the pace they learned, when she had to wade awkwardly through miles of mud while her peers swam effortlessly and gracefully to their destinations within minutes, when she hadn't thoroughly cleansed residues of her eliminations from her hands and accidentally injured the Kzizn around her, her excretory enzymes catalyzing even the tough Kzizn exoderm. Whenever these events seemed nearly overwhelming, she'd always held to the thought of one day returning to Gaea to meet the members of the Procopio family, imagining their joy in finding out that she, Lydia Procopio, daughter of Viscountess Basilissa Procopio, had survived the shipwreck and was returning home triumphant.

The one tenuous thread connecting her with Gaea, the fragile link to her past and her heritage through her parents, her mother a Viscountess and Ambassador and her father a University Professor, was abruptly severed.

And in spite of having overcome extreme difficulty in losing her parents and in adapting to a terribly foreign environment, Lydia had never let any of it defeat her.

But this?

How was she supposed to cope with this?

The one saving grace, the one place where she knew she belonged, the family left behind on Gaea, who cared for her the way her mother had cared for her, in whose arms she might find the comfort and security that she'd once found in her mother's arms.

Gone.

* * *

Colonel Melanctha Remes looked over at Lydia.

After the young woman's tearful departure with her father, a scene that had evoked a few tears even from the thick-skinned Colonel, Lydia had collapsed into the co-pilot's chair and had turned the helm over to Melanctha.

"Just get us to Gaea," she'd said.

It'd been rather eerie to watch Xsirh embrace Lydia, his bright green protoplasm wrapping its folds nearly all the way around her, as if to swallow her whole.

After muddling through a few test jumps to insure she had a rudimentary understanding of the controls, Melanctha had taken them far afield, generating random jumps to baffle any pursuit.

And then she'd brought them to Pontus XIII, a financial services sanctuary, where anyone with a fortune could go to hide it, just a few systems over from Gaea.

Melanctha set the ship adrift in the Oort cloud and swiveled the pilot's chaise toward Lydia's. Then she reached over and turned the co-pilot's chaise toward her.

"What?" Lydia looked at her listlessly and then dropped her gaze back to her hands.

Melanctha stared at her, wondering what approach would work best. "Not good news, was it?"

A tear slid down Lydia's cheek.

"If you go to Gaea now, they'll dip you in hummus and have you for an appetizer."

Another tear, and then another.

Melanctha leaned forward and took Lydia's hands.

The young woman began to shake with soft sobs, her face a wreck.

The Colonel waited, wishing she could do something to ease the other's pain. There wasn't, and it infuriated her that they'd subjected this child to such a terrible fate, sending her to her death aboard a ship set to disintegrate as it entered its destination's atmosphere. All of which begged the question: Why?

And the other question nagging Melanctha, now that they knew Lydia wasn't the Ambassador's child at all.

Was that why no one on Gaea had come forward to claim the lone survivor of the Ambassador's shipwreck? Or had the entreaties simply been ignored?

Remes didn't know, the past mystery as bewildering as the current one.

"Sorry, Mela," Lydia said, wiping her face. "I guess I'm not handling this well."

"Nothing to be sorry about, Lydia. You've been served a plate of rotten scraps. Of course you're upset." She evaluated whether the young woman was ready and suspected she was. "The question is, if you're not Basilissa and Dorian Procopio's daughter, then whose child are you?"

Chapter 17

Lydia hove into orbit around Sol IV, a cold red planet named after some long-forgotten culture's god of war, Mars.

Gaea was the next planet inward, but getting there from outside Sol's Oort cloud required a full bioscan of all ships and an auto-decontamination, or A-decon, of all travelers. Fortunately, while drifting at the edge of Pontus, Lydia and Melanctha had contacted the lawyer of Dmitri Bouras on Gaea, Chiron Likashose. To all appearances, he was a partner in a legitimate law firm whose primary focus appeared to be government lobbying, Likashose looking after the Bouras Syndicate interests in the Hellenic Parliament. From him, they'd secured false identities complete with dossiers, a contingency frequently required of the Syndicate, apparently.

"I'd think having A-decons at every stop would catch any xenopathogen, wouldn't you?"

Melanctha just shrugged at her.

"Probably wouldn't help to tell them I've been inoculated, would it?" Lydia sighed and pulled the archaeota into line behind the other passenger vessels seeking permission to land on Gaea. It extended halfway around the planet. She groaned, wondering whether they'd be stuck in orbit above Sol IV for days, no way to get around the bureaucratic red tape. She threw a glance at Melanctha. "Mela, you didn't have to do this as an IBS agent, did you?"

The other woman shook her head and glanced down at her plain formalls.

It occurred to Lydia how much Colonel Melanctha Remes was risking in coming with her to Gaea this way, as a fugitive. "This won't look good on your resume, will it?"

"No, probably not," Melanctha said. "Mind if I turn on the news?"

Lydia shrugged. "Not at all." She found it bewildering, the penchant these humans had for constantly filling their heads with extraneous information. But there really wasn't much else to do while they waited.

Melanctha reached for the holovid controls.

"And in other news," a busty anchor said, "efforts to curtail the outbreak on Cygnus Twenty failed spectacularly as the Panthovirus continues to spread, having achieved a saturation rate of ninety-five percent. Further, local contingents of the Imperial Infection Control Authority appear to be in disarray, calling upon the Gaean Central Command to take over the pathogen interdiction efforts. Evidence indicates that the quarantine is in tatters. A similar subsequent outbreak in the Maldives Constellation points to the possibility of a Typhoid Mary—some individual or agency spreading the pathogen deliberately, bringing the total number of infected worlds to twenty-five. For more on this phenomenon—"

"Imperial Infection Control, prelim inspection vessel requesting permission to come alongside," the override com said, a bespectacled bureaucrat replacing the busty anchor. A prelim inspection vessel pulled alongside theirs, the other vehicle small, a single-passenger minnow-class ship. "Any declarations?"

"I do declare this is an onerous process," Lydia snarked.

"Look, lady, make my job easier and just say no. I'm asking about offworld plants, animals, or other biologic living material, all right?" The poor, bored bureaucrat looked as if he could use a vacation.

"No declarations," Lydia replied.

"Inbound from where?"

"Eris Eleven," she replied. "It's all in the manifest."

"Yeah, saw that, gotta ask anyway. Sleek little ship you got, by the way. Expensive?"

Lydia decided to lob a wobbler. "I'm not sure. Daddy bought it for me. Must be, though. He said I should take better care of it than the last one."

The Inspector snorted, his gaze going to his screen for the first time. His eyes grew big around. "Who's your daddy, Ms. Castellanos?"

"Zorba Castellanos, Duke of Pyrgos." The lie came easily to Lydia, the name part of the dossier, but the position a complete fabrication.

"I'm afraid I have to ask you to follow me, Duchess." The image collapsed.

She exchanged a glance with Melanctha.

"Now, you've done it."

"But what have I done?" Lydia engaged the engines and followed the minnow. They passed frigates and cargo ships, huge passenger star liners, personal yachts, quite a few commuters, and several tankers.

The minnow led them to a side-dock at the inspection station, where their holo lit up again. "We'll have you both step off your ship and through the A-decon," the inspector said, "and then we'll give it a bioscan and get you on your way."

"Why, thank you," Lydia said, delighted.

"My pleasure. Please follow the signs."

They stepped off the archaeota through a compression hatch into a long corridor. In one cubicle, they had to disrobe and step into the next cubicle for the dousing. Getting doused with a demicrobiating agent was like taking a shower in a thick, clear mud. Lydia didn't mind it, having grown up in mud, but it was clear Melanctha detested the process. They stepped to the next cubicle for a rinse, and then at last one, dressed themselves in a fresh set of formals. Then back through the compression hatch into the archaeota.

"Cleared for Gaea," the ship's transponder beacon now declared.

"I wonder if they do that for all the nobility," Lydia said.

En route to the blue-gray planet, she reviewed Ezra's information again, knowing she would have to retrace his route.

First, Selene Toccim, Professor of Xenobiology at the University of New Athens.

Then, Chiron Likashose, the lawyer on retainer for Dmitri Bouras on Gaea.

Finally, picking up where Ezra had left off.

"I'm always amazed at how beautiful Gaea is each time I see it," Melanctha said, its image large on the holoscreen.

Lydia glanced at it with a fair degree of ambivalence. The place she'd been born that had once been her home, Gaea held both joy and dread for her. Joy at the possibility of being reunited with the family she'd always thought was her own, dread at discovering what really lay in welcome for her. Would they embrace her as the Viscountess's daughter, or reject her as some interloper from an alien planet at the rim of the galaxy? And what about her real family, the one she was truly descended from?

As she looked at the city of New Athens, perched on a craggy peninsula on a huge inland sea, Lydia became aware of an itch on her right forearm.

Absently, she scratched it.

* * *

"Professor Dorian Procopio? Yes, of course I remember him." Selene Toccim, Professor of Xenobiology at the University of New Athens, looked over the lectern at the pair across from her. She'd just concluded a lecture on microbial variants, and students had begun filing from the room when the two strangers had sidled their way into the lecture hall. "What about him?"

"What do you remember about his wife's appointment as Ambassador?"

Selene looked the younger woman up and down, struck by how attractive she was. Even the plain formalls couldn't obscure the fact that the young woman had the face and figure of a goddess. I wish I were that attractive, she thought. She'd always been short, blond, and skinny, with an acne-scarred face. Pumps, pads, and face-caking had never done much to obscure the fact that she just wasn't attractive.

The other, older woman was plain if statuesque, perhaps of an age with Selene, and disciplined in her mien, as though accustomed to command, her face sharp.

"I think they did it to silence Dorian," the Professor said bluntly.

The other two exchanged a glance, looking taken aback.

"Come with me," Professor Toccim said, and she strode from the room, heading toward her office on the fifth floor. The ground floor theater had disgorged its occupants into the confluence of students flowing through the corridors. She headed through the crowd for the stairs, not waiting to see if the other two would follow, knowing she'd rather be using her time to prepare for her next lecture.

It was the third time someone had inquired, and she'd have liked to dismiss them outright.

Except that she'd known Dorian well and had been hired by him twenty-five years ago to help with his research.

Except that just before the coronation, she'd had a similar inquiry from a creature whose sight, sound, and smell had been so bizarre as to be offensive.

Except that days later, the Dowager Empress had splashed that same bizarre creature with a disintegrator gun when it had stepped forward to protest.

On the fifth floor, she stopped at her door and glanced at the next door down.

His office door, once.

It hadn't helped that she'd been enamored of him, Selene a young researcher just hired as an adjunct professor by Professor Procopio to assist him with his research, highly impressionable and slightly giddy at having an office right next to one of the most prominent experts in the field of alien microbiology. It hadn't helped that Professor Procopio's wife was a Viscountess and very nearly royalty, twentieth in the line of succession.

Professor Toccim palmed the lock and pushed her way into her office, her guests not far behind. "Please, have a seat." She set her holopad on her desk and slipped off the Proctor's robe to hang it on the rack behind the door.

Shelves of Vilasian twistwood climbed to the ceiling on two sides, most of them occupied with placards of honorarium, among them a few still shots of the Professor with prominent politicians and other mementos of a lifetime in Academia. The desktop was a single slab of Istralis crystal, the milk-white rock glittering with a subdued, subtle glow. The deeply-padded chairs were upholstered with cured Gurlagian cowskin, the tanning esters making the office redolent of a bank.

The other two sat across from her.

On her holopad, Selene summoned a diagram from the research results that Professor Procopio had been finalizing for publication at the time of his wife's appointment. A blue, green, and red hologram hovered above the desk.

"I had a visitor two weeks ago, a creature from the very same planet where they banished Dorian and his family. When I showed him these preliminary results of Dorian's experiment, it got very excited."

"Ezra was here?"

Professor Toccim looked sharply at the young woman, startled. "You knew the creature?"

The woman nodded. "He and my father were close friends."

"Your father?"

"Oh, uh, sorry, my adoptive father, Xsirh. My ... human father died when I was four years old."

She sat down abruptly, the realizations cascading into her brain. "I remember ... You were so pretty then, even at four years old. You survived the crash! How ... they told us there weren't any survivors. I can't believe it! Oh, I'm so grateful." She stood and stepped around the desk and folded the young woman into her arms, remembering the delightful girl, the daughter of her colleague. You once wished you'd have a child like her, Selene remembered. And when she'd heard that the Ambassador's ship had crashed on arrival, Professor Toccim had wept in private, as though the family had been her own.

The young woman pulled away, as if uncomfortable with the embrace.

"What is it?"

"I'm ... It's ..." She didn't seem to be able to speak.

The taller woman spoke up. "Xsirh did a genetic analysis. Lydia just learned hours ago that the Procopios aren't her parents."

Selene felt the blood drain from her face. She looked at the hologram, having imagined for years that it'd been the Professor's research that had offended someone in power.

"Professor Toccim, what was so exciting about the research?" the taller woman asked.

Selene glanced between the young woman and the holo above her desk. There were layers to this situation far beyond her comprehension. "His research proved that infectious diseases were—and are—infiltrating human habitations on xenogenic planets throughout the galaxy at a rate far greater than we have the technology to track."

"I don't understand, Professor. Why's that so important?"

"The model he was devising predicted that within thirty years, a pathogen with a ninety-five percent transmission rate will infect colonies throughout the Milky Way." Professor Selene Toccim looked at both women. "A pathogen so virulent it will kill ninety percent of the population and wipe out humanity as we know it."

Chapter 18

Lydia read through her father's work, startled at its clarity and gravity.

Infiltration of human pathogens by alien microorganisms was inevitable. Humans had spread throughout the galaxy far too fast for the research on alien pathogens to keep pace. Once an infectious vector had been compromised by an alien genome or had mutated in its exposure to extreme environments, it had the potential to spread among humans with a savagery unseen for centuries.

In one pandemic on pre-diaspora Earth, a pathogen had infected a quarter of the population and had killed a quarter of its victims. The Spanish Flu of 1919 had killed fifty to two hundred million people after infecting over twenty five percent of the human population. This haemagglutinin-1, neuraminidase-1 virus, or Influenza H1-N1, an admixture of swine and avian viruses, had made the leap into its human variant and had spread throughout the world within months.

Key to any pandemic was its lethality. The rhinovirus, or common cold, despite being highly infectious and likely to reach fifty to sixty percent of the populace during any given cold season, was rarely lethal, its victims nearly always succumbing to some secondary opportunistic infection rather than the rhinovirus itself. Contrary to myth, no part of the rhinovirus was an aphrodisiac. Despite its high penetration rates and near-ubiquity in virility enhancements, it killed very few people.

A highly lethal virus, such as the haemagglutinin-120, neuraminidase-240 strain, Influenza H120-N240, otherwise known as the tyranovirus, was infamous for shredding the meat off a human skeleton in one bite. Difficult to transmit, the tyranovirus was rare, its rampages confined to prehistoric theme parks. However, if it ever developed the transmissibility of its rhinovirus cousin, a lethal pandemic would instantly ensue.

Professor Dorian Procopio had extended standard epidemiological models to the spread of humans throughout the Milky Way. Encounters with new alien microorganisms occurred daily. Professor Procopio postulated that no matter how robust the human immune response, such exposure rates would inevitably overwhelm its ability to adapt. Incorporating travel patterns, settlement rates, trade volumes, and xenomicrobial profiles, the Procopio model predicted with a ninety-five percent certainty that an alien pathogen would infiltrate one or more of the human viruses within thirty years, and cause a pandemic so widespread that interstellar travel was likely to collapse. Further, the model incorporated xenobiologic lethality potentials, a relatively young field of study, which had identified only a handful of alien microbes inimical to humans.

And it was this small proportion of inimical versus benign alien microbes that detractors had used to silence Professor Procopio's work. Peer reviewers had consistently derided the research over this weakness in his arguments.

Reading through the work, Lydia now understood the human paranoia regarding infectious diseases. She also understood that the lynchpin of the research was the lethality potential. It only took one lethal alien pathogen to infiltrate a high-penetration viral vector to create a pandemic.

One section of the work was devoted to an analysis of environments most likely to produce such a pathogen, among them water-covered planets whose temperatures ranged just below those at which the human metabolism operated.

Kziznvxrz, for example, Lydia thought. And then she read the next line.

"Kziznvxrz, just beyond Theogony in the Mnemosyne Constellation at the end of the Scutum-Centaurus arm, is a prime example of a world likely to produce a pathogen with a high degree of lethality. Its nine-tenths water surface and ambient temperature of 36 degrees Celsius make it the perfect Petri dish for culturing an organism inimical to the human physiology."

How ironic, she thought.

Lydia looked out over New Athens University from Professor Toccim's office and sighed.

Still deeply sad at finding out that the Procopios were unrelated to her, she still felt a curiously-detached pride in the work her father had done prior to leaving Gaea. The vague memories she had of her parents contained that high degree of security fundamental to any developing human. There wasn't any question in Lydia's mind that Basilissa and Dorian Procopio had been there for Lydia as parental figures. The fixed place they held in her psyche could not be contravened by something so superfluous as not sharing their genetic heritage. She was as much their child as any biological offspring might have been.

Lydia had chosen to come to the University of New Athens first, both because her mother's positions as Ambassador and Viscountess tended to overshadow her father and because the Noble Procopio family was far more intimidating and, at least in Lydia's mind, best approached last.

Before Xsirh's revelation that she was not a genetic descendant of the Viscountess, Lydia had hoped to prove she was Basilissa's daughter through a simple genetic test. She'd imagined approaching the family through an intermediary, perhaps the enturm, Chiron Likashose, the lawyer of Dmitri Bouras on Gaea.

But now, her heritage in question, Lydia didn't know how she was going to prove she was the daughter of Basilissa Procopio and therefore the rightful Viscountess.

Declaring herself the long-lost daughter of a member of a noble family was itself fraught with difficulties, a process likely to upset the status quo and invite the enmity of the current Viscountess, if not that person's homicidal intentions.

I might as well declare myself the Empress, Lydia thought.

Her other task before approaching the Procopio family was to retrace Ezra's steps on Gaea. Her father's breeding partner when Ambassador Procopio's ship had crashed on Kziznvxrz, Ezra had helped to care for the orphaned girl and later had advocated with the Kzizn government to allow Xsirh to adopt the child.

Despite transmitting regular progress reports to Kziznvxrz, Ezra hadn't been able to finish his investigation and had assembled only a disjointed, incomplete picture of the events leading up to the Viscountess's being appointed Ambassador.

Colonel Remes and Professor Toccim returned from the cafeteria with a tray full of food.

Lydia blanched. The smell was nauseating, the human propensity for animal flesh one of their most disgusting characteristics. The vegetarian sandwich they'd managed to procure from the cafeteria was a dry slab of carbonaceous fibers cooked in a vat of animal lipids and slapped onto a stale pastry made of a milled grain kneaded with more animal lipids into a puffy lump whose moisture had been baked out of it. Further, the "psomi" had been slathered with a thick yellow sauce made from the ground seeds of a known carcinogenic plant and another white sauce made from more animal lipids and the whites of a domesticated bird's reproductive embryos. The "mustard" and "mayonnaise" condiments did more to condemn the sandwich to inedibility than rescue it.

But Lydia was hungry. And they'd brought her a beverage to help lubricate her epithelial digestive tissues. The combination wasn't as bad as she'd thought, except that she had to chew more than she was accustomed to, the Kzizn diet consisting primarily of liquefied microbial proteins.

"Find anything interesting in there?" Melanctha asked around a mouthful of food, throwing a glance at the holo still hovering above Professor Toccim's desk.

Lydia nodded. "Very similar to what I studied on Kziznvxrz in college." Or what passed for college on the planet, a vastly different structure than that she'd seen on human-occupied worlds.

"Not too technical?" the Professor asked, gravy dripping off her roast beast.

She tried not to stare at the nauseating spectacle. "No, not at all. I found the commentary from the peer reviewers specious at best. They seemed bent on refuting the model based on speculative ratios of benign versus inimical xenomicrobes, as if they were in any better position to evaluate the threat."

"For having been reared by the Kzizn," Toccim asked, "you have a surprising command of Galactim."

"Xsirh was adamant that I study it. I guess he always knew I'd return to Gaea."

* * *

"Duke of Pyrgos?" Chiron Likashose III, JD, Esq., threw his head back and laughed. A doctorate in jurisprudence hadn't deterred him from taking the most lucrative position to be had: Personal counselor and governmental affairs advisor to Syndicate Boss Dmitri Bouras, a choice of position most lawyers would call imprudent.

Like any law office, bound volumes of the current code of regulations filled every shelf, de rigueur for impressing clients with the gravity of the work that lawyers did. The expense of having so much printed matter on the walls was impressive by itself, particularly since the only purpose of such an expense was to impress. He never consulted the voluminous material, his law clerks doing the legal grunt work and searching the holonet anyway.

He looked across his desk at the beautiful young woman in plain formalls. "I'd be happy to add that to the dossier, Ms. Castellanos." He glanced at the older, hatchet-faced woman behind her. The woman's bearing gave her the air of nobility and command. Accustomed to privilege,

Chiron thought. "And how about you, Ms. Giorgiadis? Is everything in your file satisfactory?"

"It certainly is, Mr. Likashose. Thank you for your assistance."

"By the way, it's pronounced Like-as-hose." He could ruin her career with a flick of his pinky. A Colonel in the Imperial Bureau of Suspicion escorting a fugitive to Gaea under an assumed name was enough to send her to prison for life. The younger woman was intriguing, daughter of a Viscountess who'd died on an ambassadorial mission gone awry to a planet at the galactic rim.

"Beyond that little modification to the dossier, Mr. Likashose," the younger woman said, her gaze piercing, "you do understand the delicacy of the issue at hand, don't you?"

"I certainly do, Ms. Castellanos. The long-lost daughter of a deceased Viscountess appearing after a quarter-century absence will upset quite a few applecarts. Let's just say that the worms will writhe when they find out they've bit into a rotten apple." He saw her brow crease. "Sorry, an old adage. It's best at this point to speak in vague generalities to preserve your plausible deniability. Don't you agree?"

"Of course she does," the older woman volunteered.

He saw from her look that she would explain in more explicit terms later. Chiron stood, stepped around the desk, and extended his hand to the young woman. "I want you to know, Miss, that restoring what's rightfully yours will be handled with the utmost discretion. Whatever you do from this point forward must compromise neither your current identity nor your purpose in having come to Gaea—particularly not using that name we both know. Please, on your way out, see my assistant for contact instructions—the how and when we will meet in the future. On this point I must be firm: You must never come back to this office. Katalavino?"

The young woman blinked at him, looking bewildered.

"Understand?" he repeated in Galactim, belatedly realizing she didn't know Greek.

"Oh, uh, yes, I understand. Thank you, Mr. Likashose."

He saw them to the outer office, nodded to his administrative assistant, and then returned to his desk.

The problem, Chiron thought, is that the current Viscountess Procopio won't be the person most upset by the return of the long-lost Ambassador's daughter.

It'll be the Dowager Empress Narcissa Thanos and her puppet, the Empress Hecuba Zenon.

But pissing off Empresses was what his boss wanted him to do.

Chapter 19

Lydia looked over New Athens and nearly cringed.

She stood in the kitchenette of their suite, as far from the balcony as she could get.

The sight of the city packing the bowl-like valley nine stories below caused her heart to thunder and her breath to rasp. Her skin crawled and grew clammy, the fine, cilia-like hair on her arms prickling.

Melanctha's standing on that very same balcony, leaning against it, and looking as if she were going to pitch over the side to the street below, didn't help.

Lydia forced herself to sit in a chair, and when that didn't assuage her panic very much, she turned her chair to face the other direction.

Her back to the window, she was finally able to relax somewhat, her heart slowing and her breathing becoming easier.

"Not a comforting sight, eh?"

She started to look Melanctha's direction, but quickly became overwhelmed.

"Here, why don't I tint the glasma?"

The room darkened appreciably and the interior lights brightened to compensate.

Lydia tried to look that direction and found the darkened wall to be a little less daunting than the precipitous drop several stories down. As though a fuscous landscape made it somehow less tangible. "Thanks, that's much better."

"Never seen anything like it, eh?"

"Actually, I have, but my response has always been the same. Father says it's a trauma response."

"To what? Your parents' ship falling out of the sky?"

Lydia nodded, knowing it a neurological flight response, something the Kzizn didn't understand, their endocrine systems under direct prefrontal control, and not subject to the vicissitudes of their basal ganglia.

Looking at Melanctha, Lydia wondered again what to do about her. I can't ask her to put herself at any further risk on my account, she thought, knowing that Colonel Remes was now vulnerable to exploitation. The law offices of Dewey, Treatem, Likashose, and Howe had surely recorded every moment of Remes' visit.

"Melanctha, I want you to know how much I appreciate all you've done. It's more than anyone could expect of another person. Thank you."

The other woman smiled. "Before you go on, I want you to know something. Whatever else happens, Lydia, remember that you have allies. In a lot more places than you might imagine." Then Colonel looked levelly at Lydia. "You were saying—?"

"But I can't ask you to risk your livelihood or your life any further."

"If I felt that way, I'd have told you."

Lydia considered her perspective. Given the degree that the aristocratic Colonel had extended herself, Lydia felt she could no longer leave unsaid how much danger there was in continuing the enterprise. "I know you're here because you feel a sense of purpose and obligation.

I really admire the depth of your loyalty in do-ing so, but I can't in good conscience ask you to accompany me further."

"You don't have to ask."

She looked at Melanctha, standing so tall, eas-ily six inches taller than Lydia, her sharp features perfect for chopping through bureaucracy, her posture as straight and proud as an axe handle. Lydia smiled sadly. "I'll miss you, Mela."

"No, you won't."

Taken aback, Lydia shook her head. "It would be foolish for you to continue, Mela."

"I know the risks, and I'll walk face first into them, willingly."

"Mela, I can't let you do that."

"Lydia, you can't stop me."

She stared at the other woman, not sure what to say, bewildered by the other's persistence.

Melanctha stepped to the table and pulled out a chair to sit facing her. "You're courageous and very considerate to take on this challenge alone. Whatever your reasons for not wanting me to continue, whether it's because my career is in jeopardy or that I'm likely to be extorted by the syndicate, they don't hold up in the face of my reasons for continuing. I can't be dissuaded."

Lydia opened her mouth to argue.

The other woman held up a single finger. "My childhood friend died a strange and tragic death." She raised another finger. "The aristocracy is being undermined in subtle and insidious ways by some erosive poison eating away at its foundation." She raised another finger. "What happened to your parents could happen to any of the noble families. Yes, I'm risking everything, but that's because everything I know is at risk." Melanctha sighed and glanced toward the balcony.

Lydia looked at the older woman and saw in her face the lines of her age. But in the creases too was the wisdom of an ancient lineage that extended deep into the past, her heritage in her wrinkles. And rather than weigh her down with the centuries, this heritage strengthened her and gave her courage in the face of longanimous suffering.

A scion's death at age ten had scarred a young Melanctha, but that scar had hardened into a callous. And the older, wiser Melanctha saw an opportunity to get at the heart of an imbalance wobbling nearly twenty-five years out of equilibrium.

Lydia saw all that and more, and saw it because it was the same fiber from which she herself was woven, the Procopios having passed along to their daughter the determination that comes with quiet resolve. They were nobility, and theirs was to endure whatever vicissitude their sovereign commanded of them.

"What if Empress Hecuba tells you to arrest me and bring me to the palace?"

"What if Metaxa were brewed from the bitter grapes of ambition?" Melanctha retorted.

Lydia smiled and took the older woman's hand. "Thank you."

* * *

"Who're you?" Baptiste Tomaras, Licensed Behavioral Technician, had just walked into his apartment to find two women waiting for him, both in dark sunglasses and utilitarian formalls.

One was tall and statuesque, with a face like a blade, and the other was the perfect height, with perfect proportions, perfect hair, and a perfect face.

The face of a goddess.

He stopped short, as taken aback by her beauty as he was by finding them both in his apartment. He was certain he'd locked his door. Further, it was a palm lock, impervious to decryption.

"Agent Giorgiadis," said the tall one from behind dark tints.

"Agent Castellanos," said the pretty one, hers equally dark.

They weren't pointing guns at him, but they might have been.

"Where are your badges?"

Their heads moved incrementally toward each other, as if to exchange glances. Then the pretty one said, "We don't need badges."

Baptiste's gaze narrowed. *What did I do, just walk onto the set of a bad immersie?*

But the fact that they were in his apartment bespoke an abridgement of his privacy by some powerful surveillance agency inoculated from the constraints of law. "Agents of what?"

"The Imperial Bureau of Suspicion," the taller one said.

Baptiste felt his scrotum crinkle. His feet grew cold and he couldn't feel his hands. He stood gaping at them, mute, not daring to speak, his teeth sure to chatter in fright and his lips sure to blurt his confession.

Here it was, the dreaded moment when Imperial law enforcement finally moved in to arrest the alien collaborator. Accomplice to the Kzizn agent who'd conspired to disrupt the crowning of Empress Hecuba Zenon. They must have retraced Ezra's steps, Baptiste thought, certain his wide, staring eyes and trembling knees gave away his guilt.

"We need your help," the shorter one said. "We're not here to arrest you. Our apologies for breaking in, but we had to make sure we weren't seen."

Baptiste heard something in her voice, the catch of a silent plea, the desperation of someone unmoored from all that anchored a person to the past. "You want to know about the Kzizn, Ezra."

She seemed relieved, her shoulders easing back a little. "Yes, Mr. Tomaras."

He caught the faint odor of an organic compound, the smell redolent of Ezra himself. "You knew him, didn't you? You aren't ... related, are you?"

"He was my stepfather, and he came here to help me."

Bewildered, he looked her over. She didn't look alien. She looked to be as delectable a human specimen as he'd ever seen, her soft, soulful eyes a window into her unusual past, her elfin, heart-shaped face begging to be cradled in loving hands. There wasn't a trace of alien-ness about her, except that she was so trusting and vulnerable. Her mien of complete trust invited him to extend the same trust to her, which he found himself doing despite multiple reasons not to.

"Stay for tea?" he asked, setting down his bag and moving into the kitchen. Comprised of three modest rooms, his apartment was comfortable, a bedroom and bath to one side of a living room, on the other a small dining-kitchenette. "Have a seat, and I'll put some water on."

He didn't even have three chairs, his guests taking the two that he did have. The water was instantly hot, and he poured them each a cup, having to wash the one that he'd used at breakfast. As cushy and well-paying as his job was, he still couldn't afford a luxurious life. Not in New Athens, the most expensive place in the galaxy to live.

"I'll stand," the taller woman said.

"You sure, Agent …?"

"Giorgiadis," the sharp-faced woman said. "Yes, I'm sure." She leaned against the window embrasure, her cup in hand.

Baptiste settled across from the pretty one, Agent Castellanos. "What do you want to know?"

"Do you know why Ezra was here?"

"He said that his people thought the Gaean Empire had been deceived."

Chapter 20

How does a person deceive an entire Empire? Lydia wondered, reviewing her mental notes.

Neurologically, the Kzizn were able to remember everything, unlike humans. All sensory input was encoded into a hextuple neuropeptide brain that doubled as a genome. Whenever a Kzizn reproduced asexually through transverse binary fission, all memory and knowledge was transmitted to both offspring. Hence, Lydia's neurological limitations had bewildered them, the alien species not understanding for years why she had such difficulty with learning. Eventually, they'd helped her to develop skills to improve her memory to the point of nearly eidetic recall.

Incorporated into her mental notes were the dossiers of the two Governesses and the Laundry Maid, dossiers that Colonel Remes had pilfered from the archives of the Imperial Bureau of Suspicion. All three of them had died on coronation day.

Baptiste Tomaras had told them he'd given Ezra a tissue sample from Princess Cybill Zenon, also on coronation day.

"What do you suppose Ezra did with it?" Melanctha asked, looking over the holo coming slowly to life under Lydia's hands.

She'd begun putting her ideas together in a gigantic holographic mindmap on her palmcom, consisting of two clusters, the small one a tight ball of clear ideas around a nine-tenths water planet known as Kziznvxrz, and the large one a tangled web of mysterious clouds around the third planet orbiting a small yellow sun.

"Took it somewhere to be analyzed, I guess," Lydia replied. She drew the orb representing Icarus Terzi, son of Count Terzi, toward her. "What did you say was the name of his governor?"

"Giles..." Melanctha began, squinting and turning her head to the side, as though she might roll the information out of her ear. "Sotir something."

Lydia looked over at the dossier on her governess, Filmena, whom she barely remembered, whom her parents had left behind on Gaea when Lydia was four years old. "Sotiropoulos?"

Melanctha's gaze narrowed. "I think so. How'd you know that?"

She expanded the dossier on Filmena, the globe enlarging enough to reveal the information contained therein. Among her vital statistics was the notation of a marriage to a man named "Giles."

Lydia and Melanctha exchanged a glance. The years of the marriage overlapped with the years Filmena had been her governess. "Can you get his file?"

"I can try, but I don't want to do it from here. If a trace is run, it'll lead directly to us. How about the Pantainos Library?"

A famous public library in New Athens, it'd been named after Titus Flavius Pantainos, a benefactor of ancient Athens who'd dedicated his private library to public use in the name of the city's patron goddess, Athena.

"Let's go," Lydia said, snapping the palmcom shut.

Three galleries surrounded an arboretum whose soaring glasma ceilings enclosed a virtual microcosm of the Gaean biosphere, nearly every type of flora represented among its sixty different microclimates.

Lydia drank in the scents as she and Melanctha wound their way toward the holonet terminals, every volume in the vast library accessible on the holonet. The heavy encryption shielding the IBS archives from public view recorded every request for access and its source. Accessing the archives from a place so public as the library might enable them to avoid being traced.

At the entrance, they'd seen the inscription above the door dictating proper library etiquette: "No work is ever to be removed from this collection, either by fiat or edict, nor to be made inaccessible out of political expediency. Down that road lies tyranny."

The library was situated to the west side of the Agora, near the Gate of Athena Archegetis, considered the most revered site after the Tower of the Winds and the Parthenon itself, the gate made of four Doric columns on a base of pentelic marble. Manufactured of synthetic pentel, the library soared thrice as high as the Archegetis Gate, dwarfing the ancient structure. Its glasma panes and geodesic roof gave the library the air of an open festival or bazaar, sans the calls of vendors endlessly hawking their wares.

Instead, under the hush of a place devoted to deep study and contemplation murmured the babbling of multiple streams, bringing their life-sustaining waters to a diversity of plants.

"Magnificent," Lydia whispered, walking the lichen-splotched flagstone path beside Melanctha.

"I couldn't get enough of this place as a child," the other woman said, stopping outside the portal leading to the holonet terminals. "You should stay here, Lydia. They're sure to have holocams."

Lydia nodded, spotting a fern-infested glade surrounded by trellis. Micromisters saturated the air with humidity so thick she could see the mist. "I'll be over here." She retreated to the chosen glade as Melanctha entered the holoterminal area.

Sitting on a damp bench under ferns, Lydia relaxed for a few moments, the microclime reminiscent of Kziznvxrz's humidity and fecundity.

"May I rest for a moment?"

Lydia looked toward the voice.

An old woman stood there, her gray, curly hair escaping a checked scarf tied tightly under her chin. She wore a long wool coat that reached her ankles, and carried a woven-straw handbag looking too insubstantial for the weight it seemed to be carrying. She sat without waiting for permission. "Not as young as I used to be, you know. Hope I'm not a bother. I'm Giorgi Lillis, by the way." She stuck out her hand.

Lydia shook the wrinkled claw, the name vaguely familiar for reasons she couldn't name. "Do you have far to go?"

"It isn't the distance ahead that tires me; it's the distance I've traveled." The old woman looked Lydia up and down with an upper body stiffened by age and infirmity. "You're a pretty one, child. You remind me of someone I once knew, someone who embodied a dream, and whose death was a tragedy long forgotten."

"Good and bad memories, all in one," Lydia said, seeing the old woman's joy and sadness.

"Our greatest triumph sometimes becomes our most humiliating defeat."

Not minding the old woman's prattle, she smiled. "The opposite is true too, sometimes."

"Yes, child, sometimes."

"You! Old woman! How many times have I told you not to bother the patrons?!"

Lydia looked up.

A uniformed security officer was bearing down on them. "Get up, and get off with your old carcass! Go on!" He reached for the old woman's arm.

Lydia stood and shoved her face into his. "Excuse me, she's not a bother. She's my grand-mother!"

He recoiled, backing away a step, blinking rapidly.

"Next time, ask! Who's your supervisor? Eh? Out with it, man! Harassing old women unnecessarily. Ought to be ashamed of yourself. Come on, Grandmama. Here, let me help you to your feet."

Later, as they approached a pneumatube station, the old woman said, "You needn't have done that, child. Here, let me give you my address. Come and see me, if you've a mind. You know, the more I hear you speak, the more you remind me of her."

"Who, Dame Lillis? Who do I remind you of?"

"My daughter, Ambrosia," the old woman said, a tear trickling its way down her cheek, "dead now nearly thirty years."

* * *

"You did what?" Melanctha recoiled as if stung.

The two of them had just stepped out of a pneumatube and now strode through the Chaidari neighborhood toward Agias Paraskevis, on the western outskirts of New Athens, a set of sharp, short peaks between them and the Gulf of Elefsina. After Melanctha had retrieved the dossier on Giles Sotiropoulos, which contained his last known address, they'd come here to this part of the old city to check the dwelling. Walking up the steep hill, Lydia wondered that the houses here still stood, packed side-by-side on narrow tree-lined streets. She marveled that they'd not slid into the valley through erosion or succumbed to the area's frequent seismic activity.

"It wasn't right, what he was doing," Lydia said.

"We're supposed to be undercover, Lydia, not drawing attention to ourselves."

"Sorry, but I couldn't let that pompous idiot treat her that way." Lydia knew she'd jeopardized their mission by defending the old woman in the arboretum.

"I'd have probably done the same." Melanctha glanced at her handheld and then looked at the apartment buildings on both sides. "This one," she said. "Let's hope Mr. Sotiropoulos still lives here, eh? According to public records, he committed suicide shortly after being dismissed from Count Terzi's service. But the IBS dossier says otherwise."

None of the houses looked in terribly good shape, paint peeling from walls, cracks in the foundations from subsidence. Melanctha had indicated a three-story structure set back from the street by only a few feet, behind a thin strip of ill-kempt grass. On either side of the walk stood a tree struggling to eke out enough nutrients. The entry held a com system for the six apartments in the building, two on each floor.

A door swung open before they'd even read the labels. "It's me you're looking for, isn't it?"

Lydia was startled by how direct he was. She saw that his face was the same as the image in the dossier.

"May we come in?" Melanctha said.

He let them inside and gestured to a darkened living room. "Please, have a seat. I'd get you something, but I don't get around so well anymore."

Lydia's eyes adjusted, and she realized that the only source of light was the shaded balcony looking out over the street, through which he'd seen them approach. The air was thick and closed, as if the occupant never opened the windows or left the apartment.

"Thank you, Mr. Sotiropoulos. We appreciate your time."

"What else am I going to spend it on? I'm retired, nothing else to do but wait for Thanatos to come claim my soul." He hobbled to the chair opposite a low table, his step infirm and his breathing heavy.

"You probably don't remember me, Sir."

"Of course I do, clear as a bell. You're—"

"Agent Giorgiadis, Imperial Bureau of Suspicion. We're here on a highly classified mission requiring the utmost discretion."

The gaze shifted to Lydia and then back to Melanctha. "They've been here three times already, asking me about her. We divorced twenty years ago, rarely saw each other since then."

It was a silent complaint. "And you already told them everything you know," Lydia said. "Agent Castellanos, by the way. The circumstances of her death were odd, to say the least."

"An alien life form attacked and killed her in her apartment on the day Princess Hecuba was crowned. A bit more than odd, wouldn't you say?"

"A bit, Mr. Sotiropoulos," Melanctha said. "We're here to ask you about another time in her life, when you were married."

"You know, my dear, you and that young man would have married."

Melanctha looked at her feet.

She and Icarus Terzi, son of Count Ilias Terzi, Lydia knew. She could tell Melanctha was struggling to maintain her composure. "Mrs. Sotiropoulos was governess to Viscountess Procopio's daughter, Lydia," Lydia said.

Giles nodded, his eyes not leaving Melanctha. "She was. Unusual for a married woman to be a governess. We were planning to divorce before the girl got much older. But Viscountess Procopio was appointed Ambassador and left for that godforsaken place on the galactic rim." He swung his gaze over to Lydia. "I can't ever remember its name."

"Did Mrs. Sotiropoulos mention anything unusual during her four years as Lydia's governess?"

"Chatted endlessly about the household scuttlebutt to any who cared to listen. Volumes, you might say."

"Anything unusual?"

Giles looked out the single unshaded window and shrugged. "There was an incident, early on, which I happen to recall for very personal reasons. Filmena told me that they expected the child to have some difficulties."

Lydia frowned. "Difficulties?"

"Yeah, you know, developmental difficulties."

Melanctha asked, "As in mental retardation?"

Giles nodded and spread his hands. "Some cluster of infirmities in her gene structure. No specific deformity, Filmena said, just a number of weaknesses. How did she say it? 'An aggregate of lesser infirmities,' I think. Odd that Princess Cybill became the functional idiot. The two were born the same day, you know."

Lydia exchanged a glance with Melanctha.

"Anything else, Mr. Sotiropoulos?"

He looked at Melanctha and shook his head. "It was nearly thirty years ago. Difficult to remember much else, after all this time."

"Did she know Eugenia Ioannou, the Governess to Princess Cybill?" Lydia asked, knowing the two governesses had both died on coronation day.

"They were friends, as I recall. And Filmena did mention taking Lydia onto palace grounds once for a little picnic with Eugenia and her charge. I thought it odd, since the two infants weren't more than two weeks old. Filmena said a third person was there, someone I wouldn't have expected."

Lydia exchanged a glance with Melanctha. "Who was that?"

"The Lady's Maid of the Empress Consort, Ambrosia Lillis, who died in childbirth."

"Lady's Maid?" Melanctha said. "Very odd that she was there. Do you remember her name?"

"Her name? Why do you want to know some Lady's Maid's name? I don't remember it. She wasn't anyone important."

Chapter 21

Near sunset, they were back at the library, Melanctha at a holoterminal, Lydia waiting for her in the arboretum.

Lydia was hoping to see the old woman again. She hadn't realized at the time that Giorgi Lillis was the mother of the deceased Empress Consort, Ambrosia Lillis, who'd died giving birth to Princess Cybill on the day that Lydia herself had been born.

A prim old man sat at the other end of the bench under the ferns, the trellis reaching high overhead. There was no sign of Countess Giorgi Lillis. Beyond him, she could see the entrance to the wing of holoterminals, where Melanctha had gone.

"Have you got a tube fare you could spare?" he asked, his voice a croak.

The request struck Lydia as odd. Earlier, she'd offered Giorgi enough money to take the pneumatube home, but Giorgi had declined, saying the tube was free to the elderly. So either she'd declined out of decorum, or this prim old man was panhandling. "How much is it?" Lydia asked.

"Ten drachma," the old man said.

She fished that much out of her pocket. "Here you go," she said. "I thought the pneumatube was free for the elderly."

"I thought everyone knew the tube fare was ten drachma," he retorted. "You some rutabaga from the provinces?"

Why she had the feeling she was being insulted, she didn't know. She did notice he'd evaded her question. "Ten drachma won't get you a pint of mead, if that's what you're after."

Melanctha emerged from the holoterms and strode toward the fern-filled enclosure, saw the old man, and abruptly turned toward the library entrance.

On alert, Lydia resisted the impulse to follow her.

"The devil mead, why would I want any of that?"

Same reason most people would, Lydia thought idly. "Better get going, old man. They don't like vagrants around here."

"Who says I'm a vagrant? Do you know who I am?"

Lydia shook her head. "Who are you?"

"Death himself, Thanatos incarnate! Impudent wench!" The old man staggered to his feet and wandered off.

What the stars was that all about? Lydia wondered, getting to her feet and going the other direction.

She found Melanctha outside the main entrance, at the bottom of the long, wide staircase, near a marble lion with one paw in the air.

"You didn't recognize him?" she asked as Lydia descended the last few steps. "That was IBS Agent Provocateur Erastus Doukas, whom I recruited on Lucina Nine, in disguise. I wouldn't have recognized him if I hadn't monitored his work for years."

Lydia went cold, frightened that IBS had managed to track them to Gaea somehow.

* * *

"Before taking over command of Lucina Nine, I was in counterinsurgency," Melanctha was saying.

Lydia was exhausted, the two of them having taken multiple tube trips across the city, changing clothes in boutique dressing rooms, splitting up and taking different routes to the next rendezvous, waiting at each stop to see if someone followed them.

It seemed hours later when they finally decided there wasn't a chance someone could have followed. Night had fallen by then, and Lydia was hungry and tired.

"We'll have to rent new lodgings each night and leave each place as if we're going to return. I'm glad Likashose gave us that encrypted holomail address. He hasn't responded yet, but in his business, he's sure to know someone who's good with disguises."

They ate awful food at a lipid utensil and rented a room in a low-down high-rise. The noise kept Lydia awake half the night, and the vermin kept her awake the other half, the comings and goings of other patrons audible through the film-thin walls. She debated which would be worse: the elevators at one end of the hallway or the restrooms at the other, the noises from each equally lurid.

In the morning, she took a look at the shared cleansall and decided she didn't need a bath. The scum-covered walls might have supplied her a meal, but she didn't have a kitchen to prepare it in.

"This way," Melanctha said, going out the back door.

The alley contained the city's normal assortment of trash: addicts, criminals, and prostitutes. Two women in formalls appearing in their midst caused a minor stir. They looked at Lydia like a delicacy, but a baleful glance from Melanctha warned them off.

The address that Likashose had commed to them wasn't far away, off another alley with equally unsavory characters loitering in its shadows.

"Somebody's got to loiter in alleys, might as well employ the trash to do something," the woman told them. "Call me Polly. You don't need to know more than that."

In a short few minutes, Polly had concocted disguises for them both. "Let me look at you." She stood back, gave them a once-over, and shook her head. "You," Polly said, pointing at Melanctha, "you're fine, but you, girl, you've got just too much of whatever you high-born types are born with. It's gonna show through any disguise I give you. The big one's got it too, but at least she hides it. You just don't know how to hide, do you?"

Lydia frowned, her brows drawn together in bewilderment.

"Here, I'll demonstrate." Polly turned to face away, wriggled her shoulders, and then turned back around. She looked completely different. Her comportment was that of a Duchess at an Imperial ball, her head held high, her back as straight as a pole, her shoulders back, her bosom stuck out proudly, her gaze traveling over everyone's head.

"That's how I look?" Lydia asked.

"It's worse than that, Rutabaga Pie," Polly said, "That's who you *are*. If I didn't know better, I'd say you were Empress Hecuba, except prettier. Ugly as pondscum, that woman."

Lydia giggled, having thought the same. "So what do I do?"

And Polly proceeded to show her, contorting Lydia's limbs in uncomfortable ways.

"Well, can't say it's a complete failure." Polly sighed. "It'll have to do. Oh, uh, and Chiron said to give you that." She pointed to a package near the door, a three-by-three-by-six inch oblong rectangle. "It was making some odd noises, so I just left it where he put it."

Lydia recognized the outer materials as Kzizn in origin. She picked it up and knew instantly what it contained. How had Xsirh obtained them? And how had he sent them here without setting off every alien biologic matter detector between Kziznvxrz and Gaea?

Outside, Melanctha told her, "Polly's right, you know."

"Huh? About what?" Walking toward the tube station beside her, Lydia tried to carry herself the way Polly had told her. It was so depressing!

"There's no hiding who you are. What's in the package?"

"Trained didinium, two of them, like the one that tried to kill me on Amphitrite Three. Our revered leader told me just before I left Kzizn-vxrz that Wrwrmrfn dissidents had tamed wild didinium."

Xsirh's note just under the wrapper indicated that these two didinium had been neuro-sensitized to Ezra's scent, but that they were still voracious predators, to be handled with extreme caution. They were trained to obey Lydia exclusively and attack any Kziznvxrfn instantly. Also in the note, he'd warned that the dissident leader, Mzixrhhz Gszmlh, who hadn't been seen on Kziznvxrz in many years, was now thought to have gone into exile for safety. Xsirh had written the note in the Kzizn script, which no Homo sapiens had ever deciphered, Lydia the only known human who could understand it.

"What now?" Lydia asked, a three-inch cube in each pocket. Her hair now blond, and a thick brow ridge giving her the visage of a throwback, Lydia resisted the urge to scratch. Polly had given them enough in supplies to last a few days, warning them to remove the disguises every night and re-apply them every morning, or they'd start to slough off.

"Now we try to track down the others Ezra saw. By the way, Lydia, what was he thinking?"

"What was who thinking?"

"Ezra, going up there and spouting off like that in front of the Gods and everybody? Didn't he know he'd be splashed?"

Now, in retrospect, it did seem to be ill-advised. Lydia would have felt compelled to do the same in those circumstances. "On Kziznvxrz, it would be expected."

"Dorothy, you're not on Kzansas anymore." She glanced at Lydia. "I don't want you doing something similar, all right?"

"Yes, Mela," Lydia said, trying not to grin.

* * *

Agent Provocateur Erastus Doukas of the Imperial Bureau of Suspicion hurled himself into the bushes as the pair of women strode past him. He felt ridiculous in his flower-delivery disguise, complete with winged helmet and winged shoes, a gold, glittery, one-piece body suit emphasizing his muscular figure and giving him the physique of a god. The outsize genital cup was the whipped cream atop the hot-fudge sundae of his humiliation, the prominent bulge emphasizing his cherries.

They must be laughing off their posteriors back at the office, he thought, peering from the bushes toward the two women who'd passed him. The dark-haired taller woman with the stooped shuffle didn't concern him. The smaller one with the troglodyte brow ridge, however, carried herself with the ease of an Empress, not at all like somebody who was irremediably ugly.

Agent Doukas had lost his quarry yesterday after seeing the pair enter the Pantainos Library twice in one day. The first time, he'd seen the young woman, the Procopio scion, on a bench speaking with a decrepit old hag. He'd shadowed the pair as they'd taken a pneumatube to a neighborhood on the outskirts of New Athens and then had followed them back to the library. There, he'd ventured to sit on the same bench with the uppity brat. How dare she imply all he wanted to do was drink his life away!

And then they'd slipped away, somehow, and he hadn't been able to find them.

With a still of the decrepit old woman, Erastus had obtained her dossier and had come to her address, on the off-chance the Procopio woman would appear.

Problem was, Countess Giorgi Lillis lived the high life, her mansion surrounded by a thick hedge of rhododendron twenty feet high. Erastus couldn't get onto the grounds, and the estate was so large, he couldn't monitor the four entrances all by himself. It didn't help that he'd been given a disguise so blatant and flashy that it was downright gauche. No self-respecting spy would be seen in such a get-up.

The two women were far enough past that he was able to extract himself from the hedge.

He emerged just in time to see them turn toward the gate. His jaw dropped as they entered the grounds.

That's them! Erastus thought, kicking himself in the cherry cup for having let them past.

And then he wondered, why are they visiting Countess Giorgi Lillis?

* * *

"Why have you come to see me?" the old woman across from them asked. "Forgive me, I'm having difficulty understanding why you're here."

Melanctha had tried in vague terms to explain the reason for their visit.

"It's delicate," Lydia said. "We don't want to endanger you, but we need your help. I need your help."

"Help with what?"

Lydia looked around the parlor, its carpet a thick Naltrexian wool, the furniture of Wirtassian origin, the elaborate moldings done in Mildanian beetle-wood. This was the kind of parlor her parents had had, where trillion-galacti deals were cemented with a smile and a toast, where truces between antagonists were discussed over sips of fine Metaxa.

Emperor Athanasios had been entertained in this parlor, an event Lydia was convinced would never be held for the wart-faced Empress Hecuba.

Lydia turned her attention back to Countess Lillis. "My parents were sent to Kziznvxrz to their deaths, their A-warp engine sabotaged to explode on arrival."

The elderly woman looked at her with a level gaze. "It was a strange time. Go on."

"I've been pursued across the delta sector by Gaean security agents and a dissident Kzizn faction for no apparent reason. After discovering the sabotage, one of my Kzizn caregivers, Ezra, came to Gaea to research my past. Twice now, that dissident Kzizn faction has tried to assassinate me. And just before coming to Gaea, I found out that Viscountess and Professor Procopio aren't even my parents."

"What?"

Lydia struggled to keep from bursting into tears. "My Kzizn father kept tissue samples from my parents' bodies in zero-kelvin cryo and compared their genomes to mine. I'm not a genetic relation to either one." A tear slipped down her cheek. "And yesterday, we were spotted by an IBS agent at the library arboretum. Somehow, they traced us all the way from Lucina Nine."

"Not the child of Basilissa and Dorian Procopio?" The old woman stood and began to pace before the hearth, its mantle carved from a single piece of cured Filgastic bone, the huge beasts five times larger than any creature ever to have roamed Gaea. The Countess Lillis looked deep in thought, her brow wrinkled and her gaze on her feet.

"We haven't told you everything, mostly because there's so much to tell."

"And you shouldn't, child. I probably know too much already." She stopped and looked at Melanctha. "Your family probably isn't in a position to help?"

"No, Lady, and I fear I've placed them in jeopardy already, simply by being here."

"Certainly true. But what's been done to the Procopios might be done to any among the nobility."

Lydia exchanged a glance with Melanctha. "Or already has," she said.

Countess Giorgi Lillis stopped in her tracks, her gaze fixed on Lydia. "How can I help?"

Chapter 22

"Somewhere in the Gaean government, a faction is conspiring with the dissident Kzizn to destabilize the Empire."

Melanctha whirled toward Lydia. "Feels that way to you, too, eh?"

They were headed toward the nearest pneumatube station after leaving the Lillis estate. Lydia felt conspicuous, the long empty stretches of wide avenue emphasizing their presence. There simply wasn't a way to access the area on foot without looking obvious. The occasional passing vehicle was inevitably a luxury-class hover. The hedge-lined streets rarely saw a vehicle worth less than the gross domestic product, and pedestrians were an endangered species.

As if to contradict her very thoughts, a flower-delivery vehicle hove around the corner, engines

353

whining, its gold-glitter exterior outlandished by a pair of blinding-white wings.

"What insensate marketing executive would subject a company's employees to parading around in such gaudy vehicles?"

The hover careened toward them and slewed to the side, skidding to a halt. A figure leapt from the cab, his musculature emphasized by the skin-tight, one-piece, gold-lame body suit, a large genital cup giving his physique a protrusive pubis. The man leveled a blasma pistol at them. "You're under arrest!"

Lydia burst into laughter, and she'd have fallen to the ground in stitches if the pistol weren't aimed at her. She recognized him as the pompous idiot who'd commandeered the Imperial Detention Center on Theogony.

Melanctha was sniggering behind her hand. "Stars above, Erastus, is that the best Clandestine could do for you?"

"Awful, isn't it?" he said. "You're still under arrest."

"All right, all right," she said, her arms up, her body half-bent over with laughter.

Erastus stepped up behind her and wrestled her wrists into cuffs. Melanctha would have looked forlorn in the glasma bracelets if she weren't laughing so hard.

"Just be careful with the didinium," Lydia said as the agent provocateur approached to cuff her.

"What's a didinium?" Erastus asked, hesitating.

"The creature in my pocket. Take a look." Lydia kept her arms above her head.

He fished the three-inch cube from the side pocket of Lydia's formalls and stepped back, keeping his blasma barrel on her. Underneath the clear material writhed a swirl of organic goop. "Ewww!"

"They're really very affectionate," Lydia said.

He looked at her, doubt clear on his face. "Do they smell as bad as those Kzizn?"

"No, sweet as ambrosia, in fact. Take a whiff."

He popped the container open, and the didinium leapt upon his face and wrapped itself around his head. Lydia grabbed the barrel and shoved the pistol at him to keep him from firing it. The two of them tumbled, his hands going to his face to claw the creature off him. Lydia fell onto him, the bulk of her weight landing right on his outsize crotch cup. She tore the weapon from his hand and got to her feet.

The pistol aimed at him, she pulled the didinium off his face. At her bidding, the creature withdrew its tentacles from around the man's head and settled onto her arm.

Erastus was too busy holding his bruised reproductive organelles to give her much attention. She nicked the key off his belt and helped Melanctha out of the glasma bracelets.

Melanctha took the weapon from her, and Lydia put the didinium back into its protective enclosure. Despite being trained to obey her commands, a creature so feral might still turn on her.

"Get into your vehicle," Melanctha ordered.

"I'm hurt, bitch! Can't you see—"

Melanctha kicked him in the gonads, and he curled into a ball. "Help me out, Lydia."

They each grabbed a handful of his gaudy suit at the shoulder and hurled his fetal form headfirst into the equally gaudy hover. Melanctha leaned into the cab and fiddled with the controls, then slammed the door shut.

The glittery hover took off down the avenue on autopilot.

"Where's it taking him?" Lydia asked.

"The palace, where he'll get a welcome reception," Melanctha replied, grinning and shoving his pistol into her belt.

"If they don't cut apart the hover as it approaches," Lydia added, turning to look at Melanctha.

The other woman met her gaze. "I guess I'm all in now, aren't I?"

Lydia nodded, knowing now there was no turning back for either of them.

* * *

Just before they stepped from the pneumatube, Lydia rigged a leash of sorts for the didinium. The glasma restraint circlet fit around the didinium perfectly. To the glasma circlet, she attached an elastoband. Any time she wanted to rein in the didinium, she reduced the band's elasticity, and the didinium snapped back toward her. Lydia had been looking for some way to leash them, not wanting to let them completely loose while tracing Ezra's scent throughout the city.

"Nice little contraption," Melanctha said, looking at the elastoband in Lydia's hand. "Is that a rash?"

"Huh?"

"Those spots on your arm, is that a rash?"

"Oh, that? I don't know," Lydia said. "It's been itching off and on since I left Kziznvxrz. It can't be anything contagious; I've been inoculated."

They stepped out of a capsule into the transit plaza closest to the palace. The maze of tubes overhead made this one of the busiest, most-chaotic tube stations on Gaea, being just east of the Acropolis, surrounded by major attractions such as the Temple of Zeus, the Parliament, and the National Gardens.

The crush of crowd swept Lydia and Melanctha toward the exit, neither able to resist the surge. This side was all exits, people popping out of tubes like gophers on an arcade game. Beyond the tube station, Melanctha stopped at a crossing, where hovers on the street whined dangerously close to pedestrians, all the machines moving at a crawl.

Ahead was the main entrance to the palace, the public entrance, multiple guards both inside and outside the gate.

Weaving her way through the crowd, Lydia walked toward the Parthenon, dominating the Acropolis above them. "Ezra was standing at the front of the crowd when he was splashed." She made her way across the plaza toward the base of the Acropolis. Relatively empty now, just a few pedestrians around, the square looked vastly different. She couldn't tell where Ezra might have been standing. "You saw the coronation too, right, Mela?"

The other woman nodded. "Let's try over here."

Lydia followed her. Oddly, her own nose alerted her to the faint ammonia esters that still lingered.

"Look at the green splotches."

Spots of bright green were splattered across a twenty-foot area, each spot showing evidence of attempted clean-up. The acidic heptoneuropeptide biochemistry of the Kzizn was a challenge for any detergent.

Lydia pulled the didinium from its enclosure and slipped the circlet around it. The slug-like blob of protoplasm bulged from both sides of the glasma ring. She set it on the ground and increased the elastoband's elasticity.

Like a dog, the creature darted this way and that, pausing momentarily and extending a tendril, as if sniffing. It was remarkably adroit at avoiding pedestrians, seeming to sense when it was about to be stepped on. It helped that most pedestrians found the creature repugnant.

A slug on a leash, Lydia thought.

The didinium then darted across the square, back toward the palace gate.

At the crosswalk stood a fire hydrant, where the didinium suddenly froze. One tendril shot straight up, and a stream of dark green liquid doused the hydrant.

Then the didinium moved to the curb, right beside the traffic lane, and prowled parallel to the sidewalk, one short tendril feeling the curb edge. Lydia and Melanctha followed. Again, it stopped, this time extending two tendrils at ninety degrees from each other, one vertical, the other horizontal. Slowly, it turned in place, and then began a frantic dance, its horizontal tendril pointed toward a building.

"Target acquired," Lydia said.

Melanctha looked that direction. "Dedalou Medical Plaza," she said, reading the sign. Her brow furrowed, and she looked at Lydia. "Why would Ezra go there?"

"I wonder …" She calculated quickly. "Baptiste said he gave Ezra a tissue sample from Princess Cybill on coronation day. This was probably the laboratory closest to the ceremony." She grinned at Melanctha. "Come on."

The didinium strained at the elastoband, pulling them at a rapid clip toward the building.

An explosion behind them echoed across the square, and Lydia whirled. Near the palace entrance, a hydrant head crashed to the pavement, a spout of water beside it reaching fifty feet in the air, people scattering in panic.

"Pretty caustic, looks like," Melanctha said. "Better not let it urinate on anything else."

Lydia nodded, exchanging a glance with her. They entered the building, strode to the elevator, and took it to the second floor to a laboratory, the didinium leading the way.

The clerk leaned over from behind steri-glasma to peer at the creature on the floor. "No pets allowed in the building."

"It's a service animal. Can't a girl get some comfort?"

Looking nonplussed, the clerk gaped at her, like a fish gasping for water.

He might look pretty cute in gills, Lydia thought. "A friend of mine dropped off a tissue sample for analysis," she said. "His name was Svkszvhgfh Ezhrozprh, but he might have just given his short name, 'Ezra.'"

Again, the clerk peered at the didinium. "Was his skin the same vomit green as that?"

"About, yes." Ezra would have been mightily insulted at being compared to a didinium, the gentle Kzizn manner antithetical to the feral creatures.

"Ah, it's been waiting for him," the clerk said. "I was wondering when he was coming back. Ezra's the name, you said?"

Lydia nodded. "He's not coming back. He's deceased."

"Oh, uh, sorry to hear that. One moment, please." The clerk retreated behind a panel, shelves visible behind the service counter. A moment later he returned, a memnode in hand. "That'll be a hundred drachmas."

"Usurious!" Melanctha said.

Lydia paid without complaint, sliding a chit into the sterile exchange tube, the irradiation cleansing it of any microbes.

The clerk slid the memnode into his side of the exchange tube.

She plugged the memnode into her handheld, and the machine beeped at the upload. "Oh, uh, I'll need another analysis." She produced the vial of blood she'd obtained from Countess Giorgi Lillis.

"There's a kiosk to your left. Put the new sample into a steri-sample envelope, please, located at the kiosk. We'll have your results in twenty-four hours."

She stepped to the deposit kiosk, filled out the form, deposited the Countess's blood sample into an envelope, and slipped it into the receptacle. The machine whirred and hummed.

"Deposit accepted," it said, and spat a receipt at her.

Lydia reeled in the didinium and returned it to its enclosure.

"Good idea," Melanctha said as they made their way toward the elevator. "Where to, now?"

"I'm famished. How about you?"

"I know a place nearby called Petit's."

"Does that refer to the price or the portion?"

The two of them made their way to the restaurant, dodging hovers and wading through the crowds. The restaurant's circular, green-and-red emblem was emblazoned upon bright orange shades. Inside, they were seated near the back, Melanctha facing the front. "We should be safe in our disguises, as long as we can see who comes and goes," she muttered, eyes on the door. Lydia ordered a Kalamata olive salad, hold the lipid-based dressing, and Melanctha ordered similar. "Guess I'm adapting a little to your diet," she said.

Lydia smiled. Someone's gorging themselves on the cooked, fleshy remains of a meaty bovine was a disgusting sight. She realized that her favorite, algae soup, was just as disgusting to them.

While they waited for their order, Lydia pulled out her handheld. On it were four sets of genetic analysis. Hers, one for each of her Procopio parents, one for Princess Cybill. She programmed in a comparative analysis of all four genomes, similar to the analysis Xsirh had already run, the one establishing that she couldn't be the Procopio's natural child.

"One more gene sample," Lydia said, wondering what they'd do for twenty-four hours while the laboratory analyzed the genome for Countess Giorgi Lillis.

She sighed and ate her salad in silence, anxious to get the results.

Chapter 23

That night, they rented a room at a posh, run-down, flea-bag hotel called the Miramare, located almost due south from the Acropolis. It should have been called the Nightmare. Its one redeeming feature was the sound of surf, which found its way in through the alley that their window faced. When the cats weren't caterwauling, and the street toughs weren't scuffling, and the drunks weren't belting out some forlorn, besotted memory. It was better than the one they'd stayed in last night, but not by much.

And the room had its own cleansall. Without moss-caked walls.

Lydia luxuriated, her parched skin sopping up the water like a sponge.

"You gonna use all the hot water?" Melanctha called after awhile.

After a few more minutes, Lydia got out. "Hand me a pair of formalls, would you?" she said around the door.

Melanctha did so, getting a glimpse of Lydia. "You've got a body to die for, girl."

She blushed, stepping into the formalls. "Thanks."

"And a face to launch a million ships."

It was wonderful to feel admired, especially given her recent travails. Dressed, she stepped out to the main room, where Melanctha was watching a news report on the holo.

"They just sterilized a whole fucking planet."

"Huh? Sterilized?" Lydia hadn't heard Melanctha cuss before.

"Watch. Maybe they'll replay it." Melanctha turned up the volume.

"...pathogen appears to have been neutralized," said the anchor, her bulbous breasts defying gravity, "but all recent travelers to Ananke Ten have been placed in mandatory quarantine for sixty days. Nearby quarantine centers are overwhelmed with the number of detainees, many of whom had relatives on Ananke Ten. At one such center on Pales Three, our very own

News Center reporter, Pompous Pompadour, spoke with one grieving family member."

The view switched to a man's face and impossible coif. They protruded from the holo into the room. Behind him was the crowded quarantine center, the low hum of multiple voices in the background. "Thanks, Bustine. We're here at the Imperial quarantine center on Pales Three with Serge Thalamis, who just disembarked after visiting his father on Ananke Ten. What was it like there, Mr. Thalamis?" Pompous shoved a microphone into a man's face.

Tears streaked his cheeks. "My father was healthy! He had no symptoms whatsoever! Why did they have to do that?" Thalamis plunged his face into his hands and wept.

The camera switched back to the bulbous-breasted anchor. "Again, breaking news, Ananke Ten sterilized just hours ago after the outbreak there couldn't be contained."

The vid switched to a blue, cloud-shrouded planet, green continental swatches across its surface. Thousands of flares began to lance the land masses from space, pinprick points of light flashing at each point of contact, until every land surface on Ananke Ten was engulfed in flame.

"I remember visiting there about five years ago," Lydia said, her gaze blurring. She sat on the bed, biting her lip.

The reporter's face replaced the burning planet, his hair easily five inches tall, curving up and out over his forehead like a tsunami. "The last outbreak of this magnitude was three years ago on Quirinus Eight," Pompadour said. "A similar loss of life ensued when Imperial Infection Control was required to inoculate its atmosphere with a caustic enzyme. Back to you, Bustine."

"Thank you, Pompous," the busty Bustine said. "Epidemiologists tracking the outbreak aren't sure about its source but do say that anyone who's traveled to Ananke Ten in the last five years should be immediately screened for symptoms. These symptoms include itching, wheezing, coughing, fluid buildup in the lungs, and increasing respiratory distress. With us in the studio to talk about the outbreak is Professor Selene Toccim, Chair of the Procopio Institute of Xenobiology at the University of New Athens. Welcome, Professor."

The holo switched to a woman in a lab-coat.

"That's not Professor Toccim." Melanctha frowned at Lydia.

She gaped at the image. Professor Toccim had been short, blond, and skinny, with an acne-scarred face. The woman on screen was medium-tall, brunette, and almost as buxom as the anchor.

"Thank you for having me on your show, Bustine."

"Tell me about this particular pathogen."

"Well, Bustine, it appears to be a hemagglutinin-sixty variant, crossbred with a xenobio organism of unknown origin and incubated in a human host for a substantial period. What's remarkable is both the virulence and transmissibility of the H-sixty variant. Further confounding the situation is our vulnerability to the pathogen. Once it began spreading on Ananke Ten, there wasn't any way to stop it."

"Explain what you mean by virulence, Professor."

"Virulence is the speed with which a pathogen causes symptoms of disease and distress in its victims. It also refers to the severity of these symptoms. The H-sixty variant causes a rapid buildup of fluids in the lungs, or pulmonary edema. The virus colonizes almost exclusively in the lungs. The onset of symptoms is so rapid, in fact, that people literally drown within hours. Further, the incubation period appears to be minutes, the onset so brief that people barely have time to seek help."

"How about transmissibility?"

"This term refers to the ease with which a pathogen spreads from one person to another. Some diseases are spread through vectors, often parasitic organisms. These pathogens are usually neutral to these parasites, on occasion weakening them but rarely debilitating them. Some vectors are inert, such as water droplets, a frequent culprit in respiratory infections such as the H-sixty variant. We cite these as 'airborne,' but in fact, standard droplet precautions are sufficient to reduce the rate of infection. But on Ananke Ten, even droplet precautions proved inadequate, as if the pathogen had evolved or had been cultured to produce its own airborne vector."

"Professor, pardon me, but the way you're speaking makes it sound intentional."

"We haven't ruled that in or out, Bustine," Professor Toccim who wasn't Professor Toccim said. "The incubation period is just one of many assumptions we've made in trying to establish how this pathogen developed."

"Professor Toccim," the anchor-breasted anchor said, "didn't the founder of the Procopio Institute of Xenobiology try to warn us of precisely these kinds of outbreaks? Didn't Professor Dorian Procopio's research predict to a ninety-five percent certainty that we would have a virulent outbreak of a xenopathogen within twenty years?"

"Well, Bustine, his research certainly did indicate that an outbreak was a remote possibility, and it remains the basis for much of xenoepidemiology today, but no, his work made no predictions with that degree of certainty or that extreme a result. No one could have foreseen the magnitude of events on Ananke Ten."

Lydia gaped at the holo, having read the research. "How dare she lie about my father's work?!"

"Hush," Melanctha said.

"But Professor Toccim, there's a small community of scientists who advocate otherwise and a slim compendium of literature to support their view. They all claim that Ananke Ten and Quirinus Eight are the natural consequence of mankind's spread across the galaxy. And that Professor Dorian Procopio predicted these events."

The fake professor put up a façade of indifference. "Not a single word from Professor Procopio's published work says any such thing."

"Earlier, we were discussing intent. Is there evidence that points to someone's having concocted this pathogen?"

"Bustine, it would be preliminary even to discuss this aspect of the outbreak. However, a review of alien visits to the planet did turn up an interesting event. In this holo segment from the main spaceport on Ananke Ten taken five years ago, you'll see an alien step off a ship."

The holo switched to an amoeba-class vessel of Kzizn manufacture. A blob of bright-green protoplasm in a two-legged egg cup tottered down the boarding ramp.

"That's Xsirh!" Lydia shrieked.

"How do you know?" Melanctha asked.

From the ship behind the Paramecium walked a pretty young woman in formalls. Lydia, five years younger.

"We've issued an all-sectors-bulletin for this pair," the fake Professor said. "Anyone who's seen them should report the sighting to their nearest Imperial Infection Control authority. Further, it's not the alien we suspect of having been the carrier, but the young woman in the background. Alien-to-human transmissibility is a relatively rare occurrence, and human-to-human transmission is nearly always implicated in a pathogen this virulent. Our Typhoid Mary in the Ananke Ten outbreak is almost certainly the unidentified companion of this giant Paramecium."

"Liar!" Lydia leapt to her feet and shook her fist at the holo. "You slimy, bottom-feeding, pondscum liar!"

Melanctha wrapped her arms around Lydia. "Hush, child," she said quietly.

Lydia struggled for a moment, straining to get at the smug face of the fake Professor.

The older, larger woman held her securely, calmly reached around her, grabbed the remote, and killed the holo.

Lydia turned inside Melanctha's arms, put her head to the woman's shoulder and wept.

Chapter 24

"Typhoid Mary," Lydia later learned, was a figure from Old Earth, Homo sapiens' planet of origin, now a gigantic archeological ruin devoid of life, rendered uninhabitable by its original occupants. The dissident Wrwrmrfn held as one of their basic tenets the belief that Homo sapiens was doing to the galaxy what they'd done to their planet of origin, fouling their own nest. Somehow Homo sapiens had managed to escape the planet before annihilating themselves.

Among the tales attributed to Old Earth was this Typhoid Mary, a Kitchen Maid in the households of primarily wealthier families. Her lack of simple hygiene had caused the spread of the salmonella typhi bacteria, the woman preparing food without washing her hands after contact with her own feces and urine.

Now I'm Typhoid Lydia, she thought, lying awake that night, the sound of surf seeping in through the alley window.

Melanctha snored sonorously beside her, oblivious.

Unable to sleep, Lydia pulled a chair to the window. An occasional puff of breeze carried the comforting scent of brine. How she wished she were home on Kziznvxrz, where the brine was rich in microorganisms and electrolytes.

Over and over in her mind, she replayed the interview. Lydia wasn't sure what bothered her more, the anchor's gargantuan breasts poking like armed missiles from her chest, the imposter's trying to represent herself as Professor Toccim, or being accused of spreading a raging contagion.

At least mine are proportional and real, Lydia thought. Hers are sure to be prosthetic and filled with helium for buoyancy. If I had breasts that big, I'd have to stand on my head!

And what did they do to the real Professor Toccim?

Why are they assassinating my character in this propagandistic hatchet job?

Unable to sleep, Lydia slipped out of her nightclothes, slipped into pair of formalls, and slipped out the door. The hotel was pin-drop silent. The last hotel had stayed raucous with saturnalia nearly till dawn. This one appeared to retire early. On the ground floor, she sidled past a snoozing night concierge, a spike-haired younger woman tattooed in brilliant colors.

A half-block away was the ocean, the coastline rocky but the seas gentle. The breeze here was stronger, bringing with it the smell of strong brine. Lydia breathed deeply and walked parallel to the ocean, an occasional hover whining past. A few streetlights along the road stole her nighttime anonymity. The stars glistened overhead, scintillating with brilliance. This close to the galactic core, nighttime skies were daunting for their fusillade of stars, so different from Kziznvxrz on the galactic rim, where only a handful of stars and the vague dust of the Milky Way hung in the night sky like a ghost.

What am I going to do? she wondered.

It was clear the government had concocted the Typhoid Mary charade to justify publicizing a still of her in its efforts to detain her. Why they sought her so avidly was a mystery. She hadn't done anything to them. Why were they persecuting her?

A hover roared past, and she nearly wet herself in fright.

She hadn't heard it coming, wrapped deeply in her thoughts. She realized how vulnerable she was. If the IBS agent had traced her before, others could certainly do the same. And out here, on a lonely strip of ocean-front road, she was easy pickings.

Lydia turned back toward the hotel.

The night concierge was awake. "Sneak out the back door?" the woman asked, her muscled arms rippling under tattoos as brilliant as the night sky. "You look better without the disguise, by the way."

Lydia grinned, stifled a yawn, and stepped to the elevator.

"Hey, uh, Ms. Castellanos, I almost forgot. There's a message here for you. Don't you have holomail?"

"Not where I come from," she said, returning to the desk. She and Melanctha hadn't dared connect to the holonet, except anonymously through a desk term at the library. She took the proffered envelope, its texture the fine flim used on Kziznvxrfn. Made from a dried and flattened colonial protist, the flim was edible, one of her favorite snacks. "Thanks," she told the concierge. How did Xsirh get this to me? she wondered, turning.

"Hey, watch out for that old curmudgeon on the top floor, ok?"

Lydia stopped to look at the woman.

"I'm Buster, by the way."

"Pleased to meet you. Who on the top floor?"

"Old guy, one of those lesser nobility, fallen on hard times, too uppity to work, too poor to continue the debauchery he's accustomed to steeping himself in. About five years ago, he bought the penthouse suite and disappeared into it. We maybe see him once a year. Nobody goes in, nobody comes out. Every once in a while, I get a complaint when he harasses somebody in the elevator. Don't take him seriously. Just an old, disaffected grouch."

A bit more information that I needed, Lydia thought, suspecting the concierge was lonely.

"Thanks, appreciate the warning. Good night, Buster."

"Good night, Lydia."

She stepped into the elevator and opened the envelope.

* * *

Lydia my darling,

I hope you're well. May you find the scum of the galaxy nourishing. I've taken great risks to get this letter to you. The outbreak on Ananke Ten made it imperative that I get you our latest intelligence information on the dissident Wrwrmrfn.

We've discovered that they're far more subversive than we ever gave them credit for. Revered leader Gzelfozirh ordered a raid on dissident headquarters. We arrested nearly a thousand Wrwrmrfn and discovered a plan to destroy the Gaean Empire and annihilate humanity. They plan to infect human-occupied worlds with a virulent pathogen that they've been incubating for over twenty years. We're working to isolate the pathogen now.

The outbreak on Ananke Ten was a test run, and by Wrwrmrfn standards, a successful one. Their plan is to infect all major settlements throughout the Gaean Empire in similar fashion, including the capital, Gaea. And while it appears the Imperial Bureau of Suspicion has accused you as the carrier in its efforts to find and capture you, we fear that the actual carrier is far more pervasive and ubiquitous.

Further, we're still not able to locate the Wrwrmrfn dissident leader, Mzixrhhz Gszmlh. She seems to have disappeared, and even her closest adherents either won't or can't disclose where she's hiding. Worse, the documentation we recovered in the raid indicates that Wrwrmrfn researchers perfected a long-acting catalyst to solidify the Kziznvxrfn exoderm years ago. If dissident leader Gszmlh is using this catalyst, it means she may be in hiding among the Homo sapiens, masquerading as one of them. She could be on Gaea itself, and no one would know it.

Oh, and on a personal note, the instability in the Empire has caused a spike in essential-goods prices, and the company profits are higher than ever. For now, I'm placing all profits in those clandestine accounts that you had me set up on Pontus XIII years ago. I'd wager you didn't think you'd ever need them, did you?

Profits should remain high into the near future, just as long as our customers don't know I'm running the company. Xenophobia is running rampant throughout the Gaean Empire. After Ezra got splashed at the coronation ceremony and a holo of you and me was shown yesterday on the interstellar news, our people have had to flee Homo-sapiens occupied planets. Some didn't make it off planet and were killed by rampaging mobs of these unsapient sapiens.

It would be easy in these circumstances to adopt the dissident philosophy and condemn the entire race as primordial bottom-feeders or some deep-ocean-trench algae, but when I think of you, and how kind and gentle you are, and how beautiful, I'm reminded that all life is worthy of respect, even these pondscum human specimens rioting and killing Kziznvxrfn.

I send you the warmth and love of all our people, and I pray to the Almighty Single-Cell Organism that you return to us safely.

Yours,

Xsirh Xlmhgzmgrmrwvh.

* * *

Lydia clutched the letter to her chest and sighed.

She stood in the corridor outside the room she shared with Melanctha, early morning light beginning to seep through the glasma door at the end, which read "fire escape."

She stepped down the hall, not quite ready for sleep, wanting to think through what Xsirh had said, but mostly wanting to bask in his warmth and affection. She stepped out onto the fire escape. Hungry, and knowing Melanctha wouldn't be awake yet for breakfast, Lydia gobbled the letter, the dried and flattened protist fizzing with effervescence on her tongue.

From her vantage on the fire escape, she saw where the avenue intersected the coastline, the white foam of the soft, gentle surf just visible in the approaching light of dawn.

"Peaceful, isn't it?" said a voice from above.

Lydia turned and looked up.

An old man leaned on the balustrade above her.

"I had no idea there were rooms up there."

"Just the penthouse suite. Care to enjoy the view and watch the sunrise with me?"

The fire escape did extend to the roof, she saw. "All right." For a gruff, old curmudgeon, he seemed awful nice. She climbed up to the roof and saw that the "penthouse" was a rundown tar-paper shack beside a conglomeration of roof-top air-conditioning equipment. Must get noisy up here in summer, Lydia thought.

"Looks better inside," he said, "but it does get noisy in the summer months, all those air conditioners going. You'd think by now we'd have come up with a more efficient heat exchange system, wouldn't you?" He was easily six feet tall and perhaps seventy years in age. His hair was jet-black with some gray at the temple, and his features were those of a patrician god, classic Athenian lines similar to the ancients depicted in statuary throughout the capital. He carried himself with the equanimity of the self-assured, as though born to privilege, and although his face bore clear indications of his age, his posture reflected none of it, still proud and straight, in spite of his plunge into penury.

"I'm Horace Drivas."

"Lydia Castellanos."

They shook, and his eyes searched the area behind her. "Curious, not a name from among the nobility—not even those in disgrace, as I am." He returned his gaze to her. "And yet you carry that nobility in the way you move. Your beauty is startling, too."

Lydia blushed. "Thank you." She remembered the make-up artist, Polly, saying something similar. She wondered about his name, thinking she'd heard it before.

"Where dost thou come from, Princess Anonymous?" he asked in an affected accent, bowing gallantly.

She giggled, not quite believing she was succumbing to his charm. "Well, you might say I went to a really special finishing school."

"Oh, pray tell, where was that? I'd like to recommend it to our new sovereign, her Highness Empress Hecuba. Oh, but her visage is incurably ugly, isn't it? No amount of charm will ever lend her a smidgen of comeliness."

"I'm afraid not," Lydia replied, "but her looks don't matter, do they? Have you noticed who's in the background of all the stills and vids of Empress Hecuba? What matters is the power behind the throne."

"Indeed, Ms. Castellanos, indeed."

Lydia looked out over the ocean, the sky slightly lighter.

"Not only do you have the carriage of nobility, your face is somewhat familiar."

Anxiety blossomed in her gut like a bloom of algae.

"The Typhoid Mary of Ananke Ten."

Now I have to kill him, Lydia thought.

"Why would they level such an accusation, except to assuage their guilt at carrying out that massive slaughter?" His gaze went to the eastern horizon. "Its transmissibility and virulence would have slowed the pathogen substantially. Kill your host too fast, and you kill your means of spreading." Then he looked at her. "Such gloomy talk does little to brighten the coming day."

"You don't think I'm the carrier?"

He shook his head. "Of course not. How could the pathogen incubate in Ananke Ten's populace for five years, spreading asymptomatically, and then suddenly activate all at once? No, child, unless there's a catalyst."

"What if it's built into the pathogen?"

"As with some RNA clock? No, because such a clock would have been reset at the time of infection, and we'd have seen a gradual spread of symptoms across Ananke Ten, not an abrupt, widespread onset."

Lydia cheered up a little. He reminded her somewhat of her father, Dorian Procopio. What little she remembered of him consisted of a warm voice and warm arms, and a gentle affection and adoration.

"Then there's the little coincidence of your looks."

She remembered with a nudge of panic that she wasn't wearing her disguise. "You, too, eh?"

"Others have said something similar?"

Lydia nodded. "Countess Giorgi Lillis."

Horace's gaze narrowed, his brow creasing between the eyes. "Mother of the now-deceased Empress Consort, Ambrosia Lillis, to whom you bear a startling likeness."

"Who died giving birth to Princess Cybill Zenon."

"The poor child, condemned to a life sentence in a mind barely capable of reason."

"A child who looks nothing like her mother." Lydia exchanged a glance with Horace. His face grew suddenly brighter, and Lydia looked.

The sun peeked over the eastern horizon and grew visibly larger as she watched. Soon it was too bright to look at, its warmth chasing away the chill of night. Lydia let the light pour into her soul, understanding why the ancients had worshipped Helios as a god.

"No, Lydia, whatever else you are, you're not the carrier. Don't believe their lies."

Chapter 25

Disguised, Lydia picked up the results at the lab the next day, Melanctha waiting outside.

"I'd swear we're being followed," the older woman had said the instant they'd left the hotel.

Lacking experience in clandestine activities, Lydia couldn't have named so succinctly that creepy feeling in her spinal column, the cilia standing on end, the skin crinkling as it twitched at the touch of a hostile gaze. She'd thought she was being paranoid until Melanctha had said something.

They'd split up, rendezvousing at random pneumatube stations throughout New Athens, surveilling each other in their attempts to find whoever was surveilling them.

Unable to ferret them out, they went to the lab shortly before noon, where Melanctha waited downstairs.

"Where's your slug-dog?" the lab tech asked.

In her backpack, but she wasn't about to tell him. "At home with my friend."

The tech looked disappointed. "If you don't mind my asking, a romantic friend? I was thinking of asking you out."

She smiled and shook her head. "No, not a romantic friend. But I am involved, sorry." She took the memnode the clerk gave her and plugged it into her handheld.

In the elevator, she incorporated the sample into the ongoing analysis, which still wasn't complete. With the additional gene sample to analyze, the projected time of completion increased to forty-eight hours. Her palmcom had a really slow processor.

Lydia sighed, wondering what she and Melanctha were going to do in the meantime.

As the elevator door opened, a young man tried to step on and then backed away at seeing her. He held the door, his skin fair and his hair dark.

"Thank you," she said, passing him. She caught a whiff of miasma, like pondscum or algae.

The didinium in the backpack lurched, tugging her to one side and nearly throwing her off-balance.

He lunged as if to catch her. "Almost tripped there, eh?"

"Almost, thanks," she said, righting herself, wondering what the didinium were doing. On a whim, she tore the backpack off her back and opened it.

Both didinium leaped onto the young man's face.

He clawed at the green slugs, his scream muffled, and fell backward across the elevator threshold. Then his hands turned into jelly, his body went flaccid inside his clothes, and his flesh morphed into a blob of bright green protoplasm. The two didinium began feeding lustily on the still-quivering Kziznvxrfn flesh, his cilia writhing in his death throes. The elevator doors thunked against the body and retracted.

Lydia backed against the wall, gasping.

Melanctha appeared beside her and whispered harshly, "Quick, get your pets and let's go."

She squelched her terror, stepped to the Kziznvxrfn, and gingerly plucked the two didinium from atop the carcass. The elevator doors thunked against the body and retracted. Tucking the didinium close to her body and walking half-hunched over to hide them, she followed Melanctha from the building, throwing furtive glances over her shoulder.

"I don't think anyone saw us," Melanctha said. "Come on, let's get the tube out of here. Keep walking hunched over like that."

At the pneumatube station, the taller woman shoved through the lines of people waiting for tubes. "My friend's hurt, sorry," she said multiple times, elbowing people out of the way, Lydia hunched over.

They stepped into a double capsule and Melanctha punched up a destination. "Why'd you have your critters loose in the backpack anyway?"

Lydia shook her head. "I was thinking they'd be easier to pull out if I didn't have to take them out of their enclosures." The image of the gnawed carcass caught in the elevator doors wouldn't leave her mind.

"Better put 'em back in now."

Lydia did so, juggling them while the capsule curved and swerved toward its destination, the two-person capsule a tight squeeze. The noon-time traffic was moderate, and they arrived just as Lydia finished containing the second didinium.

"We can bet that he wasn't alone. Take a tube to the Gerakas station, find a public restroom, change your disguise, and ten minutes later, get in a tube to the library station."

She stepped from the capsule and navigated her way to the pneumatube to Gerakas. A capsule popped to a stop in front of her. She stepped aboard, and it shot her upward. Her terror began to subside, and in its place blossomed the ugly fruit of guilt. She was grateful she'd had the didinium to help detect the Kziznvxrfn in disguise, but she felt terrible she'd killed him. As the city whisked past below, the capsule sledded through a series of tubes, upended, and plummeted toward a station in the northeast suburbs.

She found the public washroom and changed her disguise in a stall. The various getups that Polly had given them were easy to don, and with a few helpful pointers, such as changing stance and posture, the difference was startling. She changed in three minutes and went back to the tube station.

Waiting the full ten minutes before stepping into another capsule took forever. People came and went, none of them announcing themselves as spies. What does a spy look like, anyway? Lydia wondered, her doubt and ambivalence growing. Did I really need to kill the spy? she wondered. Had it really been necessary to turn the savage didinium loose on the Kziznvxrfn?

Lydia didn't know.

She saw ten minutes had passed and boarded a capsule for central New Athens, feeling terrible that she'd killed a Kzizn, never mind he'd been one of the dissident Wrwrmrfn who'd attempted twice now to kill her.

* * *

"What are we doing here?" Lydia asked.

"More research," Melanctha said, looking around suspiciously. The Colonel looked Lydia up and down. She's looking a bit shook up,

Melanctha thought. Probably the first time she ever killed someone.

The canopy of verdure under the geodesic glasma roof was snarled with all the danger of an urban jungle. Melanctha hadn't wanted to come here, knowing any pattern of movement likely to betray them to their surveillers. If the IBS had traced them once already to the library, they were sure to be monitoring the location. Now, though, with the IBS, Infection Control Enforcement (ICE), and the dissident Worm-Worm all pursuing them, Melanctha had to call upon her contacts in New Athens, no longer able to keep Lydia safe by herself. She looked over at the younger woman.

The disguise couldn't hide her beauty. Lydia had the legendary comeliness that caused the balladeers to croon love songs and poets to gush iambic pentameter. Even Lydia's obvious terror at being pursued couldn't dim the beauty radiating off of her, as though she were a blue-white star in her own right, shining with her own light.

Melanctha saw the toll the Kzizn's death was taking. There was a hollow look to Lydia's face that hadn't been there before. How many times have they tried now to kill her? the Colonel wondered. She'll have to get accustomed to eliminating her enemies pretty fast. Sympathy for one's nemesis was a self-culling trait.

"Sit down," Melanctha said inside a copse of thick olive. Adapted from the olive groves of Earth, this particular copse was engineered to grow densely, its fruit to mature simultaneously. She could barely see through the thick olive canopy to the tessellated glasma overhead.

"You're mad at me, aren't you?"

She realized she was. She sat and faced the young woman. "These Worm-Worms aren't your friends. They've tried to kill you thrice now."

"The Wrwrmrfn? But—"

"No 'buts,' Lydia. No quarter is to be given an enemy, do you hear? You have to kill swiftly and remorselessly, because that's what they're trying to do to you."

"I think you're wrong."

Melanctha blinked at Lydia, befuddled.

"I had my back turned to him, and I was off balance. If he'd wanted me dead, he'd have killed me right then."

She couldn't believe her entreaty was falling on deaf ears. "What about the other two times?"

The young woman shrugged. "I don't know, Mela. Some other faction? Some infiltrator? I just don't feel that I'm in that much danger. Yes, we're being watched, and it feels hostile, but I don't sense they want my death."

There was a kernel of truth deep inside what she was saying, Melanctha realized, a feeling that had been niggling at the Colonel ever since they'd arrived on Gaea. Even before that, when Infection Control had slapped their ship with a tractor beam while it was in A-warp. As big and powerful as the Gaean Empire was, it had chosen thus far not to eliminate them both. She knew what the intelligence apparatus was capable of, and if it really wanted to find and eliminate a minor annoyance like this pair of women, it could have done so long ago.

"You're right." Melanctha sighed, because the implications were astounding. "Well, the reason I'm here, actually, is that I need allies. I can't continue to protect you on my own. I just don't have the resources. And if the Empire doesn't want you dead, it begs the question, 'What does it want?' "

* * *

"I came as soon as I heard," said the middle-aged man across from them.

Lydia looked him over. He had that same patrician posture that Polly had told her couldn't be disguised. His hair was styled fashionably, and he wore a suit impeccable in cut and fashion, the seams just so, the spats and cufflinks twinkling in matching gold, the cravat perched under his chin like a toy poodle, the slacks creased to the floor like naval prows.

She and Melanctha were huddled under an umbrella in front of the Estiatorio Milos, a side-street café hidden from the main avenue by a screen of trees. They each could see over the other's shoulder and had spotted the man's approach from a long way away. At his approach, Melanctha had asked Lydia to remove her disguise.

"Mela, you look dreadful," he said, and then he turned toward Lydia. "And you, young lady, are

399

an absolute eyeful of radiant grace and beauty. Surely, a duke or baron has already asserted his claim on your hand in marriage?"

Lydia blushed. "You're being ridiculous, Sir, but pray tell, don't stop at my protest."

"I assure you, I wouldn't, if I weren't happily married. I'm Hadrian Kritikos, son of Hector Kritikos, Chief Admiral of the Gaean Navy."

She shot a glance at Melanctha. "You know I'm being sought, don't you?"

"Indeed, Miss. I'd be concerned if Ananke Ten hadn't been a thorn in the Empire's foot."

"So it was politically convenient to kill two trillion people?"

Hadrian nodded in acknowledgement, his eyes boring into her. "Another reason that reduces my concern. My government is—oh, how might I say it?—imbalanced."

"And your father doesn't have similar concerns?"

Hadrian's gaze darted to Melanctha, and he raised an eyebrow at Lydia. "You never knew Emperor Athanasios—a good man led astray. He'd have never sanctioned the sanitizing of an entire planet. My father would denounce me publicly if he knew I were here. And privately praise me. Such are the exigencies of political office. What he thinks is secondary to what I know. And what I know, simply by looking at you, is that a terrible betrayal has taken place."

"Why do you say that?"

"You're twenty-eight, aren't you?"

"How did you know?"

"And the daughter of Basilissa and Dorian Procopio."

Lydia stared at him silently.

The eyes probed hers. "Missing now for nearly a quarter century, and presumed dead in the crash on Kzizn."

She held herself absolutely still.

"But you're not the daughter, are you?"

She neither acknowledged nor refuted his assertion. She didn't know any longer what to think. She desperately wanted to believe she was the devoted daughter of Viscountess and Professor Procopio, but genes didn't lie. Her palmcom held the secret, churning away relentlessly on its comparative analysis of five different gene profiles.

"You were born the same day as Princess Cybill Zenon. Her genes were as pristine as a dewdrop on a summer morning, daughter of Emperor Athanasios Zenon and Empress Consort Ambrosia Lillis, the both of them breathtaking eidolons of human beauty. And yet, somehow, Princess Cybill is not fit to rule." He looked into the distance, and then brought his gaze back to her. "But you—"

Lydia felt the swelling in her throat, not ready to hear what he was saying. "Please, stop." She felt Hadrian's eyes probe her soul, his face blurring. "I'm sorry. Please, you mustn't."

Melanctha took her hand in both of hers.

All the evidence pointed toward the conclusion Hadrian was about to state, and the comparative gene analysis running on her palmcom would prove it. But it was a conclusion so far beyond anything she could have imagined, with repercussions that would shake the foundation of the Gaean Empire and poison its relations with its tiny neighbor, Kziznvxrz, that Lydia wasn't able to face it.

A conclusion likely to plunge the Empire into confusion and perhaps civil war. A conclusion certain to place in danger her home planet and the alien race who'd nurtured her since she was four years old. With only a tiny armed navy, Kziznvxrz would be immediately vulnerable, and Lydia's enemies wouldn't hesitate to exploit this weakness.

She simply wasn't ready. "We don't know anything yet, Lord Kritikos. And ultimately, it's better left unsaid."

"For now, young lady, yes. The day will come, however, when the truth cannot be denied. How will you stay safe until then?"

She met his gaze.

Hadrian Kritikos stared back at her. "And more importantly, lovely Lydia, how do you prepare for that day? How do you prepare for that truth?"

Chapter 26

"What are you here for?" a hotel-lobby denizen asked her.

She and Melanctha were in the lobby of the Value Palace. Melanctha stood at the barred-glasma window negotiating a room from the proprietor of this New Athens underworld hotel, by far the worst place they'd stayed in their traipse along their downward spiral.

Warped and stained paper with faded patterns peeled from the walls. The portrait of someone who might have been famous leered salaciously at them from a canted angle. The carpet admonished them to walk only within the blackened strips, where the nap had worn through to the warp and weft. The furniture declared itself unfit to sit upon, stains in multiple, overlapping penumbras attesting to urine-soaked occupants, the upholstery pattern long since lost in the tides of incontinence.

"What'd you say?" the man asked.

Lydia looked him up and down. The man hadn't changed his formalls in several days, and his aroma was redolent of a bovine dish left out in the alley. The dried, scaly toads of his feet poked through the frayed formall toes. His hair hung lank over a face gaunt with dissipation. His beard looked like the back side of a bear that had rubbed it too hard against a tree, the half-inch, red-brown stubble glinting in the poor light. His lips were sunk into an edentulous mouth, puckered from years without teeth. His eyes held an amused despair, a cynical ennui, as if to say, "This is what I've got to give."

"What do you mean, 'What am I here for?'" Lydia asked.

"Everyone's here for something, kid," he said, "You name it, I got it."

"I'm not interested."

"Everyone's interested in something. I've got heroin, cyclidine, opiates, cocaine, amphetamines, hallucinogens, inhalants, psychotics, cognates, cognacs, weed, worm, snake, slither, slime, slug, barbiturates, neurolytics, neuroloptics, neurolactics, and neurolumptics. I can get anything you want, 'cause when you got nothin', it's all the same."

As he named off the drugs, sensations flared in each region of her body that she imagined was involved. She'd heard about people like him, the tales so tall she hadn't believed anyone could stoop so low. "I'm not interested."

"Just a babe in the woods, aren't you?" His eyes grew round, and he rolled forward on the balls of his feet, as though to pounce. He didn't lick his lips, but he might have. The man shot a glance toward Melanctha at the window. "You renting by the hour with your friend? Too bad you go that way. A girl like you could troll the Ritz-Carlton."

Lydia blinked at him, not quite following. What's taking Melanctha so long? she wondered. "I'm not interested," she repeated.

"The questing is how you want it. Do you want to shush, push, gush, flush, blush, brush, busche, crush, cush, dush, frush, grush, hush, kusch, lush, mush, plush, rush, slush, thrush, woosh, douche, bouche, or do you want a complete and total scaramouche?"

The patter of his chatter was bamboo beneath her fingernails. "I got slugs. You want slugs?" She whipped out an enclosure. Beneath the clear exterior, the knot of green slime swirled.

"Ooohhhh, and phlegm green too, the best kind. Trade a slug for a slug?"

"Let the guy alone, Lydia," Melanctha said, stepping up behind him.

The man whirled, bewilderment in his gaze. "What did you say?"

"Sorry, was she bothering you, sir? I see she's got her soulcatcher in hand. You know you're not supposed to use that here, Lydia. Put it away."

"Soulcatcher?"

"She's from Lunoid Twelve, doesn't know any better. Left to her own devices, she'd take the soul of everyone in the building and leave behind a bunch of zombies. Come on, Lydia." Melanctha guided her toward an uneven stairwell, the steps groaning in their inclination to collapse.

Lydia threw a glance over her shoulder. The dirty, dissipated man was looking after them, befuddled as a zombie.

They went up six flights, Lydia following by a few steps, not wanting to risk both of them on a single step at the same time, a recipe for a disaster.

"People like him are the reason it's called the Value Palace, you know."

Lydia met her gaze and giggled.

Their room was in better shape than the lobby, but not by much. She stepped to the window. The hotel sat inland on a saddleback between two valleys. Far to the north stretched a pastiche of rooftops, hovels glinting under the harsh, unforgiving sun. Chaotic lines of foot traffic threaded their ways in between hovels, the slum-dwellers without hovers, and the area absent the usual skyful of pneumatubes. Hotels of similar quality as the Value Palace lined what looked to be a main thoroughfare. She suspected this hotel was no better or worse than most.

Lydia backed away from the window, sat on the bed, and nearly wept.

"Somewhat of a reduced circumstance, I'd say," Melanctha said, sitting next to her.

She leaned into the other woman, biting off her despair. "I feel so helpless."

Melanctha nodded. "It's difficult, having to wait on other people."

"I just wish we could walk into the palace openly, without a disguise, and tell the Empire that a great wrong has been perpetuated upon them."

"You don't like all this intrigue and subterfuge."

"It feels so ... dishonest."

Which, as she thought about it, was precisely the point. Reared amidst a race of beings biologically disinclined to deception, Lydia felt the wrongness of her current circumstance like a crushing weight on her chest. It pressed the air from her lungs and left her gasping for breath. As though the oxygen of truth and forthrightness couldn't be found in the atmosphere of Gaea. As if New Athens lived off the noxious odors of fraud and artifice, chicanery and stratagem.

It wasn't how Lydia wanted to live.

"Mela, if this all resolves the way we think it will," Lydia asked, phrasing it with the delicacy of avoidance, "will I be like them?"

Melanctha pulled away and adjusted her position to face Lydia directly. "Taking over the apex doesn't require you to adopt the rot. Absolutely not. You're your own person, Lydia. You always have been. Xsirh, Basilissa, Ezra, Dorian, and all your other mentors saw to it that you developed the inner resources to be your own guide and resist the blandishments of convenience and exigency. No, Lydia, you won't be like them, not at all."

It was comforting to hear her say that. Lydia's doubts stemmed not from her lack of experience with such circumstances—and she had none, a royal rutabaga indeed—but from her insecurity about what would happen next.

Seeking some distraction, she turned on the holo above the bed. The holo was mounted on an articulated joint and could be positioned to be viewed from any place in the room. Lydia saw her own face staring back at her.

"Looks as if the previous occupants enjoyed watching themselves."

Lydia blushed, guessing that antics on the bed were often pictured on the holo. She switched the channel to the local news.

"And in interstellar matters," the busty Bustine said, her twin zeppelins threatening to lift her out of the studio completely, "the Empress Hecuba Zenon arrives tomorrow, back from her tour of the Imperial Domains, having circumnavigated the galaxy. Other than some minor route deviations to avoid the outbreaks, the new Empress was received by her subjects with all the pomp and circumstance at their disposal. Today, her Royal Highness issued this statement through her shameless self-promotion department."

The holo switched to a still 3-d image of the beetle-browed Empress, the wart on her cheek at least as big as one of the didinium slugs in Lydia's possession and almost the same puke green.

"'My blessed subjects, citizens of the Empire, Gaeans all, on the evening of my return tomorrow night from touring the Imperial Domains, I do declare a holiday in celebration of the effusive welcome I received from all my loyal subjects. Further, since I so love a masquerade, all the attendees will come dressed up as members of the royal family and a contest will be held to determine who has most closely masqueraded themselves as one of us. Everyone is invited and no one shall be turned away."

The still image appeared to be looking directly at Lydia, as if daring her to come.

* * *

She and Melanctha were at breakfast the next morning when they heard the news.

The restaurant was a Spanish bistro. On its walls pranced beefy male bovines with outsized horns, waltzing to the strains of a soft violin on a warm summers' day. Lydia was having a breakfast berry crisp topped with creamy salmon spread and a side of radish hash browns with a cucumber-avocado shake, a fair compromise to the meat-laden dishes that these Homo sapiens seemed to consume at every meal.

In the corner, above all the patrons and drowning out the threnody-wailing violin, was a holonews broadcast, full of market-opening ticker numbers and sniggering about the up-coming Imperial Masquerade, none so brazen to comment on the one currently in progress.

"Coming up: An outbreak of a virulent respiratory infection this morning on Amphitrite III, and what Imperial Infection Control is doing about it. But first, this word from our sponsor."

Lydia frowned, raising an eyebrow at Melanctha. "Do you think the Syndicate will let the Imperium proceed with its usual blasma-cannon approach?"

"I'll bet Likashose is busy this morning," Melanctha replied. "Speaking of whom, we need to get more supplies for our disguises. I didn't realize we were out. You shouldn't be seen in public without one."

Lydia didn't mind, having grown tired of slapping the rubbery props onto her face, of the itching and sweating and worrying whether the make-up was sloughing off. She'd known they were running low and had forgotten to say anything. She and Melanctha had left their things in the hotel room, intending to fetch a quick breakfast and return afterward for their effects, Lydia bringing only her palmcom.

With both Countess Lillis and the Admiral's son Hadrian gathering support among the noble families, and the genetic comparison nearly finished, Lydia couldn't wait to get on with things. The last thing she wanted was to attend an Imperial Ball.

"You should waltz into the palace and claim the throne," Melanctha quipped.

Her palmcom on the table beside her plate beeped. "Comparison finished," it flashed.

Lydia just stared at the machine.

"Are you going to look at it? Most people would be anxious."

A life hangs in the balance on the thread of its result, she thought, knowing what it would say, knowing she wasn't prepared for its conclusion. There simply wasn't a way to prepare. Hadrian had said as much. What does a person do to gird herself for the moment she finds out that she isn't who she thought she was, but someone far more important, someone fated to change the course of the Empire, someone fated to restore a balance thrown into a chaotic wobble by someone so wicked that all innocence and purity was disillusioned and sullied.

I am who I am, even if I never knew it, Lydia thought. The existential swirl of sophistry and supposition, of who was who and who was perceived as whom, threatened to consume her in its solipsistic slobber.

I am, she thought, and my only task is to be the very best person I can.

She punched up the results.

Princess Cybill Zenon, purported daughter of Emperor Athanasios Zenon and Empress Consort Ambrosia Lillis, was no relation to her supposed grandmother, Countess Giorgi Lillis, to a ninety-five percent certainty. Princess Cybill Zenon was a direct descendant of Professor Dorian and Viscountess Ambassador Basilissa Procopio, their daughter to a ninety-nine percent certainty. Lydia Procopio, purported daughter of Professor Dorian and Viscountess Ambassador Basilissa Procopio, was no relation to them whatsoever to a ninety-nine percent certainty. Lydia Procopio was a direct descendant of Countess Giorgi Lillis and was, to a ninety-five percent certainty, her granddaughter.

A tear trickled from her eye.

Lydia wiped it away and handed the palmcom to Melanctha.

The Colonel read the results, her face growing sharper with disdain. "I'm sending this to Countess Lillis, if you don't mind."

Lydia nodded her to go ahead, her mind aswirl with the implications.

Somehow, the two girls, Lydia Procopio and Cybill Zenon, born the same day, had been switched shortly after birth.

And the daughter of Emperor Athanasios Zenon and Empress Consort Ambrosia Lillis was supposed to have died in the wreck of the vessel carrying Ambassador Procopio and her family to Kziznvxrz. A vessel sabotaged with the intent of killing the Emperor's daughter.

But she'd survived the crash.

Lydia, the Emperor's daughter, looked across the table at Colonel Melanctha Remes, Commander of the IBS Outpost on Lucina IX.

The Emperor's daughter, Lydia told herself.

"Your Highness," Colonel Remes said, bowing her head. "It's my privilege and honor to offer you my everlasting fealty and service and those of my descendants in perpetuity, may you rule wisely and well."

The doors crashed open. A beam zapped Melanctha in the back and hauled her toward the door, her arms flailing, the palmcom flying. Blasma barrels shattered through windows on all sides, every rifle aimed at Lydia. Patrons hurled themselves to the floor.

A uniformed man stopped just inside the door as Melanctha was towed past, the tractor beam hauling her out of the restaurant.

"Nikitas!" she snarled at him, her arms now pinned to her side by her captors.

The uniformed man approached Lydia. "I'm Lieutenant-Colonel Urian Nikitas, and you, Lydia Procopio, are under arrest."

Lydia considered attempting to flee but knew she wouldn't get far. "I'm a sovereign citizen of Kziznvxrz," she said. "You can't arrest me."

"I don't care if you're the Empress, bitch. You're under arrest." And he clapped a glasma bracelet on one wrist, spun her around and cuffed the other, and then hiked them both up between her shoulder blades. "Come quietly, and you won't get hurt."

The Emperor's daughter, and rightful heir to the throne.

Not much good it'll do me now, Lydia thought.

Chapter 27

The cell wasn't any worse than the others she'd been in. I've become a connoisseur of confinement, Lydia thought.

What differed was the level of security surrounding it. The Bogiati Military Prison on the island of Aegina was encircled with the elite corps of brigadiers. The island itself was surrounded by a fleet of ocean-going vessels whose combined deck space exceeded the island's square footage. Overhead circled a fleet of aircraft whose sides bristled with so many guns they looked like porcupines. In subspace orbit was an armada of spacecraft equipped with so many blasma cannon that they could have seared the surface of Gaea with one fusillade.

You'd think they were greeting an arriving Imperial, Lydia thought sardonically. Oh, that's right, the Empress Hecuba returns from her Imperial tour tomorrow.

The booking process seemed more akin to a military induction, with strip, shower, body scan, medical screening, cavity searches, cuticle cutting, toe-jam inspection, and a variety of unmentionable indignities.

"What's that rash on your forearm?" the doctor asked.

Lydia looked at her blankly. "What rash?"

"Right there, those red spots."

She looked closely at the area indicated. On the interior of her forearm, three inches in from her wrist, tiny red dots sprinkled an oval patch of skin one inch wide and two inches long, each dot so small as to look like a pinprick. "That's a rash?"

"How long has it been that way?"

Lydia shrugged. "I don't know, a while, I think." She tried to remember if she had it the last time she'd left Kziznvxrz.

"Does it itch?"

She shook her head. "Well, on occasion," she amended, remembering having scratched it before.

"Bioscan is clear, no infectious pathogens aboard," the doctor said, looking at her handheld. "Must be a histamine response to some allergen."

Then they gave her an orange pair of formalls and hustled her to a cell deep underground.

A grill in the ceiling high above issued a stream of chilly air. The solid granite block walls yielded no clue to what lay beyond. The door was set in a wall of carbo-nick alloy reinforced glasma, the door itself a single sheet of clear glasma. Beyond the door stood four guards, two more than she usually had. The bunk was a thick slab of travertine sitting directly on the floor. The toilet was a ring of porcelain on a pedestal in the corner, the sink an indentation in the wall sticking its lower lip into the room. Two bare loomglobes hung near the ceiling, in excess of the requisite lone-source lighting.

Fancy, Lydia thought, feeling spoiled to have so much light.

She put her face in her hands and wept in despair.

* * *

The woman appeared without warning outside the cell door.

Lydia had been in the cell for about four hours, without a way to mark the passing of time. She'd looked away from the door for a moment, and when she looked back, the guards were gone and the woman was there, unannounced.

She needed no announcement.

Her face had lurked in the background of every appearance by Emperor Athanasios or Princess Hecuba for the last twenty years. A hawk face, watching relentlessly. A predatory face, ready to pounce at the least sign of intransigence, resistance, or disobedience. She was the Dowager Empress Narcissa Thanos.

She wore a slick jacquard uniform, similar in style to the ones worn by all the Imperial Guards, but hers of a far finer material, with embroidered accents at hem, knee, waist, breast, and neckline. Her shoes were form-flow flats, meant for mobility and comfort, whose only concession to style was a sequined clasp. On one hand she wore a brass ring that was green with corrosion. Her hair was tied tight at the nape and fell straight to her mid-back, leaving the hawk face sharp and ready to peck.

She stood there, silent, staring at Lydia through the clear glasma door, like a patron at a zoo watching a confined animal. She did not move nor evince any change in expression for five full minutes, her eyes boring through Lydia like lasers through granite.

Lydia didn't have in her the ramrod steel hardened in the forge of politics, but she knew the purpose in such stares.

And she refused to cower, not to this one, not to the usurper. Not to the mastermind of the scheme that had put the Princess and Heir to the Throne on a ship bound for the galactic rim, its engines sabotaged to explode on arrival. Not to the scoundrel who'd subsequently eliminated any other proximate claimant to the throne through cunning, stealth, and intrigue, one of those victims having been Icarus Terzi, son of Count Terzi, Melanctha's betrothed.

No, Lydia would not cower to the usurper.

The silence stretched between step-daughter and step-mother, neither ceding ground by speaking first, two she-wolves pissing on opposite sides of the same tree.

"I served your mother, once." The voice was sultry, an octave lower than expected.

Lady's Maid Narcissa Thanos to her Imperial Highness, the Empress Consort, Ambrosia Lillis, whom the Emperor Athanasios Zenon had married posthumously. The Lady's Maid hadn't had a solid enough grip on the Emperor's affections to stop the post-mortem nuptials, the marital obsequies.

"You killed her, didn't you?"

Thanos laughed softly, not a hint of smile reaching her face. "Of course, dear Lydia—or perhaps I should call you Cybill, since that's your birth name. How else could I claim my place? But my deeds of yore are such a bore."

Lydia saw no one behind the woman and sensed no one else in the corridor outside the cell. Was she completely alone, no one to bear witness to her acknowledging Regicide? Had she turned off the holocams?

"No, dear Lydia, there's no one listening and no devices recording. We're alone, child, just you and me."

Completely alone meant completely vulnerable. So why doesn't she kill me? Lydia wondered.

"Why don't I kill you? You're of use to me, a distraction for the masses. Oh, they'll never know I switched you and the retarded Procopio whelp when you were infants only two weeks from the womb, but they *will* know of your conspiracy with the Wrwrmrfn when you attempt to assassinate the Empress Hecuba. Homo sapiens will finally declare war and stir those indolent Kziznvxrfn from their centuries-long slumber."

Lydia was taken aback at the woman's perfect pronunciation of the two foreign words. I thought I was the only person who spoke perfect Kziznvxrz. She smelled the faint miasma of an algae-rich tidal flat. Her Kzizn father Xsirh had asserted in his last letter that the dissident Wrwrmrfn leader might be in hiding among Homo sapiens, masquerading as one of them, using the long-acting catalyst to solidify the Kziznvxrfn exoderm. Lydia stared at the Dowager Empress.

"I see you're beginning to understand, Lydia. You humans are notoriously stupid and impulsive. Not that the Kziznvxrfn are absent all flaw, certainly. Yvuliv blf zxxfhv nv, gzpv z ollp zg blfi-hvou."

Lydia automatically translated the aphorism. "Before you accuse me, take a look at yourself."

"Our tolerance of your pesky race has gone on far too long. We should have ground your endoskeletons down to calcium centuries ago, before you managed to escape the cesspit you'd made of your own nest."

"You're her, aren't you?" Lydia asked, gasping. "Mzixrhhz Gszmlh, the Wrwrmrfn dissident leader!"

This time, a smile did reach the face of Narcissa Thanos, but there was no humor in it, only the simple necessity of inflicting death. "Now, Lydia, I have to kill you. But not before I use you to wipe out three-quarters of humanity and stir those lazy pacifist Paramecium brethren of mine into wiping out the other quarter."

And then she was gone.

Lydia had been looking right at her and had not seen her leave. The Wrwrmrfn Leader in human disguise had simply vanished. And she'd vanished so quickly that Lydia was surprised she hadn't heard the pop of a vacuum suddenly filling with air.

Staring at the spot where the woman had been, Lydia wondered how to stop her. I'll escape and denounce her at the Imperial Ball! she thought, realizing instantly how idiotic it was to think she might escape the most secure prison on Gaea.

Somewhere, a door slammed open, an order was given, and a contingent of guards marched in, halting in front of her cell door at another order.

The woman at their fore turned toward the cell door. She alone among them wore a single, floor-length robe of fine, shimmering, night-black silk. "Lydia Procopio, daughter of Viscountess Ambassador Basilissa Procopio and Professor Dorian Procopio," the woman announced in grave tones, "you are hereby found guilty of conspiracy to spread virulent pathogens to numerous worlds, including but not limited to Amphitrite Three, Pyrgos Five, Quirinus Eight, Lucina Nine, Ananke Ten, Eris Eleven, and Cygnus Twenty, requiring their sterilization. You are sentenced to death."

"But I plead not guilty!" she protested. "Besides, you missed four, six, and seven." She wondered why Erato IV wasn't mentioned, a planet she'd visited several times, the planet where she and Xsirh had been detained, known locally as Theogony.

"Great stars above, Ms. Procopio, what do you think this is, some backward style of government, like a democracy? Now that you've nothing further to say for yourself, you're to be taken to the steps of the Parthenon for public execution by a firing squad of your peers."

"But I was reared on Kziznvxrz," she protested. "Where are you going to get twelve of my peers to shoot me?"

"Uh, well, uh, I hadn't thought of that. We'll have to consider that, but of course it won't delay your execution by a moment. Come with me."

"Who are you? You haven't introduced yourself."

"Me? Oh, sorry, I'm Daphne Carras, Chief Justice of the Gaean Empire. I thought everyone knew my name."

A legend in her own mind, apparently, Lydia thought. The cell door swung aside with a whoosh. She stepped forward to the indicated place in the midst of the soldiers, the Chief Justice beside her. They placed a pair of glasma circlets on her wrists.

For the second time that day, Lydia smelled the faint miasma of an algae-rich tidal flat.

On the Chief Justice's order, the contingent did an about-face and escorted her from the facility.

* * *

Aboard the military ferry between the island of Aegina and the mainland, Lydia stood encircled by guards near the prow, the ship shrouded in thick fog, the thrum of engines under her feet. Gulls circled the vessel overhead, calling out antemortem laments. To starboard, port, astern, and ahead, barely visible, were auxiliary ships in the flotilla escorting the prisoner to the mainland.

They can't even wait until Empress Hecuba returns, Lydia thought bitterly, despair threatening to overwhelm her.

The Chief Justice in her floor-length robe stepped into the circle of guards and nodded amiably.

It's not your execution, Lydia wanted to say.

"It's not your time, child," Chief Justice Carras said with a wink. "Hold your breath."

Astounded, Lydia took a deep breath and held it.

The flock of gulls dispersed, the sky above them shimmered, and the guards surrounding Lydia fainted, each of them slumping to the deck unconscious. Lydia caught the faint odor of a soporific.

A boarding ramp dropped from nowhere, and Daphne nudged her forward. The diaphanous hull made the Kziznvxrz ship nearly invisible in the thick fog.

Her heart thundering with excitement and disbelief, Lydia ascended the ramp and boarded the vessel, Daphne right behind her. The sub-ether drives engaged, Lydia bracing herself against a bulkhead.

Daphne's human physique melted into a blob of green protoplasm, which squirmed from beneath the robe and sat up on its exoderm. Xsirh swung his optical organelles at Lydia and opened his tentacles toward her.

Weeping, Lydia stepped into her father's embrace.

* * *

"Father, no, I can't let you do that. Don't you understand? I'm the one who has to expose her. Remember what I told you about Homo sapiens? They're as likely to crucify me as to crown me. Some politician could blame me at any time for infecting all those planets. As much as I'd like your help, this is something I have to do on my own."

Lydia and Xsirh were sitting across from each other in a corner table in the ship galley, the gigantic Kzizn Armada Flagship half in sub-ether, half in the physical universe, hovering in the shadow of the moon. The Kzizn Naval Commander, Chief Admiral Svxgli Pirgrplh, sat to one side of the table. The way he watched them reminded her of a Licensed Family Counselor doing therapy for a kid from a broken home.

Lydia wanted to tell him she wasn't broke. She had just told them about Mzixrhhz Gszmlh, the Wrwrmrfn dissident leader, and her grand plan to destroy humanity by inciting a war between the races.

"Well, yes, I guess I understand," Xsirh said, taking her hand in his tentacles. "Who am I lying to? Of course I don't understand. You humans are beyond understanding. But I don't need to understand. I just need to let you handle this the way you feel is best. They're your people and it's your planet. One of my people may have messed up your life terribly, but you're in the best position to fix it—or even know how."

Well, at least he understands part of it, she thought, sighing. Would he ever understand the rest? The human group-think, the prideful face-saving, the urinary competition? Probably not.

"Here, take this, Lydia." Xsirh pushed an ampule toward her.

The vial was soft-surfaced and compressible, with a spout formed on one end. "What is it?" she asked, picking it up. It had an organic feel, clearly made from the outer membranes of a large, single-cell protozoon.

"It's an antidote to the exoderm-solidifying catalyst. Squeeze the ampule to spray her with it, and she'll melt into her natural shape."

Lydia tucked it into a pocket. "I hope I can get close enough to use it. She's pretty slippery."

Admiral Pirgrplh got Lydia's attention. "So you won't need me to attack the palace?"

"No, Admiral, I'm afraid not."

"Oh, thank the One-Cell-Over-All for that! I thought for certain I'd have to fire a weapon. Ghastly things. We only have them aboard in case of a hostile confrontation." He swung his optical organelles toward Xsirh. "You know, Xsirhglksvi, I'm not even sure they work."

A warfaring race, the Kzizn were not.

"So, your Imperial Highness," Admiral Pirgrplh said, "tell me where I can let you off, and signal me if some need arises."

"Thank you, Svxgli, that's very kind," she said, knowing it'd take her years to become accustomed to the title. "And please, just call me Lydia."

"But I could never do that, your Highness, not now, not with—"

433

"It's not official until it's official," Lydia interrupted. "When they crown me their Empress, then it's official." She sighed. They were such sticklers for protocol. "You can set me down in Countess Lillis's garden."

"Yes, your Highness." He bowed to her, rolled onto his exoderm and squirmed toward the door.

Xsirh looked at her from across the table, his tentacles intertwined with her fingers. "Promise me you'll be careful."

"I'll be careful, Father, I promise." And she leaned across the table to kiss him somewhere in the vicinity of his cheek.

Chapter 28

The bedroom on the fourth floor of the Lillis Estate in central New Athens was bedecked in silks, satins, sequins, and squawkadoodles.

"I don't know why Ambrosia liked squawkadoodles," Countess Giorgi told Lydia. "She was half-crazy for them and insisted on wearing them everywhere she went. I persuaded her to forego them for the Imperial Ball the night she met Prince Athanasios, and I'm sure she'd have worn them at her wedding if she hadn't been ..." The older woman turned away, her voice catching.

Lydia had stepped off the Kzizn Armada Flagship into the garden behind the Lillis mansion. By the time she'd turned to wave, the ship had already vanished, and the old Countess had swept up Lydia into her arms, weeping profusely and squealing in delight. The comparative analysis results had reached Countess Giorgi Lillis that morning, just before Lydia's arrest at the Spanish Bistro. Then, arm-in-arm, grandmother and granddaughter had entered the house, Grandmama taking Lydia directly to Ambrosia's suite on the fourth floor, where the Consort-to-be had prepared herself for the fateful Imperial ball. "Where you're going to prepare for quite another Imperial ball," Countess Giorgi said.

The two of them stopped in front of the dressing dummy that still displayed the gossamer, robin's-egg gown Ambrosia had worn, its silicoid-alloy threads impervious to the depredations of time and inattention. A sash of similar material trailed to the floor on one side, and a bodice of gathers barely covered the dummy mammaries.

Lydia eyed the dress doubtfully, knowing her bust already the object of too much testosterone titillation. The ballroom floor will be awash in hormones if I wear that! she thought.

"Not nearly inadequate enough to show off your fine figure," Grandmama leered, "but it's what your mother wore. In the palace, there's a portrait of her wearing that dress, you know. Makes me weep to think about that night, when it seemed that every girl's dream was to be in her shoes, and every boy's dream to be in his." Countess Lillis put her palm to her chest. "Oh, and when they kissed, the stars burst with joy and brilliance!"

For a moment, Lydia thought the old biddy was going to swoon.

"But you won't have your prince tomorrow night. It'll be just you and all the other guests against that bitch upstart Lady's Maid."

Lydia smiled and patted the ampule in her pocket, wondering whether she should tell Grandmama Giorgi about the alien in disguise who'd ruled the Gaean Empire from behind the throne for the past quarter century. Better let it be a surprise, Lydia thought, guessing the Countess wouldn't be able to keep it to herself.

"I've invited a few friends over for dinner this evening, my darling. I hope you don't mind."

"Oh, no, not at all, Grandmama," Lydia said. "Uh, who would that be?"

"Her Excellency, Bishop Dea Papadopoulos of the Divine Orthodoxy, Admiral Hector Kritikos,

Chief of the Gaean Naval Forces, the honorable Elke Drivas, Speaker of the Gaean House Assembly, his honor Flavian Galanis, Premier of the Gaean Administration, and her right honorarium herself, Daphne Carras, Chief Justice of the Gaean Empire."

Lydia blanched, particularly at the latter, the Chief Justice certain to be under suspicion for having let such a high-value detainee escape from her custody.

"What's the matter, dear? It's important we have their support before the coup, don't you think?"

"Uh, well—"

"Did you think the five most powerful people in the Empire besides the Dowager herself were going to throw their weight behind you the instant you expose that rotten, bottom-feeding, scum-sucking rutabaga for the deceitful, power-hungry, concupiscent slut she is?"

"Uh, well—"

"They're a bunch of—"

"Grandmama, that's enough."

She stared at her granddaughter, her eyes wide.

As if I've roused her from a trance, Lydia thought. "You're right, of course. It's important that I have their support. I just hope they don't get distracted by the lure of power, too. It's certainly corrupted the Dowager Empress, hasn't it?"

The eyebrows rose and furrowed together. "I hadn't thought of that. I guess we'd better tread carefully. They'll be here in an hour."

* * *

Lydia greeted each in the atrium of the Lillis mansion with a perfect smile and a perfect manner, wearing a lime-green evening gown whose neckline curved modestly down toward her cleavage to give just a hint of its promise without flaunting the proud, full bodice. She wore a didinium like a corsage, slung over one shoulder, the creature's protoplasm hanging elongated to her hip and attached to the slim belt of emeralds encircling her waist. The greens complemented her skin, giving her the vibrant glow of a blushing bride, offsetting the hue given her by her chlorophyll-rich diet.

First among equals, her Excellency Bishop Dea Papadopoulos of the Divine Orthodoxy was the first guest to arrive, ordering her passel of priests to wait outside. She was bedecked in layers of vestments, an elaborate chasuble over an intricate dalmatic, and beneath it all the humble alb, a pure-white robe reaching her ankles. The miter she wore atop her head was a modest cap of intertwined gold bands, a far cry from the church steeple she'd sported at the coronation.

"Lady Giorgi, who is this dear, beautiful child?" Bishop Papadopoulos asked, her eyes wide as she took in the sight before her.

"Your Excellency, may I introduce my granddaughter, Lydia," the Countess said.

The Bishop's head whirled so fast that her miter almost took flight. "But you don't have ..." She swung her gaze back to Lydia. "My darling, it's such a pleasure. Surely, Grandma Countess will explain herself in due course."

"The pleasure is all mine, your Excellency," Lydia replied, curtseying and kissing the ring of the Bishopric. "And with luck, all the mysteries will be revealed tomorrow evening."

Admiral Hector Kritikos, Chief of the Gaean Naval Forces, was next to arrive, a contingent of commanders marching in lockstep up to the entryway behind him. He doffed a gold-rimmed tricorn, tassels dangling merrily from the two rear horns, and bowed to her elaborately. His uniform was so bedecked with medals that it tinkled like a windchime as he straightened. His spats shone like mirrors and brass tacks trimmed his slacks.

"Did you say 'granddaughter,' Dear Countess? Wherever on Gaea . . . ? Pardon my discomfiture, my child, it is a shock, to say the least, to behold the apparition of one so dear to us all. A pleasure to meet you, Lady Lydia."

"Mutual, Lord Kritikos," she said, curtseying and not minding the way his gaze traveled the length of her body. "I so enjoyed lunch with Lord Hadrian a few days ago. Please give him my regards."

The honorable Elke Drivas, Speaker of the Gaean House Assembly, arrived next, a bunch of bureaucrats bickering bitterly amongst themselves behind her. She looked relieved to be shut of their banter as she stepped through the portico into the atrium. The jacquard jacket and herringbone skirt seemed somewhat at odds with the business pumps on her feet, but then pumping the flesh was a politician's occupational hazard. The precise cut of her pageboy and no-stick, perfect face signaled how impervious she was to ridicule and blackmail, like an immaculate angel devoid of taint.

"Lydia, dear, so honored to make your acquaintance. Where has the Countess Lillis been hiding you all my life?"

"A pleasure, Honorable Speaker," Lydia replied, curtseying.

Her right honorarium herself, Daphne Carras, Chief Justice of the Gaean Empire, swept in moments later on robes made of wings, like a wraith on strings, floating into the atrium from within a coterie of legal aides, their faces planted in giant tomes of legal codes.

"Your Honorarium," Lydia said forthrightly, before Countess Lillis introduced her. She knelt at the feet of the Chief Justice and bowed her head. "Please forgive me for the debacle earlier today aboard the ferry."

"Oh, that?" A light laugh tittered off her tongue. The woman helped Lydia to her feet and clasped her by her shoulders. "Never you mind, dear girl. It'll take more than that to tie my robes into knots. Her Highness Empress Hecuba owes me some latitude. After all, I crowned the bitch. Very nice to meet you, Lady Lydia. Did you say, Lady Countess, that she's your granddaughter? You didn't have to, since it's so clear. Lydia, my child, you look just like your mother, who was beholden by Gaeans everywhere."

Lydia smiled and sighed, basking in the Chief Justice's regard.

"Oh, but where's our colleague, his honor, Premier Flavian Galanis?" Justice Carras asked.

Countess Lillis dropped her hand from her ear. "I've just received a com from him, your Honorarium. He sends his apologies that he's been delayed, and he's asked that we not wait dinner for his arrival."

Grandmother Giorgi extended her arm to Lydia, and together they led the way into the dining room.

Tablecloths of damask and napkins of silk cushioned silver flatware so shiny it might have burned through the table. The seven-place setting of fine Hardassian cerasteel service scintillated under a chandelier of Crgrtrzm crystal, its thousand bulbs so diffuse and subdued that illumination appeared from thin air. The centerpiece of Litressan lilies sprouted from slim, graceful stalks, a single flower spreading its pure, pale petals in front of each plate, the flower the family namesake.

"A toast and a prayer," Bishop Papadopoulos said, standing and raising her Crgrtrzm crystal chalice. "To the return of Countess Lydia Lillis to the warm embrace of her family, may all her rightful privileges and positions be restored forthwith! Eis igian!"

"Eis igian!" everyone repeated.

Lydia raised her chalice with the others, in hers water tinged with a dye to make it the same gold-brownish color as the Metaxa in their chalices. She metabolized ethyl alcohol so quickly it was disorienting for her to drink. And she knew she'd need a clear head tonight.

And so it went, each guest toasting Lydia with praise and good wishes so effusive it was intoxicating. And finally it came round to her.

Lydia stood and smiled demurely. "I'm honored and humbled by your welcome. In some ways I know you honor the memory of my mother, Ambrosia, and if I have any regret, it's that I'll never know her as you did, to bask in the warmth of her smile and the grace of her presence. I am my mother's daughter, and I'm also the child of Viscountess and Professor Procopio, who reared me until I was four, and the child of the Kziznvxrfn, who reared me after that. Equally Gaean and Kzizn, I'm a child of the galaxy, and I pray I'll be able to serve the people of the Gaean Empire to the best of my ability. Thank you for honoring me tonight. Long live the Empire!"

"Long live the Empire!" everyone repeated.

"And let's eat before the Metaxa goes to my head," Speaker Drivas drawled.

On a signal from Countess Lillis, servants began to bring out appetizers.

"What is that thing you're wearing on your shoulder, Lady Lillis?" Admiral Kritikos asked. "It almost looks alive."

Her laugh was light, and the night felt like magic. "It *is* alive, Admiral. It's a didinium, a single-cell protist ciliate from Kziznvxrz." She took it off her shoulder and rolled it into a ball to hand to him. "It's an excellent hygienator, since it feeds on all microorganisms it comes into contact with. On Kziznvxrz, it's a fierce predator."

The Admiral peered at the ball of protoplasm skeptically. "If I may, I'd rather pass, but thank you."

Sounds of a disturbance came from the atrium.

The bombastic voice of the Premier Flavian Galanis floated into the room. Suddenly, he was at the doorway. "Pardon, Lady Countess, for my tardy arrival. Fashionably late and all that, eh?" Over the top of his suit, he wore a silk tabard embroidered with the Imperial Crest, as clear a declaration where his loyalties lay as the scorn upon his face, his eyes immediately finding Lydia.

The ball of protoplasm in Lydia's hand sprouted spikes as it bristled, shot out two tendrils, one at the chandelier and the other at the far edge of the table, and it slung itself like a rocket right at Galanis.

The Premier clawed at the alien stuck to his face as he stumbled backward and fell with a whump to the floor, pulling at the goop. His hands turned to goop themselves, going green, and his body melted into a mass of slime, the didinium snacking lustily on the Premier's Kzizn face.

"What in Hades?!" Members of the dinner party crowded around the quivering mass in a tuxedo, gawking.

"Stand back," Lydia said, reaching over to pull the didinium off its victim. The ball of protoplasm strained against her hold, trying to leap from her hands to return to its feast.

The Kzizn corpse quivered in its death throes, and then was still.

"What's that horrible smell?! Is that a sewer leak?"

"Where did this alien come from?"

"That creature at the coronation, the one that the Dowager Empress splashed, wasn't it similar?"

"What has it done with Flavian, the poor boy?"

"Lydia, dear, do tell us what's going on, please?"

She looked among them and sighed. "This is a dissident Kziznvxrfn who disguised itself as a human, one of several Kziznvxrfn who are conspiring to topple the Gaean Empire. It's such a long story that I don't know where to start."

447

"Well," Bishop Papadopoulos said, "start from the beginning. How about, 'In the beginning …'?"

"Maybe not that far back," Countess Lillis said.

"Probably not a good idea," the Bishop said. "I always get bogged down in the begats. But go on, my girl, take all the time you need."

Lydia looked among them, sighed again, and told them what was happening.

* * *

Waking the next morning in the suites that had once belonged to her mother, Ambrosia, Lydia felt both elated and encumbered: Elated at the warm reception and near-unconditional support she'd received from four of the most prominent Gaean citizens, and encumbered with guilt for the havoc created by the Wrwrmrfn faction from Kziznvxrz.

As much as she tried, she couldn't shake the feeling that she was somehow responsible for their having suborned at least two high-placed Gaean officials. It was guilt by association, and with that guilt was the worry that regular, peaceful Kziznvxrfn would be blamed for the betrayals perpetrated by a few dissidents.

And the question left in everyone's mind last night after Lydia had finished her story was, how many more dissident Kziznvxrfn had infiltrated the nobility?

Further, the Imperial Masquerade Ball was tonight, and Lydia was overwhelmed with the preparation and the coming confrontation with the Dowager Empress, Emperor Zenon's second wife, Narcissa Thanos, otherwise known as the Wrwrmrfn dissident leader, Mzixrhhz Gszmlh. The confabulated cabal of conspirators last night had all agreed: Bish Pap and Admiral Kritikos would investigate Premier Galanis's disappearance, and Lydia herself must publicly expose the fraud.

No one knew how long the alien had occupied the Premier's position. A factor most humans overlooked was longevity. The Kzizn lived such long lives that subsuming oneself into the life of a comparatively short-lived human was not nearly the sacrifice that it would be for a Homo sapiens.

The combined guilt by association and the anxiety about tonight's confrontation weighed heavily on Lydia.

"I have to get out of the house, Grandmama," she told Countess Giorgi at breakfast. The weight of luxury around her added to the burdens she already carried, the mansion palatial.

"Certainly, take a stroll down at the docks. The fish market is not to be missed, and perhaps it'll remind you somewhat of home. But do take the scullery maid Melpomene with you. She's a sharp eye for miscreants and a sharper knife she keeps hidden in her bodice."

"Thank you, wonderful suggestion, Grandmama."

Melpomene was a substantial woman easily two inches taller than Lydia and nearly twice her weight. And it was weight well proportioned, the woman thick through both limb and torso. "It's my big bones, they say," she said, clasping her own meaty forearm in demonstration.

Lydia mocked herself up in the smock of a Scullery Maid and pulled a bonnet tight to obscure her looks.

450

The pneumatube ride was uncomfortable, the double capsule still not quite large enough for them both, Melpomene complaining she was too large for a single capsule and had to pay double to get anywhere. The tube popped them out just one street over from Pireas Bay in Attica, where smaller sea-going vessels clotted the small inlet's waters, pontoon wharves branching out in between. Many among these were private fishing trawlers, their captains and crew weathered by a life at sea. Stalls lined the streets facing the inlet, fishmongers calling out their catch for sale, screeching to be heard over the gulls. Brine and sea floated off the bay in the light breeze.

Toward one end were larger fishing trawlers, the industrial size, their cargo holds wheeled directly onto transport hovers for shipment to the canneries.

"Why we goin' here? They won't be sellin' none of their catch to the likes of us."

Reminiscent perhaps of a not-so-distant time in her life, Lydia mused, trawler hulls towering over them on either side of the wide quay.

A vaguely familiar man was stepping down a gangplank. He stared at Lydia and Melpomene as they strolled past. "Pardon, aren't you …?"

She knew the voice. "Orrin, right? Orrin Stamos of Titanide Aquafoods, yes? We met on Theogony. I'm Lydia."

"Of course, yes, now I remember, much as I might like to forget," he said, looking abashed. "Terrible, the way they treated you and your father. How is he, by the way?"

"None the worse for the experience, thanks for asking. What brings you all the way to Gaea?" She was pleased to see someone she knew who didn't suspect her of Imperial ambitions and wasn't wanting to arrest her.

"Those didinium you were going to buy from me, as a matter of fact," he said, grinning. "I'm researching a possible niche market for them as a hygiene product."

"Surprised you got here, as paranoid as everyone is about these outbreaks." He seems genuinely pleased to see me, she thought. "How'd you get past Imperial Infection Control?"

"They're the ones who may be buying them. Despite the outbreaks on several planets in the

452

Delta Quadrant, I noticed Theogony is virtually unaffected. Given its industry, nine-tenths water and all, I suspect the didinium might have a role, they're so ubiquitous. We're researching their anti-contaminant properties now."

"The ones on Kziznvxrz are so ferocious they'd be lethal. They're tamer on Theogony?"

"Certainly are. Say, Lydia, do you want to have lunch? My next appointment's not until three ...?"

"I can't, Orrin, sorry. I have an engagement tonight I'm preparing for." She sighed and shrugged, seeing Melpomene was anxious to go. "But thank you, Orrin, very kind of you."

"Maybe tomorrow? How long are you on Gaea?"

She didn't know whether she'd be alive tomorrow, much less what her availability was. "I'm committed to a project for the next several days, but send me a holo, and I'll see what I can do. Very nice to see you again, Orrin."

"Nice to see you too, Lydia." He nodded and headed up the quay.

She watched him go, lamenting that she couldn't take him up on his offer. She'd sensed more than a desire to talk business, and she couldn't exactly say she'd had much of a social life recently.

"We're going to stand around here all day for what?" Melpomene said.

Lydia signaled she was ready to go. On their way back to the Lillis estate, she pondered the encounter, knowing her simple wish to go to lunch with a friend a distraction from the terrifying fate that awaited her at the palace tonight.

Not knowing its outcome.

Chapter 29

She wore the same dress her mother had on the night she met Emperor Athanasios.

The blue chiffon glowed with the color of the sea at high noon, the back open to the waist and gathers at the shoulders. In the front, the neckline dropped to the base of her sternum, the mountains on either side forming a rift valley hinting at the delights to be found there. A slim belt in sky-blue sequins trimmed the waist, and the material dropped to the floor, slit up the sides to mid-thigh, edged with a strip of azure lace. Matching heels in sequined straps winked from beneath the hem.

Around her neck she wore a single string of aquamarine and lapis lazuli, and from each ear dangled a two-inch trail of the same, a matching bracelet at one wrist. The jewelry was the same as her mother had worn, except for a few touches

Lydia had added. Dangling from the bracelet was the green ampule given to her by Xsirh, and around one ankle was a lime-green ring of didinium, contained in an elastoband torus.

Grandmother Giorgi wore a dress similar to Lydia's but more modest in mien, exposing considerably less in both skin and form. Lydia and Countess Lillis were among thousands of guests heading toward the palace, the streets jammed with hovers. Traffic was stopped intermittently and hovers were moved aside as escorted hovercades were given room to pass, the glitterati getting favorable treatment.

"I could have insisted we get an escort, I guess," Countess Giorgi said.

"No, it's all right, Grandmama," Lydia said. "The less attention we get, the better, eh?"

But the longer it took, the more her anxiety mounted, her bowels tied up in knots by the time their vehicle floated up the long drive toward the palace entrance.

The Zenon Palace sat just north of New Athens, filling the saddleback between the Acharnes and Kamatero neighborhoods, the ridges on either side funneling winds off the

Bay of Elefsina. The sprawling complex climbed both sides of the saddleback, all servicing the main palace structure. The palace itself brooded like a toad, framed on four sides by towering, black-stone turrets out of some medieval nightmare. The architecture was some deranged architect's blend of random historical themes. Multiple minarets poked their domes above the main roofline like obstinate children, none so bold as to challenge the corner turrets. Framing the main portico was a colonnaded walk between marble columns marching out from the entry like sentinels. And for the Imperial ball, miniature lights sprinkled every surface, the palace aglow like some tawdry house of depravity and dissolution.

And inside skulked Lydia's nemesis, the Dowager Empress Narcissa Thanos.

"Whatever happens, child, remember to smile," Countess Giorgi said.

Their hover pulled up to the entrance, and servants swarmed to assist them from the vehicle.

"If you could step this way for a bioscan, your Excellencies?"

Lydia followed the Countess under an arch. The glowing biodetector flashed green as she passed through it, the didinium at her ankle escaping detection.

One step behind the Countess, Lydia followed along the colonnaded walk toward the main portico, the columns on either side growing ever larger. By the time she reached the soaring doors, she felt extremely small.

Smile as Grandmama told you, she admonished herself.

The concierge took the Countess's calling card, swiped at a holodisplay to find their names, and passed the card to a footman. The footman's tails flapped happily as the servant led them deeper into the palace, the soaring ceilings and thick plush carpet absorbing the noise of their passage. The corridors were so sound-absorbent that had Lydia spoken, Countess Giorgi wouldn't have heard her. Walls of alabaster and marble leaned heavily inward, many showing signs of pictures recently removed.

The footman led them into the main ballroom, a vast hall already crowded with thousands of people. Twenty-one chandeliers hovered above, the central chandelier so ponderous she was convinced it had to be supported by antigrav units. At various points on the walls and on pillars throughout the hall perched portraits, hundreds of portraits, each one of a past member of the royal family, all mounted above head-height. Moved from the corridors into the ballroom for this occasion, Lydia guessed.

People nearby fell silent and stared at her.

The footman handed the card to the maitre d'. He glanced once at the card, glanced down his nose at them, and glanced at the card again, his brow furrowing. He gestured the footman close, pointed to a place toward the front of the hall, and whispered something.

The footman's eyebrows shot up. "Yes, Sir," he said. The footman handed Lydia a small flag on two-foot stick and said in a low voice, "Here is your number, Lady. At the time of the voting, hold your number just above your head, and good luck in the competition. This way, your Excellencies."

As he led them through the crowd, people turned to look, falling silent as Lydia walked past.

Countess Lillis nodded to many of them, her smile never faltering.

Lydia nodded to those who would meet her gaze, letting the hint of a smile reach her face. She caught up with the Countess and murmured, "This is all too easy, Grandmama."

"It is, isn't it?" The Countess shot her a look, her smile slipping not a notch.

The footman led them to the front of the hall, near a semi-circular dais raised three steps above the ballroom floor. Just yards from the dais stood two pillars. On one was a portrait of the Emperor, Athanasios Zenon, resplendent in full uniform, his spiked helmet tucked under one arm. At the pillar base stood a coterie of at least thirty imposters, each dressed as elaborately as he who was pictured. Mounted on the second pillar was a portrait of the Empress Consort Ambrosia Lillis stunning in a chiffon dress the blue of the sea at high noon. No one stood at the base of this pillar.

Countess Lillis looked up at the portrait above Lydia, and then brought her gaze down. Her hand leaped to her mouth, and her eyes filled with tears.

That was when Lydia realized that the ballroom had gone silent.

"Ravishing!" rang a voice. "Absolutely ravishing!" From the crowd stepped Orrin Stamos, CEO of Titanide Aquafoods, bedecked in uniform, a spiked helmet tucked under his arm. He stopped a few paces away and bowed elaborately. "Lady, I had no idea I'd find you here. A pleasure to see you again."

"Mutual, Mr. Stamos, and I see you're dressed the part." She gestured at portrait of Emperor Athanasios. "Good luck this evening, especially since it appears you have quite the competition."

"There's no competing with you, Lady. Tis clear you've already won." He stepped close to her and murmured, "What do I call you?"

"Lady Lillis is fine, or your Excellency. Mr. Stamos, this is my grandmother, Countess Giorgi Lillis." She introduced them, noticing that conversation in the room was returning to its previous low-level rumble.

"A business associate?" the Countess asked Lydia, looking flustered.

She can't help it, Lydia knew. The thought of working for a living was antithetical to the very ethos of nobility. "It wasn't long ago, Grand-mama, that I discovered who I was."

"Thank the stars, you did. Wouldn't want your backside calloused from a chair, heaven spare you that terrible fate."

Lydia didn't roll her eyes at Orrin, and she saw he was trying not to grin. Suddenly, his grin faltered, and he went to his knees. Everyone else in the room bowed too, silence falling again.

Only Lydia still stood, feeling the stab of eyes in her back like a knife. She didn't need to be told who was there. Deliberately, impertinently, she remained standing in the presence of her royal Highness the Dowager Empress, not caring what offense it implied.

Had Narcissa Thanos wanted her dead, it would have been done, and Lydia would not now be standing beneath a portrait of her mother, wearing the same gown. The former Lady's Maid would have quietly rid herself of Lydia long ago, had she wanted it.

So Lydia remained with her back to the Dowager Empress, the only person in the room on her feet.

"Yes, he's right," hissed the soft, sultry voice, the lower octave menacing. "You do look stunning, dear Lydia."

The didinium around her ankle strained against its elastoband containment. Lydia fingered the ampule on her bracelet. Lydia pitched her voice so everyone in the room would hear. "And who, Lady Dowager Empress, are *you* impersonating?" Then she turned.

Beside Narcissa Thanos was Empress Hecuba.

Immediately, Lydia went to her knees. "I humbly beg your pardon, your Highness, for my unforgivable breach of protocol. I thought it was just the usurper behind me."

The Empress Hecuba Zenon threw a glance at her mother, her eyes going wide. In her hand was the royal scepter, a gold staff three feet long with a fist-sized diamond capping its head. She was sitting upon the semi-circular dais three steps above the ballroom floor, the Dowager Empress standing beside her. Second child of Emperor Athanasios Zenon, Hecuba wore a dress identical in design and materials to that in the portrait above Lydia, complete with lapis lazuli and aquamarine jewelry. The bright green wart the size of a banana slug on her cheek dispelled any hint of resemblance. Her dishwater hair was done up in spiraling vertical coils like some cultured, miniature plant. The single brow was almost a precipitous cliff above the close-set eyes. Her perpetually pouty lips puckered, as if in displeasure at the confrontation suddenly brewing in front of her.

"Why do you call her the usurper, Lady Lillis?"

"Because, your Highness, she murdered my mother, the Empress Consort Ambrosia Lillis," Lydia said.

The narrow gaze went to the Dowager Empress, Narcissa Thanos.

The former Lady's Maid to the Empress Consort gazed placidly back at the Empress.

"You don't deny this, Mother?"

"No, your Highness, why should I? Oh, perhaps not my proudest moment, but after all, I did it for you, dear. If I hadn't, her child would now be sitting where you are."

Lydia couldn't believe what she was hearing. The brazen admission of murder was so unexpected, laid out in so forthright a manner, without the slightest hesitation and with only the slightest compunction, that Lydia gawked at her nemesis.

"Do spare me the theatrics, Lady Lillis. Surely, your mother taught you better than that?" Then Narcissa issued an impertinent little laugh and put the back of her hand to her forehead. "Oh, sorry, I forgot about your upbringing. An orphan reared by giant slugs at the galactic rim. How desultory, how utterly despicable, how incredibly rutabaga!"

"Your Highness," Lydia said, keeping her voice under control, "the usurper switched the Emperor's first child with that of Viscountess and Professor Procopio, and four years later, sent Ambassador Procopio and her family to their deaths in a vessel sabotaged to crash upon arrival on Kziznvxrz."

Empress Hecuba looked quizzically at Lydia and then turned her gaze toward her mother. "You did all that, Mother?"

"I'm assiduous in my efforts not to be so industrious, I really am. Do I look like the kind of person who would do such dastardly deeds? Of course I did them. But not everyone died in the wreck, did they, Lady Lillis?"

"You mean ..." Hecuba glanced between her mother and Lydia, looking befuddled.

"Yes, your Highness," Lydia said. "I'm your half-sister, Cybill Zenon, daughter of the Empress Consort Ambrosia Lillis and firstborn child of Emperor Athanasios Zenon."

"Well then, who's that?" Hecuba pointed toward the forward corner of the ballroom to her left, where a woman in a blue evening gown scribbled furiously on a wall with a crayon, attendants attempting to sop up endless ribbons of drool.

"That is the child of Viscountess Ambassador Basilissa and Professor Dorian Procopio," Lydia replied. "I have the genetic analysis to prove it."

Empress Hecuba turned her stare upon the former Lady's Maid. "Mother, you could have warned me at least."

"What, and spoil the fun? But you're absolutely right. My apologies for not telling you sooner, your Highness." Narcissa peered slyly at Lydia.

"Your Highness," Lydia said, bowing, "what's done is done, and you're the Empress now. None can gainsay that, nor undo it. I'm not here to claim something that's not mine, but I am here to beseech your Highness to bring to account the perpetrator of these foul deeds and to administer justice both swift and merciless upon the person responsible." Lydia straightened. "Thank you for considering my request."

The Empress scowled at the Dowager Empress. "What do you say, Mother Highness? Are any of these foul accusations true?"

Again, Narcissa Thanos laughed, the low, sultry voice carrying over the crowd. "I've already admitted to these deeds, Daughter. You act as if you don't believe me. What would I gain by denying I did them?"

"Utterly wretched and despicable acts, Mother. Of course I believe you did them. I just can't believe you'd admit to them so readily. What am I supposed to do with that, Mother?"

"Who am I to tell you, Daughter? *You're* the Empress. I've always said you'd be on your own one day. It's happening a bit sooner than you expected." Narcissa glanced toward Lydia. "Aren't you going to greet your half-sister, your Highness?"

Lydia and Hecuba both stared at the woman as if she'd lost her mind.

"Your Highness!" Daphne Carras, Chief Justice of the Gaean Empire, stepped forward. "Forgive me my intrusion into this little family reunion. In light of the admissions made freely by the Dowager Empress Narcissa Thanos, I must insist that she be detained immediately."

Empress Hecuba's eyes darted to Narcissa, then to Lydia, and then finally rested on the Chief Justice. "Your honorarium, please administer to this supplicant before me the sacred oath of fealty."

"Yes, your Highness, it would be an honor." Daphne Carras stepped to the base of the dais. "Your Excellency Lady Lillis, kneel before me."

Lydia stood and knelt before the Chief Justice. She was five feet from the Empress and a similar distance from the Dowager Empress.

Almost close enough.

Chief Justice Carras raised her right arm. "Raise your right arm, your Excellency."

Lydia dutifully raised her arm. From the bracelet on her arm dangled the ampule, practically begging her to use it on the Wrwrmrfn dissident leader Mzixrhhz Gszmlh, standing but feet away in the guise of the Dowager Empress Narcissa Thanos.

"Do you, Countess Lydia Lillis, daughter of Empress Consort Ambrosia Lillis and first-born child of Emperor Athanasios Zenon, swear upon all that you hold sacred to serve the crown and uphold the laws of the Empire to the best of your ability as a citizen of Gaea, with all the rights, responsibilities, and obligations thereto implied?"

"I do, your Honor."

"Swear it to her Highness, the Empress Hecuba."

Lydia bowed to her half-sister Hecuba. "I swear, your Highness."

"She must foreswear any claim to the crown," the Dowager Empress said.

The Chief Justice glanced at Empress Hecuba, who nodded. Carras turned to Lydia. "And do you, Countess Lydia Lillis, swear to forego all claims, past and future, upon the throne of the Gaean Empire, for as long as you shall live?"

"I do, your Highness."

This time, it was the Empress herself who spoke. "And now to the truth."

Chief Justice Carras nodded. "And do you, Countess Lydia Lillis, swear to the veracity of what you have attested today?"

"I do, your Highness."

"One more, your Honor," Empress Hecuba said, throwing a glance at her mother.

The judge nodded gravely and turned. "Your Highness, Dowager Empress Narcissa Thanos, you stand accused of the murder of Empress Consort Ambrosia Lillis, to which you have admitted. Do you swear to that admission?"

"I do, your Honor," Narcissa Thanos said nonchalantly. "For the record, I killed Empress Consort Ambrosia Lillis with the full intent of murdering her. I admit this deed volitionally with the expectation that the most severe of punishment is to be levied upon me in penalty. Would you like to know how I killed her?"

"Spare us the despicable gloating of this foul wretch!" Countess Giorgi Lillis wailed, dissolving into tears, collapsing into the arms of Orrin Stamos.

Lydia wanted to run to her grandmother and hold her.

"Your Highness," the High Justice continued, "you also stand accused of kidnapping Princess Cybill Zenon, conspiracy to commit regicide upon her, attempted regicide of her, and of the murder of Viscountess Ambassador Basilissa Procopio and Professor Dorian Procopio, to which you have also admitted. Do you swear to these admissions?"

"I do, your Honor." Narcissa smoothed a wrinkle in her evening gown, as though bored with the proceedings.

"Guards, contain her," Empress Hecuba ordered.

A contingent of guards converged on her and began to haul her away.

"No, we're not done with her," Lydia said.

Empress Hecuba held up her hand to stop the guards and looked at Lydia. "Lady Lillis ... Sister Lydia, kneel before me."

Lydia stood and stepped forward, approaching the dais and stopping the requisite five paces away. She began to kneel.

"Closer, please." Hecuba tapped a spot in front of her with the butt of the royal scepter. "Here."

She kept her astonishment off her face and stepped to the indicated spot. She knelt, her knee against the royal scepter. Then she bowed her head. "How may I serve thee, my Sovereign?" She could feel the gaze of the Dowager Empress burning upon the right side of her face. The ampule dangled from the bracelet on her right wrist.

"You said, Sister Lydia, that you're not here to claim something that isn't yours."

"Yes, your Highness."

"You don't want the throne, despite being deprived of it through intrigue and machination?"

"I do not, your Highness."

"You said you want justice, Sister."

"Yes, your Highness, that's all I desire, if it's possible for justice to be administered."

Empress Hecuba stared at her and then nodded slowly. "But there's more, you say."

"Yes, your Highness, quite a bit more, I'm afraid."

"More foul than what we've already witnessed? How can this be, Lady Lillis?"

"Much more foul, your Highness, sorry to say."

"Expose the rot, please, so that we may cut it from our midst, Sister."

"Yes, your Highness. If I may divagate for a moment to describe what I'm about to show you?" At Empress Hecuba's nod, Lydia continued. "Among the Paramecium who reared me is a faction of dissidents known as the Wrwrmrfn—"

"Were-wormer-what?"

"—who hold as a basic tenet that Homo sapiens is an invasive species deserving only extermination. The leader of this faction has been in hiding for many years, using a long-acting catalyst to solidify her exoderm and disguise herself as a human."

Empress Hecuba threw a glance toward her mother. "Her? Unbelievable! Completely without basis in fact!"

Lydia indicated the ampule on her bracelet. "I have the antidote, your Highness."

"Please, Lady Lillis, show us this dissident leader."

Lydia bowed and rose. She stepped toward the woman being restrained by guards. Bending, she pulled the didinium off her ankle. "You know what this is, don't you?" The creature squirmed and writhed, trying to get at the Dowager Empress.

Some emotion besides utter boredom manifested on Narcissa's face. "How dare you bring such a foul creature into the palace?!"

"How dare you bring your foul backside into the palace?!" Lydia replied. "This is a didinium, your Highness," she said over her shoulder to the Empress, "a carnivorous unicellular ciliate protist native to the Kzizn homeword, one that feeds voraciously on Paramecia."

The didinium struggling in her right hand, Lydia reached for the ampule with her left. The rash on her right forearm flared, and she scratched the itch. Then she grasped the ampule between two fingers, aimed it at Narcissa Thanos, and squeezed.

A cloud of fine, green mist enveloped the Dowager Empress. Her face began to melt and change color, livid chartreuse spreading across the flesh. The melting spread up over the head and down the neck. The head sank into the upper torso and the arms retracted into the body as the upper half became what looked to be a giant yellow-green...

"Slug! Ewww!"

The transformation spread to the torso, and the evening dress fell away, the legs fusing and the torso sinking to the floor onto them, until all that was left was a potato-shaped lump of ugly green protoplasm.

The didinium strained against Lydia's grip, frantic in its efforts to feed.

"This, your Highness, is your culprit. Her name is Mzixrhhz Gszmlh, and she remained disguised as a human with the ultimate intent of provoking Homo sapiens into attacking Kziznvxrz."

"But why?!" Empress Hecuba asked.

"So we could wipe our asses with your faces," Mzixrhhz Gszmlh blurted, her words oddly clear through her burbling intake orifice, despite her physiology's lacking the parts necessary to produce human speech.

"You have asses?"

"Asses far cleaner than yours, you wart-faced runt."

"Why, you little ball of slime, I—"

"Your Highness, forgive me," Lydia interrupted. "But this creature only wants to provoke you. If we succumb to the temptation and go to war against her people, she and the other dissidents win. The Kzizn technology is far superior to ours, your Highness, and they'll quickly defeat us in any war we launch against them."

"Is that what she's been after all these years? To provoke us into attacking their world? To incite these peaceful if repulsive slugs to destroy us?"

"Yes, your Highness."

"Well, then we just won't attack them, will we?"

Lydia sighed and shook her head. "I wish that were all, your Highness."

Empress Hecuba groaned audibly. "Can't I just stage an Imperial ball? Stars above, Sister, what else could there be?"

"I suspect that Mzixrhhz has ulterior motives for admitting so readily to my mothers' murder and my kidnapping. I'm not completely sure, your Highness, but I think she's trying to hide the fact that she's behind these recent outbreaks of disease."

Hecuba stared at her, looking pale. "How so? She's never been to any of those worlds."

"No," Mzixrhhz Gszmlh said, "but my agent has, and we'll wipe you Homo sapiens off the ass of the galaxy one way or another!"

"Agent? What agent?"

"Your low-brow Highness, allow me to introduce the Typhoid Mary of my disease." Mzixrhhz Gszmlh pointed a tentacle at Lydia. "Her!"

Lydia stepped back as if struck by a physical blow. The room began to warp and skew, a nightmare threatening to envelop her.

"You short-sighted humans have it all wrong." Mzixrhhz Gszmlh laughed, the sound similar to a severe bout of flatulence. "I didn't try to kill you, Lydia. Far from it! No, just those uppity Procopios, so you'd have to live among my people throughout your life. Excellent way to incubate a pathogen. You're a walking Petrie dish, darling. Fifteen years in the primordial soup of the Kziznvxrz mudflats was more than adequate to gestate a viral strain strong enough to kill off eighty percent of Homo sapiens. Too bad you don't have the insight to exterminate the other twenty percent yourselves. Wherever you've gone, Lydia, disease and death has followed!"

Of course! she thought, a dark cloud beginning to engulf her. Why didn't I see it? They virtually told me I was the carrier. The media had levied the accusation after the Ananke Ten outbreak. I've been to every one of the infected worlds. The itch on my right forearm! Lydia thought, the blood draining from her face. She stared at the rash, the tiny red bumps so faint they could hardly be seen.

Professor Dorian Procopio had predicted such an outbreak. Her father's research had proved clairvoyant, prognosticating the development of a highly-infectious and highly-lethal pathogen. Except for one small detail: It hadn't developed spontaneously. The dissident Wrwrmrfn Mzixrhhz Gszmlh had developed it, her intent to exterminate humanity.

Lydia felt someone at her side. She was so disoriented she didn't know who it was. The person eased her to a seat, the ballroom swirling around her like a typhoon. The colors in her eyes tasted bad, the sounds in her ears felt like sandpaper, and the taste in her mouth looked black and ugly.

Melanctha was at her side, whispering assurances.

"Mela?" Lydia wondered where she'd come from. Lydia's anchor in the recent weeks of chaos, Mela had been the one person she'd been able to count on when all else had come crashing down around her.

"I'm here," Melanctha said. "Come on, Lydia. Don't let her win. You've survived so much. You're so strong and courageous. You can't be defeated. You've been through so much that you can get through anything. And you know it. All you have to do is to reach deep inside for that extra dose of strength and courage. Let's see what you've got."

The ballroom settled around her, the maelstrom subsiding.

She was sitting on the dais, the didinium struggling to free itself from her right hand, the rash on her right forearm itching terribly.

Over one shoulder was Empress Hecuba. "Are you all right, Sister?"

"I think so. Sorry, just a bit of shock." She looked around.

Melanctha was nowhere to be seen among the spectators.

"Where's Colonel Melanctha Remes, your Highness?"

"I'll have to look into that." Empress Hecuba shot a look at a staffer, who took off running. "I'll find out."

"Thank you, your Highness." She looked at Hecuba. "Forgive me, Sister. I didn't know I was the carrier. I thought I was inoculated."

"It wasn't you, Lydia. You didn't cause this to happen."

"I know, your Highness, but somehow… somehow …" Lydia frowned at the blob of protoplasm lazily waving its cilia just a few feet away, unable to dispel the feeling that somehow she should have known. She looked at Empress Hecuba. "I've now infected Gaea too, your Highness. There must be something we can do to stop the outbreak."

"There's nothing you can do," Mzixrhhz Gszmlh said. "If we had enough time, we Kzizn could simply sit back and watch you exterminate yourselves, but you'll turn the galaxy into a trash heap if we wait. Kill me now, if only to deprive me of my delight in watching your pathetic race die."

Lydia got to her feet and looked down at the oval mass of slime.

"Narcissa Thanos," Empress Hecuba said, drawing herself erect, "in the interests of swift and merciless justice, I sentence you to death by diddily, or whatever that thing is in Lydia's hand." She lifted the gold, diamond-topped staff and brought the butt crashing to the floor. "Go ahead, Sister," Empress Hecuba said. "Kill it! Kill the filthy creature now!"

* * *

It was surreal.

And in that moment, as she gazed upon the dissident Wrwrmrfn who'd condemned her to a fate worse than death, who'd marooned her on an alien planet, who'd incubated a pathogen inside her, who'd chased her across the galaxy to turn her into an interstellar Typhoid Mary, Lydia realized that she wanted nothing more than to destroy the agent of her transmogrification.

And yet ... Exhorted by the Empress herself to carry out a death sentence, Lydia hesitated.

It was all too surreal. Too pat. Too tidy.

Too convenient.

She glanced between mother and daughter, between Dowager Empress Narcissa Thanos and Empress Hecuba Zenon. The didinium in her hand strained first the mother's direction, and then the daughter's.

Lydia pivoted and hurled the didinium into Empress Hecuba's face.

The slug parachuted and wrapped itself around her head. Her hands came up to claw it away from her face, the staff falling aside. A muffled scream emitted from the beneath the green-slime facial, and the Empress's hands lightened, morphed, and turned into tendrils. The didinium sank into the alien as its head sank into its body, green exoderm replacing human flesh. The tentacles flailed one last time and then were still. The dead Kziznvxrfn's limp mass sloughed off the throne onto the dias. The slurp of a happily-feeding didinium filled the ballroom.

"She was one of them," someone said in a breathless voice.

Lydia looked over at Mzixrhhz Gszmlh.

The dissident leader's cilia looked wilted, as though with disappointment.

"She was your daughter cell, wasn't she? And you planned this all along, didn't you?"

"Yes, we did." The frank admission was uttered with the monotone of fact. The Kzizn were incapable of lying, per se, but they could certainly be deceitful. Mzixrhhz Gszmlh didn't seem bereaved at her daughter's death, only disappointed in the mission's failure.

"Gaeans all," Dea Papadopoulos, Bishop of the Orthodoxy, called out to the silent ballroom, "I hereby propose that Lydia Procopio, also known as Lydia Lillis, also known as Cybill Zenon, be granted immediate authority to act as Empress until such time as we can hold a proper coronation."

"I second that motion," said Chief Justice Daphne Carras.

"I too back her candidacy," said Hector Kritikos, Chief Admiral of the Gaean Naval Forces.

"The hell with it! Let's crown her now!" said Elke Drivas, House Speaker of the Gaean Assembly. "The Empress is dead. Long live the Empress!"

A roar filled the ballroom, hats and scarves flying into the air.

Lydia blinked the tears from her eyes, shaking her head.

Countess Giorgi Lillis stepped to her side and took her to the pillar where the portrait of Empress Consort Ambrosia Lillis was mounted. "Do it for her, Lydia. Your mother would have wanted to see this day."

Lydia looked among their faces, seeing a people cast adrift by the deep-seated betrayal perpetrated upon them and the sudden demise of their sovereign.

If I don't become the Empress, they'll launch a war on Kziznvxrz and the dissident Wrwrmrfn will have won.

"Your Honorarium," Lydia called to the Chief Justice, "Swear me in as Empress, please."

Chapter 30

In fairy tales, they live happily ever after, Lydia thought, frowning at the blob of green protoplasm through the cell door, carbo-nick alloy bars reinforcing the glasma between them.

"Hasn't said a word since we put ... it in there, your Highness," the guard said. Beyond her, the detainment center Commander nodded in confirmation.

The optical organelles stared at the floor, not even pivoting to follow the conversation, laying flat against the upper torso above an intake orifice as limp as the rest of the creature. Mzixrhhz Gszmlh looked defeated.

"I don't think she's going to help us," Orrin said. After the ball, he'd spent the night at the palace in one of the bazillion guest rooms and, at Lydia's request, had joined her to see if they might extract information from the dissident leader imprisoned in the dungeon. Beside him stood Colonel Melanctha Remes, whom they'd found last night in a cell nearby, forlorn and forgotten.

Lydia surmised that Mzixrhhz Gszmlh had gotten pregnant by self-insemination. The records indicated that the Imperial Laundry Maid, Drucilla Kanelos, had indeed verified Narcissa Thanos's loss of hymenal tissue on the night of the her wedding to Emperor Athanasios, but an alien as crafty as Mzixrhhz could easily fake the bloody sheets. The greater difficulty must've been fabricating the development of a human child with a Kziznvxrfn body, not an impossible feat given the advanced biotech available to the species.

Lydia hadn't slept well, going over and over in her mind the terrible suffering being inflicted by a pathogen beginning its rampage across the Empire. "She has to know something," she said. "We've got outbreaks on thirty worlds, and we have to find some way to stop the infection."

Automatic quarantines had been ordered for any planet where signs of respiratory distress were reported. Another thirty worlds, Empress

Lydia thought, and I'll have to order an Empire-wide quarantine. Two million occupied planets in the Gaean Empire depended on a swift containment of the disease.

"Mzixrhhz," Empress Lydia said, "look at me."

The optical organelles shifted slightly, now aimed in her direction.

"You've lost, and you'll never achieve your goal. Your daughter cell is dead and your resistance movement has been dismantled. Humanity is going to survive this plague, and you know it. How do we stop the pathogen?"

"Go dump yourself in the deep blue sea," the creature burbled listlessly at her in Galactim.

"Where the feral didinium reign supreme." Lydia sighed, knowing they'd get no help from the creature.

"What about your father's research?" Melanctha asked.

She looked at the Colonel. "Certainly worth looking through. Maybe he had some ideas. Let's go."

The Empress visiting the University of New Athens was no simple task. The campus was locked down immediately, as if a mass murderer had gone on a rampage. "Surround the building," she ordered as her hover approached the University. "No one's to go in or out."

"Yes, your Highness."

Within seconds, the building was sequestered. The Royal Hover dropped into the quad.

Empress Lydia with her inevitable entourage swarmed the building that housed the offices of Selene Toccim, Professor of Xenobiology. She who still had a closet-full of Professor Dorian Procopio's effects. She who had appeared on a galactic broadcast, looking very different from the Professor whom Lydia had spoken with when she first arrived on Gaea.

An advance guard penetrated the office, blastols ready.

The short, blond, skinny Professor with an acne-scarred face stared wide-eyed from behind her desk at Empress Lydia, clearly petrified by the multiple barrels aimed at her. "Your Highness, it's an honor, I think."

She took the chair across from the other woman. The guards all stepped back at her wave.

Orrin took the chair beside hers, and Melanctha stood behind her.

Lydia introduced Orrin. "And you remember Colonel Remes, Professor Toccim. Everything my father predicted has come true, except that the pathogen is worse than he thought and it's been manufactured rather than incubating naturally on its own. I know what the media is calling me. Typhoid Bloody Lydia." A conflation of Typhoid Mary, the typhoid carrier from Earth's nineteenth century, and Bloody Mary, a murderous queen from Earth's fifteenth century. "But I'm also in the best position to stop the contagion. By the way, who was that on the interstellar news?"

Professor Toccim shrugged her slight, bony shoulders. "Some fatuous idiot the administration selected, didn't know her ass from an infectious disease."

"I'm glad you're all right, given the spate of abductions. Do you know of anything in my father's research about the likely means of transmission, the structure of the viral sheath, the RNA sequence—anything that could give us some edge in containing this contagion?"

The woman gave Lydia a mirthless smile. "Dorian didn't speculate too much on the internal viral structure, but he did speculate on the means of transmission, or vector, which every plague has—some way of getting from one victim to the next. The Bubonic Plague used fleas, and Lyme disease was carried by ticks. Most influenza viruses are transmitted by droplets, but they can also live on an open surface in the right conditions for about forty-eight hours.

"Dorian speculated that the next virulent contagion would adapt to live on an open surface for far longer, perhaps by entering a dormant phase, much as ticks do. He also speculated that such adaptation to extant conditions might include its viral sheath becoming impenetrable to the most commonly-used antiseptics, even bleach."

"Rendering contact precautions ineffective," Orrin said.

"Exactly," the Professor said, glancing at him. "If either one is true, your Highness, then the infection is going to be far more difficult to stop than any plague we've ever seen. And given this pathogen's eighty-percent death rate, if it has developed both dormancy and an impenetrable sheath, humanity is doomed."

"And every world I've ever visited is now infected." Lydia dropped her face into her hands. Empress to a dying Empire. How ironic. She forced herself to look at the Professor. "What about the other twenty percent?"

"Who develop immunity or aren't infected?"

"The ones who develop immunity," she said. "Can't we engineer an inoculation or immunization?"

"By the time you develop an antigen, your Highness," Professor Toccim said, "seventy-five percent of the victims will be dead. The incubation period appears to be minutes, and after the onset of symptoms, death follows within hours. I was looking at the statistics just before you arrived." She gestured at the air, and a holograph appeared above her desk. A tally of infected worlds and the number of dead from influenza. The graph was steep already. "These are only the reported numbers. The actual numbers, your Highness, are sure to be worse. And mounting."

"Please look again at my father's research, Professor. There has to be something."

"Yes, your Highness, I'll keep looking." Suddenly, she turned her head into the crook of her arm and sneezed. "I'll look right now, in fact. Your Highness?"

"Yes?"

"Is it true you aren't even Dorian's daughter?" Her voice was mangled by a stuffy nose.

Lydia nodded sadly, her memories of Professor Dorian Procopio obscured in a thick haze. She blinked away her tears, the loss of her parents at four years old still hurting. "He was as much a father to me as anyone. Thank you, Professor Toccim."

"You're welcome, your Highness." Professor Toccim sneezed into her arm again.

* * *

Outside, Empress Lydia headed toward the Royal Hover. Nearly every person in the Royal Entourage was sneezing.

Except her and Orrin. Even Melanctha two seats over was seized with a fit of sneezing, sweat beginning to bead on her forehead.

Buckling herself in, she looked at Orrin. "Not quite the lunch date you were expecting, is it?"

He chuckled gently despite the despair evident in his eyes. "Your Highness, would you marry me if I were the last man on Gaea?"

She threw her head back and laughed. "Even if you weren't," she replied, warmed by his affection. Then she gave him a bewildered look. "Doesn't the CEO of Titanide Aquafoods have business he needs to be conducting?"

"Oh, I suppose," he said. "Given the circumstances, not too many people are interested in buying my hold full of didinium."

Lydia seized his arm. "Didinium! That's it!" Her heart thundering in her chest, she threw her arms around him and hugged him tightly. "That's what we need!"

"What—?"

"Where's your ship?"

"Huh? My ship?"

"That hold full of didinium you're trying to find a buyer for. Where is it?"

"Uh, at the spaceport. Why? What's going on?"

"Pilot, New Athens Interstellar, immediately!"

The Royal Hover banked sharply toward the north.

"Your Highness, are you all right?" Melanctha asked. She sneezed again. "Have you lost your mind?"

"Not yet, Mela. Orrin, didn't you tell me that the populace of Theogony is virtually un-affected? Nearly everyone on Theogony handles the didinium. They're in every trawler hold, they cling to the nets, they get in your fishing boots. If you're a fisherman on Theogony, you can't avoid the didinium. They're everywhere. Didn't you say you're researching their anti-contaminant properties?"

His eyes went wide, his hand to his mouth. "I'll send the crew a com." His cargo vessel sat on the tarmac near a distant corner of the spaceport, guy lines and grav units holding it in place, its engines running at a dull hum to keep its cargo hold refrigerated.

Her guards insisted on sending a contingent aboard first, their noses running, sneezes seizing them. Lydia followed Orrin and Melanctha aboard.

On the cargo-hold deck, the symptom-free crew stood around a vat full of a thick, swampy liquid, its smell redolent of Kziznvxrz. Inside the vat swam several hundred globules of bright-green protoplasm, each didinium about as large as two hands held tightly together in a double-fist.

"I need a volunteer. Colonel Remes?"

"Certainly, Lydia, uh, your Highness." Melanctha turned and sneezed into the crook of her arm. "My apologies. If this bug is going to kill me within hours, I'll do anything to get better. What do you need me to do?"

"Here," Lydia said, putting her hand into the thick muck. One of the six-inch balls of green slime swam over to investigate her hand. She grabbed it and put it against the Colonel's neck. More tame than the didinium on Kziznvxrz, the one from Theogony settled complacently into the curve between the chin and collarbone. "Let it spread out, Mela."

Her eyes wide with fright, her hands trembling, she nodded. "Yes, your Highness."

It slithered down her chest under her uniform, worked its way all the way down to her toes, then up her backside, and up to her shoulders again. She squirmed at its progress, her face contorting with disgust.

"Now into your lungs."

"Eh?" And she sneezed, sneezed, sneezed again. Sweat beaded on her forehead, and her complexion grew red.

She's already getting a fever, Lydia thought in despair. "Let it crawl into your lungs, Mela." To a crew member, she said, "Get her a chair."

One appeared instantly, and she sat.

"Just relax, Colonel."

Terror in her eyes, Melanctha nodded and leaned her head back.

The didinium crawled onto her chest and slid a pair of tentacles up her neck and into her mouth. She began to squirm, a strangled gargle emitting from her throat.

"Just relax," Lydia said again, glancing at Orrin.

The CEO's face was white. He signaled to two of his crew.

Colonel Remes put her hands to her face as if to tear the didinium away.

The two crew converged on Melanctha and pulled her arms back.

The two tendrils grew turgid. The gargle intensified. It sounded as if she were strangling. Then the Colonel passed out. Lumps of gray-green phlegm surged through the tentacles, the didinium's mass swelling.

The didinium gave a final slurp and withdrew its tentacles from Melanctha's throat.

"She's not breathing!" one crew member said, his cheek near the Colonel's mouth.

"I'll start compressions!" Orrin said.

They laid her out on the deck, and Lydia took the didinium off the Melanctha's chest. Oh, Mela, she thought, terrified at the thought of losing her friend.

Orrin ripped open the shirt and positioned himself over the Colonel. Ribs crackled at each compression. "Where's that defibrillator?!" Orrin shouted.

The machine wheeled itself into place and attached its pads to the Colonel's chest while Orrin continued to give compressions.

"Get help. Stay calm," the defibrillator said. "Analyzing heart rhythm, do not touch the patient."

Orrin brought his hands up and leaned back. "Everyone clear, analyzing rhythm!"

"Shock advised, stay clear of patient. Administering shock, stay clear of patient."

The body leaped six inches off the deck.

"Resume compressions," the machine said.

Orrin leaned forward and put his palm to the sternum, about to restart compressions.

Melanctha twitched, and her eyelids fluttered open. "What happened?" she asked, her voice a whisper.

"Analyze rhythm," Orrin shouted at the defibrillator, withdrawing his hands.

"Analyzing heart rhythm, do not touch the patient," the machine said.

"Why does my chest hurt?" Melanctha looked down at the pads, her eyes wide.

"Normal sinus rhythm detected. No compressions needed. Get patient to hospital immediately."

Other than her sweat-soaked brow, Melanctha looked all right, her color returning to normal.

"How do you feel?" Lydia asked.

She took a deep breath and coughed experimentally. Her cough was dry, her lungs sounding clear. Melanctha looked at her in wonder. "I'm in pain, but it worked."

The Empress stepped back and looked among the other members of her entourage. "Who wants to go next? How many defibrillators do you have aboard, Orrin?"

He grinned at her and turned to a nearby crew member. "You, get the other defibrillators, every single one of them." He turned to a cluster of other crew. "You, you, you, and you, go get the defibrillators off every vessel nearby." Then he looked at Lydia. "You did it, your Highness."

She knelt beside Melanctha and embraced her. "Thank you, Mela. On behalf of the Empire, thank you."

The Colonel sat up, wiped the sweat from her forehead and pulled her blouse closed. "What are you thanking me for? Getting sick?"

"For volunteering."

"You're welcome, your Highness, but you were the one who thought of it. You're the one we owe our gratitude." And Colonel Melanctha Remes bowed from the waist to her.

"I'm glad I could help." Empress Lydia bowed back, relieved.

Epilogue

The fleet of five hundred Kzizn vessels filling the air above the New Athens spaceport fired off a brief blast of their retrorockets simultaneously.

A tiara upon her head, Empress Lydia Lillis saluted the fleet, and then waved as the diaphanous vessels slowly rose and faded into the sky. "Goodbye, Father," she whispered as the fleet disappeared, feeling as if she'd never see Xsirhglksvi Xlmhgzmgrmrwvh again.

The Kziznvxrfn of the impossible name who'd reared Lydia since she was four years old was going home and taking the Kzizn fleet with him.

Wiping away a tear, Lydia chided herself for thinking such disastrous thoughts, knowing he'd be at her side instantly whenever she asked, knowing she would see him again.

Maybe it's because I've spent so much time with him in the past six months, the Empress thought, Xsirh at her side nearly every moment throughout her battle with the virulent contagion.

Receiving a salute from her escort, Empress Lydia descended from the bunting-clad platform, her entourage preparing for departure. The Kziznvxrfn had endured hours of speeches as the assembled humans had honored the Kziznvxrfn for their assistance in the battle.

We couldn't have done it without them, Lydia thought, reaching the tarmac.

"Well, your Highness," Orrin said, bowing from beside the steps, "stopping a plague in the first six months of your reign was quite the feat, wouldn't you say?"

She flashed him a grin. "A plague today, poverty tomorrow, and the next day, who knows?" she replied. "Maybe I can cure ambition, too." They shared a laugh.

Lydia felt exhausted as she walked along the red carpet toward the Royal Hover.

On the seven hundred worlds that the plague had eventually spread to, nearly five hundred million people had died, but another two hundred billion on those same worlds had survived.

Only with extreme quarantine methods had they kept the pathogen from spreading to more worlds. The Kziznvxrfn with their sub-ether drive vessels had been central to the quarantine and the didinium distribution, risking their lives to get trillions of the creatures to the infected worlds.

Very few patients had needed a defibrillator, they'd discovered early on, most people easily cured within minutes. Further, the didinium thrived off the virus, phlegm, and other pathogens that they removed from patients and underwent binary fission after treating three to four patients, making more didinium. Study of the didinium exoderm had helped the Kzizn and Homo sapiens researchers to develop a biochemical agent able to penetrate the pathogen's tough viral sheath, improving antisepsis dramatically.

She stopped at the door to the Royal Hover and looked over her shoulder.

Orrin was deep in conversation with Melanctha near the bunting-clad platform.

"One moment," she told her staff. And Lydia walked back over to the pair, both of whom immediately bowed to her. "Did I remember to say thank you to you both?"

The two of them exchanged a glance. "You're welcome, your Highness," Melanctha said, grinning.

"You're welcome, your Highness," Orrin said with a nod.

"And by the way, Lord Stamos," Lydia told him, "I've been considering your offer, and I'd like very much to have lunch with you. Are you free tomorrow, by chance?"

Dear reader,

We hope you enjoyed reading *Inoculated*. Please take a moment to leave a review, even if it's a short one. Your opinion is important to us.

Discover more books by Scott Michael Decker at https://www.nextchapter.pub/authors/scott-michael-decker-novelist-sacramento-us

Want to know when one of our books is free or discounted? Join the newsletter at http://eepurl.com/bqqB3H

Best regards,
Scott Michael Decker and the Next Chapter Team

About the Author

Scott Michael Decker, MSW, is an author by avocation and a social worker by trade. He is the author of twenty-plus novels in the Science Fiction and Fantasy genres, dabbling among the sub-genres of space opera, biopunk, spy-fi, and sword and sorcery. His biggest fantasy is wishing he were published. His fifteen years of experience working with high-risk populations is relieved only by his incisive humor. Formerly interested in engineering, he's now tilting at the windmills he once aspired to build. Asked about the MSW after his name, the author is adamant it stands for Masters in Social Work, and not "Municipal Solid Waste," which he spreads pretty thick as well. His favorite quote goes, "Scott is a social work novelist, who never had time for a life" (apologies to Billy Joel). He lives and dreams happily with his wife near Sacramento, California.

Where to Find/How to Contact the Author

Websites:
http://ScottMichaelDecker.com/
http://www.linkedin.com/pub/scott-michael-decker/5b/b68/437
https://twitter.com/smdmsw
https://www.facebook.com/AuthorSmdMsw
http://www.wattpad.com/user/Smdmsw

Inoculated
ISBN: 978-4-86750-325-6 (Large Print)

Published by
Next Chapter
1-60-20 Minami-Otsuka
170-0005 Toshima-Ku, Tokyo
+818035793528
4th June 2021